Once again, Kathy Harris
the pages turning. Perfect for readers who love dogs, nature, and edge-of-your-seat plot twists.

—Julie Cantrell
New York Times and USA Today best-selling author of *Perennials*

Deadly Conclusion, the final installment in Kathy Harris's Deadly Secrets series, is full of twists and turns that will keep her readers turning the page well past their bedtimes. Readers will cheer for a cast of likeable characters who must confront past family secrets as they struggle toward a happier future. Lovers of canine search-and-rescue stories won't want to miss this one!

—Kelly Irvin
best-selling author of *Trust Me*

I enjoy a book with action and suspense. My wife prefers romance. *Deadly Conclusion* is a brilliant combination of both. For the first time, we had one book with two placeholders in it. A great read.

—Dave Watson
television producer/host

Kathy Harris brings her Deadly Secrets series to a satisfying ending in *Deadly Conclusion.* If you love canines, reunion romances, and buried secrets coming to light, then grab your copy of *Deadly Conclusion* today!

—Sarah Hamaker
2022 Selah romantic suspense winner and author of *Protecting Her Witness* and The Cold War Legacy series.

Fans of heart-stopping suspense need to carve out a day for this absolute page-turner. Lives and hearts are on the line, and from the first page until the last, it's a race to find a killer.

—Mindy Steele
best-selling author

Action-packed romantic suspense! One chapter in, and I knew *Deadly Conclusion* (Deadly Secrets book 3) by Kathy Harris would be a page-turner. This book gripped me from the beginning. When dog trainer Keely Lambert and Beau Gardner of the TBI set out to find a missing child, they also stumble upon a clue in the woods that could help unravel the case of Keely's missing father from years earlier. Through their heart-pounding journey to uncover the past, they quickly discover there is someone else out there who will do anything to keep the truth buried . . . maybe even kill again. Keely and Beau's race to find answers will keep you guessing until the very last page.

—Christine Clemetson
thriller author

Other Books in The Deadly Secrets Series

Deadly Commitment
Deadly Connection

DEADLY CONCLUSION

The Deadly Secrets Series

KATHY HARRIS

IRON STREAM FICTION
An Imprint of Iron Stream Media
Birmingham, Alabama

Deadly Conclusion

Iron Stream Fiction
An imprint of Iron Stream Media
100 Missionary Ridge
Birmingham, AL 35242
IronStreamMedia.com

Library of Congress Control Number: 2022941341

Cover design by Hannah Linder Designs

ISBN: 978-1-56309-595-5 (paperback)
ISBN: 978-1-56309-596-2 (ebook)

Printed in the United States of America
1 2 3 4 5—26 25 24 23 22

To those with a warrior's heart.

In all these things we are more than conquerors through him who loved us.
—Romans 8:37 NIV

In Memoriam

Erma Smith

Tina "MaShiloh" Barber

ACKNOWLEDGMENTS

Thank you to:

The Iron Stream team—for believing in this series.

Ramona Richards—the best editor a suspense writer could have!

Susan Cornell and Sue Fairchild for copyediting—you rock!

Julie Gwinn—a super agent, super encourager, and super motivator.

Debbye Scroggins—for hours of brainstorming, inspiration, and laughter.

Debbie Layman—for the grand tour of Leiper's Fork and our years of friendship.

Dave Watson—for research and editorial input.

Sandy Squires Robertson Bennett—for your wisdom and your grace. You have a warrior's heart, and you inspire me.

Jamie Bacon and her dog Darttania—for real-life German Shepherd search and rescue inspiration.

Thank you to former War Dog handlers Larry Chilcoat and his Military Working Dog (MWD), Geisha, and John C. Burnam and his MWDs, Timber and Clipper. I first met Larry and John when they were working to raise money for the US Military Working Dog Teams National Monument, which became a reality in 2013 at Lackland Air Force Base (JBSA), San Antonio, Texas. MWDs and their handlers are both a legacy and a treasure to our nation.

Ed Laneville, Tom and Letha Edwards, Donna Jean and Britt Kisshauer, Peter and Gracie Rosenberger, Jim and Minisa Halsey, Lee and Denene Lofland, Powell Hedley, Marco Conelli, Regena Richardson, Linda Kirkpatrick,

Stacie Bertram, Mitch Wernsing, Paul Jackson, Tana Wilhelm Cromwell, and Janet Bozeman—for your encouragement and your support.

Everyone at JustRead and the *Deadly Conclusion* Launch Team.

My Seymour Agency author family—you exemplify the biblical directive to *encourage one another and build one another up.*

Very special thanks:

Oasis Audio and Aimee Lilly—for giving The Deadly Secrets series a "voice."

Linda Veath—my BFF since second grade.

My late husband, Larry—for loving me and our three Shiloh Shepherds, Baer, Glocken, and Jazz, predecessors to my fourth Shiloh Shepherd, Gabriel.

My parents—for showing me sacrificial love.

My hope is that this story will reflect the Word, Jesus Christ, who was, is, and will be forever. I write to the rhythm of His song.

CHAPTER 1

Tuesday afternoon, December 28

Titan paced back and forth in the rear compartment of Keely Lambert's white SUV. The black German Shepherd seemed to know instinctively this was no training session. Keely's lead S&R dog, Ruby, had strained a ligament and couldn't work for at least another week. And Pearl, her second in line, was within three weeks of delivering a litter. That left Titan, Keely's two-year-old prodigy, to do his best. A six-year-old boy's life depended on it.

Connor Wells had wandered away from his family while visiting A. G. Beaman Park near Ashland City, just north of Nashville, and the timing couldn't have been worse. Not only because this was Titan's first run, but because today's seventy-degree weather, unusual for Nashville in late December, would be dropping below freezing tonight and several inches of snow were expected tomorrow morning.

Keely glanced at the clock on the dashboard of her Forester Wilderness. It was already after three o'clock. She would soon be running out of daylight.

Where was Adam? She hit redial. This time he answered.

"Did you get my message?"

"No, why?"

"We've been called to a search. Connor Wells is missing."

"Emma's son?"

"Yes. I have Titan with me. How soon can you meet me at Beaman Park?"

Adam hesitated. "It will be at least an hour. I'm on my way to the airport."

"The airport?"

"To pick up Sergeant McAlister. Remember, he changed his flight? He's coming in today."

Keely groaned. How could she have forgotten? Sergeant Greg McAlister, who was assigned to Lackland Air Force Base in Texas, was flying into Nashville to assess her breeding program. If he was sufficiently impressed, she might soon be supplying working dogs for the military.

"Did you hear me?" Adam interrupted her thoughts. "The sergeant's plane is landing in a few minutes, and I need to run. We'll meet you at the visitor's center in about an hour."

"That's too late." Keely merged into the right lane. "I'll make the run without you."

"Keely, I don't think that's a good idea. You could be out there all night."

"I hope not for Connor's sake." She glanced at the clock again. "I can't believe I forgot the sergeant was coming in today. I have too much on my mind."

"Yes, you do," he said. "With Pearl's litter and your mom's problems. Just remember you have Sara and me to help."

"I know, and I appreciate it." Adam and Sara, now married, had been her best friends since elementary school.

"I'll see you in about an hour. Keep your phone handy."

"Adam, I don't know what I'd do without you."

"You'd never make it." He teased and ended the call.

Keely laughed and turned onto Eatons Creek Road. The rugged hills and forested ridges of the Highland Rim now loomed in front of her. Beaman Park, with its deep hollows and thick undergrowth, was no place for a six-year-old boy to spend the night alone.

A few years ago, an adult hiker had been lost at the park for three days. Keely and Ruby had been one of the teams participating in the search. Thankfully, the man was found alive, but that had been in the warm months of the year. Connor wouldn't be so lucky if they didn't find him before the temperatures dropped tonight.

She followed the narrow tree-lined road up the ridge to Old Hickory Boulevard and then took a right into the park entrance.

Vehicles from the Metro Police Department, the Urban Search and Rescue Crew, and Metro Parks were already on the scene, along with an ambulance from the Nashville Fire Department.

Ten or fifteen people had gathered in a circle in front of the nature center. Connor's dad, Devon Wells, a tall man with wavy dark hair and glasses, stood out among them. As soon as he saw Keely, he rushed toward her.

Keely grabbed her backpack and hopped out of the SUV. "Any word?"

The answer was already written on his face. "Nothing."

"We'll find him." She gave him a quick hug.

Devon nodded. "The police have called in the mounted patrol . . . And bloodhounds. Two crews are already on the ground."

"That's good." Keely looked up to see Emma, Connor's mom, walking toward them. She stopped beside her husband and slipped her arm into his.

"Thank you for helping." Emma wiped away tears.

"I came as soon as you called." Keely reached to embrace her old high school classmate. It had been a while since they had seen each other. After Emma and Devon married, they had moved to Franklin, about twenty miles from where Keely lived in Leiper's Fork. Connor had been no more than two years old when Keely saw him at Emma's mother's funeral. And Jessica, his two-year-old sister, hadn't been born yet.

"Where's Jessie?" Keely looked around the parking lot.

"Devon's mom picked her up. I have the best mother-in-law in the world." Emma looked at her husband. "I'm grateful for her."

Keely turned to Devon. "Can you give me some idea about what happened?"

"Of course." He nodded. "It was a beautiful day, and I'm not in the office this week, so Emma and I decided to bring the kids out here for a picnic lunch." He wrapped his arm around his wife's waist and pulled her closer to him. "The kids had never seen the nature center."

Emma smiled and wiped her eyes.

"I parked at the Highland Trailhead. We ate lunch in the picnic area, and we were about to set out for the nature center when Emma decided to change Jessie's diaper. I went back to the car with her to get a bottle of water, and when I turned around Connor was missing."

"At first, neither of us was overly concerned," Emma said.

"He's a big boy, very mature and responsible for his age, and we didn't think he would go far." Devon glanced to Emma and then back to Keely. "But after a few minutes of looking and not finding him, we knew we had a problem."

Keely nodded. "What did you do next?"

"I asked Emma to stay with the car in case Connor came back, and then I ran as fast as I could here. To the nature center. I was hoping that Connor might have found his way by himself." The lines in Devon's face deepened. "But when he wasn't here, we notified authorities and started calling everybody we knew."

"That's when I called you," Emma said.

"So, it has been three hours since you saw him?" Keely asked, looking at her watch.

"More than three hours now."

"Is there a chance he left with someone?"

"No. I'm certain of it." Devon's voice didn't waver. "Connor wouldn't do that. Besides, there was no one else around."

Keely turned to Emma. "Do you have any idea why he might have run away?"

"He didn't run away." Emma frowned. "He's lost." She visibly shuddered. "He probably saw a deer or some kind of wild animal, started running after it, and then got turned around. He loves animals."

"And he's full of himself," Devon added. "Connor isn't afraid of anything."

"But he's also respectful." Emma looked at her husband. "He wouldn't just run away and leave us. He has to be lost."

"How was he dressed?" Keely asked.

"He had on brown shorts, a beige t-shirt, and red sneakers."

Keely winced. Unfortunately, those colors provided the perfect camouflage in the winter woods. "So, if he has been gone three hours—"

"He could easily be three or four miles from where he started."

Keely turned to see who was speaking and saw a park ranger walking toward them.

She stuck out her hand. "Keely Lambert."

"Dan Rodgers with Metro Parks, ma'am." He shook her hand. "Are you and your canine ready to go?"

"Yes, sir. Is there a specific area of focus? I've been here for one other search, about three years ago, so I'm somewhat familiar with the park."

"I thought I had seen you before." He smiled and held out a map.

Keely took it and refamiliarized herself with the circuitous trails running through the park.

"We have a team working here." Rodgers pointed to the place on the map where Connor was last seen and traced down to where they were standing now.

Keely nodded.

"There's a service road up here." He pointed to a dotted line running parallel to the top of the park's northernmost boundary. "We have two motorized teams driving up and down this road looking for him."

Keely glanced to Devon and Emma. Both were intent on what Rodgers was saying.

"So, right here." The ranger called Keely's attention back to the map. "If you and your dog will start here . . ." He pointed to where Henry Hollow Loop and Laurel Woods Trail intersected. "And work your way around as far west as you can." He backed away. "Ideally that will be all the way to the Shortcut Trail, along Long Hollow, and on around the South Fork."

"Do you have drones in the air?" Keely asked, folding the map and slipping it into her pocket.

"We do. But drones aren't a hundred percent effective for us because of the heavy overgrowth and the rugged terrain of the park. They also have limited battery power."

"Thank you, Ranger Rodgers, I'm ready to get started. My partner will be here soon. When he arrives, would you please give him the same information you gave me? His name is Adam Hunt, and he will most likely have someone with him."

"I certainly will." Rodgers held out a clear plastic bag with a scarf inside. "And you'll need this. It's Connor's. His mother had several pieces of his clothing in her car."

Keely took the bag, traded phone numbers with the ranger, and offered a word of encouragement to Devon and Emma, before hurrying back to her SUV.

When she opened the hatch door, Titan began pawing and whining inside his crate. He was ready for his chance to run.

If he only knew how important this run was.

Within a few minutes, she had him leashed and on the ground, and they were headed up the trail. The big dog tugged at his lead, head held high and anxious for what, to him, was a game that would ultimately be followed by a reward. Keely hoped they would both be rewarded with finding Connor safe.

A half mile later, she steered the shepherd to the left at Henry Hollow Loop Trail. And although they had a way to go before reaching their assigned starting point, Keely commanded the dog into a sit position, opened the scent bag, and let him smell.

"I want you to find," she said.

Titan's ears tilted forward, and his body shook with excitement. If excitement translated into success, they had this one handled.

Please, God.

"Go find!" Keely ordered, as she unsnapped the leash.

Titan took off down the trail, veering off-path to the right and then to the left. Stopping, sniffing, assessing, and then taking off again.

After securing the scent bag, Keely started after the dog.

"Good boy, Titan," she shouted. "Make us all proud."

CHAPTER 2

Tuesday afternoon, December 28

Beau Gardner pulled his Chevy Colorado to a stop along the right-of-way of Little Marrowbone Road, left a voicemail with his office, and tucked his pistol into his belt. Then he grabbed his jacket and a flashlight and climbed out of the truck. Looking right and then left, he locked the truck, and pocketed the keys, before jogging toward the north-side perimeter of A. G. Beaman Park.

He had been here before, several times for pleasure and twice for training. He hoped his experience could help him find Connor before someone—or something—else did, because he knew all too well that predators roamed this area. Some of them carried themselves on two legs, rather than four.

After searching for a shallow spot in Little Marrowbone Creek, he waded across. The next half mile would be straight up through a wooded area to the top of the ridge. If he had calculated correctly, he should be heading directly toward Laurel Woods Trail, near the Shortcut, some two hundred feet above him.

He checked his phone before starting his climb. *No bars.* With any luck, he would have service at the top. This wasn't the time, or the place, to be without cell service. Less than a half hour later, after steady climbing, he made his way to the crest of the ridge.

He stopped to catch his breath and turned to take in the view that had been behind him as he climbed. Especially in the wintertime, the panorama from the top of the Highland Rim could be spectacular, as it was today.

But there was no time for sightseeing right now. Connor was in danger. Beau checked his phone again. *Two bars.* He should call

Emma but decided to wait until he knew his exact location. He turned and hurried toward his intended goal.

Acres of trees of all kinds, from white oak to shortleaf pine, reached toward the fading light in the western sky. And hibernating, brown perennials covered the hillside barrens ahead of him. In the spring, Beaman Park's outcroppings of shale and limestone would boast of wildflowers and wind-whispered, green grasses. But now, in the midst of the Tennessee winter, despite today's unseasonably mild temperature, nature lay dormant.

Both the warm temps and the daylight would soon be gone. He glanced at his watch. He had an hour before the sun went down. He could almost feel the beginning chill of the promised first snow of the season.

Within twenty minutes he saw the bend of a path in the distance ahead. It had to be Laurel Woods Trail. Whatever it was, he hoped it was the right path to Connor.

As he made his way toward the trail, dry grass and broken bits of tree limbs crunched beneath Beau's feet, and the flutter of wings stirred overhead. He looked up to see a flock of turkey roosting in the treetops. It was their way of staying safe from the predators that came out at night, a reminder that this was no place for a six-year-old boy to be after dark.

As if on cue, the call of a distant coyote—perhaps some three to five miles away—announced its presence. Beau stumbled on a small outcropping of rock, reminding him to keep his eyes on his feet.

His phone rang. It was Emma.

"Where are you?"

"I'm inside Beaman, near the Shortcut." He looked for a sign that might confirm his location. "How are you?"

Emma sniffed back tears. "I'm scared."

"We'll find him, sis." Beau took in the landscape around him. The woods and the darkness were closing in. He swallowed his emotion. "I promise. Remember, that's what I do."

"I know. I just . . ." Silence and the sound of the phone being shuffled.

"Hey, man. It's Devon. Emma gave me the phone. She's having a hard time." His brother-in-law hesitated. "We both are."

"We'll find him." Beau repeated the words he had used with Emma—and many times before when trying to encourage the parents of missing children.

Somehow, those words felt empty now.

"I hope so. Emma is worried about the darkness setting in. That's why she wanted to talk to you. She wanted to know if the rescue teams will call off their search at dark and come back in the morning."

"Tell her not to worry." Beau scanned the landscape as he walked, looking past every rock and every tree for a sign of the boy. "I'm here, and I'm sure everyone else will be, until we find Connor." He shook off his fear. "But I can tell you right now that I hope to get to him first, because I'm going to give him a great big bear hug when I do."

"That would be an answer to prayers." Devon breathed the words into the phone. "Having his uncle Beau find him would be less traumatic for him."

Devon's words stuck in Beau's gut.

"Connor will be found safe. If not by me, then by one of the other search teams . . . *He has to be.*" The last four words were almost inaudible.

"Where are you now?"

"I parked my truck on Old Marrowbone Road and entered the park from the north. I crossed Little Marrowbone Creek and made my way to the top of the ridge. I wanted to start where everyone else would ultimately be heading, cover different territory, and hopefully get to Connor sooner." He pulled his flashlight from his jacket. "There's a trail up ahead, and if I've calculated correctly, it's Laurel Woods Trail near the Shortcut." He watched as the last light filtered into darkness.

"You're a good man, Beau, but you always were a rebel."

"I would like to think that most of that is in my past." Beau chuckled, thankful for his brother-in-law's attempt at humor, because he needed to stay strong for Emma's sake. Another rock tripped Beau up. "Bro, I'll let you go. I'm in rugged terrain right here. I need to watch my footing. I'll keep you posted."

"Before you go," Devon said. "Speaking of your past. You should probably know that you may run into Keely out there."

"Lambert?"

"Yes. She's here with her dog. Emma called her."

Beau stopped walking. He hadn't allowed himself to think much about Keely in two or three years. Once he started, he could spend too much time thinking about that part of his life.

"Did you hear me?" Devon interrupted his thoughts.

"Yes. That's good." Beau shook off the memories. "I'd forgotten that Emma and Keely have kept in touch." He started moving forward again. "I've heard she's good at what she does. And we need all the help we can get."

"Agreed . . . ," Devon said. "I'll let you go now. Stay safe out there and check in once in a while."

Beau put his phone away. Maybe what he had said wasn't completely accurate. Of course, he knew that Emma and Keely had stayed in touch. He just did his best to not think about it.

CHAPTER 3

Tuesday, December 28

Keely waited until she reached the Shortcut Trail before stopping to assess GPS coordinates. She called Titan back to her, examined his coat for burrs or injuries, then looked around the landscape. Dusk had settled around them, distorting the images of the distant trees and rock outcroppings, giving them a ghoulish, unearthly appearance. Even the sounds of day had segued into night. The eerie trill of an eastern screech owl and the distant howl of a coyote now replaced the chirping of birds and rustle of leaves.

She pulled a flashlight and the scent bag from her backpack. After giving Titan another sniff of Connor's scarf, she switched on the dog's LED safety collar to make it easier to follow him in the dark.

Then she directed him forward. "Go find."

Even though there was still some daylight, Keely cast the high-powered beam of her flashlight from one side of the path to the other as she picked her way up the trail. Although it was unlikely that Titan would miss audible or scent evidence of Connor, Keely scanned the nearby foliage for anything the dog might have missed. A shoe, a piece of clothing, or even Connor himself. Unfortunately, she had to divide her attention between site searching and her footing, because, in many areas, tree roots and rocks protruded from the dirt and gravel path.

She had trained Titan, as she did all her dogs, to stay in range of her voice, while exploring one hundred and eighty degrees in front of her. Occasionally, she would call him back to reinforce her control. After he was rereleased, he would bound away, intent on finding his target.

Prey drive was one of the most important characteristics of a good search and rescue dog. They had to stay focused on their task. Keely evaluated each puppy in a litter when he or she reached six weeks old. By eight weeks, the pups were being trained. First in basic obedience and then in S&R techniques.

She trained her dogs to search by both scent and sound. A dog's sense of smell is forty times greater than a humans', and a dog can hear sounds four times farther away. Both were important attributes, because Keely and Titan—and any of her dogs—would be working in extreme environments, from dangerously hot temperatures to circumstances when snow covered the ground. If she and Titan didn't find Connor tonight, they would be working in snow tomorrow. She hoped that wasn't necessary.

She caught a glimpse of the big shepherd, standing at the peak of the rise in the trail up ahead. His nose was in the air, and he had one ear cocked backwards. Something had piqued his interest. He was processing either a scent or a sound or both. Then, without warning, he took off running.

Keely rushed up the hill behind him, trying her best not to trip. Once she reached the top, she stopped and rotated her flashlight beam across the span of dormant trees and gray rocks in front of her. But the dog was nowhere to be seen.

She waited, afraid to hope he had found Connor, and afraid to worry that something had happened to Titan. She listened. The only sound in the woods was an owl in the distance and the crackling of the leaves behind her.

"Keely?"

She turned on the spot, now afraid for her life, her only weapon the tactical flashlight she held in her hand. She wished it had been equipped with a stun gun, as some of her others were. The intruder stood ten or twelve yards away holding his hands high above his head.

"I'm TBI, ma'am." He flashed a badge in one of his hands. "I'm here looking for Connor."

Keely eased. She flashed her beam of light from the man's badge to his face.

It was Beau Gardner.

Beau's heart pounded as he waited for Keely to recognize him. He would have known her anywhere. She looked the same. Except the shy, awkward teenager he remembered from school now carried herself like a woman in charge.

"Keely, you know me," he said, lowering his arms. "It's Beau Gardner. Connor's uncle."

The slender brunette appeared to let down her guard.

"Beau?"

"Strange place to meet after all this time, isn't it?"

She opened her mouth to speak when a black German Shepherd ran up to her, barking and jumping. Keely wheeled around to look at the dog, and then took off running, shouting over her shoulder. "He's found him!"

Beau ran after her, and the dog led them over the rise, around a bend in the trail, and then off-trail toward an outcropping of rock. That's when he heard the sound of rushing water below. It was Little Marrowbone Creek.

Please God. No . . .

"Connor!" Keely screamed.

Beau hurried to her side and followed her gaze down to the water. But Connor wasn't in the water. He was lying on a narrow ledge that overlooked the creek.

Keely dropped to her knees and reached for him. But the boy was too far away.

"Connor, don't move until I can get to you," she pleaded. "OK?"

"OK." The boy's voice sounded thin.

Keely fell to her stomach and crawled closer to the edge of the bank. With her arms out and her shoulders down, she tried to grab ahold of the six-year-old.

He was still too far down.

"Let me help you." Beau kneeled beside her. "I'll hold on to your waist, so you don't fall."

Keely nodded and inched forward, her upper torso dangling in mid-air. She tried again to grab Connor, as the German Shepherd hovered closer, keeping watch on all of them. Especially Beau.

"Connor, it's Uncle Beau." Beau peered over the edge of the rock. "We're going to get you out of there. OK?"

"K." The little boy's frown turned upward to a smile.

Now that he was closer to the end of the embankment, Beau could see that his sister's son was clinging to a small Paulownia tree that had grown out of the limestone. The boy was positioned precariously between the rock face and the tree, which was keeping him from a twenty-foot drop into the rocky creek bed below. One wrong move and Connor would free fall to his death.

Keely turned to look at Beau. "Do you have me?"

"Yes."

"I'm scared!" The little boy cried.

"It's OK, Connor. Hang on one minute more," Keely told him.

"I have your legs." Beau loosened his grip on her waist. "Go for it."

Keely nodded and moved forward until her waist was hanging over the edge. Only Beau's strength held her to solid ground.

"Connor, can you help me?" Keely shouted.

"Yes." The six-year-old nodded but turned to look over his shoulder.

"Don't look down! Look at me," Keely ordered. "Keep your eyes on me."

The boy returned his attention to her, and she reached for him.

"Grab my fingers, Connor!"

"I can't—"

"Yes, you can!" she reassured him.

Beau prayed silently and spoke calmly. "Try one more time, Connor. You've got this."

The six-year-old stretched his hand upward as Beau braced Keely.

"I have you anchored," he told her.

She stretched both arms and clamped both sets of fingers around Connor's small wrist. "Good," she said. "Now I need you to trust me. OK?"

Connor didn't respond.

"Connor, turn loose of the tree branch and let me lift you."

The boy's face clouded, tears tracking down his dirty cheeks, and then he released himself to her.

Beau reinforced Keely, as she pulled Connor slowly toward the top. He could feel her straining, the front half of her body suspended in midair as she worked. He wanted to help her lift Connor, but he didn't dare shift his weight. His job was to brace her, so she didn't fall. So, *they* didn't fall. All he could do was watch and wait until Connor's shoulders reached ground level.

"Can you crawl back toward me?" he asked Keely, his words breathless.

"Can you pull?" Her voice quivered, and her arms appeared to falter.

Beau knew he had to make a move. If not, Keely might lose her grip, dropping the boy, and maybe even falling with him. He covered her body with his own to anchor her to the ground and reached with both hands to grip Connor. The boy cried out, and Keely shuddered beneath him.

"Crawl backwards, if you can," he shouted to Keely.

"I don't think I—"

It was then that the big shepherd, that had been hovering close, grabbed Keely by her belt and tugged.

"Pull, Titan. Pull!" Keely's urging motivated the dog, and he tugged even harder.

Feeling Keely move beneath him, Beau made the decision to trust the dog. He shifted his weight to make it easier for her to inch backwards, while quickly lifting Connor to the bank.

"Are you OK?" he asked.

The boy nodded. His eyes were as big as half dollars.

"Don't move, OK?"

Connor nodded, and Beau turned to grab Keely. With the dog's help, he pulled her to safety. She sat back on the ground, breathless, and gave him a weak smile. "I'm glad you showed up when you did." The dog licked her on the face and settled next to her.

Beau relaxed into a sitting position beside Keely and took Connor in his arms.

"I promised your dad that I was going to give you a bear hug when I found you," he whispered into the boy's ear. "And this . . . is . . . it. *Grrrr.*" He growled like a bear.

Connor laughed and relaxed into his embrace.

Beau turned back to Keely. "It took all three of us. But we did it."

"I helped," Connor said.

"You sure did, buddy. You did a lot, especially after everything you've been through today."

Beau marveled at the child's courage. He had been separated from his family for hours, walked three miles by himself, and then clung to a tree branch over the water for who knows how long. He was lucky to be alive.

Keely sat up, opened her backpack, and dug through it. "Here, Connor." She held out a bottle of water. "Take slow sips."

Beau helped the six-year-old open the bottle and watched him drink.

"How long have you been here?" Beau asked, looking around for clues.

"A little while," Connor said. "I was trying to see the water, and I slipped."

"Well, you certainly landed in a good spot. If that ledge hadn't been there, you would have been swimming home."

"You know I can't swim, Uncle Beau."

"I know, buddy. I know." He ruffled the blond hair on the child's head, relief finally settling in. "I'm sure glad you're safe. Let's call your mom and let her know you're OK."

CHAPTER 4

Tuesday, December 28

Keely's phone played the theme song from *Friends*—Adam's ringtone.

"Where are you?" she asked.

"I was about to ask you the same thing."

"We found Connor."

"You did?"

"He's safe. A little banged up, but he's fine."

Keely could hear Adam talking to someone in the background, and then she heard Emma crying.

"Let me give you my GPS coordinates." Keely paused to look at her phone and then read the numbers to Adam. "We're getting ready to head back now."

"You and Connor?"

"Beau Gardner is with me too. He found Titan and me on the trail just before we found Connor."

"Beau is with her," Adam said to someone on the other end of the phone. That brought a round of applause in the background. "I'll ask you about Beau later." Adam chuckled. "There are EMT waiting for your return."

"See you in a bit." Keely ended the call and turned to Connor. "How are you feeling?"

"I want to go home." He had a tear in his eye.

She glanced to Beau, who had stepped a few feet away for a phone call. "We'll leave as soon as your uncle Beau finishes his call."

"OK." Connor swiped his eyes.

"You're really brave, did you know that?"

Connor nodded. "I was scared when it started to get dark."

That gave Keely an idea. She searched through her backpack and pulled out an LED headlamp. She held it out to him. "Look! I have something for you."

Connor's eyes widened. "Is it a light?"

"Sure is." She smiled. "It's a light that you wear on your head. Do you want me to help you put it on?"

"Sure!"

Keely lifted the band over Connor's head, placed it across his forehead and adjusted it to fit him. Then she switched it on.

"Wow!" His face lit up.

"What do you have there, buddy?" Beau asked, walking over to them.

"It's a light!" Connor tilted his head from side to side to see how far the beam would go.

"It's yours to keep," Keely said. "And I have one for your uncle Beau too." She pulled two more headlamps from her pack, gave one to Beau, and placed the third on her head. "Now we're all lit up!"

The boy giggled and pointed to the LED lights on Titan's collar. "He is too."

"I almost forgot!" Keely reached inside her backpack and pulled out a ball, holding it out for Connor. "Do you want to give this to him? His name is Titan."

Connor took the ball and held it out for the dog. "Here, Titan."

The dog took the ball from the boy's hand and started running circles around them.

"That's his reward for finding you," Keely said. "I think he's happy, don't you?"

Connor nodded.

"How about we get going?" Beau said. "I just talked to your mom. She and your dad are waiting for you."

Connor jumped with renewed enthusiasm, and the three of them started up the trail.

An almost moonless night had settled in around them, so Keely lit their path with the high beam of her tactical light, while Beau carried Connor. Titan led the way a few yards ahead of them.

The dog had an unmistakable swagger to his step, knowing he had accomplished his mission.

"Good job, Titan," Keely told him again. "You made me proud. Good boy."

"Good boy," Connor repeated her words.

"He sure is, buddy." Beau cradled the six-year-old, who appeared to be fighting sleep. He had reason to be tired after the day he'd had. "We're glad Titan found you."

"Me too," Connor said. "Good boy."

Beau chuckled and then grew serious. "Why did you walk into the woods on your own, Connor?"

The boy shifted in his arms and looked at Beau. "There was a man talking to me."

Beau stopped walking and glanced toward Keely as he stroked Connor's hair. "Did you know him, buddy?"

Connor shook his head. "No."

"Have you ever seen him before?"

"Maybe."

Beau looked to Keely again. "When? When did you see him before today?"

The boy shrugged. "I don't know . . ."

Beau started walking again. "If you remember, will you tell Uncle Beau?"

Connor nodded. "Yes, sir."

"You're a good boy, too, Connor."

"Good boy," Connor repeated and then yawned, leaning into Beau's shoulder.

Keely chuckled and refocused on the uneven path in front of them. "Be careful," she told Beau. "This section of trail has a lot of roots jutting out of the ground. I noticed it earlier when . . ." Her light reflected off a dull metal object.

"What is that?" Beau asked.

"I don't know." She scuffed at it with her foot, then bent forward to tug on it, and pulled it from the ground. It was a military dog tag. Her heart fluttered. "Beau . . . look at this."

She pulled it closer to her, wiped dirt from it, and then shined her light on it. The letters strained to be seen in the semi-darkness, but she knew exactly what they said. She read them out loud as her hands began to tremble. "Sergeant First Class William J. Lambert."

It was her father's dog tag.

Beau readjusted Conner in his arms and studied Keely's face. Even in the white light of their LED headbands, he could see her pale.

She turned her face to him. Moisture filled her eyes. "What does this mean?" She handed the dog tag to him, and he rolled it around in his fingers. It looked like the real deal. Then again, why would someone want to fake a dead man's dog tag?

"I don't know," he said. "Maybe nothing. But it looks real."

Keely fell to her knees, took a small shovel from her backpack, and started digging.

"Keely, I'm not—" He tried to pull her to her feet. "This isn't the right time."

She jerked away from him. "Twenty-two years later isn't the right time?" Her voice was frantic.

Realizing something was wrong, Titan came running back and started barking and hovering again. Connor roused.

Beau settled the boy down, and then reached for Keely. Titan growled, and Beau backed off. The six-year-old, who now understood that something was amiss, started crying. "Uncle Beau, what's wrong?"

"It's OK, buddy." He turned his body slightly, so the boy faced the other way. "Keely, we need to get Connor back to his parents. Why don't you mark your GPS coordinates, and we'll come back tomorrow?"

She blinked back tears. "But what if—what if?"

This time, she let him pull her to her feet.

Titan leaned into her, and she rubbed the top of the dog's head. "It's all right, boy." She turned to Beau. "Please, let me be . . ."

He nodded.

She dried her eyes, bent forward, and planted her shovel upright in the dirt. After checking her phone for coordinates, she jotted them down, and finally whispered. "Let's go."

Beau put his arm around her shoulder and started walking her up the trail. They traveled in silence for the remainder of their journey, finally seeing lights approaching from ahead. As they walked closer, Beau recognized Adam Hunt. He had Devon and Emma Wells with him.

As soon as Connor saw his parents he started crying. They ran to their son and, one after the other, took him into their arms. At the same time, Keely pulled away from Beau and ran to Adam. He embraced her.

Old memories punched Beau in the gut. Was this the way it would end again? Except last time, he had walked away from her.

A few minutes later, Adam stepped up to him and stuck out his hand. They had been friends in high school, but time and distance had separated them.

Beau, who was a year older, had moved away to college. Adam had stayed closer to home, graduated from a two-year technical school with a degree in finance, and helped Keely build her business.

"It's great to see you." Adam slapped Beau on the shoulder. "It's been too long."

"You're looking good," Beau said. "Married life must agree with you."

"You heard?" Adam grinned. "Sara finally let me talk her into it." He stepped back. "How are you?"

"I'm good. Especially now that we've found Connor." Beau looked toward the little boy, who was being attended to by an EMT. Keely, Emma, and Devon were with them. "The Bureau has kept me busy."

"I have no doubt. I've seen your name in the paper a few times."

"Those are just the high-profile cases. A lot of our work is less than newsworthy." Beau lowered his voice. "I would like to have your help with something that has to do with Keely."

"Keely?" Adam stepped closer.

"We found something on the trail that needs to be investigated, and we made plans to return tomorrow. Do you have time to go with us?" He hesitated before continuing. "I'll also have a forensic crew there. We may have stumbled onto her dad's remains."

Adam gasped. "Where? Are you sure?"

"I'm not sure. But I think it's possible. We found his dog tag partially buried in the dirt, just off the main trail."

Adam turned to check on Keely and then looked back at Beau. "That's all she has wanted for years." His voice drifted off. "I hope she can handle it if it happens."

"She didn't take it well back on the trail. That's why I want you to come with us. If I'm right, and we have found the remains, I'll need you to take her away while we excavate the grave."

CHAPTER 5

Tuesday evening, December 28

Keely walked with Adam from the parking lot to the nature center. Beau and Emma's dad, Deputy Sheriff James J. G. Gardner, and Devon were already inside, along with Air Force Sergeant Greg McAlister. Emma had accompanied Connor to the hospital for his evaluation.

Once inside the nature center, Adam introduced Keely to the sergeant. "Sergeant McAlister, I'd like you to meet Keely Lambert."

"It's a pleasure, Ms. Lambert." The sergeant stuck out his hand.

Keely wiped hers on her khakis before extending her own. "It's a pleasure for me, too, sir." She glanced to Adam. "We both appreciate your making the trip to see our dogs."

"They're her dogs," Adam teased. "I'm just the kennel boy."

McAlister laughed. "I know teamwork when I see it, and it looks like you have a good team. Congratulations on your success today."

"Thank you." Keely saw Beau walking in the door and motioned for him to join them. "Sergeant, this is Special Agent Beau Gardner with the Tennessee Bureau of Investigation. He had a lot to do with Connor's rescue today." She turned to Beau. "Beau, this is Sergeant Greg McAlister from Lackland Air Force Base. He's here to look at my dogs."

"Special Agent Gardner. Nice to meet you."

"Likewise," Beau said. "I'm thankful it's under good circumstances."

"These are some very special people, Sergeant," Devon said as he stepped up to the group. "We're proud to call them friends, as well as family." He gestured toward Beau. "Beau is my wife's brother."

"And this is Titan," Keely said. The dog was leaning against her, and still holding his reward ball in his mouth.

"He's a good-looking canine," McAlister said. "The main thing is that he knows how to do his job. He proved that today."

"Thank you." She stroked Titan's head. "This was his first official run."

"Really?" McAlister stepped back and assessed Titan from head to tail. "Impressive. Congratulations."

"Keely does good work," Beau said. "Her dogs are widely regarded in this area. The Bureau has called on them several times."

"How long have you been breeding shepherds?" Sergeant McAlister asked.

Keely brushed a lock of hair from her face. "Since I was twenty, about eight years—"

"Keely," Beau's dad, Deputy Gardner, interrupted. "Dan Rodgers and one of the Metro officers would like to speak with all of us in the office." He pointed down the hall.

"Of course." Keely led the way and the group followed.

"Everyone, please have a seat. We've pulled in a few extra chairs, but they're not very comfortable. I'll make this as brief as possible." Rodgers chuckled. "I'm sure you're all tired and ready to go home. I know I am."

He took a seat behind the desk.

"First of all, good work on everyone's part, especially the two of you." He looked to Keely and then to Beau. "And to your dog."

Keely smiled and nodded.

"We appreciate your efforts and your expertise. One look at the overnight weather forecast, and we all realize this could have ended differently."

"Ranger Rodgers," Devon said. "I'm sorry to interrupt, but Connor's mom and I want to thank you and the Metro police for your help too." He glanced from Rodgers to the police officer in the room, who had been introduced as Max Salem.

Rodgers nodded and continued. "I've sent the other search teams home. We appreciate their efforts as well, but I wanted to have a quick meeting with all of you to go over the facts while they're still fresh."

He looked to Officer Salem. "I'm certain that the police, and possibly the TBI, will be doing an investigation of their own, and I want you all to know that we will cooperate to the best of our abilities."

"Thank you," Beau said. "I talked with my boss a few minutes ago and shared the abbreviated version of what happened today, including that Connor is my nephew. He and I will be meeting in the morning to go over details."

"Just let me know how I can help," Rodgers said.

"Officer Salem," Beau added. "I'll exchange contact information with you before I leave."

Salem nodded.

Rodgers took the floor again. "All of us have had a chance to talk to Connor briefly but, Special Agent Gardner and Ms. Lambert, you spent the most time with him. I'd like to know what he told you about his decision to go into the woods by himself."

"Would you like to go first, Keely?" Beau asked.

She shook her head. "You can."

Beau nodded and leaned forward. "I met up with Keely and Titan just before the dog indicated that he had found Connor. Keely and I immediately followed him to the edge of Little Marrowbone Creek." He read the GPS coordinates of the site out loud, then continued. "Connor had fallen onto a narrow, rocky ledge halfway between the top of the bank and the water below." Beau hesitated, glancing to Devon. "He was in a precarious position, holding on to the branch of a small tree."

Keely shuddered. The situation could have turned out so differently.

"After the two of us—more specifically, Keely—were able to lift him to safety, he told us he had been on the ledge for a little while." Beau looked to Keely again. "Connor told us he fell off the bank while trying to see the water."

Keely nodded and added. "He said he hadn't been scared until the darkness began to set in, which wasn't too long before we found him."

Beau continued. "Once we checked him out, and Keely gave him something to drink, I asked him why he went into the woods on his own." Beau glanced to his brother-in-law again. "Connor said he saw a man in the woods."

"Did he describe that man?" Rodgers asked.

Beau shook his head. "He didn't. But he said he may have seen the man before."

A collective gasp filled the room.

"Let me be clear. He said he didn't know who the man was or where he had seen him, but that he may have seen him." Beau glanced at Keely, and she nodded her agreement. "When I asked him where, he said he didn't remember."

"Did he say anything else?"

"Only that the man was talking to him . . ."

"Did he say what the man said?"

"I didn't pursue that," Beau said.

Rodgers turned to Keely. "Ms. Lambert, is Mr. Gardner's description the same as you remember?"

"Yes, sir," Keely said. "I don't remember anything different or in addition to what Agent Gardner told you. We didn't ask too much. Connor was exhausted, and we wanted to get him back here so he could be reunited with his parents and evaluated for health concerns."

"Of course," Rodgers said.

"I don't understand why he didn't run to us instead of a stranger." Devon frowned. "It doesn't make sense. Connor knows he can always depend on his mom and me."

"Sometimes when we are confused or scared, we make bad decisions." James Gardner twisted in his seat and spoke for the first time. "Let's not be too hard on the kid. He's only six years old. I'm sure he did what he thought was best at the time."

"Good point, J. G.," Rodgers said.

Several others in the room nodded, but Beau sat poker faced while his dad spoke.

"The main thing is that he's safe now," Devon said.

"Before we wrap up, does anyone have anything else to add?"

No one spoke.

"OK," Rodgers said. "Officer Salem and I have one more thing to discuss."

Keely turned to Adam, who raised an eyebrow. *Where was this going?*

"Late this afternoon, while the search was in progress, one of my rangers was making rounds in the parking lot and discovered something." Rodgers looked to Devon Wells. "Mr. Wells, am I correct that you have a silver Toyota Sienna?"

"Yes, sir. It's Emma's car. I usually drive my truck."

"Have you noticed any unusual noises coming from the back of the vehicle?"

"No, why?"

"Are you familiar with the new tracking devices that can be purchased over the counter at electronic and hardware stores?"

"You mean those things that have been used to stalk people?" Keely asked.

"Yes, ma'am. We found one under Mr. Wells' back bumper."

CHAPTER 6

Wednesday morning, December 29

Beau opened the door to his office, pulled up the window blinds, and took off his jacket. He set the evidence bag containing the tracking device on his desk, placed his cup of coffee beside it, and sat down. After filing a case report, he logged the device as evidence and put in a call to the runner who would deliver it to forensics. If they were lucky and this guy was an amateur, they would soon know the owner. And perhaps, the identity of the man who had enticed, or chased, Connor into the woods—if, in fact, it was the same man.

Yet none of this made sense. Why would a stalker plant a device on Emma's car, follow her and her family to the nature center, scare Connor, and then leave? It was also possible that the device had been planted while Emma's car was at the park.

Beau made a note to have Dan Rodgers send over all the video footage that had been captured by park cameras yesterday, both inside and outside the nature center. He would run a background check on the owner of every vehicle in the parking lot. He also planned to check the possibility of known pedophiles or career criminals who were at the park or lived in the area.

He set down his pen. What were the chances they might be dealing with two different perpetrators? Was the person Connor saw the same person who had placed the device on Emma's car? Was someone trying to kidnap Connor for ransom? Or could they be dealing with another human trafficking ring, similar to the case he had worked last year? Young boys were trafficked as often as young girls.

Of course, there was also the possibility that some deranged person had taken a fancy to Connor and wanted to raise him as their own. All of these things happened. But you never thought it would happen in your family.

Not that his family was alien to misfortune. Or even dysfunction. God knows he had been raised by a mother who was the salt of the earth. Rachel Gardner's untimely death in a freak automobile accident five years ago had devastated all of them. Even his dad, a man who had defined dysfunction all of Beau's life, had been changed, and in a good way, by the loss. He had even stopped drinking. Cold turkey. If only Beau's mother had lived to see that.

Fortunately for Connor, Emma was exactly like Rachel. Kind. Generous. God fearing. And Devon was a textbook dad. He adored both of his children.

Although though Beau had followed his father into law enforcement, he had done everything else in his power to live a life that was one hundred and eighty degrees from him. Yes, he had rebelled. But only against his father.

He had avoided drinking. And carousing. He had tried to act responsibly . . . and now that almost everything a person did was captured on video and archived forever on the internet, his clean lifestyle had paid off, helping him land the job of his dreams at the Bureau.

Whatever had gone wrong in the Gardner family had almost always been self-inflicted by his father. James Gardner had lived his life, or at least as much of it as Beau could remember, as if he were being chased by demons. Beau had come home countless nights to a drunken, melancholy man, who was being helped into bed by his wife. At least he had never laid a hand on her or Emma. Beau had decided as a young boy that J. G. Gardner would have paid the price if he had.

Neighbors and coworkers—even Beau's mom—had always made excuses for his dad. *It was the Gulf War that destroyed his life. He was a hero for serving his country. He was never the same after he returned home from overseas.* Rachel Gardner had told Beau these things over and over, trying to instill a love for his dad that had never existed.

And never would.

Out of respect for his mother, Beau had done his best to play the part. He had shown his dad the semblance of respect she wanted to see. But after Beau left for college in Knoxville, he only returned home for holidays. A choice that still stabbed him in the gut. It was the part of his life he would like to do over.

Especially now that his mom was gone. He should have come home more often to visit her. And Emma. He was thankful his sister had a forgiving heart like their mom. They had not only forgiven Beau for being a less than adequate son, but they had also forgiven his dad. Maybe someday Beau would be able to do both.

A reminder buzzed on his phone. He needed to call Keely as soon as possible. He had promised her yesterday that they would go back to Beaman Park today. But that wasn't about to happen. The weatherman finally got one right. Temperatures had plummeted overnight, and Tennessee looked like a winter wonderland. It was the stuff of a child's Christmas dreams and a workday commuter's nightmare.

Outside his window the snow showed no signs of letting up. Freezing rain had moved in after midnight and turned to snow in the early hours of the morning. Big flakes threatened visibility as it swirled from high above his second story window to the parking lot below. The roads were covered and had been since he climbed out of bed this morning. Six to eight more inches were expected by nightfall. Tennesseans had been advised to travel only when necessary.

It was not a good day to excavate a grave, even if, in fact, that was what they had found, and Beau's gut told him it might be. Only forensics could answer that question for sure. And it would be another two or three days before his team could get there. What had been buried for twenty-two years would have to wait a little longer. Right now, he was dealing with the life or death of one six-year-old child—and maybe others.

As soon as he had finished up with the preliminaries of Connor's case, including jurisdiction issues, he would call Keely and make her promise not to go to Beaman by herself. Maybe he would invite her to lunch to make certain she didn't. He would enjoy that.

But first he had to meet with his boss.

Ten minutes later Beau stepped into Chris Enoch's office.

"Have a seat, Beau," Enoch said. "What kind of a mess have you gotten yourself into this time?"

Beau laughed.

Six years ago, when he first started working at the Bureau, he had been fortunate to have Christopher Enoch assigned as his supervisor. Most of the time, the two of them agreed on everything.

"I have an interesting case," Beau said. "I stumbled onto it because of family involvement."

Enoch sat back in his chair. "You know the rules . . ."

"Yes, sir. But what started out as my six-year-old nephew getting lost at the park on my day off turned into something completely unexpected." He stopped to collect his thoughts. "Let me start from the beginning. Some of this you already know from our conversation yesterday.

"I was running a few personal errands when I got a call from my sister, Emma. Her son, Connor, had wandered off from her and her husband while the family was exploring Beaman Park. She was in tears, and understandably so. You don't want your kid wandering around Beaman Park—or any other place these days—without supervision."

Enoch nodded, and Beau knew he understood. Enoch had two children of his own under the age of ten.

"So I turned my truck around and hightailed it out there. I parked on the right of way off Little Marrowbone Road and entered Beaman from the northwest side. I figured, by doing that, I could cover some ground other searchers hadn't yet reached. We were losing daylight quickly, and . . ." He pointed out the window. "This was coming overnight."

Enoch leaned forward. "So you found Connor, and he was safe."

Beau nodded. "Yes, sir. He's banged up a bit from his fall. But he's home and doing fine. I talked to my sister this morning."

"What happened after you found him? Did he give you any indication as to why he wandered off?"

"Yes." Beau sat back in his chair. "He said he saw a man in the woods and followed him."

"Did he tell you what the man was doing? Or if he knew him?"

"He said the man spoke to him, but he didn't tell us what he said. He also said that he may have seen the man before, but that he wasn't sure." Beau rubbed the back of his neck. "I'll be honest. We didn't push him for much more. Our main concern at that time was to assess his physical condition and get him back to his parents and medical care as soon as possible."

"You said 'we.' Who was with you?"

Beau thought about his answer. "It's complicated."

"Why is that?"

"Just before finding Connor, I met up with another searcher on the trail, and she had a search and rescue canine with her. Without the dog, I'm not sure that either of us would have found him, considering where Connor was—on a rocky ledge hidden by the creek bank. He was either in shock, or exhausted, or both because he wasn't making a sound. The dog saved his life, no doubt about it."

"Very fortunate."

"Yes. And especially interesting, or as I said a minute ago, *complicated*, because I knew the woman with the dog."

His boss furrowed his brow. "Why is that complicated? We've all met and worked with search and rescue teams in the line of duty."

"I hadn't worked with her." Beau shook his head. "I used to date her." He laughed.

"Used to date her? I hope it ended well."

Beau laughed again, this time nervously. "It didn't."

Enoch chuckled. "We all have a few of those in our past."

"Thankfully, she's the only one in my case, because I was a jerk back then . . ."

His boss raised a brow.

"Right after I graduated high school, I left town and didn't even say goodbye to her."

"You *were* a jerk." Enoch didn't cut him any slack. Now . . . or ever.

"The good news is that she didn't leave me on the trail or knock me into the creek."

"You're both professionals, but that speaks highly of her."

"Yes, it does."

"Your day in the creek, so to speak, is probably coming, if you ever see her again." Enoch laughed.

Beau grimaced. There were so many parts to this story. "Actually, I am planning to see her again soon." He hesitated. "Because something else happened yesterday. On the way back to the nature center, Keely—her name is Keely Lambert—found a clue to a cold case from more than twenty years ago."

Chris Enoch's eyes widened, and his lips parted to speak, but he didn't. Not until he had picked up a pen from the top of his desk and leaned back in his chair. "Fill me in."

CHAPTER 7

Wednesday, December 29

Chris Enoch sat quietly, listening to what Beau had to say.

"We were on our way back in the dark when Keely's tac light flashed on something metallic. She picked it up and saw that it was an old military dog tag. She showed it to me immediately."

"Could you still read the name and ID on the tag?"

Beau nodded. "Yes. It read 'Sergeant First Class William J. Lambert.'"

Enoch startled. "Are you positive?"

"Yes. It was her father's dog tag. He disappeared in the summer of 2000 and was never heard from again."

"What are the odds of her finding *that* dog tag?" Chris Enoch shook his head.

Beau leaned forward. "I would say zero to none." He hesitated. "I think it was left there for her to find."

"Are you saying your nephew's disappearance—and the man who led him into the woods—had something to do with the dog tag?"

"Yes." Beau locked eyes with his supervisor. "And possibly with William Lambert's disappearance."

"I don't know. That's an interesting set of circumstances."

"Exactly," Beau said. "And I don't believe it was coincidence. I believe it was planned."

"Because?" Obviously, Enoch wasn't convinced.

Beau sat back. "I've thought a lot about that. Right now, my best guess is that the man responsible for Lambert's disappearance grew increasingly concerned that Keely knows something that could hurt him. Or, and this is a stretch, it could be that he has a vendetta against her that has been festering."

"How old was she when her father disappeared?"

"She was seven. Her father disappeared on her seventh birthday. And she was with him when it happened."

Enoch cursed under his breath and looked out the window. "That's pure evil. A person who would do that has no regard for the innocence or the emotional state of a child." He turned back to Beau.

"I agree," Beau said. "But we both know there are people like that in the world."

"Unfortunately, plenty of them." Enoch tossed his pen onto his desktop and waited for it to roll to a stop before looking up. "So, let's get to the bottom line. I'm assuming you are asking to work this case, correct?"

"Yes."

"And you don't see a family conflict?"

"I don't. It's my theory that Connor was only a pawn, that this case is not about him at all. I believe everything that happened yesterday was tied to the cold case of William Lambert's disappearance." He chose his words carefully. "Remember, Keely isn't family. In fact, until yesterday, except for my mother's funeral, I hadn't seen Keely in more than ten years."

Enoch swiveled his chair toward the window and said nothing for a few minutes. Beau waited, hoping for a win but bracing himself for the loss.

Finally, after another spin of his chair, Chris Enoch broke the silence. "Is there anything else I need to know before I make my decision?"

"Yes, one more thing. And I think it further proves my theory."

"OK. What is that?"

"Before we left the nature center last night, one of the park rangers told us that he had found a tracking device on my sister's car."

Enoch's eyes widened, and he was slow to speak. "You have an interesting case on your hands, Gardner."

"I know, it's—" Beau stopped mid-sentence, realizing what Chris Enoch was intimating. "Are you telling me that I have the case, sir?"

"Yes." Enoch stood to walk Beau to the door. "But I want you to keep me updated on every little detail. If this becomes a conflict, I will need to reassign it."

"Thank you, sir." Beau turned to leave and then turned back around. "I have one more question."

"What is it?"

"Does giving me this case mean that you agree with my theory?"

"I do," Enoch said. "For two reasons. Actually, three."

"And what are those reasons?" Beau asked.

A slow smile spread across his boss's face. "First, and most importantly, I think it's highly unlikely that anyone, even someone with a psychosis, would lure a six-year-old into the woods just to leave them."

Beau agreed. "And?"

"I don't like coincidences. Show me a crime that was solved with coincidences, and I'll find you a dozen good defense attorneys who can beat it in court." Enoch paused momentarily before continuing. "I don't think Keely Lambert found her father's dog tag by accident. It's too easy, and it doesn't make sense. How is it that something that was buried so conspicuously—and for twenty years, at that—had never been found?" He shook his head. "And what's more, Laurel Woods Trail wasn't built until 2020. There are more than two thousand acres in that park, and a trail just happens to be built right next to our evidence. Why wasn't it found when the trail was built?" He took in a long breath and then exhaled. "Of course, the rain and water from the creek could have slowly uncovered it through the years. But thousands of hikers have been through there, myself included. Why is Keely the one who found it? That's too much of a coincidence."

"I agree," Beau said and waited for his boss to continue. When he didn't, Beau prompted. "You said there was a third reason?"

"Yes. Your mother's funeral."

"What?" Beau took a step backwards. "You'll need to explain that one to me."

"That's because you know it intuitively." Enoch smiled. "But for outsiders like me, we can see that it either took a long-tenured relationship—or extraordinary compassion—for Keely Lambert to show up at your mother's funeral after what you did to her."

"Probably both, regrettably." Beau felt heat rise to his face.

"Everything you've told me this morning indicates that the perpetrator knows your family and Keely's relationship with it. Even Connor said he may have seen the man before." Enoch paused before continuing. "I believe that person knew, or had good reason to believe, that Keely would be called into the search yesterday."

"I'm with you on all of this," Beau said. "What do you think the tracking device found on Emma's car has to do with all of this?"

Enoch thought for few minutes before answering. "It's either an outlier or a red herring."

Beau chuckled. "So this guy is playing games with us?"

"Either that or the tracker is completely unrelated to the case."

"Maybe," Beau said. Although he had another idea. One he wasn't ready to share until he knew more. He prepared to leave, but Enoch stopped him.

"One more thing, Gardner. I'm sure you've thought about this, but I would find out who assigned Keely to that particular trail for the search and have that person checked out."

"Good point. Thank you, sir." He closed the door and took off down the hall. It was time to call Dan Rodgers.

Rodgers picked up on the first ring.

"Dan, it's Beau Gardner at the TBI."

"How can I help you?"

Beau got straight to the point. "Can you lock down a trail for me?"

"Of course." Rodgers hesitated. "Would it be possible to share the reason for your request?"

"Yes, sir. But please keep this information close. If you don't have to share it with anyone else, I would appreciate it if you didn't."

"I can keep it between us," Rodgers said quickly.

Beau took a breath. "When Keely Lambert and I were walking Connor back from Little Marrowbone Creek yesterday, we stumbled onto something concerning." How much should he tell Rodgers? He was most likely the person who assigned Keely to Laurel Woods Trail. "We found a personal artifact, a necklace belonging to someone who has been missing for a while."

"I will, of course, comply. But I'm not sure why that would concern you. We're always finding personal artifacts out here."

"As soon as the weather clears up, I would like to send a forensic team to the site to excavate."

"So you think there's more?"

"I'd like to find out for sure."

"Of course."

"And in the meantime, I would like to keep everyone else away from Laurel Woods Trail."

"Do you want me to lockdown the park as a precaution?"

"Can you do that without a problem?"

"In this weather? Yes, of course," Rodgers said.

"I'll be back in touch as soon as I have a crew scheduled. Thanks for your help."

Beau disconnected the line, and then placed a call to Chuck Hailey in the forensics lab to explain what he had found and what he wanted to do.

"Can we make it happen?" Beau asked.

"Sounds doable to me," Hailey said. "I'll get started on the paperwork. That should take two or three days unless you're in a hurry, and I can expedite it."

Beau looked out the window. The snow was still coming down. "That should work out just fine. I'll check with you later this week." He hung up and leaned back in his chair.

It was time to call Keely.

Why was that so hard? He had seen her yesterday, and they had broken the ice.

Just keep it business, he reminded himself. He wasn't looking to renew a relationship. Not that it mattered. She wouldn't be interested after the way he left ten years ago.

There had been no goodbye. He had just rushed off to school to get as far away from his father's house as he could. But also leaving behind the woman he still loved.

Even more than he wanted to admit.

CHAPTER 8

Wednesday, December 29

"Keely Lambert." She answered the call without looking at her phone.

"It's Beau."

Keely's heart took a dive. The sound of his voice had a way of bringing it all back. Every bad memory. Not just those from ten years ago when he left her, but now . . . Her hand flew to the dog tag she was wearing. "Hey."

"Am I interrupting?"

She straightened. "No. You're fine. I'm having lunch with Sergeant McAlister at The Country Boy, but the waitress hasn't brought our food yet." She made an attempt to lighten the mood. "It's still the best place in town."

"Always has been. Maybe I can meet you there sometime."

"Sure." *Whatever . . .*

"Anyway . . ." He cleared his throat. "I'm following up on our plans for today. We need to reset because of the weather."

"I agree." She turned to look out the window. It was only mid-day, and the snow was already several inches deep. She glanced to Sergeant McAlister across the table. "We haven't had the chance to work the dogs as I'd hoped."

"He saw Titan in action yesterday."

Keely relaxed her shoulders. "That's what he said." She looked again to the man sitting across the table from her. "I hope I'm not misspeaking, but I think he likes my dogs."

Greg McAlister laughed and gave her a thumbs up.

"That's great, Keely. I'm happy for you."

"Thanks. My dad would be proud—"

"Yes," Beau said. "You're keeping his legacy alive."

She wiped her eyes and bolstered herself. "I told the sergeant that Dad had been a dog handler."

"I have a feeling this is God ordained. One of those little blessings that has been waiting for a while to surprise you," Beau said.

She held the phone away from her ear. "Who are you? You sound like a preacher."

"I'm a long way from that. You know better than anybody."

"Truth."

Beau had been the most rebellious boy in school. And at church. She had always been attracted to the bad boys. One reason Adam had never been more than a friend.

"I'm working at doing better."

"I'm sorry if I offended you."

"No offense taken. I'm just trying to start over."

She sat back in her chair. "Good luck with that."

"I deserved that." He paused, presumably to lick his wounds. "Why don't I call you back when the snow clears, and we can schedule a time to meet at the park?"

"OK. Maybe tomorrow . . . or Friday?"

"We'll see."

"Beau." She stood and paced toward the back of the restaurant. "You'd better not leave me out of this."

"What do you mean?"

"You know what I mean. You had better not go out there without me." She studied the quilt hanging on the wall near the bathrooms.

"I'm not so sure you—"

"Beau! I'm a big girl. I've seen a lot of things in my work. I have . . ." *Could she say it?* "I have a cadaver dog, and I know—" She swallowed back tears. She *would* not cry. Not here.

"Keely, this is your dad we're talking about."

"I should be the one who decides whether I'm strong enough to handle this."

"OK."

"Can I trust you?"

He hesitated. "Yes," he said. "You can."

"Thank you." She ended the call, tucked her phone into her pocket, and wiped her eyes before hurrying back to the table. Her time with Greg McAlister was too important to let Beau Gardner mess it up.

An hour later, after they had eaten lunch, Keely took her guest on a tour of the little village. For years, Leiper's Fork, with its population of four hundred or so, had been no more than an afterthought to most Nashvillians if they had heard about it at all. The town's only claim to fame was its inclusion on the National Register of Historic Places, and that was partly because of its location at the northern end of Natchez Trace Parkway.

But things had changed in the 2000s when tourists and Nashvillians had "discovered" their little town, a funny thought for the locals whose families had been born and raised here for a number of generations. Outsiders were drawn to its small-town charm, big front porches, trendy boutiques, eclectic art galleries, and country music celebrity sightings. On any given Saturday morning, a well-known music star might be seen eating breakfast at The Country Boy. That same night another celebrity might be jamming with a local band at Fox & Locke, formerly known as Puckett's Grocery. Puckett's, as the locals still called it, featured mismatched tables and chairs, shelves of canned goods, and southern food during the week, and added authentic country music at the week's end.

Judging from his reaction, Greg McAlister appeared to be as intrigued by Keely's hometown as he was by her dogs. "I think you've got something here," he told her on their way to his hotel in Franklin, which was about ten miles away. "As soon as I get back to Lackland, I'm going to recommend that we include you on our preferred list of breeders."

"I don't know what to say," Keely gushed. "Everything I do is a tribute to my dad, and he would be proud to know that his dogs—my dogs from the kennel that bears his name—may be serving the country he loved."

"Let's hope that happens. We'll take it a step at a time."

"Thank you." She glanced his way as she drove. "This has been a dream of mine for almost a lifetime."

"It's obvious that you've worked hard for it," he said. "And that you love your dad."

"Did I tell you that Titan is the namesake of his working dog in the Gulf War?"

"You didn't." McAlister studied her. "What division was your father with?"

"He served with the 502nd Regiment 101st Airborne Division out of Fort Campbell, Kentucky." She slipped the dog tag off her neck and handed it to him.

He turned it over in his hands.

"My dad served with the Screaming Eagles too. I've heard so many stories about their—" He stopped mid-sentence. "I'm sorry," he said. "I'm fortunate to still have my dad. You've missed a lot."

Keely wiped moisture from her eyes and shook her head. "No. I'm sorry to be such a mess. This has been an emotional two days for me." He nodded, and she collected her thoughts. "I would love to hear some of your dad's stories someday."

"I plan to return and, you never know, my dad might agree to come with me. When do you expect to have your next litter of puppies that might match what I need?"

"This spring for sure. Ruby will be bred in April. I've found the most amazing match for her." She stopped herself. "As you can tell, I love talking about my dogs."

"It's OK." He smiled. "Your secret is safe with me."

"It's hardly a secret, Sergeant McAlister." She shook her head. "I'm quite the conversationalist at dinner parties." She pulled the SUV to a stop in front of the hotel. "People scatter in every direction when they see me walking their way."

He laughed and opened his door. "I doubt that. Oh, before I forget." He gave the dog tag back to her. "This is a treasure. I'm glad you found it."

She nodded and bit her lip.

"I'll be right back," he said. "My bags are packed. All I need to do is check out."

"Take your time." Keely folded her fingers around the metal ID. "I'll be here watching the snow. We don't get to see it that often in Tennessee."

After he left, she settled into her seat and stared out the window. In the last twenty-four hours, a lot more than the weather had changed for her. She had been on a roller coaster ride of emotion, from the elation of finding Connor, to the bittersweet blessing of finding her dad's dog tag.

And then today, she had experienced the fulfillment of the dream she had set out to achieve almost ten years earlier. From the very beginning, her goal had been to raise dogs good enough to serve alongside the men and women of the military, like her father and others who had served beside him.

Beau had been right. Only God could orchestrate something so perfectly timed. She had been given just enough good news to balance out the dread that nagged at her gut. The dread of finally knowing for sure if her dad was dead. The dread—and yet the blessing—of possibly having found his grave and gaining closure for herself. And for her mother.

Since Keely had been seven years old, despite any lack of evidence for it, she had hoped that Will Lambert was still alive, and that he would eventually come home to them. She had imagined every scenario that might have kept him away through the years.

Now decades.

Maybe he had been struggling with memory loss and didn't know where to find them. Or, maybe, the men who had hijacked their car that day had detained him against his will, but he would eventually break free.

Whatever the truth, she might know it soon. And no matter what joy or pain would come from it, she was confident that it would happen according to God's perfect plan.

A tear slid down her cheek. She brushed it aside and hoped that she would be strong enough to handle everything coming her way.

Something in her gut told her that the roller coaster ride had just started.

CHAPTER 9

Monday, January 3

Monday morning, Beau took a left into the Beaman Park Nature Center visitor's lot, parked, and got out. Ranger Dan Rodgers was waiting for him at the front door.

"Good to see you, Beau. Would you like a cup of coffee?"

Beau checked the time. He had fifteen minutes before his crew arrived. "Sounds great." He rubbed his hands together and followed Rodgers inside. "Looks like we may be setting another record today."

Rodgers chuckled. "I'd be happier if we didn't set records for low temperatures. My wife keeps telling me it's time to retire so we can move to Florida." He closed and locked the door behind them. "Today, I might agree with her."

"Retirement isn't in my vocabulary at this point."

"That's great," Rodgers said, directing Beau toward the back. "I'm sure you'll do a lot of good—and help a lot of people—before you're ready to retire."

Beau considered that thought. It was a good one to remember when he was having an especially hard day.

"I appreciate your being here on your day off."

"Not a problem. Go ahead and have a seat in the office. I'll get the coffee." He turned to leave and then swung around. "Do you take cream and sugar?"

"Just cream."

"I'll be right back."

Beau looked around the office, finally taking a seat next to a large panoramic window. From his desk, Rodgers had a direct view of the wooded area and trail behind the nature center. The brown landscape, with its skeletal tree branches and languid undergrowth, allowed Beau to see several hundred yards into the woods, where nothing stirred. The absence of life was almost eerie.

"Here you go." Rodgers reached around and handed him a cup filled with dark brew. "Government issue. Strong and hot."

"Thanks." Beau turned and watched the older man walk toward his desk.

"What are your expectations today?" Rodgers asked.

Beau took a sip of the coffee. Rodgers had been right. It was hot. He set the cup on the table beside him. "I'll go ahead and tell you that we're looking for a grave."

The older man shook his head. "What makes you think there's someone buried on this property?"

Beau related a few details about Keely's father's disappearance. "If we should happen to find human remains, it will take a day or two to excavate it properly."

"And if you don't?"

Beau studied the ranger, whose background check had not only come back clean, but it had been exemplary. "You seem to think that will be the case."

Rodgers raised an eyebrow. "I've walked this park for more than a decade. I'd be surprised if you stumbled onto anything like that. It would have already been found."

Beau reached for his coffee again. "You could be right."

"For the sake of the family, I hope I'm not." Rodgers glanced at the clock on the wall. "Closure is the beginning of the grieving process."

"And it's a long process. I know from personal experience."

"I'm sorry to hear that, Agent Gardner. You're too young to be dealing with that kind of loss in your life."

"My mother died in an automobile accident five years ago," Beau said. "She was on Old Natchez Trace and veered off the road into the Harpeth River. Somehow, she missed every tree between the highway and the water. But the impact of the landing knocked her unconscious and she drowned."

"I am sorry."

Beau finished his coffee and tossed the cup into a nearby waste can. "My crew will be here any minute. I appreciate the hospitality."

Rodgers stood. "Do you mind if I go with you?"

"Of course not," Beau said. "This is your domain. I would expect you to protect it."

The ranger grabbed a coat from the back of his chair. "I'm eager to know if my theory is correct."

Beau stopped and looked at him. "You don't believe anyone is buried here, do you?" He studied the lines in the older man's face.

"No, I don't." He clapped Beau on the shoulder. "But we need to find out."

A black SUV was pulling into the parking lot just as Beau and Rodgers stepped onto the deck. While the forensics crew was loading tools into the back of one of two four-wheelers, Adam drove up. He had Keely with him.

Beau hurried to the car and opened the passenger side door. "Good morning."

"Good morning . . . and thank you," she said.

"For what?" Beau asked.

"For keeping your word."

"You've waited a long time."

She nodded and took his hand. He escorted her to one of the four-wheelers and helped her take a seat. "Do you mind if I ride with you?"

"Of course not." She glanced toward Adam, who was still at the car. "Do we have room for Adam?"

"Yes. I'll see if I can help him." Beau met Adam halfway. "Thank you for being here today."

"I'd do anything for Keely, and she knows that," Adam clenched his jaw. "But just so you know, she's a strong woman. Never doubt that."

"Duly noted."

"Are you aware of her mother's situation?"

"You mean the accident she had a few years back?"

"No. The after-effects of that accident. Maggie started having problems a few years ago and was eventually diagnosed with early-onset Parkinson's Disease. The doctors think it was brought on by the head trauma."

Beau winced. "I'm sorry. I didn't know . . ."

"There's a lot you don't know." Adam set out toward the four-wheelers. "You left, remember?"

Keely rode in silence as the four-wheeler navigated the roughshod and winding trail. It was always more pleasant walking than riding, but then again, this trip wasn't for pleasure.

Once they reached the place where she had found the dog tag, like a makeshift cross, the shovel marked the spot. She turned her head away and said a silent prayer. Could this be the end of her search?

"Why don't you wait in the four-wheeler, while my crew sets up?" Beau suggested.

"I would prefer to walk around and look for other artifacts." She addressed the ranger. "Is that OK with you, Mr. Rodgers?"

"Yes, ma'am. Just be careful. There are a lot of rock outcroppings and fallen branches around here that can trip you up."

Keely stepped out of the four-wheeler and set out to walk a perimeter around the site where the men would be working. About two hundred yards out, she turned and started walking a clockwise circle, looking for anything that might be out of place. Hoping for another piece of evidence that could be linked to her father.

Even in the middle of winter, the undergrowth was thick and entangled. It would be almost impossible to find something out here. Not unless it had been recently discarded. If the dog tag hadn't been right beside the trail, and only partially hidden by dirt and dead leaves, she wouldn't have found it last week.

The obvious question was why someone hadn't found it before now. Had it been here for years, waiting for her to discover it? An answer to her prayers? And if it that answer was the one they had always dreaded, how would she tell her mother? Maggie Lambert was fighting a battle of her own and might not fully comprehend the news.

Keely had almost completed her third rotation when she saw Beau, Rodgers, and Adam gathering in a semicircle around the excavation crew. She could see the men talking among themselves, but their words faded into the woods around them.

She pulled a small white flag from her pocket and stuck it into the ground to mark the point of her search and then started walking directly toward the men. As she got closer, she could make out the sound of a shovel penetrating soil, its sharp blade piercing the grass and undergrowth and pinging against an occasional rock. She watched as two men dug and one man sifted. Their work slow and tedious. Suddenly, the man with the shovel stopped digging and knelt in front of the trench they had made.

Keely took a deep breath and hurried forward. A pile of dirt obscured the hole in the ground just past it. She had to see. She had to know.

But before she could pass, Beau Gardner turned and reached out to her. She sidestepped, but he grabbed her arm.

"Wait," he said.

Keely pulled her arm away and started to protest. But the expression on his face stopped her. She had never seen such compassion in his eyes.

"It's not what you think," he said.

"What—?" She looked from Beau to Ranger Rodgers to Adam and then back to Beau. "Just tell me."

One of the two men stepped aside so Keely could look into the grave. Or what should have been a grave. But there was nothing—no one—there.

"We're three feet down right now, ma'am," the stranger said. "And we're not finding anything that would indicate that someone has been buried here."

"Then why . . . ?" Keely pulled the dog tag necklace from the pocket of her jacket and looked at each of the men.

"That's what we have to find out," Beau said, then turned to Rodgers.

"As soon as I get back to my office, I will be filing paperwork to put this area—from the nature center to where we're standing and beyond, under temporary TBI jurisdiction. I would appreciate your immediate cooperation."

Rodgers nodded.

"Why?" Keely asked.

Beau turned to her. "I don't think it was Connor who was targeted last week. I think it was you."

CHAPTER 10

Monday, January 3

Keely turned around and hurried up the trail toward the place where they had found Connor. It had been a place of victory. For Titan. For herself. For her daddy, the man who had not only inspired her dreams, but given them wings.

She would never give up hope of finding him. *Never.*

But until then, how many times would she have to lose him? How long would it be before this nightmare ended, and she could finally bring him home?

"Keely!" It was Adam walking up behind her. "Are you OK?"

"I'm good."

She raised her hand in the air and waved it. A silent plea to let her be for a time. To let her grieve on her own. She would pull herself together and be back. Fighting again. Ever the warrior like her daddy had told her she could be.

Like the warrior she was.

She slowed her pace, inhaled the fresh air, and let it out slowly. A tear streamed down her face. She wiped it away. She wouldn't let Beau, or anyone else for that matter, see her cry. *That included the man who had left the dog tag for her to find, whoever he was.* He may have thought he was taunting her, but he had only empowered her.

A few minutes later, when she reached the edge of the upper bank of Little Marrowbone Creek, she looked down at the empty ledge. *Thank you, Lord, for helping us find Connor in time.*

"Keely . . ."

She wheeled around, startled by the intrusion. It was Beau. Adam was standing beside him.

"You scared me half to death."

"I'm sorry. We just thought . . ."

"That you needed to follow me? Why?"

"Keely, did you hear what Beau said back there? You could be in danger." Adam frowned.

She wrung her hands. "And just *why* do you think I'm a target?" She addressed her question to Beau.

"It's only a theory, but it makes sense." He pointed to the dog tag still in her hand. "This was obviously a plant put there to provoke you."

"Why would someone do that?"

Beau looked to Adam, who didn't speak. "I think the man responsible for your father's disappearance has resurfaced," he said.

Adam shook his head. "There's just no way."

"I agree with Adam. It's been over twenty years. Those men may not even be alive now."

"Or they could be in prison for some other heinous crime," Adam said.

"If they are alive, I don't think they're in prison." Keely turned toward the creek to watch the waters run. "But it could be someone else who found the dog tag and wanted to hurt me."

"Who would want to hurt you?" Adam joined her at the creek bank's edge.

"I'm not immune," Keely whispered. "No one is."

"So, you agree with me that it wasn't a coincidence?" Beau stepped around her, quickly pulled his arm back, and hurled a rock into the water.

Keely watched as a ring of white ripples dispersed from the point of impact. "I don't believe in coincidences," she said.

"Then we have some common ground?"

"I suppose we do." She looked at him.

"I don't agree." Adam threw his own rock.

"Keely." Beau hesitated. "I believe he may have come back for you."

Adam frowned again. "That's ridiculous. It's obvious he must have had a vendetta against Keely's dad, but it's not like he can hurt him now by going after Keely. I don't understand why he would return after twenty years."

"That's easy . . ." Keely looked from Adam to Beau. "Because I was a witness. I was in the car with Daddy before he disappeared."

"So was Levi," Adam argued. "Is he on this guy's list too?"

Beau shrugged. "We don't know that he isn't."

"Levi is vacationing in Hawaii with his family right now," Keely said. "And besides, Levi was only five when Daddy disappeared. He doesn't remember anything."

"Keely, I don't think any of us is certain what's going on, but we're here for you . . ."

"Thanks, Adam. But it's OK." She bent to pick up a stone and hurled it into the water. It landed close to where Beau's rock had submerged. "I can handle this." She turned to Beau. "You aren't telling me anything I haven't feared all along. That it was my fault."

"What could you have done? You were only seven," Adam argued.

"I agree," Beau said. "That doesn't make sense."

"It does to me," Keely said matter-of-factly. "Why else would he choose to take my daddy on my birthday?" She looked from one man to the other. "Coincidence?"

Beau frowned. "I think you're taking that idea a little too far."

"Really?" she challenged him.

"He couldn't possibly have known it was your birthday." Adam shook his head. "I'm not buying it."

"Keely, I think it's more likely that he has returned because he's a sick man," Beau said. "Some people fuel their sickness by preying on others."

She wrapped her arms around herself. The temperature had to be dropping.

"He would have to be sick to do what he did to Keely and her family," Adam said.

"Because of that, we need to be especially cautious."

"So, what is your plan?" Keely asked.

Beau seemed happy to change the subject. "My men will continue to dig. Not just there, but around that area to be sure they don't miss anything. They will also take soil samples." He motioned to her and Adam to start walking back.

Keely nodded.

"We will be looking for any evidence that human remains may have been there at one time. And we'll preserve soil samples for future comparisons."

"OK," Keely said, turning toward the trail.

Beau lowered his voice. "I would like to keep all of this to us. Have either of you mentioned any of this to anyone else?"

"Only Sara," Adam said.

"No one," Keely said. "Of course, Greg McAlister knows because he was here that day. But I haven't told anyone else. I didn't want to bother Levi on vacation until I knew more about the possibility of finding Daddy. . . . And it looks like we're back to square one on that."

"How is your brother?" Beau asked. "I haven't seen him in years."

"All grown up." Keely smiled. Perhaps for the first time today. "He's doing great. He owns a music publishing company in Nashville, and it has been quite successful."

"Good to hear." Beau walked to her right. "I'd like to catch up with him sometime."

"I'm sure he would love that," Keely said. "He always admired you when he was a young boy."

"I'm not sure I deserved it." Beau sobered.

"You didn't."

"Adam!" Keely admonished.

"He's right," Beau said. "I wish I had, but I didn't." He checked his watch and looked to Adam. "I think it would be a good time for you to take Keely home. I'll ask Rodgers if I can borrow his four-wheeler to run you back to the nature center."

"You're not leaving? But you want us to leave?" Keely stopped walking.

"I promise. I'm not hiding anything."

She met his gaze and nodded. "I believe you. But please call me this evening or in the morning to let me know what's going on."

"If the two of you don't mind, I would like to do more than that," Beau said. "Can I meet you at the kennel in the morning and take you to breakfast?"

"OK with me." Keely started walking again.

"I should be available. What time?" Adam asked.

"Nine o'clock?"

"That works." Keely glanced to Adam and then back to Beau. "But just so you know, that's more like brunch. We eat breakfast at first light in the country."

CHAPTER 11

Tuesday, January 4

Keely silenced her alarm, threw off the covers, and reached for her robe. The old yellow farmhouse she had inherited from her grandparents had good heat and adequate insulation, but she could save money on her utility bills and keep her three live-in shepherds happier when her thermostat was set to a frosty sixty-two. That made for some cold mornings. But she was used to it. Besides, she wouldn't be hanging around the house for long—she had eighteen kennels to clean.

Ruby, Pearl, and Titan lived in the house with her. But eighteen other dogs in various stages of life—from puppy to two years old—were housed in her state-of-the-art kennel with its twenty-foot outdoor runs, indoor training arena, and outdoor play yard. She had spared no expense when designing the kennel, which included a small business office and a whelping suite with a cot, mini-kitchen, and bathroom. After a litter was born, either Adam or she would stay in the whelping suite until the mama dog and her pups were settled. The first seventy-two hours were especially important, in case the mother or one of her babies developed problems.

After pouring a cup of coffee, Keely fed her four-legged roommates, before changing into a pair of faded jeans and a lightweight sweater. She grabbed her coat and keys on the way out the back door to the kennel, which was several hundred yards away from the house.

On a typical weekday morning, she would let the dogs out to run in the play yard, while she cleaned the kennels. Adam usually arrived mid- to late morning to start the exercise, training, and socializing routine. Because of their breakfast with Beau, Adam came in early to help with the kennels and to get an early start on training.

"If you want coffee, grab a cup from the house," Keely told him as she wiped her hands on a towel.

"I'm good," Adam said. "I'm saving myself for breakfast on Beau's dime."

Keely laughed. "You don't like him much, do you?"

Adam sobered. "I like him just fine. I just don't like him bossing you around."

"It's not that bad." Keely stopped working and looked at him.

"Whatever you say."

"Adam, I've never seen you like this. I think we should give him some respect. He has worked hard to get where he is."

Adam continued to work and never looked up. "I respect him. I just don't want him breaking your heart. Again."

Keely laughed. "Hey, I'm a big girl. Let me take care of my own heart."

He stopped and looked at her. "I'm sorry. I know you can. I'm just not sure I buy into his theory."

"You mean that I'm the target?"

"Yes."

"That may be the one thing I agree with him on the most—" Her phone rang. Greg McAlister's number was in the caller ID.

"It's Sergeant McAlister," Keely whispered and pointed to the phone. "Lambert Kennels . . ."

"Hey, Keely. Greg McAlister. How are you today?"

"I'm doing well, Sergeant. I hope you had a good trip back to Lackland."

The small talk was going to kill her. *Please God, let this be good news.*

"I have good news," McAlister said. "You're on our breeder's list."

"That's amazing!" Keely gave Adam a thumbs up, and he silently high-fived her.

"I'm happy about it too," McAlister said. "You have my email address. And my number. Keep me updated on your next litter."

"I will." Keely did her best to hide the excitement in her voice. "Thank you for letting me know."

"I'll talk to—" He stopped mid-sentence. "Oh, I almost forgot to tell you. My dad said he remembers your father."

"He does? That's crazy! Please let him know that I would love to meet him." She swiped moisture from her eyes. "And that I would love to hear some of his stories."

"I'm sure he would like that too."

"Thank you so much, Sergeant. I'll stay in touch."

Adam high-fived her again as soon as she ended the call. "Congratulations."

She laughed and wiped another happy tear. "That's not the best part. He said his father remembers my dad."

Adam's expression softened. "I hope you can meet him some day."

"Wouldn't that be perfect? I have so many questions I would like to ask him. I just can't imagine." Keely took a deep breath. After twenty-two years, her dad's presence was becoming almost real again.

The next two hours passed quickly. Keely cleaned, while Adam worked with the dogs, and Beau arrived at nine o'clock.

"Anybody here?" he asked, opening the main kennel door.

"We're just finishing up. Come on in," Keely said.

"Wow." He stepped inside and closed the door behind him. "This is something else."

"Thank you. It works for what I need," Keely said.

"Are you kidding me?" He looked around. "It's incredible."

"Let me give you a quick tour before we go to breakfast." She turned to Adam. "Do you mind giving my inside crew an outside break, while I give Beau a tour?"

"Happy to." Adam offered a short greeting to Beau on his way out.

"Let's start in here," she said, leading Beau to the whelping suite. "I rarely have two litters at one time, but I wanted to be prepared in case that happens."

"Nice," he said.

"It's a fairly comfortable cot—although that doesn't matter, because you don't get a lot of sleep when the babies are first born." She laughed. "Here's a kitchenette." She opened a door. "And the bathroom is in there."

"I don't know how you do all of this on your own."

"I don't," she corrected him. "Adam works with me full time. If I have a litter, that includes working weekends."

"Forgive me for asking, but is there much profit in dog breeding?"

"Not really," she said. "But there's good money in dog training. And Adam is one of the best."

"Really? Where did he learn the trade?"

"He's self-taught like I am," Keely said. "What we've learned, we've learned together."

"So, you have your own method of training?" Beau appeared to be completely captivated.

"You could say that."

He shook his head. "I can't tell you how proud I am . . ." He hesitated. "Of you."

She felt heat rise to her face. "Well, thank you, Beau Gardner." She put her hand on her hip. "You did pretty good for yourself too."

"Me?"

"Absolutely! I was telling Adam earlier how much I respect what you've accomplished."

It was Beau's turn to blush.

"Maybe Independence High did a decent job. Go green, blue, and gold," she said.

"I think I owe all that I am to Mrs. Arnold at Hillsboro Elementary." Beau chuckled.

"She was something, wasn't she? We were lucky to have such a good teacher." Keely caught his gaze. They had made a lot of memories together.

"Can I see the rest of the kennel?" he asked, looking around.

"Follow me." She led him to the indoor play area, which was the size of a small basketball court, but the floor was covered in epoxy instead of wood.

"This is our inclement weather exercise and training area. We're a lot like the post office," she said. "We don't stop just because it's raining. It takes two thousand hours to get each dog to the level we want."

"Incredible."

"I have a full house right now. Eighteen dogs ranging in age from six months to two years."

"Are they all yours?"

"About half of them," she said. "I also take in a few outside dogs for training. But only German Shepherds because that's my expertise."

She led him to the boarding area. "I have eighteen kennels, and each kennel has an outside run."

Beau shook his head but didn't speak.

She opened the side door. "Behind the runs is our outdoor training area and play yard." She pointed to the football-field-size area beyond the runs. "As you can see, it's completely fenced." She turned to him. "That's not because I worry so much about my dogs leaving, but I want to keep other critters out. Especially big ones, like coyotes and foxes."

She motioned for him to follow her. "And thanks to my grandparents, we have this large search and rescue training area." She pointed to the woods that ran behind the kennel building. "I have five acres of wooded land back here. Adam and I have turned it into our own private hiking trail. It's also fenced to keep hunters and trespassers out."

"You probably have to shoo tourists away," Beau joked. "I can't believe how our little hometown has turned into a vacation destination."

"It's crazy, isn't it?" Her stomach rumbled.

"I'm ready for breakfast, if you are," he said.

"Sounds good."

He escorted her to a black SUV.

"I thought you had a truck."

"Company car." A slow smile spread across his face, and he opened the passenger side door for her. "I confess. I've been looking forward to breakfast at The Country Boy since talking to you last week."

A few minutes later, Adam joined them in the vehicle.

"I can't tell you how much I've missed this place," Beau said, engaging the engine.

"Then why haven't you been back?" Keely asked.

"I'm not sure I can answer that." Beau turned the vehicle around and glanced her way. "There are a lot of bad memories here."

She nodded.

"But I think it's finally time I face them."

"You either face them, or they will eventually run you down, bro," Adam said from the backseat.

CHAPTER 12

Tuesday, January 4

Beau turned left out of Keely's driveway on the way to Leiper's Fork. "The Fork," as he and other locals had always called it, wasn't much more than a collection of old buildings lining a short section of Old Hillsboro Road. But he had missed it.

The unincorporated little village had its original Glory Days more than two centuries ago. The second renaissance of Leiper's Fork had begun in the late 1990s and early 2000s, about the same time Keely's dad disappeared. Something Beau hadn't previously considered. *Could there be a connection?*

He glanced to Keely, who was sitting in the front passenger's seat. "What happened after your dad disappeared? Did you move?"

"We did." Keely nodded. "I remember Mom telling me a few years later that she couldn't afford the mortgage on the house where we were living, so she sold it. We moved to a place farther out of town."

"Do you know who bought it?" Beau asked.

Keely crinkled her nose. "I have no idea. Why do you ask?"

"It just occurred to me that there was a rush on property at that time. Accumulating large pieces of land into huge trusts was the popular thing." He glanced to her again. "Old homes near the village, like where you lived when your dad disappeared, were particularly attractive to buyers."

"I remember when all that property redevelopment and restoration started happening," Adam said from the back. "Although I can't say I paid much attention to it at the time."

"I call it the beginning of the end." Keely shrugged. "It was the end of our sleepy little village, and the beginning of what has become a steady stream of people moving into town."

She turned to Beau, "Although Mom has always said we left the house for financial reasons, now that I'm older and understand more about grief, I think she also needed to get out of there. There were too many memories in that place."

"I apologize for not remembering, but what did your dad do for a living?" Beau asked.

"He was a real estate agent. He and another man started their own agency."

"Even I don't remember that," Adam said.

"Where was their office?" Beau asked.

Keely thought for a few seconds. "Somewhere in Franklin. I'm not sure exactly where."

"Did your mother earn a residual income from the agency after your dad disappeared?"

Keely shook her head. "I don't think so. At least not for long. As I understand it, there were no real assets when Daddy disappeared. And he and his business partner had a resolution clause in their contract that pretty much cut Mom out after Daddy became inactive in the business."

Beau nodded.

"The worst part for us was the waiting period to collect Daddy's small life insurance benefits. If someone disappears, they aren't immediately assumed to be dead."

"Your mom is to be admired," Beau said.

"She's a fighter." Keely sighed. "Daddy taught his girls to be fighters."

Beau drove slowly past the restaurant. "Looks like there's no place to park in front."

"There usually isn't," Keely said. "You're better off to park at the church."

"Just ahead on the left?" Beau asked.

"Yes. But, so you know, it's paid parking."

Beau chuckled. "Something about that seems wrong."

"Right?" She laughed. "I suppose it's the price you pay for living in a tourist town."

"They don't charge on Sundays," Adam countered.

Beau glanced at his old friend in the rearview mirror. Adam had a disagreeable look on his face. They had at one time been good friends, but apparently Beau had messed that up too. He shrugged. He had a big job ahead of him if he was going to take back their friendship, but he was willing to put in the work. Seeing this old town, and his old friends, for the first time in too long was enough to convince him of that.

After parking the SUV in the church lot, Beau stepped out of the car and hurried to the other side. He opened Keely's door, and they walked together toward The Country Boy, a place that had been a big part of his childhood.

"I see a table!" Keely made a beeline for the back of the room.

"Good choice," Beau said, pulling a chair out for Keely and then taking the seat next to her. "We can talk with a bit of privacy here."

Adam took off his jacket and laid his phone on the table. "I'm going to run to the restroom." He looked to Keely. "If the waitress comes while I'm away, I'll have a glass of sweet tea. No lemon."

Keely nodded and picked up her menu. "What are you having, Beau?"

"I'm here for breakfast," he said, not even glancing at his menu. "I've missed the biscuits."

Keely smiled.

He had missed her brown eyes too. He set his menu on the table and looked at her. "Back to what we were discussing in the car. Is there somebody you can ask who might know the name of your dad's real estate partner?"

"My uncle Peter would. Hang on . . ." She waved an index finger in the air. "I'll send him a text."

While Keely typed, Beau took in everything around him. Not much here had changed except the clientele. The checkered curtains, the red fifties chairs, and the old wood bar were the same. But more than half of the people in the room appeared to be tourists.

"Here you go," Keely said, holding her phone closer for Beau to see.

He read the name out loud. "Roy T. Peyton Real Estate, Franklin."

"Ever heard of him?" she asked.

"No, but I'll check him out." Beau typed the name into his phone for reference later. "Thank you."

"May I take your drink orders?" It was the waitress.

"Just water," Keely said.

"Sir?"

"A cup of coffee for me, and a sweet tea, no lemon, for the gentleman who will soon be joining us." He pointed to the chair across the table where Adam would be sitting.

"I'll be right back to take your food order," she said before leaving.

Beau studied Keely. "Now for the hard question. Do you have any idea who might want to harm you or cause you trouble?"

Keely shook her head. "None."

"Have you ever suspected that someone was watching, or following, you?"

"No."

"Any suspicious or threatening phone calls, texts, or emails?"

"Nothing at all . . ."

"How about your family? Have they had anything happen that could be considered suspicious?"

"No," she drew out the word. "There's nothing."

Beau nodded.

"Other than what I told you yesterday, I have no idea why anyone would want to hurt me or my family." She turned to Beau. "And I don't understand—"

The waitress brought their drinks just as Adam returned. After taking their food orders, she left.

Adam took a sip of tea. "Keely, what was Beau asking that you don't understand?"

"He wanted to know if there has been anything usual or suspicious that has happened in my family."

"Did you tell him about your mom's accident last year?"

She sat back in her chair. "No . . . why? That was an accident."

Beau turned to her. "Please tell me what happened to Margaret."

Keely stared at him, her eyes dark. "It was only an accident. I'm not sure why Adam wants to make something more out of it."

"So, what happened?"

"She fell." Keely focused over Beau's shoulder, and then back to him. "She was working in her garden and fell."

"When was that?"

"About two months ago. It was November 8. The weather was unusually warm for that time of year, and that's why she was in her garden."

Beau nodded.

Keely continued. "She shouldn't have been out there. She's been unsteady on her feet since she was diagnosed with Parkinson's. Actually, before."

"When was that?"

Keely turned to Adam. "She was diagnosed six months ago?"

"Probably," he said.

"Or maybe eight months . . ." Keely stopped to consider. "It was in May or June of last year when she was given the diagnosis. Apparently, it can take months and even years to identify Parkinson's. Before that, and since then, she has had a battery of tests."

Beau stirred cream into his coffee.

"We've known for a while that something was wrong. Mom has been in decline for a year or two."

"Does Parkinson's run in your family?"

"No," Keely said. "It's the craziest thing. The doctors believe her case was triggered by head trauma. I didn't even know that could happen."

"Head trauma?"

"Yes." She hesitated. "Did you not know about Mom's car accident a few years ago?"

Beau nodded. "Yes, Adam and I talked about it last week."

"Her doctors believe the Parkinson's came about because of that accident. She was unconscious for almost a day. We were worried about her at the time."

"And then she hit her head again in November?"

"Yes."

Alarm bells went off in Beau's head. "Does that strike you as coincidence? Or suspect?"

Keely shrugged. "I don't think it's either. Anyone can have an automobile accident. And she fell in the garden because she wasn't being careful."

"That's a fair answer," Beau said.

"So, I'm being graded on my answers?" She raised an eyebrow.

Adam chuckled.

"I'm sorry. I shouldn't be talking when I need to be listening. I was trying to say that makes sense." Beau thought about his next question. "What are her other symptoms?"

"Related to Parkinson's?"

"Yes. And otherwise."

"She has memory and speech issues. At this point, her memory is probably better than her speech." Keely looked down at her hands. "Don't get me wrong, her memory is failing her. But we don't know how much because of her lack of communication skills. It's a bad situation to be in." She smoothed a wrinkle in her napkin. "It's frustrating for Mom. But it's frustrating for the rest of us too. The doctors refer to it as aphasia."

"Did that start in November?"

"It's worse since then."

Beau was almost certain he knew the answer, but he had to ask. "Does your mom live alone?"

"Oh, no," Keely said. "Her sister, my aunt Gigi, moved in with her temporarily to help her . . . and us."

"First of all, I'm really sorry, Keely." Beau took a breath. "Your mother has had more than her share of troubles in life."

"She's a strong woman." Keely looked up.

Like mother, like daughter. Adam had used similar words yesterday to describe Keely.

"Hot breakfast!" The waitress set a steaming plate of food in front of Beau. It was a feast for his eyes—scrambled eggs, bacon, hash brown casserole, and biscuits. The savory, sweet smell of bacon caused his stomach to rumble. He hadn't had a breakfast like this in a year.

"I'll be right back with the other food," the waitress said.

"I had forgotten how big these biscuits are."

Keely smiled. "Catheads. My mother used to make—"

Beau's phone rang. It was Emma.

"Is everything OK?"

"Stop worrying . . . we're good," Emma assured him. "Connor is back to being a spunky six-year-old. Devon and I have been trying to temper him with reminders about his birthday party on Saturday. That's why I'm calling. He asked me to invite Uncle Beau to his party."

"What time?"

"One o'clock. Unless you want to eat hot dogs with us. In that case, noon."

Beau chuckled. "I'll pass on the hot dogs and see you at one."

"Thank you. He'll be so excited." She hesitated. "He's asking for Keely to come to the party too—and to bring her 'hero dog.' His words, not mine. Before I call her, I wanted to make sure you were OK with that."

"Of course. I'm sitting here with her right now. Do you want me to ask?" He glanced to Keely.

"Oh . . . sure. That would be great."

"I'll call you back this afternoon."

Beau placed his phone on the table and looked to Keely.

"I have been asked to pass along an invitation to you."

"From?"

"From Connor."

Keely smiled.

"He wants to know if you and Titan will come to his birthday party on Saturday."

"Really?" Her eyes danced. "That will be a first! But there's no reason we can't." She sat back in her chair. "We don't do dog tricks. I hope that's not a problem."

"I don't think he's expecting that." Beau laughed. "I think it's more about showing Titan off to his friends and telling them about his adventure in the park."

"We're happy to do it."

"Do you want to ride with me?"

Adam coughed and took a drink.

"That depends." Keely frowned at Adam and turned back to Beau.

"On . . . ?"

"On how much dog hair you want in your car."

"That bad, huh?"

"That bad."

"OK . . ." he said.

"We'll drive separately then." Keely turned to Adam. "You might need to ask your doctor about that cough."

July 6, 2000

"Who wants to go for ice cream?" Will Lambert asked.

"I do. I do." Seven-year-old Keely jumped up and down, her brown curls bouncing.

"Me too, Daddy!" Levi bounced with her.

"Can the puppy go?"

"No, Punkin'. Let him stay with Mommy. We'll be right back."

Will Lambert grabbed the car keys from the kitchen counter, kissed his wife, and swept Keely into his arms. "Did you have a good birthday?"

She nodded and grinned.

"I love you, honey. You're a big girl now. Almost too big for Daddy to carry." He turned to his son. "Let's go, buddy. What kind of ice cream do you want?"

"Can I have chocolate and vanilla both?"

"Of course." Will Lambert ruffled his son's hair, and the three of them walked out the door.

CHAPTER 13

Wednesday, January 5

Keely browsed the aisles of Unique Toy Store near Cool Springs Galleria in Franklin looking for a gift. *What would a seven-year-old want for his birthday?*

A talking ATM? No . . . *Cute but too juvenile for Connor.* Maybe a replica multi-story parking garage? *Ninety-nine dollars? I don't think so.* Although it should be something electronic. Isn't that what every kid wanted these days? Technology.

She thought back to her childhood. The only thing she had ever wanted was a puppy.

A puppy? No. That was something Emma and Devon would need to do for their son. But maybe . . . ?

Keely hurried to the stuffed toy section. Bears . . . Cats . . . Dinosaurs . . . There they are! Stuffed dogs. Shih Tzu. Pugs. Boxers . . . German Shepherds. *Perfect.* There was even a bonus box that included a stuffed shepherd-looking dog, a dog bed, a brush, and a certificate of adoption. It would be a great way to teach Connor how to care for a puppy if he ever had one.

She picked up the box and took off for the front of the store.

"Are you buying for yourself, ma'am?" the clerk asked.

Keely laughed. "I don't think so. I have a whole lot of the real thing at home. This is for a seven-year-old."

"I'm sure he'll enjoy it."

He? "How did you know it was for a boy?"

"I'm sorry." The man chuckled. "I have a seven-year-old grandson, and I guess I just assumed that everyone was that lucky."

She smiled. "You sound like a wonderful grandpa."

"Thank you." He handed her the receipt. "I hope you have a nice day."

Keely took the receipt from his hand, picked up the package, and walked out the door as her phone rang.

"Hi, honey. It's Aunt Gigi. Are you still picking your mom up for lunch?"

"On my way right now." Keely looked at her watch. "It'll be about twelve-fifteen. Is that OK?"

"Works good, honey. See you when you get here."

Keely ended the call and slipped the phone into her pocket. She opened the rear compartment of her Forester to stow the gift, and then hurried to the driver's side of the SUV to get in. What would she have done if Aunt Gigi hadn't moved here, at least temporarily, to look after her sister? Maggie Lambert would never willingly leave her home, the place where her children had grown up.

The toy store and Cool Spring Galleria were about twenty miles from her mother's house. With traffic, it was a forty-minute drive. Gigi greeted Keely as soon as she arrived.

Not much had changed in the old ranch style house since Keely and Levi had moved out. Their school pictures still hung on the wall over the sofa. And the family Bible had kept its time-honored spot on the mantel. Even the smell of the place—lavender from her mother's garden, fresh in the summer and dried in the winter—was the same.

Every time Keely stepped inside of the small, brick ranch house it brought back memories of Friday night pizza parties, sleepovers with her girlfriends, and baking cinnamon rolls out of a can, while watching Saturday morning cartoons. Keely smiled. The pizza and the cinnamon rolls were the only thing about those sleepover weekends that had made them tolerable for Levi.

She and her brother had always been close. They still were. Sharing the bittersweet memory of being the last to see their dad had created an inseparable bond. Together, with their mother, they had gotten through it.

Keely had often wondered, especially now that she was older, why her mother hadn't remarried. It would have been the easiest thing to do. Or so it seemed. Raising two children on her own had been difficult financially. And even if Keely and Levi had never caused any trouble, having a father figure around might have helped insure that.

Beau Gardner was the closest to trouble that Keely had ever been. He had been a rebellious teenager. Never at cross purposes with the law, but always headstrong. And a free thinker. Probably a lot like her dad was at his age, if the stories her uncle Peter had told her were true.

And Keely had no problem visualizing Will Lambert as a wild child. It had taken grit to make it through the Gulf War. And to return home when others hadn't. Even though she had lost him early, she had always considered herself blessed to have known him at all.

"Have a seat, honey." Gigi pointed to the sofa. "You're here right on time. I was just about to wake your mama. She takes a nap in that chair every morning after breakfast. I'm not sure how she sleeps as much as she does."

Seeing her mother in her present state tugged at Keely's heart. Maggie Lambert had aged ten years in less than one. If that accelerated, she couldn't imagine what the next five years would bring.

Her focus drifted to the rocking chair where Aunt Gigi had taken a seat. Her fifty-five-year-old aunt loved to knit. Skeins of bright colored yarn filled a basket on the side table next to her with the excess yarn spilling onto the floor.

"What are you making?" Keely asked.

Her aunt's face lit up. "It's a baby blanket. Did you know that Meagan was pregnant again?"

"No! I hadn't heard! Congratulations on being a grandmother again! Is it a boy or a girl?"

"Another little girl." Gigi's blue eyes sparkled. "Little girls are a lot of fun."

Keely smiled. "I hope you enjoy her." She glanced in her mom's direction and then back to Gigi. "Would you like to go to lunch with us? We'd love to have you."

Her aunt folded the blanket and placed it, along with her needles, inside a larger basket on the floor. "Oh, no, dear. You two go ahead on your own. I need a break." She laughed. "I love her. She's my sister, and I've always told her I would take care of her after our mama died."

Keely nodded.

"Maggie would have done the same for me if it had gone the other way."

"She would have. She loves you."

"Love helps, but you also need a good sense of humor." Gigi stood and stretched her back. "Some days as a caregiver are easier than others."

"Mom always quoted a Bible verse about not getting discouraged in doing what is right." Keely looked at her mom sleeping in the chair and then back to her aunt. "I don't know what I'd do without you, Aunt Gigi."

Her aunt chuckled. "Well, you're going to find out for the next two hours, because I have a lot of errands to run. I need to go to the grocery store. And to the bank. I can't get any of those things done when I'm watching Margaret."

"Thank you," Keely said.

"You're welcome, honey." Gigi's expression softened. "You have a good time with your mom today. I'll see you back here at two o'clock." She walked across the room to her sister's chair and placed her hand on her shoulder. "Wake up, Maggie. Keely is here."

Maggie Lambert opened her eyes. "Hi, honey." She smiled.

"Hi, Mom. Would you like to go to lunch today?"

"That would be OK."

Keely bit her lip. "Are you hungry?"

"Not that much. But I want to go with you."

"OK. We'll go. And we'll have fun."

With Gigi's assistance, Keely helped her mother stand and put on her coat.

"I've got it from here," Keely said and then slowly walked Maggie out the door and to the Forester. Keely helped her climb into the vehicle.

When Keely reached across her to buckle her seatbelt, the older woman planted a kiss on her daughter's cheek. "Thank you."

"You're welcome, Mom."

Keely hurried around to the driver's seat and climbed inside.

"How is Levi?"

Keely started the car and backed it out of the driveway. "He's fine. He's out of town right now, but he'll be back next week."

"OK."

"Where would you like to eat today?"

"Wherever you want to go."

"How about the Puffy Muffin? You like their quiche."

"Sounds OK."

"Will you share some of your fries with me?"

Her mother giggled. It had long been their private joke. Something uniquely theirs. A moment in time remembered from Keely's first trip to McDonald's and forever their bond.

They had shared a lot of fries since then. Fries and long conversations. Fries and tears. Fries given with motherly advice. Some wanted. And some not. But always offered in love.

Within a half hour, the two of them were seated inside the Puffy Muffin in Brentwood, a small community close to Franklin. Keely ordered the quiche for her mom and a sandwich for herself.

After their food arrived, Keely snatched a French fry from her mother's plate. "Thank you, Mom." She wrinkled her nose, and her mother giggled again.

Laughter had become Maggie Lambert's emotional default. A random reaction to the world as a result of the brain injury and Parkinson's. But it had also been one of the best random blessings Keely could have chosen. What if a predisposition to tears had set in instead?

Giggles were good.

Keely snapped a mental picture of her mother sitting quietly across the table, enjoying her lunch. It was a moment she wanted to remember forever. She pulled her phone from her handbag and took a few photos to document the occasion. Her mother was still a beautiful woman, even if she had aged in the past six months.

Maggie's greying hair had been swept back and her clothes were neat and trendy. All thanks to Gigi.

When first diagnosed with Parkinson's, Maggie had talked almost incessantly, but she would often confuse her words. The doctors had called it aphasia and told Keely it was common among brain injury patients. Maggie might substitute the word *coat* for the word *dog*, or the other way around. Or the word *blanket* might be the word she chose when intending to say *water* or *medicine* or *wallet.* There was no real pattern. And it would often make communication difficult.

Now that Maggie's disease had progressed, she would rarely initiate conversation. And when she did speak, her response wasn't always appropriate to the topic. Whether from hearing loss or internal brain processing malfunction or both, the doctors didn't seem to know for sure.

Keely might ask, "How are you today, Mom?"

And Maggie would reply, "The clouds are pretty today, aren't they?"

"There's a lot of traffic today, Mom."

"I don't like white cars, do you?"

White cars always seemed to be an issue.

Keely would nod her head and respond to the reply she was given. Aunt Gigi had taught her to do that. "Don't argue or cause frustration," Gigi had said. "Jump into her world and enjoy the time you have with her there."

And in fact, Keely did enjoy spending time in her mother's world. But she also questioned how much of it was based in reality. She decided to take a deep dive into that uncertainty and ask her mom about her dad's former business partner.

"Mom, do you remember Roy Peyton?"

Maggie slowly smiled. "He was a good man."

"Who was he, Mom?"

"He sold property."

"Real estate?"

"Yes."

"Is that all you remember about him?"

"He helped us."

"That's good to know," Keely said and took a bite of her chicken salad sandwich. "How is your quiche today?"

"OK."

Keely smiled. At this point in her life, "OK" was her mother's highest—and only—approval rating. Qualifiers and inflection were no longer a part of her skill set, and that contributed to her monotone, stilted, and often difficult to comprehend communication style.

"That man is back." Maggie Lambert pulled Keely back to the real world.

"What man, Mom?" Keely turned and looked around. There were several men in the room, but none had familiar faces.

Maggie cowered. "You know . . ."

"Mom, I'm sorry. I don't know who you mean." Keely scanned the room a second time.

"He's back."

"Who's back?"

"He hurt me."

"Mom, I wish I knew who hurt you. Is he here?"

"No," Maggie said.

Keely caught the attention of the waitress. "Check, please." She wasn't about to take any chances.

CHAPTER 14

Saturday, January 8

Beau voice dialed his office on the way to Connor's birthday party. "It's Beau Gardner. I missed a call about an hour ago."

"Yes, sir. Chris Enoch asked me to call you. We received a tip from hikers who were at the Beaman Park Nature Center the day your nephew disappeared."

Beau's pulse accelerated. "Thank you. Please, go ahead."

"After they left the park that afternoon, they noticed a white Toyota Camry parked alongside Eatons Creek Road, about a half mile past the park entrance. They were unaware of Connor's disappearance, but the location of the vehicle seemed suspicious, so the car passenger snapped a photo of the license plate. Apparently, they are regulars at the park, and when they found out yesterday that a boy had been reported as missing that day, they told the guard on duty what they had seen, gave him the plate number, and a rough description of the Camry."

"Who owns the vehicle?"

"Unfortunately, the plate came back as stolen."

Beau pounded his fist on the steering wheel. "Do we have any details about the theft of the plate? The whereabouts of the vehicle when it was taken? The possibility of security cameras capturing the theft? Anything?"

"Unfortunately, no. Or, at least, not likely. The real owners had no idea their plate was even gone until they were pulled over by a Metro police officer. It could have been stolen anywhere."

"Let's stay on that," Beau said. "Maybe start with a list of the times, dates, and locations where they had parked their vehicle up to twenty-four or even forty-eight hours prior to Metro pulling them over. If we can get that, we can contact each business establishment and ask for security camera footage."

"Yes, sir. But that will take some time."

Beau sighed. "If you can get me the list of places, I will follow up as I can."

"I'll work on it."

"Thank you."

Beau ended the call. So far, he had nothing but dead ends.

The tracking device that had been found on Emma's car had come back as registered to an anonymous owner. And the serial number and purchase information hadn't brought any leads. Enoch was probably right. The tracker was most likely an outlier, and not related to the case.

Beau engaged his turn signal as he approached Devon and Emma's driveway. Someone had tied brightly colored balloons to the mailbox. Children's birthday parties had a way of bringing you back to the basics. Lots of balloons, sugar, and laughter awaited at the end of the drive.

Keely would be there too. He checked his hair in the mirror. *Beau, you're looking older.* He would be thirty his next birthday. Where had the time gone? It seemed like only a year or two ago he and Keely were taking midnight rides down Natchez Trace Parkway. Now Emma and Devon had two kids. Somehow, he had let ten years slip away. Was there any chance at all that he could make up for lost time?

Connor ran out to meet him when he parked in front of the house. "Uncle Beau! You're here!"

"Hey, buddy. Happy birthday." He gave the seven-year-old a hug and then a high five. "Seven . . . you're almost grown up."

Connor's smile reached from ear to ear. He grabbed Beau's hand. "Come on in the house. I want you to meet my friends." His eyes twinkled. "Keely and Titan are already here!"

"What do your friends think of Titan?"

"They think he's pretty cool. I do too!" He released Beau's hand and took off running, reaching the front door about ten seconds ahead of Beau. "Hey, everybody. My uncle Beau is here! He's in the TBI."

Beau laughed and instinctively looked for Keely in the crowd. She was standing in the back of the room talking to Emma. Titan sat beside her taking in the noise and chaos as it if were just a part of his everyday life. That was good training.

Keely waved.

Beau nodded and started making his way across the room.

"Hey, brother. How are you?" Emma hugged his neck. "Thanks for taking time to make our seven-year-old happy. He couldn't wait for you to get here."

"He met me in the driveway."

"I know. He's been looking for you since lunch."

Beau laughed. "Sorry I missed the hot dogs."

"My brother, the food critic." Emma sighed.

"They were good," Keely said. "Titan loved them."

"You let your dogs eat hot dogs?" Beau shook his head.

She laughed. "Only when the birthday boy insists."

"Hey, guys." It was Emma again. "We're going to open presents now. Keely, do you want to help?"

"Sure! Whatever you need," Keely said. "If Beau will watch Titan for me." She held the leash out to him.

"We'll be right here." He took the leash from her and pulled up a folding chair. "Titan, it looks like it's you and me. You might as well get comfortable."

The dog gave him a sideways glance and settled onto the floor.

"Good boy." Beau gave the dog a pat. "We'll watch from here."

As soon as Emma and Keely reached the far side of the room, Keely walked around to the back of the long gift table. Emma stood in front of it and clapped her hands. "Hey, everyone. It's time for gifts. After that, we have a surprise."

"A surprise!" Excited giggles echoed across the room.

"Connor, come up here and open your gifts."

"Cool!" The seven-year-old ran to the table and rubbed his hands together.

"Silly boy." Emma laughed and turned him around. "Why don't you run back behind the table with Keely. She'll hand you the gifts."

Instead of running around the table, Connor scrambled underneath and popped up on the other side.

Beau shook his head. The kid had spunk.

"Here you go, Connor," Keely said. "Your first gift is from . . ." She read the tag. "Scarlett."

Connor took the box from her and quickly tore off the paper. It was a game. "Thanks, Scarlett!"

Beau heard a giggle and "you're welcome" come from somewhere in the center of the room.

"Connor, this gift is from Travis." Keely gave him a gift bag, and Connor immediately pulled out some sort of lightsaber.

"Where are you, Travis?"

A blond-haired boy in the back of the room waved.

"This is cool! Thank you!"

Keely continued to hand out gifts until they were all opened except one. "Here you go, Conner. I saved Titan's and my gift until last."

The little boy looked up at her and grinned. "What is it?"

She gave him the box. "Open it and see."

Connor tore off the giftwrap and gave it to his mother, who had a large trash bag already full of paper. The boy's hand went to his mouth and he jumped up and down. "It looks just like Titan!"

Keely nodded, and Connor spontaneously hugged her. "Thank you!" He waved to the dog in the back of the room. "Thank you, Titan!"

Emma stood and set aside the trash bag. "OK. Are you guys ready for a surprise?"

Excited squeals echoed around the room, and Emma pointed to the front door. Beau saw the door open and a clown walk in. Connor immediately ran around the table toward the clown and when he did, Titan, who had been lying calmly on the floor, jumped up and bolted, pulling the leash from Beau's hand.

"Come back here!" Beau shouted.

"Titan!" Keely screamed. "No!"

The dog reached the clown just as she did, and she grabbed him by the collar. "No, Titan. Back off."

The dog lunged forward, held back only by Keely's hold on his collar, which pulled his front legs and head into the air. Big jaws threatened the clown, who backed against the wall in a fetal like position.

"Titan! No!" Keely finally got the dog under control, took hold of his leash, and escorted him out the door.

Beau hurried across the room, around the crowd of kids, and followed her. She was in the front yard walking the dog when he caught up with her.

"What was that about?" He pointed over his shoulder.

Her cheeks flushed. "Apparently, I'm not as good of a dog trainer as I thought I was." She shook her head. "I can't believe he did that."

"Don't be so hard on him," Beau said. "It's not like he's seen a lot of clowns before."

"It doesn't matter. He should never . . . I just can't believe he reacted like that."

"I don't know." Beau looked back at the house. "My money's on the dog. Something just wasn't right."

"Beau, it was the clown suit. I know my dogs. They're not used to seeing people in costumes." She sighed. "So, I've learned something today. I need to step up my training to include clowns and intergalactic warriors and everything in between. This has been a good lesson for me."

That's when Beau saw it.

"What?" She turned. "What are you looking at?"

He walked quickly to the back of her SUV and bent forward. "This." He pointed to a small black object that had been secured to her bumper. "It's a tracking device. Just like the one we found on Emma's car."

CHAPTER 15

Saturday, January 8

While Beau went inside to find Emma, Keely waited with Titan beside her car.

"We have a lot of serious work to do, young man."

The dog looked up at her with big brown eyes.

"You did great last week, but don't let it go to your head."

Titan brushed her leg with his paw.

"I still love you." She bent down to hug the dog. "Everybody makes mistakes."

"Is everything OK?" Emma asked, walking up to them. Beau had returned with her.

"Titan and I were just having a discussion. I'm sorry about what happened inside," Keely said.

"No worries." Emma laughed. "The kids will be talking about Connor's birthday party for days, and he will love that." She turned to Beau. "Is there a problem out here?"

"I wanted to show you something," Beau said.

She gave him a sideways glance.

"Do you see anything unusual about Keely's car?"

"Did somebody damage it?"

"No." He walked her to the back of the Forester.

"Do you see anything unusual or out of place?" He pointed to the tracking device.

"Yes! What is that?" She reached for it.

"Don't touch." He stopped her. "I need to take a photo and dust it for fingerprints."

"Is that one of those things you found on my car?"

"Yes. A tracking device."

Emma's hand flew to her mouth. "Oh, Keely! I'm so sorry." She turned to Beau. "Is this my fault?"

"Why would you ask that?" Beau said.

She shrugged. "I guess I assumed it was put there by the same person who was stalking me."

Keely stepped forward. "It's not your fault, Emma. In fact, it may be the other way around."

"How is that even possible?"

"Keely may be right." Beau bent to snap a photo. "In fact, that's my working theory."

"I'm anxious to hear more, but . . ." Emma looked back over her shoulder. "Can we talk after the party? When I left the house, the clown was making balloons for the kids, but they may have him tied up by now."

Keely chuckled.

"That's fine," Beau said. "I've called the Williamson County Sheriff's Department. Someone is on their way here to file a report and dust Keely's car for fingerprints. We'll see you inside."

Emma started to walk away.

"Oh, sis, before you go, one question. Do you have security cameras on your property?"

"Unfortunately, we don't." Emma pointed toward the front of the house. "We have a doorbell camera, if that helps."

"OK. Thanks." He nodded and turned to Keely. "It's chilly out here. Why don't you go inside with Emma? I'll be in as soon as I'm finished."

Keely shook her head. "No way I'm taking Titan back inside. I'll stay out here with you. How long will you be?"

He looked at his watch. "It shouldn't take long. They have a unit in the area."

"OK. See you both in a bit." Emma turned and hurried up the sidewalk toward the back door of the house.

Two minutes later, a Williamson County sheriff's car pulled up the driveway and stopped. The deputy got out of the car and sauntered over to where Beau and Keely were standing.

He stuck out his left hand. "Beau, how are you? I was just asking your dad about you the other day." He glanced to Keely and back to Beau. "He's one proud papa having a son in the Bureau."

Even in the afternoon sunlight, Keely could see Beau's cheeks flush. Was he embarrassed or upset? She knew him well enough to know it could be either.

"I don't do anything different than what you've done every day, Russ." Beau shook the deputy's hand. "For what? Twenty-five years now?"

"Thirty-one." The deputy shook his head. "Almost as long as you've been alive." He laughed.

"Russell, this is Keely Lambert," Beau said turning to her. "You may remember her family. They've had a place in Leiper's Fork for years. Keely, this is Russell Wallace. He and his wife used to live not too far from your grandparent's place."

"Nice to meet you, Deputy." Keely held Titan on a tight leash in case he should decide he didn't like police uniforms either.

"Was your granddad Gene Lambert?"

Keely nodded and smiled.

"I used to hunt on his farm. I was sorry to hear about his passing. He was a good man."

"Thank you, Mr. Wallace. I was lucky to have him in my life. I live on his and Grandma's farm now."

"You do? Great place. No doubt it's worth a fortune in this day and age with the price of land going up in our county." He shrugged. "I wish I had held onto my place longer."

"Mine is definitely not for sale." Keely smiled and looked down at Titan. "I keep my dogs on the property now. Lambert Kennels. I raise and train working dogs."

"And she does a great job," Beau said. "Actually, Russ, it's Keely's vehicle that was being tracked." He pointed to the back of the Forester. "I found it about an hour ago."

Wallace frowned. "We've seen a rash of those lately. I'm not sure what has gotten into people. They don't know how to mind their own business." He scratched his head. "We're finding out that a lot of them are being used by kids, mostly teens, who enjoy playing with new technology."

"I wish that was the case with this one," Beau said. "However, I'm concerned otherwise. Would you mind dusting her car for prints?"

"That's why I'm here. Let me get my briefcase."

While Beau watched the deputy dust for fingerprints, Keely walked Titan up and down the long driveway. At the end of her third rotation, she nearly came face to face with the clown, who was climbing into his truck to leave. Titan growled and pulled at his leash.

"Titan, stop that." She forced the dog to sit and then apologized to the man—or woman?—in the clown suit. But he shook his fist at her and drove away.

Can't say that I blame him.

"Titan, you need to learn how to tell the good guys from the bad ones. We have a lot of work to do."

She led the dog back to her car and said goodbye to the deputy as he was leaving.

"If you ever have any problems, ma'am, please call me. Here's my card."

She reached to take the business card from his hand. "Thanks so much. That means a lot."

"See you later, Beau. Call us when you need us."

"Will do, Russ. Thank you." He turned to Keely. "Let's go talk to Emma for a few minutes before we leave. It looks like most of the parents are here for their kids, so they'll be leaving too."

Keely saw a line of cars pulling into Emma's driveway from the main road. "Let me put Titan in the car first. He's had a trying day. First entertaining thirty seven-year-olds and then fighting off clowns." She laughed. "He just tried to take that guy out again before he left."

"He did?" Beau helped her secure Titan in the vehicle and started walking her to the house. "There's something about that situation that bothers me."

"So you're a clown hater too?" she teased.

"Very funny."

"Maybe you need to spend some time in my classroom too."

He smiled and put his arm around her waist, escorting her up the sidewalk.

As soon as they stepped inside the back door, they could see that most of the children were on the front porch waiting for their parents.

"It looks like Emma is about to get her sanity back," Keely said. She started picking up paper plates, plastic utensils, and cups and stuffing them into a trash bag.

"We missed the cake." Beau looked around the room. "I'll go find us fresh plates and forks so we can have a piece."

"OK . . ." Keely suppressed a laugh. One minute he was chasing down the bad guys. The next minute he was chasing down a sugar craving.

She had disposed of the trash and was starting to sweep the floor when Emma and Beau returned.

"Your cake is good," Beau said. He handed Keely one plate and kept the one that had a half-eaten piece on it.

Emma laughed. "I'll be happy to send the leftovers home with you. It's the last thing I need to keep around here."

Keely took a bite. "It is good. What kind is it?"

"Family recipe." Emma winked at her brother. "A boxed mix with canned frosting."

"Mom's cakes weren't from a box," Beau argued. "She was a great cook."

"She was definitely a great cook, but I can tell you for certain that this is her special birthday cake recipe."

"You mean, all of these years I've thought she spent hours in the kitchen making our birthday cakes and they came from a box?"

Emma laughed. "As far as I'm concerned, it is a special birthday cake recipe. You can't beat family traditions, even when they're out of a box."

"Whatever," Beau said. "I'll be right back. I'm going to the kitchen for another piece." He stopped and turned to Keely. "Do you want another piece too?"

"No, thanks. One is plenty."

As soon as Beau had cleared the room, Emma turned to Keely and whispered. "It sure is good seeing the two of you together again. You always made him so happy."

Keely felt heat rise to her face. "Well, apparently not. He left and never looked back."

"Trust me. That was all Dad's fault." Emma frowned. "He was always good at destroying relationships."

"What do you mean?"

Emma bit her lip. "No . . . I'm sorry. I've already said too much. I'll leave it up to Beau to tell you."

"Girls," Beau said, walking into the room with a plate and fork in his hand. "Let's sit over here and talk for a minute." He looked around. "Where's Connor?"

"He's upstairs in his room," Emma assured him. "He will be up there for a week playing with his new toys." She grinned. "That's one benefit to big birthday parties. In exchange for two hours of screaming and a little bit of cleanup, you can get a week's worth of peace and quiet."

Keely laughed.

"Speaking of that." Beau pulled an envelope from his back pocket. "Please give this to him. It's a card and a twenty-dollar bill. I wasn't sure what to buy him."

"Trust me," Emma said, taking the card. "He will like the money just fine. They learn early."

Beau set his empty plate on the table in front of him. "Em, how did you hear about the clown who entertained the kids today? Did one of your friends refer him to you?"

"Not at all. But I thought he did a good job, didn't you?"

"We were outside, remember?"

Emma nodded. "He did a good job . . ."

"If a friend didn't refer you, then how did you know about him?" Beau persisted.

"Actually, I saw one of his business cards pinned to the bulletin board in the front lobby at church."

"So, you didn't have a reference?"

She looked at him. "Why does that matter? It's not like we weren't with him the whole time he was here." She hesitated. "Does that make me a bad mom?"

"No!" Keely said. Then she turned to Beau. "Beau, give your sister a break. Everything worked out just fine."

"I guess I just assumed if his card was on the bulletin board at church that one of our members had put it there because they had used him and liked him." Emma shook her head. "Maybe I should have researched him more."

"You did a great job with the party," Keely said. "Beau's just suspicious because Titan reacted so violently to him. I keep telling him that's a dog problem, not a clown problem."

Beau rubbed the back of his neck with his hand. "I can see I'm not getting anywhere with the two of you. I'm only trying to follow up on every angle. There's somebody out there putting tracking devices on your cars, and that's not acceptable."

CHAPTER 16

Saturday, January 8

Keely glanced in her rearview mirror before taking a left into her driveway. Beau had insisted on following her home so he could check her house and kennel for intruders. While the possibility was certainly real—as real as the device Beau had found on her car, the thought of someone breaking into her place when she had twenty-one German Shepherds on duty seemed reckless at best. Ludicrous at worse.

She parked her Forester, hurried to the back, and opened the hatch door, freeing Titan. The big, black shepherd jumped to the ground, and Beau stepped up beside them.

"Kennel or house first?" she asked.

"Let's start with the kennel."

"Since you're here, you might as well help me feed and exercise the dogs."

"That sounds like fun."

"We'll see how you feel in two hours."

"Two hours? Really?"

Keely walked to the front of the kennel building, unlocked the deadbolt, cracked open the heavy door, and realized what she had done. She had assumed he wouldn't be busy. And on a Saturday night when most people had a date or a party to go to. She had been hanging out with dogs for so long, she had forgotten what normal people did.

Heat rose to her cheeks, and she stopped. "I'm so sorry. How presumptuous of me. You probably have plans."

"No plans." He grinned.

"Really?"

"None. How about you?"

She shook her head. "Are you sure you don't want to change your mind? This is hardly your best option for a Saturday evening."

"Nope. I'm good. Teach me what I need to know." He had a glimmer of mischief in his eyes. "You did say I needed to spend time in your classroom, right?"

"Well, probably. But I was only halfway serious." She laughed.

"Which means . . . you were *somewhat* serious," he countered. "Let's get started."

Keely led Beau to the feed storage room and showed him how to dispense food from the giant bins. "While you're filling bowls, I'll run to the house and let my other two dogs out."

"I can't let you do that."

"Why?"

"I need to check your house first."

"Beau . . ." She put her hands on her hips. "I hardly think that with two one-hundred-pound German Shepherds in the house that anyone would break in."

"Can you guarantee that?"

"No." She sighed.

"Then, let's go do it."

The two of them, along with Titan, walked uphill to the house, which was about two hundred yards away from the kennel.

"Were you ever here when my grandparents were living?"

"One time, as I remember."

"It looks a lot different now."

"Did you renovate it?"

"No. I just emptied it out . . . a lot." She unlocked the mudroom door and opened it slowly. Two big German Shepherds met them just inside the room.

"Ruby and Pearl, this is Beau. Beau, meet my two best girls."

"Well, hello, ladies—" He was immediately stopped in his tracks, while the dogs sniffed him up and down.

"Sorry about that. It's the standard greeting. My dogs make a living with their noses."

"I surrender." Beau threw his hands in the air and gave Keely a sideways glance. "I wish I had one of Emma's hot dogs in my pocket."

She laughed. "It wouldn't help you. They wouldn't eat them until they checked you out first. And only then if I told them that it was OK."

"Are you serious?"

"Absolutely." She took a step back and studied him. "Are you sure you went through law enforcement training? Not taking food from a stranger is a critical lesson for working dogs. We don't want them to be easily bribed . . . or poisoned."

"Makes sense."

"Come on, girls," she said. "Let's go out!"

Apparently satisfied with their assessment of Beau, the dogs took off running into the main part of the house. Keely followed them, and Beau followed her into the kitchen, through the dining room, and out the sliding glass doors into the sunroom. Once in the sunroom, she opened the backyard door and the three shepherds, Titan now with them, charged through it.

Then she turned to Beau. "That's my three-hundred-pound security system. What do you think?"

"Admittedly, impressive," he said. "I also see that you have good locks on your doors."

"No offense, Mr. Gardner. But my business is based on discipline and detail."

"I didn't mean to offend you," Beau said. "I just want you to stay safe."

Keely backed down. "That sounded worse than I meant it. Would you like to see the rest of the house?"

"Sure."

"It's a short tour. My grandparents built this house as a retirement home, and it's the perfect place for me." She led him back into the house, through the dining room and down the hall. "There's a half-bath here, and back here is my master bedroom, bathroom, and laundry room."

He followed her through the suite, paying particular attention to the windows on the east wall and in the nook on the far side.

"As you can see, I turned my grandmother's reading room into a 'sitting room' for my dogs." She emphasized the two words with air quotes. "It's the right size to accommodate three oversized crates. And in case you're wondering, I rarely crate them. There's no need."

He nodded.

After a quick tour of the master bath, walk-in closet, and laundry room, she led him back through the hall and into the great room. "Let's go upstairs." Keely took two steps at a time on the way up, and Beau followed her in lockstep. "I have two small bedrooms and a Jack and Jill bathroom up here."

"Nice," he said.

"It's small. But it was built, and passed on to me, with love by my grandparents. It's everything I could ever want."

"Really?" Beau asked. "You don't have aspirations for a big house on a hill?"

"Are you kidding? And what would I do with that? I might want to build on to the kennel." She laughed. "No, really. This is all I need."

He grew serious. "What if you marry someday and have kids?"

She studied him. "So, you don't think the man I marry will like my little house?"

His expression softened. "I'm sure he would. But it's hard to imagine two teenagers in this small place."

Keely laughed. "I agree with you. In fact, after that birthday party today, I'm not sure about two seven-year-olds."

"Don't tell Emma I said this," Beau said. "But I'm not sure how they do it, even in a big house."

Keely started walking down the stairs. "Right? I have my hands full with my business." She hesitated. "How did you end up in law enforcement? I would have never thought you would follow in your dad's footsteps. I don't remember the two of you agreeing on anything."

"You're right," he said. "But funny enough, I think it was because of my dad."

They reached the main floor, and Keely stopped to look at him. "How is that?"

"I wanted to best him. To show him I could do what he did—but better." He shrugged. "That's a terrible attitude, isn't it?"

"Can I be honest?"

"Yes. But be gentle." He laughed. A self-deprecating laugh.

"I always knew you were running from your dad. When you left me after graduation, and almost without a goodbye, I was hurt." She looked away and then back to him. "The only thing that got me through it was knowing in my heart that you were running from him and not from me."

"Keely . . . I'm sorry. I didn't mean to hurt you."

She nodded and started walking toward the sunroom door. "I forgave you a long time ago. But it's really hard to forget."

When she opened the door, the dogs came running into the house. "Come on, babies. Let's get you fed."

Beau followed Keely and the dogs back to the mudroom on the far side of the house and watched as she scooped dry food from a large pull-down canister built into the wall of cabinets near the outside entrance. She filled three large bowls, sprinkled something from another smaller canister on top of the food, and set the bowls on the floor.

Everything in her house had been customized for her dogs and her lifestyle. There was nothing pretentious or excessive here. She had pared everything down on the basis of need. If it wasn't needed, it wasn't here.

The only family photos on the walls were in her master bedroom. One of her holding a German Shepherd puppy when she was about Connor's age. And another of her parents that could have very well been taken on the day her dad disappeared. But nothing else. An outsider might easily conclude that Keely's life had effectively stopped on that day.

But Beau knew better. He knew she was a survivor. A strong woman who wasn't about to let bad things stop her. From what little he knew about her parents, he guessed it was probably a family trait. Will Lambert had made it through the war and managed to return whole, unlike Beau's own father.

And despite losing her husband, Maggie Lambert had raised two small children to adulthood. And she had raised them well. From what Beau had heard about Levi Lambert, he was a successful businessman and a family man. And Keely. She was—

"Are you ready?" Keely beckoned from the mudroom door. "We need to feed and exercise the kennel dogs before dark."

"I'll follow you," Beau said and then closed and locked the back door behind them.

"Where do you live?" Keely asked as they headed down the hill to the kennel.

"I have a small condo in Capitol View downtown."

"I know that area," she said. "That's a great place for you. How far are you from your office?"

"About six miles, depending on which way I go. It's an easy commute."

She laughed. "As you can see, I have the easiest of all." She unlocked the kennel door, and they stepped inside. "Are you ready for my version of a seven-year-old's birthday party?"

"What do you mean?"

"You'll see," she said. "Wait here."

She took three steps to the left, opened a wall-mounted cabinet, and pulled a small cylindrical-shaped Kong toy from the inside. She reached into a bag of soft treats and stuffed two or three into the toy. "I'll be right back."

Beau watched as she exited the side kennel door that led to the backyard play area. In a few minutes, she returned. "Come with me," she said.

As soon as they were standing in the play yard, she pulled her phone from her pocket, showed him an app on her home screen, and clicked on it.

"Now . . . watch this." She pressed a button on the app that read Master Open, and all of the kennel gates lifted at once. "Go find!" she yelled.

Immediately, eighteen shepherds of various sizes dispersed into the play yard, sniffing, chasing, and almost running over each other, presumably to find the treat ball.

"I call this search and rescue war games," she told him. "It not only stretches their legs, it gets their blood pumping and their minds—and noses—working. And it teaches them to work together, while also nurturing their competitive spirit. But it must be friendly competition. If a fight breaks out, the perpetrators have to go back to their runs—and they miss the treat for that game."

He watched what was, in essence, controlled chaos. It took him back to the days when he'd had to learn offensive—as well as defensive—moves in law enforcement war games. This was Street Fighting 101. And the woman in charge was standing next to him, beaming with pride.

"How do you teach them to understand what you want?"

"Instinct. Theirs, not mine," she said. "Wait until you see the obvious pride of the dog who finds the toy. He or she will carry it around the yard like a prize. Because it is." She looked at him. "Then, after a few seconds of gloating, they'll bring it to me and lay it at my feet."

"I'm blown away, Keely."

"It's easier than you think. They're intelligent creatures."

"What about the others who looked for the treat ball but didn't find it?"

"They will follow the 'winner' at a respectable distance when he or she brings the toy to me, because they know they'll be rewarded as well.

"So, they all receive a treat?"

She nodded. "Every one of the dogs who plays fair and stays in the yard through the competition will receive the same treat after the winner is rewarded with his. The winner also gets to keep the ball."

"So, although they all want to find the prize, they also know that, once it's found, they will all be rewarded." Beau summarized.

"Exactly! It teaches them to work together, or at least work respectfully. If I have my dog out in the field, and we're looking for a lost hiker, there will likely be several dog teams working nearby. In some cases, those teams may be other shepherds, and in some they may be bloodhounds or another breed. I teach them that we all need to get along, even if we want to be the team that finds the 'prize.' Does that make sense?"

"It makes a whole lot of sense." He stifled a laugh. "I wish you could teach that to a few of my coworkers at the TBI."

"Are you serious?"

"Halfway," he said, using the same word she had used earlier.

"Which means you're *somewhat* serious." She smiled, somewhat mischievously.

A sudden outburst of barking shifted their attention to the play yard. One dog, a big, black and tan shepherd, was parading around with her head held high—and a toy in her mouth. The other dogs were barking jubilantly behind—and alongside—her.

"That's Kuma," Keely said. "She's one of my best students. I'm training her for a police department in Mississippi. I'll give her another ten or fifteen seconds to prance around, but then I'll call her to me. We don't allow excessive celebration."

Beau laughed. "That's football jargon."

"And I'm coach, manager, and referee," she said.

Almost immediately, perhaps instinctively, knowing her time was up, Kuma came running to Keely.

"Good girl! Good girl!" Keely danced with the dog, calling her name, and praising her. "You win!" Then normalizing her body language, Keely flipped an invisible switch. "Kuma, drop the ball."

The dog dropped the ball and lowered herself to the ground.

"Good girl," Keely soothed and reached to pick up the toy. She immediately dispensed the treats to the dog, and then gave the toy back to her. "Good girl!"

Kuma jumped up and started running circles around the other dogs, who were now lining up for their treats. Keely pulled a handful from her pocket and dispersed them one by one along with a "good boy" or "good girl."

A few minutes later, each dog returned to its personal run for supper. Beau followed Keely into the feed room. He filled the bowls while she carried to the dogs, and they were done in less than twenty minutes.

"What about water?" he asked.

"I check each of their dispensers when I feed them. It's automated, but I never rely on equipment when it's critical to the dog's well-being."

"You amaze me," Beau said out loud almost unintentionally.

"Why do I amaze you?" She studied him.

"You are probably the only person I've ever met who was always sure about what they wanted to do with their life. Have you ever had any doubts?"

Keely leaned against the entrance to the main hall and thought for a minute. "Honest answer?"

"Yes."

"No. I've never thought about doing anything else except marrying and having kids someday."

Her answer both stung him and gave him hope.

"Keely, I'm—I'm sorry about us." He shook his head. "No. I'm sorry about me. You deserved better."

She straightened. "I told you earlier. I forgive you."

"Do you think we could start over again?"

She bit her lip and looked away, wiping a tear from her eye.

"If we do, we have to start from the beginning."

"I'm not sure what that means. We already have so much history together . . ."

She stared at him in disbelief. "That's the problem, Beau. Our history. It ended with you walking out on me for what seemed to be no reason, without explanation."

"But . . . but I thought you said you understood why I left. That I was running away from my father."

"I did. And I do." She placed her hand on his chest. Right over his heart. "Now, *you* have to understand that. And learn from it."

"Face my demons before they run me down, like Adam said the other day?"

"Yes."

"I can do that. I want to do that." He focused on the wall behind her. Could he forgive his father—and then forgive himself?

"It may take a little bit of time," he said, looking at her. "But I can't start from the very beginning."

"Why not?" She frowned.

"Because I loved you the day I left, Keely. And I have never stopped."

CHAPTER 17

Sunday, January 9

After locking the main kennel door behind her, Keely hurried up the slight incline toward her house. Kennel work didn't stop on Sunday, but she could keep it to a minimum. With her morning errands now completed, she had twenty minutes to change into her church clothes. Beau would be picking her up at ten o'clock to take her to church and then lunch, followed by a visit with her mother.

He had suggested the idea last night before leaving, presenting it as an opportunity to interview her mother. But Keely knew it was also his attempt at starting their relationship over—quite literally from the beginning. Their first date in high school had been to church. That thought brought a smile as Keely opened her mudroom door.

"Hey, babies. Did you miss me?" The three shepherds greeted her as if they hadn't seen her in a week when it been less than three hours. The dogs playfully nipped at her heels, herding her through the house and into the sunroom.

As soon as she opened the outside door, they took off running to the far end of their half-acre backyard. They would work their way back to the house after a security check for squirrels as well as unwelcome human intruders.

Keely latched the door and hurried to her bedroom closet. It had been chilly this morning when she left for chores, but the temps were already climbing toward today's expected high of fifty-five.

Once inside the closet, she picked out a pink sweater and a pair of fresh blue jeans. After changing clothes, she pulled her hair into a loose ponytail, brushed her teeth, and added a touch of lipstick. She was ready to go in ten minutes.

By the time she had let the dogs in the house, checked their water bowl, and issued treats, Beau was texting that he was in the driveway. She closed and locked the mudroom door behind her and hurried down the hill.

Beau stepped out of the truck and walked around it to open the passenger side door. "You look nice, as always," he said.

"I got some sleep last night, despite everything that's been going on. How about you?"

"Good." He helped her into the truck.

"Are you sure you're OK with this?" she teased.

"Church? Absolutely." He shrugged. "The preacher's not going to call me out any more than my supervisor does every day."

"We'll slip into the last row with Adam and Sara so we can get away if needed."

He smiled. "Sounds like a plan."

Before they were out of the driveway, Keely received a text from Sara saying that she and Adam weren't going to make it to church but inviting Keely to have lunch with them afterward. Keely texted back to ask if Beau could join them.

Sara replied, "Of course!"

"Turns out we're not sitting with Adam and Sara after all. They won't be in church this morning, but they have invited us to lunch at The Country Boy. Are you good with that?"

He nodded. "Of course, it will be nice to see Sara again."

Two hours later, Beau opened the front door to the restaurant and followed Keely inside. Adam was waiting for them.

"Great timing," he said. "We just found seats. Our table is in the back." He stepped aside so Keely could take the lead.

As soon as she saw Sara, Keely waved and hurried to the table. "Do you remember this guy?" She turned to Beau, who was right behind her.

"Beau!" Sara's mouth flew open. She stood and laid her napkin on the table. "It has been years."

Beau reached to hug her. "You look great. Married life must be good for you."

Sara blushed. "We're having a lot of fun."

"I'm happy for both of you," he said, helping Keely take her seat.

"I can't wait to hear more about what's been going on with you," Keely said. "It has been a while since we've caught up."

Sara nodded. "My work has been busy. I know yours has too." She picked up her menu. "How about we order lunch first? I can't seem to get enough to eat lately." She blushed again.

Fifteen minutes later, after the food had been ordered and served, Adam took a drink of his iced tea and glanced from Beau to Keely. "So how did the birthday party go?"

"Titan did great," Keely unfolded her napkin. "Until the clown came into the room."

"Clown? What do you mean?" Adam stared at her.

Keely exhaled. "Emma hired a clown to entertain the kids, and as soon as he walked in the door, Titan went ballistic."

"I can't believe that." Adam shook his head and set down his glass. "He's too well-trained for that to happen."

"Why do you say that?" Beau asked.

"I've worked him with clowns several times."

"You have?" Keely gasped and sat back in her chair. "I don't remember that."

"It might have been when you were out in the field," Adam said. "I can't remember. But my friend Rob has several clown suits. He collects them. I've had him come over more than once to work with the dogs." Adam shook his head. "I would have bet money a clown suit wouldn't have upset Titan."

Beau nudged Keely. "I knew something was wrong."

She looked from him to Adam. "Adam, he went crazy. Not just once but twice."

"What? And you didn't call me about this?" Adam frowned.

"I'm telling you now—"

Beau interrupted. "Let's get back to the clown for a minute." He turned to Keely. "What happened the second time?"

"You know me . . . I can't sit still for very long," she said. "I decided to exercise Titan, while you and Deputy Wallace were dusting my car for prints."

Beau nodded.

"I walked him up and down Emma and Devon's driveway. We were on our third round when I looked up and saw the clown climbing into a truck."

"Do you remember what kind of truck?" Beau asked.

Keely tried to recapture the moment. "I think it was an older model Ford. I'm not sure."

"OK . . . so what did Titan do?"

"As soon as we were within twenty or thirty feet of the guy, Titan went crazy for the second time. I was afraid I wouldn't be strong enough to hold him back."

"Did the guy say anything?"

Keely shook her head. "No. I apologized. But he shook his fist at me."

Adam almost came out of his chair. "He shook his fist at you?"

"That's not good," Sara said. "Someone with that kind of attitude doesn't need to be working with kids."

"I agree," Keely said.

"Did you get his license plate?" Beau asked.

"No. Sorry."

Beau nodded, and Adam broke his silence. "Why was there a deputy sheriff dusting your car for prints?"

Keely glanced to Beau, and he picked up the story. "After the first episode with the clown, we wanted to get Titan out of the way, so Keely and I walked him outside to calm down. While we were out there, I noticed something underneath the back bumper of her SUV. It turned out to be a tracking device like the one we found on Emma's car."

Sara swiveled in her seat. "I hadn't heard about any of this." She turned to Adam.

"I never got around to talking about it, honey. We've been so focused on other things." He glanced to Keely and then to Beau. "We've had some excitement in our family this week."

Sara smiled. "I'm pregnant."

"Sara!" Keely squealed, jumped up, and ran around the table to hug her friend. "When are you due?"

"In June. We found out relatively early."

"I'm so happy for you!" Keely hugged her again before taking her seat.

"Congratulations, man," Beau said.

"Thanks." Adam smiled. "We're both happy about it." He glanced to Sara and then back to Beau. "Please go on. I want to hear more about the tracker."

"I hope to know more tomorrow or Tuesday. Williamson County gave me permission to take it to the TBI lab." He looked to Keely. "But I'll tell you now, we may not find out much. Those devices can be configured anonymously."

"That's not good." Sara's face clouded.

"It's a right to privacy thing, which I completely understand," Beau said. "But it's a handicap when it comes to law enforcement investigations. Tracking falls under stalking laws, which is a Class C Felony in the State of Tennessee."

"Keely, this isn't good." Adam shook his head and then looked to Beau. "Man, I have to admit I thought at first that you were on a wild goose chase with this whole thing, but I'm glad you're helping Keely."

"I agree," Sara said. "Please keep her safe, Beau."

"Hey . . . let's stop talking about me." Keely looked across the table to Sara. "Have you had any weird cravings yet?"

Sara laughed. "Funny you should ask . . ."

While the women talked about babies, the men paid the lunch tabs.

"Will you help me fix the room up?" Sara asked Keely.

"Of course! But I'm better at implementing than I am at planning. You decide what you want, and I'll help you do it."

"Deal." Sara picked through the leftovers on Adam's plate. "I've been starving lately."

"That's because you're eating for two, Mama."

Sara smiled. "That reminds me. How is your mother doing?"

Keely sobered. "Not great but holding her own. She knows me and, of course, my aunt Gigi. But she has a difficult time communicating." Keely dotted her lips with her napkin. "And she's sometimes paranoid."

"What do you mean?" Sara asked.

"She told me at lunch last week that there was a man in the room, and that he was the one who had hurt her."

"What did you just say?" Beau had apparently been listening.

"She makes things up, Beau. She's done it for a while now."

Sara shook her head. "But Keely, what if she's right. Maybe the man who hurt her is the same man who put the tracking device on your car." She gasped. "Do you think he followed you to the restaurant?" She looked around the room.

"I didn't mean to scare you." Keely straightened. "You just never know with Mom." She turned to Beau. "What do you think?"

He stood and placed his hand on her chair. "I think it's time we paid a visit to her."

CHAPTER 18

Sunday, January 9

Beau opened the passenger side door of his Colorado and helped Keely inside.

"Does your mom still live in the ranch house off Garrison Road?"

"Yes. The place where we moved after my dad disappeared."

He took a right out of the parking lot and headed toward the Trace. It had been a while since he had driven Natchez Trace Parkway, which was among the most scenic drives in this part of the state.

"I'm not sure you're prepared for what you're going to see," she said. "Mom has changed a lot since you were with her last."

"We all have."

"I don't mean natural aging." Keely sighed. "I wish I did. She's a shell of who she was. The bad things that happened to her took a terrible toll."

"I'm sorry. I know that's hard for you."

"I feel like I've let her down."

"Why?"

"I don't know. Because I couldn't save her from everything that has happened? Or because I can't make it right. Aunt Gigi and I have taken her to one doctor after another and no one seems to be able to help her. They just add medicine."

"What about Levi? Has he been involved with her care?"

"Definitely. But he's not as hands on as Aunt Gigi and I are." She looked in his direction. "And the truth is, Aunt Gigi has handled most of it. I don't know what I would do without her."

"Isn't she your mom's oldest sister?"

"She's her only sister. And they have one brother, my uncle Peter. Mom's the youngest of the three, but she looks the oldest."

He glanced toward her. "How was she doing when you took her to lunch last week?"

"About the same. She talked a bit more than usual, but still not a lot."

"Is that the first time she has talked about a man who hurt her?"

"Yes. In the past, when talking about her accident in the garden, she has always insisted that she tripped and fell. Or blamed it on her clumsiness." Keely turned to him. "Lack of balance and issues with mobility are symptoms of Parkinson's, and we've never had any reason to doubt she was telling the truth."

"Do you doubt it now?"

Keely shook her head. "Mom has her own version of the truth. Hallucinations, delusions, and paranoia can be symptoms of the disease. Mom is, unfortunately, one of those unlucky ones who has suffered from all three." She looked at him. "We're not sure if it's part of her illness or a side effect of her medications."

"What exactly did she say about her 'attacker' when you saw her last week?"

"Something about 'be careful,' and that 'he's back . . .' I asked her if he was in the room right then, and she said, 'no.'"

"Interesting."

"And frustrating."

"Did she say anything else?"

"Oh! I forgot to tell you, I asked her about Roy Peyton, the real estate guy."

"What did she say?"

"She remembered him. I was surprised," Keely said. "When I mentioned his name, she said he was a 'good guy,' and that he had 'helped us.'"

"So, she had a positive reaction to his name?"

"Very much so."

"That's helpful. I left a message for him, but no one has called me back." Beau stopped at a four-way intersection where he would take a right on the narrow road that led to Maggie Lambert's house. "She has been through a lot, and so have you."

"It has been a long journey, beginning with her car accident," Keely said.

He turned to her. "Before we get to her house, tell me again about the head injuries she sustained in that accident. How long ago was it?"

"It was about nine years ago. It was dark, and Mom was coming home from work when the back wheel fell off her car, throwing her into a ditch. Her head hit the door frame. Although she was belted in, her car was older and didn't have airbags."

Beau nodded.

"A passerby saw the accident and stopped to help her. He called for an ambulance, and Mom was taken to the hospital. We weren't sure for a while if she was going to make it. Evidently, she had some brain swelling, and she was unconscious for several hours."

Keely paused to breathe.

"Thankfully, she survived and even thrived after that. There was no real indication of permanent damage. Not until a few years later when she began having speech problems. By that time, she had also started the trembling that is common with Parkinson's." Keely wrung her hands. "Mom's hands were particularly weak, but she was also unstable on her feet." She turned to him. "That led to the second accident."

"In her garden?"

"Yes. She was alone, and although she can't remember what happened, we were able to piece it together. She was most likely watering or weeding, even though it was late in the evening, almost dark. But Mom loves her garden, and we couldn't keep her out of there, not even after she was diagnosed with Parkinson's."

Beau nodded.

"Aunt Gigi still lived at her own home, because Mom was able to stay by herself until after the second accident."

"You said you were able to piece the details together. Did anyone from the Williamson County Sheriff's Department do an investigation?"

"Yes. They looked around, took some photos, and filed a report. But Mom insisted it was an accident, so everybody accepted that."

"Were they able to determine what caused her head injury?"

Keely nodded. "When she fell, she hit her head on a rock. She wasn't unconscious for very long, but her Parkinson's symptoms accelerated after that."

"And that was last November?"

"Yes. November eighth."

Beau pulled his truck into Maggie Lambert's driveway and turned it off. "Keely, I don't know how much you knew about my mom's car accident a few years ago. But something similar happened to her."

"What do you mean?" Keely turned to him.

"She was leaving work and driving home on Old Hillsboro Road when the wheel fell off her car. She lost control, and her car traveled through a lightly wooded area. She landed in the Harpeth River and drowned."

"I'm so sorry, Beau. I don't think I'd ever heard the exact circumstances of her accident."

"What are the chances?" He asked.

"You mean that both of our mothers would be injured or killed in car accidents?"

"No. That both accidents were caused by a wheel falling off their cars?"

Keely frowned. "Do you think there's a connection?"

"Either that or coincidence. And neither of us put much stock in those."

She stared at him but didn't speak.

"And now, in the past week, you and Emma have had identical trackers put on your cars."

"But . . . why? There's no real connection between our families except you and me . . . and that has been over for ten years."

"*Was* over," Beau corrected her.

She nodded.

"Keely." He turned to her. "Are you aware of the connection between your mom and my dad?"

"You mean that he asked her out after your mom died? I had heard those rumors, but—"

"No," he interrupted. "I hadn't heard about that, but I'm not surprised."

"Then what are you talking about?"

"Your mom and my dad were engaged when he went off to war . . ."

"They were not! I've never heard that in my life." Keely's face paled.

"That's interesting. I'm not sure how something like that managed to evade the Leiper's Fork rumor mill."

"What makes you think it's true?"

Beau stared into the distance for a moment then returned his gaze to her. "I know it's true, because my mom told me."

"Why would she tell you that?" Keely's hand flew to her mouth.

"She wanted me to know why my dad was so set against us dating."

"He was? I never knew that."

"He was . . . he *is* a bitter man, Keely." He took her hand. "That's why I had to leave Leiper's Fork. I couldn't let his bitterness destroy me too."

"Hey, you two. Are you going to sit outside all afternoon? Come on in the house."

"Is that your aunt Gigi?"

"Yes." Keely waved and opened the truck door. "We can talk about this later."

Beau pocketed his keys, got out of the truck, and followed Keely and her aunt into Maggie Lambert's house. It looked exactly the way he had remembered. The photos on the wall, the pillows on the sofa. Even the clock on the mantel.

But Maggie looked completely different.

Keely had been right. Her mother was a shadow of her former self. Even as she slept, her hands trembled.

"Mom, wake up. It's Keely." Keely gently massaged her mother's shoulders. "I have somebody with me you haven't seen in a long time."

Maggie's eyes slowly opened and went directly to him.

"Beau?"

Keely's jaw dropped. "She knows you!"

"Hello, Mrs. Lambert." He knelt beside her and took her trembling fingers in his. She squeezed his hand, albeit lightly.

"I'm so happy to see you again." He glanced upward to Keely. "Keely has been telling me all about you."

Maggie smiled, and Beau was struck by her innate beauty, which hadn't been taken away by her cruel illness. "My girl is special."

"Yes, she is," Beau agreed. "May I sit here with you for a minute?"

Maggie nodded.

Beau reached for the ottoman near the sofa, pulled it across the floor, and placed it beside her. He took a seat and beckoned for Keely to sit next to him.

After Keely had taken a seat, Beau took Maggie's hand again. "You may not know this, Mrs. Lambert, but I work for the State of Tennessee Bureau of Investigation. Keely told me that a man hurt you. Is that right?"

Maggie twitched, and Beau soothed her hand. "It's OK. I'm here to protect you." He glanced to Keely. "And Keely."

She gave him a hesitant look.

"If you can tell me who he is, Mrs. Lambert, I will do everything in my power to see that he never hurts anyone else."

Maggie nodded and lightly squeezed his hand again.

"Take your time."

"He hurt me."

"Where were you when he hurt you?"

She pulled her hand away and raised it toward the back of the house.

"In the garden?"

She nodded.

"Have you ever told anyone else about this?"

She shook her head.

"Why haven't you told anyone?"

"Because . . ."

"Were you afraid he would hurt you again?"

Her hand twitched.

"Were you also afraid he would hurt Keely?"

"Yes!" she cried out.

Keely leaned forward and took her mother's other hand. "It's OK, Mom. I have Beau to protect me. You need to tell him everything you can."

She smiled. "I'm . . . glad you . . . have Beau."

Her words punched him in the gut. *Why had he been away for so long?*

"I'm here to stay this time, Mrs. Lambert," he said, and he took Keely's free hand in his. "And I'm here to help you both."

Maggie's hand twitched again.

"Did you see the man at the restaurant with Keely?"

"No." She tried to pull away.

"Do you know his name?"

She shook her head.

"Can you describe him to me?"

She shook her head again.

"If I showed you a picture of him, would you tell me it was him?"

This time she nodded.

Beau squeezed her hand. "Why don't we do that? I will bring you a picture, and you can tell me if it's him."

"OK . . ."

"You look tired," he said. "Keely and I will leave now, but I want you to remember something very important."

"OK."

"I want you to remember that I am going to keep you and Keely safe."

She squeezed his hand again.

"Do you trust me to do that?"

"OK," she said.

Within a few minutes, she had drifted off to sleep, and Keely's aunt Gigi, who had been sitting quietly in a chair across the room, beckoned for the two of them to take a seat on the sofa.

Once they had obliged, Keely made the proper introductions.

"It's nice to meet you, Ms.—"

"Bradley. But please call me Gigi. Everyone does."

"It's nice to meet you, Gigi. I've heard a lot of good things about you."

"I do my best," she said. "When family needs help, you do your best."

Beau nodded, not sure if he had lived up to those standards.

"I've heard a lot of good things about you too, Beau." She gestured toward her sister. "And I can tell that Maggie adores you. I've never seen her respond to someone like that. She obviously trusts you."

"I will try to deserve that trust," he said. "And yours too." He glanced sideways to Keely. "In the meantime, I want to give you my contact information."

He gave her detailed instructions, along with his phone number, and told her that he would be requesting security for their home. A few minutes later, he escorted Keely to his truck.

Once they were seated inside, she looked at him and simply said, "Thank you."

He engaged the engine and put the vehicle in reverse, then turned to her. "I wish I had been here earlier. Maybe she could have avoided that second injury."

"Beau, you're here in God's time. You couldn't have known that Mom would be attacked. No one could have." She looked beyond him and then back again. "I have beaten myself up about that same thing since November. But there was no way to know."

He nodded.

"Whoever is trying to destroy my family—and apparently yours now too—showed up again after fifteen or twenty years." She hesitated. "If, in fact, he's the same man who took my father and who scared Connor at the park."

"I agree." He backed the truck out of the drive. "We have no way of knowing right now if it's the same man, but . . ." He hesitated. "I need to tell you something about that visit we just had with your mom."

"What?" The word caught in Keely's throat.

"She knows who her attacker is. She reacted differently when she told me she didn't know his name."

"Are you sure?"

"Yes. I have no doubt about it." He exhaled. "I have interviewed a lot of people—the good guys and the bad guys—and your mother is hiding that man's identity. She may not know his name, but she knows who he is."

"Why won't she tell us?"

He glanced to her. "Because she's afraid for your life. And her own."

July 6, 2000

The 1990, blue Chevrolet sedan slowed to a stop alongside the road.

"What's wrong, Daddy?" Levi asked.

Will Lambert shook his head in disbelief. "It looks like we've blown a tire, son. The left front. You kids stay in the car, while I check it out."

Watching from the backseat of the car, Keely saw her daddy's head and shoulders disappear behind the front fender. Then, stepping back from the vehicle, he tilted his Vanderbilt baseball cap—the one he always wore—toward the back of his head. He wiped his brow with his arm and then replaced the cap.

He ambled to the open driver's side window and asked Levi to reach into the console and pull out a bright orange emergency sign. As soon as her brother found it, Will Lambert asked Keely to put it in the back window of the car, visible from the road.

"We'll have to walk to a gas station. I don't have what I need here to fix it. And I didn't bring my phone with me." He looked toward the west. "We need to hurry. It looks like a storm is coming."

CHAPTER 19

Monday, January 10

As soon as Beau walked into his office the next morning, he filed the paperwork required for tracing the owner of the tracking device. He expected the same results as they'd had with the first device, but he was hoping to be proven wrong. After calling for a runner to take the device to the lab, he put in a call to Chris Enoch requesting a meeting. Enoch agreed to see him immediately.

Following a polite exchange of greetings, Beau got down to business, taking a seat in the chair opposite Enoch's desk. He told him about finding another tracking device. Then he went into detail about Maggie Lambert's accidents. The first one, the result of a loose tire. The second of which may have been an assault, based on Maggie's cryptic statements to him over the weekend. Beau then went on to explain, in as much detail as he knew, about Maggie's diminished communication skills and her cognitive disabilities.

Enoch sat quietly and took it all in, so Beau continued. He went back in time to give his boss an overview of the William Lambert cold case they had discussed in their last meeting. And then he brought him up-to-date on the investigation so far.

"I have a couple of leads, and I can follow up on both of those with one call." Beau said. "At the time of his disappearance in 2000, William Lambert was a partner in a real estate sales firm, Lambert and Peyton, based in Franklin. Lambert had one business partner, Roy T. Peyton. Peyton is now listed as the sole owner of that firm."

Enoch nodded.

"I've just started looking into Peyton's background—criminal priors, newspaper stories, and personal references, and he's coming up clean." Beau rubbed the back of his neck with his hand. "Keely Lambert, Mrs. Lambert's daughter, asked her mother about Peyton last week, and her mother's reaction was positive."

"And your second reason to talk to Peyton?"

"At the time of Mr. Lambert's disappearance, the price of real estate in Leiper's Fork was just starting to pop. In fact, it was well on its way to a boom." Beau shrugged. "I grew up there, although my family lived a few miles from the center of the village, and I can tell you that many of the locals were shocked—and not sure what to do about the sudden popularity of their community."

"Financial gain. One of the two root causes of crime. The other being passion," Enoch said.

"Yes, sir." Beau nodded. "Passion being defined in many ways. I remember when you first shared this insight with me, and it has always proved to be right."

Enoch smiled.

"It's too early in this case to determine the root cause. I believe both could be equally debated." Beau paused. "Shortly after Mrs. Lambert's husband disappeared, she was forced to sell her home near the center of the village."

"She couldn't afford the mortgage?"

"That's correct," Beau said. "A clause in the agreement William Lambert had with his partner, Roy Peyton, quickly and significantly reduced the Lambert family income, so Mrs. Lambert's personal income was all she had to support herself and her children. She sold their family home and used the equity to buy a less expensive home several miles away."

"There was no life insurance?" Enoch asked.

"Nothing for a while. Tennessee law at the time required that Mrs. Lambert prove beyond a reasonable doubt that her husband was deceased." Beau shook his head. "And from what I understand from Mrs. Lambert's daughter, Keely, her mother was hesitant to push for that declaration—even if she could have proven it without a body or physical evidence of a crime—because she wanted to cling to the possibility that her husband was alive."

"That's a shame."

"Yes, sir. Tennessee law corresponding to this kind of thing was changed the year after Lambert disappeared. However, even then, the family was required to wait seven years before a legal declaration could be made."

"So, back to the real estate sale, you want to find out who purchased the property and what they stood to gain from that purchase?"

"Exactly."

"Do you have reason to believe it was significant?"

"I'm not sure yet."

Enoch nodded. "Any other leads?"

"Nothing concrete, sir, unless we get a break on the owner of the second tracker."

"Nothing concrete? Does that mean you have another direction of interest?"

Beau laughed. "You know me well, Chris. Yes, there is one more thing I want to investigate. It's not exactly a lead. It's a hunch."

Chris Enoch leaned back in his chair. "This should be interesting."

Beau told him about Titan's reaction to the clown at Connor's birthday party. "Although Keely is convinced the dog overreacted to the clown suit due to a lack of training, the man who helps train her dogs disagrees. According to him, Titan has been trained specifically to ignore clown costumes, hair, and makeup, as well as other kinds of uniforms and disguises. I tend to agree with the co-trainer. I'm not yet prepared to write off the dog's reaction as a mistake."

"Do you have background information on the clown or service provider for the clown?"

"That's where it gets interesting. My sister hired the clown without references. She found his name and phone number posted on her church bulletin board, called him, and booked him for the party."

"Have you followed up with him?"

"Not yet. But I will," Beau said.

"To be clear"—Enoch steepled his fingers—"you suspect the dog reacted to the person, specifically to the scent of the person in the costume, and not to the costume. Is that correct?"

Beau nodded. "Yes."

"It certainly doesn't hurt to follow up," Enoch said.

Beau started to speak, but Enoch stopped him.

"Before you move on, I need to ask you why, if there is no personal relationship, Ms. Lambert and her dog were at the party."

Beau sat straight in the chair. "I knew you would ask me that," he said. "It's the obvious question, isn't it?" He paused to gather his words. "Ms. Lambert and Titan were invited to the party by Connor. He apparently wanted to impress his party guests—all who were six- and seven-year-olds—with stories about his recent adventure in the park. And the presence of his rescuers."

Enoch shook his head. "Don't let these visits become habit, Gardner, or you'll be off the case."

"Yes, sir." Beau stood to leave and then remembered. "Sir, do you have any problem with my calling the Williamson County Sheriff's Department to request extra patrols on Mrs. Lambert's house?"

"That would be their jurisdiction."

"Yes, sir."

"Is your father still with that force?"

"Yes, sir."

"That will be fine."

"Thank you, sir. I wanted to be sure."

Beau had his hand on the door to leave when Enoch stopped him. "One more thing."

Beau turned around.

"Has there been a return to a romantic involvement between you and the Lambert woman?"

Beau hesitated and then shook his head. "None so far, sir."

Enoch cocked an eyebrow and shook his head. "See to it that there isn't, or I will take you off this case. Immediately."

"Understood, sir."

"After what you did to her the first time, I can't believe she would have you anyway."

"It would take a saint, sir."

Enoch frowned. "That sounds to me like you have already discussed the matter."

Beau wasn't sure what to say. "I can promise you this—there will be no romantic involvement until this case is resolved."

"So, you have that intention?"

"As you said, that may very well depend on her."

"Gardner . . ."

"Yes, sir."

"I will take you at your word. Don't let me down." Enoch lowered his voice. "Let me give you some advice."

Beau nodded.

"If you care at all for this woman, and you think you're the best man to keep her out of danger—and to find out who murdered her father, because he was most likely murdered—you will stay away from her right now."

"I agree, sir." Beau opened the door to leave and then turned back. "And thank you."

"Keep me informed," Enoch shook his head.

A few minutes later, after returning to his desk, Beau placed a call to the Williamson County Sherriff's Office, a number he knew by heart.

"Russell Wallace, please. It's Beau Gardner at the TBI."

"He's not here right now, Agent Gardner. Would you like to talk with your dad?"

Beau hesitated. "Yes. Please put him on."

A few minutes later J. G. Gardner answered. "This sounds official. What's going on?"

"I need to ask for a favor."

"Business or personal?"

"Business."

"Of course, the answer would have been the same either way. How can I help?"

"Do you have the personnel to assign a security detail to Maggie Lambert's house?"

"Is this an official TBI request?"

"Yes."

"I'll do everything I can, but a good reason would help. What do you have?"

There was so much history between his father and Maggie Lambert, Beau wasn't sure where to start—and said so.

"Why don't you start from the beginning?"

"You already know about Connor's disappearance and the tracker we found on Emma's car. I found the same kind of device on Keely's car."

"That could be coincidence."

"Yes, it could. But there's more to it than that, and I'm convinced that the same man—or woman—planted both trackers."

"And that's because . . . ?"

"Because we found Will Lambert's dog tag at Beaman Park not far from where we found Connor."

"That makes no sense."

"What do you mean?" Beau asked.

His father hesitated. "Beau, I thought you were a good law enforcement officer, but you're reaching a conclusion, making a connection, without any evidence and, quite honestly, that's negligence. It's something you should have learned in Investigation 101 class."

"Are you through lecturing me?"

"What do you mean?"

"You know what I mean, Dad. You also know a lot more about Will Lambert's disappearance that you will ever admit. I've known that since I was old enough to understand that situation."

"What are you trying to say?"

Beau counted to ten. "I'm saying I know how much you hated Will Lambert. It was a badge you wore with honor a long time before you ever put on a law enforcement badge."

"Son, I don't have to take this from you."

"And I don't have to care anymore," Beau said. "There was a time when I cared about what you thought. Or, to put it more succinctly, there was a time when I lived underneath your roof that I was supposed to care. But your hatred for Keely and anyone or anything that had to do with Will Lambert was so evident, it tainted everything around you." He paused and took a breath.

"Are you finished now?"

"Maybe."

"I'm sorry you feel the way you do. I've told you over and over again since your mother died that I'm sorry for carrying a grudge. It's never the right thing to do."

Beau leaned back in his chair and willed himself to relax. None of this was helpful to his case. His long-time feud with his father didn't matter when Maggie Lambert's—and maybe Keely's or even Emma's lives—were at stake.

"OK . . ."

"I will do everything I can to have an officer assigned to Maggie Lambert's house."

"Thank you."

There was nothing more to say, so Beau ended the call. But he still had two more calls to make—and the first would be the hardest, almost as difficult as talking to his dad. He searched in his contact list for Adam Hunt's number.

Adam answered on the first ring.

"Hey, it's Beau. Am I calling at a bad time?"

"No, not at all," Adam said. "Let me walk over here so I can have some privacy. I'm at Keely's right now . . ."

Beau waited.

"OK," Adam said. "I'm standing out back. What's going on?"

"I wanted to let you know that I'm officially reopening Will Lambert's case. And that I'm asking for security for Maggie Lambert's house. I will be asking the sheriff's department to check on Keely from time to time too."

"Good to hear," Adam said.

"I appreciated your help yesterday, and I want to ask for your forgiveness."

"Beau, you don't have to—"

"Please, let me finish. This has been too long in coming. I know I was a jerk when I left town. I owed Keely, and all my friends, more than that. But I just had to get away."

"Done."

"I appreciate—"

"And I hope you will forgive me," Adam said.

"You? For what?" Beau asked.

"For carrying a grudge since then. I was a jerk last week."

"Like you said, it's over."

"Thanks. You have my number, Beau. I hope you'll let me know how I can help with your investigation. There isn't anyone who loves Keely who doesn't hope she will eventually find closure with her dad."

"I'll keep you in the loop. Talk soon."

Beau hung up the phone. He had a lot to think about, and he wasn't sure where to start. Digging into the file on Will Lambert's disappearance was as good of a place as any. But before he did that, he placed one more call.

Deputy Sheriff Russell Wallace had given him a business card, which Beau had stashed in his jacket pocket. He found the card and dialed Wallace's mobile number. Wallace answered on the second ring.

"Russ, it's Beau Gardner. I'm following up on the fingerprints from Saturday. Did you find anything worthwhile?"

"Hey, Beau. We ran it through the database, but there were no matches. At least not so far. My gut says we won't find anything."

"I figured as much," Beau said. "Will you let me know if you hear more?"

"You have my word. Is there anything else I can do to help?"

"Yes. There's another reason I called," Beau said. "I'd appreciate it if you would check on Keely's house from time to time. I'm reopening her father's disappearance case, and well . . . when you stir up a hornet's nest, they don't usually go down without a fight. I may need backup."

"Just as I told Keely the other day, I thought a lot of her grandparents. If there's anything I can do to help her, or you, I'd be honored."

"Thank you. I'll stay in touch."

It was now time to dig into that file. And to track down Roy Peyton.

CHAPTER 20

Monday, January 10

"Who was that on the phone earlier?" Keely asked.

Adam shrugged. "Beau."

"Oh? What did he want?"

"He wanted to bury the hatchet."

"What did you tell him?"

"I told him that I also owed him an apology."

"Good. So . . . you're both good?"

"We are."

"Do you know how happy that makes me?"

Adam smiled. "It makes me happy too, Keely. Life is too short to let something so little come between friends. I'm not even sure now why I was mad at him." He hesitated. "And besides . . ."

She stared at him. "Besides?"

"I want to be best man at your wedding."

She picked up the closest thing she could find, which was one of the dogs' treat balls, and threw it at him. "You can stop now."

He caught the ball with his left hand and threw it back to her. "Are you going to deny it's not a possibility?"

"I'm denying nothing," she said. "But I will tell you that he has a long way to go before that would ever happen."

"You sound like Sara. Why are you girls so hard to convince? I thought every woman wanted to drag her man to the altar."

"You are seriously in for another pounding with a treat ball." She sighed. "Hey, I have an idea."

"And . . . ?"

"Do you think your friend Rob would have time to come over in the next few days? I would like to see for myself how Titan reacts to his clown suit."

"I'm sure he wouldn't mind at all. In fact, I'll call him right now."

While Adam made his call, Keely walked to the main kennel door and stepped into the sunshine. It was a beautiful day. Perfect for working the dogs outside. But first she would check on Ruby and Pearl. And maybe fix a sandwich for her and Adam.

She hurried up the hill to the house, unlocked the mudroom door, and stepped into a mess. Pearl was in labor, and it was too early. Keely would have moved her to the whelping room if she had known, but it was too late for that now.

Keely screamed for Adam to come quickly, and then closed the mudroom door and kneeled beside the dog. She was obviously in trouble.

One pup lay beside her not moving, and another appeared to be breach. Keely reached for her phone and speed dialed the vet. *Come on . . . answer.*

"Hang on, Pearl. I'm here for you."

Adam threw open the door and rushed inside. "What happened?"

"She's in labor," Keely said. "She needs help, or we'll lose her too."

Adam pulled his phone from his pocket. "Did you call the vet?"

"They're not answering. We're going to have to do this on our own."

Adam rolled up his sleeves. "It's not like we haven't done it before." He kneeled beside her and the dog.

"Breathe, Pearl," Keely soothed. "Breathe . . . you've got this. We're here to help, girl. We're here . . ."

An hour later, Pearl was resting comfortably, and Keely and Adam were cleaning the mudroom. They had lost six puppies. Two had survived.

"What do you think? Should we let her stay here for the night, or move her to the whelping room now?"

"We have to move them," Adam said. "We're better prepared out there, especially if something goes south."

"Agreed."

"If you want to carry the pups, I'll walk Pearl down the hill."

"OK. Do you have a towel? Preferably a large one? And maybe a laundry basket?"

"Got it." Keely opened the dog gate and ran into the laundry room for a clean towel and laundry basket. Ruby and Titan, had been gated inside the main house, and they ran with her to the laundry and back.

"Here." Keely handed the two items across the gate to Adam. "Give me a minute to feed these two. They've had a rough morning. If I know Ruby, she'll be grieving over the loss of Pearl's puppies."

As soon as Keely had Ruby and Titan fed, she leashed Pearl and tried to lead her to the door. The dog refused until she saw that Adam had the puppies. "Trust us, girl. We've got this."

Keely had been grateful many times for the way her grandparents had designed the farmhouse. The big front porch was accessible by stairs, but the back entrance had been built at ground level. Pearl had to simply step across the threshold. There were no stairs for her to navigate.

Keely took it easy on the way to the kennel. Adam walked beside her, continually reminding Pearl that her puppies were right there with her. Within fifteen minutes, they had mama and babies settled into their new living quarters.

"I'll spend tonight here," Keely said. "You go home and get some rest. If I need you, I will call you."

"I'm not leaving until I've helped you with the other dogs. Obviously, we won't be training much today, but they need exercise and feeding."

"Let's do it," Keely said. "I'll grab the baby monitor and be right there."

Beau dialed Keely on his way home. "What are you doing tonight?" he asked.

"You'll never believe it." She appeared to be breathing heavily.

"Are you OK?" He glanced in his rearview mirror to change lanes in case he needed to high tail it out to her house.

"Yes . . . I'm watching newborn puppies."

"Pearl had her litter?"

"Yes, and unfortunately too soon. We lost all but two."

"I'm sorry, Keely. I hope they both survive."

"They look to be healthy," she said. "And Pearl is doing OK. But she scared me this afternoon when I found her in the middle of delivery in the mudroom."

"What did the vet say?"

"I couldn't reach him. Apparently, they had a phone outage. I managed to reach his office later this afternoon, and Adam drove over there to pick up a prescription for Pearl."

"Did you deliver them by yourself?"

"Adam and I did."

"You are superwoman. Did you know that?"

"I'll be super tired woman by morning. Tonight's my night to stay in the whelping area with the babies."

Panic rose in Beau's chest. "Is it secure out there? I can be there in thirty minutes and stay all night if you need me."

"That's probably not a good idea. Two of us don't need to lose a night's sleep. I'll be fine. Adam will stay with them tomorrow night. We'll rotate until we're beyond the first week."

"I was hoping you could go with me to your mother's tomorrow."

"Really? What's up?"

"I've thought of a few more questions I'd like to ask her. She's our best witness, at least at this point, unless somebody else comes forward."

"I don't expect that to happen."

"I don't either, but I can always hope."

"Do you think we'll ever get to the bottom of this, Beau?" She hesitated. "You know . . . to the real bottom. So, I can finally find out what happened to my dad?"

"I'm not planning to stop until we do. I just hope the man who's behind it is still around to pay the price."

"Beau . . . I remembered something this morning. It's not a big deal. But I remembered that there were two men in the car that picked us up the day my dad disappeared."

"Do you remember their faces?"

"I didn't see one of them. And I can't remember the other one. Not clearly. I was seven years old . . ."

"Can you please refresh my memory about what happened that morning?" he asked.

"It was later in the day. Almost sunset. My parents, Levi, and I had just celebrated my birthday. Mom and Daddy gave me a puppy, the one I named Jax. After supper, Daddy asked if Levi and I would like to go for ice cream, so we left Mom at the house to watch the puppy, and we took off. Daddy had car trouble about halfway into town, so we started walking."

"Why didn't he call for help?"

"I think he had forgotten to bring his phone with him."

"OK . . ."

"We had walked a little way—not far—up the road, and a man in a black car stopped to ask if he could help us. I sensed fear coming from Daddy, which in retrospect is hard for me to comprehend. I mean, Daddy wasn't afraid of anything. But he agreed to let them drive us into town for help."

"So, the men drove you to a gas station?"

"No. The ice cream shop."

"What happened then?"

"The man in the driver's seat handed me money. I think it was a ten-dollar bill. He told me to take Levi inside and buy ice cream for both of us."

"Did you see his face any better when he gave you the money?"

"No. He just stretched his arm over the backseat and shoved the money at me. I looked at Daddy and he nodded, which meant he was OK with it. So I got out of the car and took Levi with me to buy ice cream."

"Did you see your dad after that?"

"No . . . Levi and I ordered our ice cream. I paid for it, and we ran outside to get back in the car. But it was gone."

"Then you called Maggie?"

"The shop owner did. He knew something was wrong when he saw me crying in the parking lot and came out to help us."

"Does Levi remember anything more, or different, than you?"

"Levi doesn't remember any of it. He was only five at the time."

"Does he remember your dad?"

"I wish he did, but he doesn't. Not that much anyway. He only remembers the things we told him when he was growing up. And, of course, we have a few pictures of all of us together."

"What do you remember about the black car?"

"Not a lot. I remember it was big."

"Is that all?"

"I think so."

"Do you think you would remember it if you saw it—or one like it—again?"

"I doubt I would. I've not thought about it before, to be honest."

"I'm sure the police interviewed the shop owner. Did he, or anyone else, see the car? Or the men inside?"

"No. I remember specifically that we parked on the side. The ice cream shop only had windows in front."

"That most likely means they drove in on one side of the shop, and then exited in the same direction . . . Never passing in front of the store."

"Maybe."

"Did the shop owner have video cameras?"

"I would assume not. I don't remember anyone ever talking about it."

"And there were no other witnesses? No one saw you in the ice cream shop parking lot or alongside the road when the black car picked you up?"

"Nobody."

"If you remember anything else, please remember to tell me."

Silence.

"Keely?"

"Yes. You know, it's funny. I haven't had these flashbacks about Daddy's disappearance for years. But in the last few days, I've had two. I think . . . I think finding the dog tag and renewing my hope that we will solve his case, has brought them all back."

"Is that a good or a bad thing?" he asked.

"It's both," she said. "When I flash back to that time, it's like I get to spend the day with Daddy again. Then I wake up . . . and I realize it was just a dream."

Her words punched Beau in the gut. He had thought about his mother a lot since she died, but he had never dreamed of her. Did he have too much guilt about not seeing her when she was fully here?

Unlike Keely, was he afraid of facing his fears?

"Are you on your way home?" Keely brought him back to the moment.

"Yes . . . unless you need me."

"I'll be fine, Beau. Stop worrying about me." She sighed. "What time do you want to pick me up in the morning?"

"Is eleven o'clock OK with you? We can get some lunch afterward."

"That shouldn't be a problem. I'll ask Adam if he can come over early."

CHAPTER 21

Tuesday, January 11

After changing out of her work clothes into clean, but faded blue jeans and a blue sweater, Keely was walking back to the kennel when Adam pulled into the driveway.

"You're early!" She walked over to his car. "I'm sorry to ask you to do this, but I promised Beau I would ride with him to my mother's place this morning."

"No worries," he said. "You're the one who will be spending another night with the puppies."

She shrugged. "I found out last night that two is a lot easier than ten or twelve."

"Sad, but true. I'm sorry you lost so many of them, Keely. How is Pearl doing?"

"She's OK. I have no doubt she is grieving for the ones she lost, but her instinct reminds her to take care of the living."

"A life lesson for all of us."

"Did you ever see the movie *Little Boy*?"

Adam shook his head as he walked with her toward the kennel door. "Not that I remember."

"It's about an eight-year-old boy whose father leaves for World War II and doesn't return. Seeking help in his time of grief, the boy befriends a priest, and the priest gives him a to-do list, which he says will help the boy become a better person—and to one day realize his dream of seeing his father again."

"Sounds like a sad movie."

She nodded. "The priest tells the boy to 'feed the hungry, shelter the homeless, visit those in prison, clothe the naked, visit the sick, and bury the dead.' Of course, the movie reminded me of my dad, because I understood the little boy's loss. But it also inspired me. Everything on the list—except for the last—is about helping others, easing their pain. It's about taking care of the living." She looked at Adam. "And to do that, we have to bury the dead."

Adam nodded. "You're having a hard time revisiting your dad's disappearance, aren't you?"

"I am," she said. "I need to bury my father, Adam. And that's why I'm hoping that Beau can finally solve this case."

"There he is now." Adam shifted his attention to the black SUV pulling into Keely's driveway.

Beau got out and walked over to them.

"This looks like an official visit." She gestured toward his car.

"Not so official I can't take you to lunch afterward." He grinned then reached to shake Adam's hand. "How's it going today?"

"I'm good . . . Sara's good. Keely is the one who is overworked and underpaid. She spent the night in the whelping room."

"Do I look that tired?" she asked. "Maybe I need to run back to the house and put on makeup."

"You look beautiful," Beau said. "I'd be honored to take you anywhere."

"See what I mean?" Keely laughed. "He's a charmer."

"Always was," Adam teased. "You two have fun . . . and I hope you can make progress on the case."

"Thanks, Adam. I'll be back as soon as I can to relieve you," she said.

"No hurry. I'm here all day." He laughed.

Beau escorted Keely to the SUV and opened the door. "Your coach awaits, Cinderella."

"I like your pickup truck just as well," she said, stepping into the vehicle.

Beau hurried around the front of the car and climbed in.

"How has your morning been?" she asked.

"There's not a lot to tell." He turned the car around and took off for the main road. "Things are moving slowly on the case. We don't have much to go on at this point. Like I said yesterday, your mom is our best witness." He glanced at her. "But I'm beginning to think that your memories of the day he disappeared may prove to be helpful in the end as well."

"I wish I could remember more."

"If we talk about it enough, maybe you can. Are you up for that? If all of this is too much, let me know."

"I'm OK." She folded her hands in her lap. "I was just telling Adam, the thing that will help me the most is being able to bury my dad." She looked at him. "If, in fact, he's dead."

He nodded.

"I just need to know."

"How do you think your mom feels about that?"

"What do you mean?"

"Does she think your dad is living or dead?"

"That's a good question. It's not something I've ever been comfortable asking her."

"Why?"

Keely shrugged. "I guess I just hate to bring up such a bad memory."

Beau glanced her way. "You don't think your mother ever thinks about your dad?" He shook his head. "That's highly unlikely."

"I suppose."

"Would you be OK if I ask her?"

Keely studied him. "I'm not sure we can trust her memory."

"Are you sure of that?" he asked.

"I've just always assumed it because her communication skills are so bad."

His focus returned to the road in front of them. "I took some time this morning to read about Parkinson's Disease and traumatic brain injury. They are two separate things with two separate sets of issues. I wish we could determine which of the two is more responsible for her problems."

"I had assumed it was both," Keely said. "But there I go, assuming again. I don't know." She sighed.

"All we can do is ask the right questions, remind her that she can trust us, and be patient." He glanced her way. "Did I tell you

I called my dad yesterday and asked him to put in a request for someone from the sheriff's department to watch her house?"

"You didn't. What did he say?"

"He said he would do what he could. You know my dad. It would have been better if it had been his idea."

"I'm sure he's proud of you, Beau. What father wouldn't be?"

He reached to cover her hand with his. "That's one reason I love you. You've always believed in me."

"Always did. Always will." She cocked her head. "So, what are the other reasons?"

"What do you mean?"

"You said that was one reason you loved me. What are the other reasons?" she teased.

"How much time do you have?"

"Lots," she said.

He laughed.

"At least I can make you laugh," she grew serious. "I like that."

He squeezed her hand. "When are you going to let me take you on a real date?"

"You mean the kind where you pick me up in the evening, and we go dancing?"

"Is that what you want?"

"No. I'd rather we just go for a drive in your truck and find a little Italian restaurant—or a country diner—somewhere."

"I'm in. When can we do that?"

"Thanks to Pearl, it will be at least a week."

"Disappointing, but I can wait."

"I'll look forward to it." Keely smiled and looked out the window.

"Me too."

They rode in silence until he turned onto the road that led to her mother's house.

"You said your grandparents used to live here?"

"Yes. My mom grew up in this house. And, subsequently, I did too. It's the only house my brother remembers."

Beau pulled into the driveway. "Does Gigi know we're coming?"

"I texted her earlier, but I didn't hear back. I have the key if we need it. But I can't imagine why we would. She never leaves unless someone is here to watch Mom."

They got out of the SUV and walked to the front door. Keely knocked lightly, and they waited. When no one answered, she rang the doorbell.

Still no response.

"I'm not sure what's going on." She dug through her handbag for her keys. "Let's walk to the back. My key fits that door."

On their way around the house, Keely peeked in the garage window. Gigi's car was inside. None of this made sense. When she turned the corner to the back of the house, her heart took a plunge. The back door was wide open.

Before she could run inside, Beau stopped her.

"No!" he whispered and grabbed her arm. "You stay out here with your cell phone in your hand. Be ready to call 911 if I need you . . . or if I don't come out within five minutes."

She stared at him.

"Keely, do you understand?"

She nodded.

"Here." He motioned for her to stand on the far side of the door so she could see in every direction. "Keep watch for me."

"OK."

Beau pulled back his jacket and reached for the gun in the holster at his waist. He checked it, and then slowly walked into the house. Keely made note of the time on her watch and then pulled her phone from her pocket. She held her breath, dialed 911, and positioned her finger above the green send button. She wasn't sure if her right hand or her left hand was shaking more.

After three minutes, with no sound coming from inside the house. Keely looked around. There wasn't a bird in the sky, even the breeze had forgotten to blow. She was on the final countdown before she had to hit the send button.

Forty-five seconds . . . thirty seconds . . . fifteen seconds . . .

"Keely!"

She jumped back. "Beau."

He stepped through the back door jam and looked around the backyard, his gun still drawn. Finally satisfied that everything was OK, he walked over to her.

"Try your aunt's phone one more time."

"OK." She exhaled. *Had she been holding her breath for five minutes?*

Clearing the numbers on her dial pad, she hit the speed dial number for Gigi's phone and almost immediately heard a ringing sound, faint but clearly a ring tone, coming from inside the house.

"I heard that too." Beau darted back inside the house and in a few seconds returned with Gigi's phone in his hand. "This is why she wasn't answering. Now to figure out where she and your mom have gone . . ."

"I don't understand. Gigi's car is inside the garage." Keely took another look through the garage window. "And so is Mom's. There must be an explanation."

"Hopefully a good one," Beau added.

Keely's heart dropped to her stomach again.

CHAPTER 22

Tuesday, January 11

Beau escorted Keely around the side of the house while watching for the possibility of intruders. Either Gigi or Maggie had left the back door open. Or some unknown—and possibly ill-meaning—person had opened it.

He hoped the former was the case.

"Don't panic yet," he told Keely. "The obvious is sometimes the hardest to see. Off the top of your head, give me five possibilities for a reasonable explanation."

"Five? I can't think of one."

"Humor me. We need to figure this out."

"So, you're convinced nothing is wrong?"

"Let's just say I didn't see any sign of a struggle. Wherever they went, and whoever they went with, they went willingly."

"OK. Let me think. Maybe Uncle Peter picked them up."

"Good one. Call him."

Keely stared at him in unbelief. "That was too easy. Why didn't I think of it?"

"Because you're worried."

"Probably." She dialed the phone and a few seconds later he heard someone answer on the other end.

"Uncle Peter, it's Keely. Do you know where Mom and Gigi might be?" Keely frowned as she listened to his response. "No idea? I don't know either and it's worrying me. I'm at the house right now. They're not here, and both cars are in the garage. I'll call a few more people. If you hear from them, would you let me know? OK . . . thanks."

She hung up.

"Now he's worried. He has no idea where they are."

"OK . . . Give me your second-best scenario."

She furrowed her brow. "If they'd gone to the doctor's office, Gigi would have driven. Same for the hairdresser. Or the grocery store." She looked at him. "Beau, there's just nothing. They're too far from anyone or anything to have walked there. We're four miles from the nearest town."

"Could they be visiting a neighbor?"

"They would have driven. Besides, Mom never has liked the woman who lives up the street. She's always said she was a busybody."

"We could use a good busybody right now. Maybe we should ask her if she knows what's going on."

Keely stared at him again. "I don't know—"

"Well, then give me another idea."

"Wait! Levi was coming back into town today. What if—?"

"Call him!"

"Hang on." She bit her lip and dialed the phone. "No answer . . ." She mouthed. And then she jerked back. "Levi! It's Keely. Do you know where Mom is?"

Beau watched as a smile spread across her face.

"She's with you?" She gave Beau a thumbs up.

"Is Aunt Gigi with you too? OK, good. I was worried. I'm at Mom's house right now. When we got here the back door was open and there was no sign of either one of them."

She nodded and listened.

"Beau is with me."

More listening.

"How far away are you? OK, great. We'll wait."

She ended the call. "It's all good. I'll text Uncle Peter and let him know."

After her uncle had acknowledged her text, Keely stuffed her phone in her pocket and focused on Beau. "They're on their way home from lunch. Levi said they're only ten minutes away." She took a deep breath. "That scared me half to death."

He cocked a brow.

"What?"

"What about the other half of you?"

"Beau Gardner, I'm going to kiss you."

"Do it," he urged.

"You wish . . ."

He grabbed her by the waist and started dancing with her in the driveway, contemplating what it would be like to kiss her again when she was ready. But he was willing to wait. She had waited for him for years.

"You've lost your mind," she said.

"No, I'm just doing what you said you wanted . . . taking you dancing."

She laughed and gave in to his silliness, and he whisked her across the limestone chert. "Thank you for reminding me to live. You were always good at that."

Levi's car appeared over the crest of the hill and pulled into Maggie's drive, coming to a stop beside Beau's SUV. Beau hurried toward the passenger side of the vehicle to open the door for the ladies, and Keely went to the driver's side door.

"Is it just the three of you?" she asked her brother through his open window.

"Yes. Anna is home with the kids. They're exhausted after the trip, but I wanted to see how Mom and Gigi were doing. We made a last-minute decision to go to lunch."

"And that's why I forgot my phone," Gigi said. "How many times did you try to call me?"

"Several," Keely said. "You probably have a few missed calls from Uncle Peter too. I called him when I couldn't find the two of you."

Gigi shook her head. "I would have sworn I locked the back door."

Keely's brow furrowed. "Beau, do you think we should check the house again?"

"It wouldn't hurt." He turned to Keely's aunt. "Would you mind walking through the house with me so we can be sure nothing is out of order?"

"Or course," Gigi said. "Keely, why don't you see if anyone wants a drink. We'll join you all in the living room after we do a quick check." She hurried to the front door and unlocked it.

Keely escorted her mom into the house with Levi following.

Beau led Gigi around the house to the back door. He opened it. "It was just like this when we found it."

"Not just unlocked, but open?"

He nodded.

She shook her head. "I have no idea where my head was. I can't believe I let that happen."

"It can happen to the best of us." Beau motioned for her to step inside and then closed and secured the wood and glass door behind him.

It took no more than ten minutes for them to walk through every room. And nothing appeared to be missing or out of place.

"I'm sorry to have worried you and Keely." Gigi held her phone in front of her. "If I had remembered to take my phone, it would have helped."

"As long as you're both safe. That's the important thing," Beau said and then walked into the living room.

As soon as Levi saw Beau, he stood and stuck out his hand. "It's good to see you, man. We're all so proud of everything you've accomplished. That's a good-looking SUV in the driveway," he teased.

"We get a few perks," Beau laughed. "I've heard great things about you too. You're managing entertainers, is that right?"

"Actually, songwriters. I own a publishing and publishing administration company in town. We work with a lot of up-and-coming songwriters, as well as a few of the top names."

"You always were into the music thing."

Levi grinned. "I guess I was. I thought at one time I was a decent guitar player. I found out differently when I started meeting some of the musicians in town. I still like to pick around on it occasionally though." He turned to Keely. "Sis, you and Beau should come to our campfire party at the house this weekend. We sit around the fire and listen to some of Nashville's best songwriters while raising money for a good charity."

"We might," Keely said, looking to Beau.

"Great! If you come, maybe you can bring Mom and Aunt Gigi with you too. The weather is supposed to be nice this weekend."

"We'll talk about it." Keely looked to Beau again, and he nodded. "It really depends on what Adam has lined up. One of my dogs had a litter yesterday, and one of us will have to stay at the kennel."

"Just let me know. I'd love to have you there." He turned back to Beau. "Seriously. Good to see you. I hope to see you again soon." He walked across the room to his mother. "Mom, I love you. Maybe I will see you this weekend."

"OK." Maggie nodded and gave him a big smile. Levi bent to kiss her on the cheek. "See you all." He waved and left through the front door.

"Levi was always bigger than life. Still is," Beau said, standing near Keely's chair.

"He reminds me a lot of Dad," she said. "Although Levi is more of a charmer. Daddy was more brusque. Uncle Peter once told me that Levi is like Daddy before he went off to war."

Beau thought about that and then turned to Keely's mom. "How are you today, Mrs. Lambert?"

"OK," she said.

"Do you mind if I ask you a few more questions?"

When she didn't answer, he took it as a yes. He walked to the dining room and grabbed a chair. He placed it next to hers. "Did you have a nice lunch with Levi?"

"Yes. I love my children."

"I know you do," Beau said, nodding to Keely. "And they love you a lot."

Maggie's eyes teared up.

Beau reached to gently wipe away the drop that was running down her cheek. "I didn't mean to make you cry," he said. "But sometimes it's good to talk about how blessed we are."

Maggie nodded.

"You've gone through a lot since your husband passed away." He chose his words carefully. "But you've remained strong for your family." Another drop trickled down her cheek. He looked to Keely. She quickly stood and knelt beside her mom.

"Do you think Daddy will come back to us, Mom?" she asked.

Maggie shook her head.

"Mrs. Lambert," Beau said. "Do you believe your husband was killed the day he disappeared?"

The older woman turned to him and for the first time her eyes seemed clear. Her distant stare was gone, and she looked directly at him. "Yes," she said.

Beau nodded. "I understand," he said. And as quickly as the fog had lifted, Maggie disappeared behind it again. She had broken through long enough to let him know.

"I think we've done enough for the day," he said to Keely. "Why don't we let your mom rest, and we'll get some lunch before I take you back to your place."

Keely nodded and stood. "Mom," she said. "I love you, and I'll see you soon, OK?"

"OK," Maggie said.

Beau walked to the door and waited for Keely to say a quick goodbye to Gigi.

"She looks tired today," he said, escorting Keely to the SUV. "Probably too much excitement with Levi coming back into town. But, at least, we got our answer."

"Do you really think so?" Keely turned to him.

"I'm sure of it." He opened the car door. "I think she knows that your dad was killed."

"Knows or suspects? There's a difference."

"Knows," Beau said.

Keely winced and buckled her seatbelt. "If that's true, I hope we find out who did it." She looked up at him, her dark eyes growing darker.

"I want you to trust me, Keely." He held her gaze. "I won't stop until we find the man who is responsible for your dad's disappearance, and I won't rest until he is brought to justice."

She nodded, and he hurried to the other side of the vehicle, climbed inside, engaged the engine, and turned toward the main highway. When she didn't speak, he reached for her hand, covering it with his own. They rode in silence. They both needed time to think, and once this ordeal was over, they would need time to heal. He would need to stay vigilant until then.

CHAPTER 23

Tuesday, January 11

Keely was grateful for the silence. There was nothing left to say, and she had a lot to think about.

Had her mother known since the beginning that Daddy was gone? If she did know, who had told her? And if she knew all of that, did she also know who did it?

Keely watched as the monotone landscape sped past her window. Bare trees reached upward toward a gray sky, and muted green grass, now dormant, waited for spring to revive the Tennessee pastureland that surrounded her childhood home.

This had been her whole world. It always would be.

"Do you want to eat at Puckett's or The Country Boy?" Beau broke into her thoughts at the intersection of Highway 96 and Garrison Road.

Keely turned to look at him. "Puckett's changed its name to Fox & Locke, but it's closed today. Do you want to try something different?"

"I'm good with whatever," he said.

"How about The Davis General? It's not far from here."

"Is that the little place in Boston?"

"Yes. On Leipers Creek Road."

Beau took a left.

"They have deli sandwiches."

"Sounds good."

"I already know what I'm having . . ."

"What's that?" He flashed a smile.

"The Hot Italian Hillbilly with Capocollo."

Beau laughed. "Who knew there was Italian food in Leiper's Fork?"

"We're uptown now," she mused. "If you want you can take me dancing in the driveway beside the gas pumps."

"You can have it all with me, baby." He squeezed her hand, and her mood lifted.

They rode in silence again for the next few miles. Beau Gardner had brought hope back into her life. But would he stay? Only time would tell. In the meantime, she would guard her heart and accept his help.

While Beau drove, she took in the white fences and pastureland where Herford cattle and thoroughbred horses grazed. Williamson County was the wealthiest county in Tennessee. Beau and she had been blessed to grow up here. A lot of lower- and middle-class families had owned land in this community, much of it inherited from generations before, prior to the influx of money into the area.

Beau's parents had sold their home in Leiper's Fork and moved closer to Franklin shortly after Emma married. On the other hand, Keely's mom had stayed in the country. Her property, which was off the beaten track, hadn't appreciated in value on the same scale as the Lambert family property on the main highway where Keely now lived.

Levi and Keely had been the sole heirs of the Lambert family farm. Because Levi had no interest in Leiper's Fork, she had made amicable financial arrangements with him so she could move there and build her kennel.

"It's right up here," Keely said, pointing to the old country store ahead.

Beau slowed. "On the left?"

She nodded.

He pulled into the parking lot. "I remember this old place."

"It has new owners. And they have great food," Keely said.

Beau got out of the car and hurried to open the door for her.

"You look tired," he said. "I shouldn't have insisted we see your mom today."

"It's OK if we're making progress." She studied him. "We are, right?"

"Every day." He locked the doors, took her arm, and escorted her into the old market and deli.

"This place looks like it hasn't been touched by time." Beau looked around. "Do we order at the counter?"

She nodded.

"Find us a seat, and I'll order the food. What do you want to drink?"

"Water is fine."

A few minutes later, Beau joined her at an old wood table set up next to the potbelly stove. "What have you been thinking about since we left your mom's house?"

Keely pulled several napkins from the holder in the middle of the table. "I have a lot of questions. And concerns."

"Like what?"

"I know you're convinced that you got to the truth, but I'm still withholding my judgment."

He popped the top off a soft drink.

"Mom is capable of manufacturing things. I'm not saying they're intentional lies. It's just that reality for her looks different than what you and I see."

"Has she always been like that?"

"Oh, no. Not at all. What I'm saying is that she doesn't have the ability to understand, or articulate, reality. She hasn't had that since her first accident."

"Her head trauma was that bad?"

She nodded. "The car accident changed her a lot. But the biggest changes have come in the past six to eight months. Even in the last year."

"You would know better than me."

"Aunt Gigi, on the other hand, is solid. She has a mind like a steel trap. I'm not sure she's capable of leaving the back door open."

"So what do you think happened?"

She shrugged. "Maybe she didn't pull it hard enough to latch and the wind blew it open. Or maybe someone picked the lock and went into the house—"

"Hang on . . . the food's ready." Beau stood. "Hold that thought."

Momentarily, he was back with their sandwiches. The Italian for her and a Reuben for him.

He settled into his seat. "This looks great."

"Hope you like it." She took a bite. "Mine is delicious."

He picked up half of his Reuben. "Your first theory isn't feasible because it was opened outward. The wind couldn't have done that."

She nodded, and he shifted in his chair.

"On the other hand, your second theory is entirely possible. But explain to me why the house wasn't ransacked. If not to steal something of value—or find something of importance—why would someone want to break into her house?"

She shrugged again. "Maybe someone has a key?"

"But who?"

"We know it's not Uncle Peter. There's no—"

Her phone rang. It was Adam.

"Where are you?" he asked.

"We're just finishing up lunch."

"Any idea when you'll be home?"

She looked at her watch. "Sometime within the hour. Do you need me sooner?"

"Sara just called me. She has a work-in doctor's appointment, and she wants me to take her."

"Is everything OK?"

"Yes . . . Sorry. It's routine, but she changed the day of the appointment. She's hoping we can see a picture of the baby."

"That would be amazing, Adam. Why don't you go ahead and leave when you need to? We'll be there soon. Pearl and the puppies will be OK if I'm not there exactly when you leave."

"Are you sure?"

"Yes. No problem. You go with Sara."

Keely ended the call and looked at Beau. "Adam is leaving soon. I need to get home after we finish lunch."

"Is everything OK at your place?" Beau took a bite of his Reuben.

"Yes. But Adam wants to take Sara to her doctor's appointment."

"I'll eat the rest of this at my desk." He wrapped up his sandwich and grabbed his keys from the top of the table. "They're understandably excited about the baby."

"I'm excited for them." She stood and took a final drink of her water while Beau asked for two bags to carry the sandwiches. They hurried out the door, and within twenty minutes they were pulling to a stop at the top of Keely's driveway.

Beau's phone rang with a call from his office.

"I'll talk to you later," he mouthed, as she got out of the car, carrying the rest of her sandwich. She waved and hurried down the hill to the kennel as he drove away.

Once inside, she found that Pearl and the puppies were content. But one look at the clock—and the horizon to the west—convinced her it would be best to go ahead and exercise the rest of the dogs and feed them. She checked water bowls while the eighteen kennel dogs ran and played. Then she filled the feed bowls.

After another check on the puppies, she secured the door and walked up the hill to the house. The clouds were moving in quickly. An early darkness would be setting in soon.

Ruby and Titan were there to meet her when she unlocked and opened the mudroom door. She spent a requisite couple of minutes with each one of them, petting and fawning, while they sniffed, and then she remembered the impending storm.

"Let's go out before the rain starts," she said, sliding past the two dogs and hurrying toward the sunroom.

As soon as she turned the corner from the kitchen into the dining room, she saw it. There was a clown suit spread across the dining room table, legs dangling off the side to colorful shoes on the floor. The eyeless face stared up at her with a blank expression. And misshapen bright red lips turned awkwardly up and then down.

Keely screamed, threw open the sunroom door, and ran out of the house into the backyard with the dogs following her. Once safely outside, she pulled her phone from her back pocket and, with trembling hands, attempted to dial Adam's number. It rang once and then went to voicemail.

She hung up and dialed it again. *Please . . . Adam, pick up.* This time it rang.

"Keely? What's going on?"

She fought to catch her breath. "Did you . . . Did you lock my house when you left?" Her voice shook as much as her hands.

"Yes, of course. Why?"

"Because there's a clown suit on my dining room table."

He laughed. "I know. I left it there."

"You what?"

"Rob came by while you were gone, and we put the dogs through a training session. Keely, not one of them reacted negatively except for the six-month-old puppy we just took in. I'm not sure he's going to pass muster."

"Titan didn't react at all?" She willed herself to calm.

"Did he react for you when you walked by the dining room table."

"No."

"There's your answer."

"Then . . ." Her stomach churned. "Then why did he react so violently to the clown at Connor's party?"

He hesitated. "You know the answer to that as well as I do. He wasn't reacting to the suit. He was reacting to the person in it."

CHAPTER 24

Tuesday, January 11

The headlights on Beau's Chevrolet Colorado reflected off the Arzo Carson TBI State Office Building sign as he took a left onto the main road. He voice-dialed Keely's number to check on her on his drive home.

She answered on the second ring.

"How was the rest of your day?"

"How long do you have?"

"As long as you need."

"Pearl and the puppies were fine when I got home, so I took care of the kennel dogs before walking up the hill to the house . . ."

He engaged his wiper blades as he drove into rain.

"I had quite the surprise when I went inside."

"Why? What happened?"

"There was a clown suit on my dining room table."

"A clown suit? Keely . . . ?"

"Before you panic, like I did, I called Adam immediately. He had left it there."

Beau's heart settled down. "Why?"

"His friend Rob was there while you and I were gone. He said they went through a training exercise with all the dogs to test and acclimate them to the suit. And, specifically, to Rob wearing it." She took a breath. "Adam said none of the dogs reacted to it, except for one young dog we have just started working."

"How about Titan?"

"No reaction. In fact, he and Ruby ran right by it on their way out to the sunroom." She hesitated. "Adam and I agree. It was the person inside the clown suit at Connor's party that set Titan on edge."

"I'd say it did more than set him on edge."

"Agreed."

"So, I was right?"

"Looks like you were."

"I need to talk to Emma. I'll call you back." He hesitated. "Actually . . . I'll just meet you at your house in about forty-five minutes. Does that work for you?"

"Of course."

"See you then."

He ended the call and dialed Emma.

"Hey, big brother."

"How are things? How's Connor?"

"We're good. He's good."

"I need to get a number from you. You gave it to me the other day, but I left it at the office."

"The clown?"

"Yes."

"I'm assuming you're not hosting a birthday party?"

He chuckled. "You're correct. But I may tell him I am."

"Can I give you some advice?"

"Sure . . ." he said, wondering where this was leading.

"You might want to block your Caller ID before you do. I'm thinking he might not pick up if he sees it's the TBI on the phone."

He laughed, thankful for the two women in his life.

"His name is Mr. Mike." She read the phone number, and then repeated it. Beau committed it to memory. "Thanks, sis. Love you. See you soon."

Beau took the next exit and pulled into a parking lot. Then he dialed Star 67 followed by the number. The call immediately rolled over to a recording. "The number you have dialed has been temporarily disconnected."

Why was he not surprised?

He eased back onto the highway and stepped on the gas pedal. That clown—Mr. Mike, or whatever his name was—was a scammer at best. And William Lambert's killer at worse. He had potentially been stalking both Emma and Keely—and terrorizing Connor. The only scenario that made sense was that Titan had picked up on the guy's scent when he tracked down Connor at the park and associated that scent with Connor's fear.

Within thirty minutes, Beau pulled into Keely's driveway. He grabbed his phone and gave her a call. "Are you in the house or the kennel?"

"The kennel," she said. "I'll open the door."

Beau got out of the truck, locked it and hurried to the kennel entrance. "Lock the door behind us," he said.

"OK . . . Are you all right? You seem to be spooked about something. I'm the one who saw the clown suit, remember?"

"Are you hanging out in the whelping room?"

"Yes. Come on back. I have two chairs, a pot of coffee, and a package of sweet rolls I'll share."

"Both sound good. I haven't eaten supper." He followed her to the back of the building.

"Me neither. Supper coming right up."

A few minutes later they were sitting in the whelping room listening to two black and tan pups whimper as they explored their pen-sized world.

"So, I'm guessing the puppy with the blue ribbon around his neck is a boy?"

"Yes. And the puppy with the pink collar is a girl," Keely said. "It was an easy choice for ribbons with this small litter."

Beau took a sip of coffee and accepted a sweet roll from the package Keely had opened. "I remember eating these as a kid."

"Comfort food." Keely took a bite of hers. "Good memories."

"My mother's chocolate chip cookies were the best though. Emma has the recipe, although they're just not the same." He cringed. "Don't tell her I said that."

"Your secret is safe with me." She teased, and then sobered. "So, what's worrying you? I could tell when you stepped out of the truck tonight that something was wrong."

Wondering where to start, he shrugged. "I have few leads on this case, and that concerns me. The less I know, the more I know I need to learn. And I'm always worried about how hard that lesson will be." He looked at her. "Does that make sense?"

"Yes. Surprises aren't always a good thing."

"Exactly." He took another bite of his sweet roll, thinking as he chewed. "I talked to Emma right after I hung up with you. She gave me the clown's number, and I called it. It's been disconnected."

"Not helpful," Keely said.

"Also, disconcerting. Things aren't adding up well for that clown, starting with the way Titan reacted toward him." Beau picked up a napkin and wiped sugar icing from his fingers.

She waited.

"What's your professional opinion about Titan's aggression toward him?"

Keely sighed. "Now that I know it wasn't the costume, my best guess is that Titan could smell maleficence."

"Dogs can do that?"

"Without a doubt. Remember the old saying, 'Never trust someone your dog doesn't like'?"

"Sure . . ."

"Have you ever heard of pheromones?"

"Aren't those hormone-like chemicals in our bodies? It has something to do with perfume, right?"

"Yes, somehow. But what I know more about is that we all secrete them. And dogs don't just pick up on them, they read them."

"You think the guy in the clown suit was giving off bad vibes, so to speak."

"Yes, probably."

"I have a theory too." He studied her. "Don't laugh, OK? I'm not trained in dog psychology like you are."

She bit her lip and smiled.

"My theory is that when Titan was tracking Connor, he also picked up on the stalker's scent. I'm guessing the man followed Connor much farther than Connor knew. And if all of that is true, it makes sense that he's the same man who dropped the dog tag for you to find."

Keely considered what he had said. "I think that's a solid theory. It's not that different than my pheromone explanation."

He nodded. "So, we both agree that Titan was on to something."

"Unfortunately, yes."

"I think he deserves a dog biscuit. So far, he has given us the biggest lead we have for the case."

She stood. "Would you like more coffee?"

"That depends," he said.

"On what?"

"On whether or not you want me to stay with you tonight. Are you afraid to stay alone out here in the kennel?"

She grinned. "Not at all."

He stood. "In that case, no more coffee for me. I'll go home and try to get some sleep. I'll check with you first thing in the morning."

"Remember," she said. "First thing in the morning is probably earlier for me than for you."

"In that case, I should definitely leave." He looked at his watch. "If you're going to get any sleep tonight."

"We'll see what Pink and Blue have to say about that. Although, they've been good so far. There's really not a lot they can do at this age. But I can't help but worry about them. They had a stormy entrance into this world. Once they get through their first week, I'll feel better about them."

"Come on then. Walk me to the door, beautiful." Beau took her elbow and escorted her out the whelping room door and into the main part of the building. "I want you to lock yourself in when I leave."

As soon as she opened the main entrance door, a streak of lightning shot across the sky in front of them. The rain was pouring down.

"You're the one who needs to be careful," she said. "That's not good driving weather out there."

"Last chance to keep me here tonight."

She motioned for him to step closer. "Take this with you," she said and then leaned forward to kiss him on the lips. She lingered for a few seconds, and then pulled away. "Now go . . . and be safe. I'll see you tomorrow."

He nodded and ran through the pouring rain to his truck.

Keely had just locked the door when her phone buzzed. She pulled it from her pocket.

It was a three-word text from Beau.

"THAT WAS NICE." In all caps.

She held her index finger over the message, hesitated, and pulled down a heart emoji. Then, stuffing the phone back inside her pocket, she ran toward the whelping room.

She was losing her heart to him. Would he stay this time? She knew she could trust him to keep her safe, but could she trust him with her heart? She was an emotional wreck. There had been too many close calls in the last two weeks.

Connor's disappearance. Titan's violent reaction to the clown. Tracking devices. Almost losing Pearl . . . and her mother and Aunt Gigi's disappearance today. Not to mention the looming possibility of having to face that her father was really gone.

She rushed through the open whelping room door and closed it behind her. Then falling back against it, she covered her mouth with her hand and gulped for air.

The tears started to flow, and she allowed herself the release.

She was exhausted. She needed sleep. And the dogs were requiring more energy than she had right now. But the memory of Beau's lips on her own would be keeping her up all night.

Of all that had happened, her feelings for him were what scared her the most.

July 6, 2000

A shiny black car coming from the opposite direction slowed as it approached. It passed by, and then, a few minutes later, returned and pulled to a stop beside them.

"Car trouble?" the driver asked. Keely thought he had a pleasant face, but her father seemed concerned about him.

"Flat tire," her dad said. "Would you mind sending a repair truck back for us?"

The driver turned to confer with his passenger, then turned back to Will Lambert.

"Why don't you and your kids jump in the backseat? The weather doesn't look good," he

said, pointing to the western sky. We'll take you to the first gas station ahead."

William Lambert looked again at the sky and then opened the back driver's side door of the vehicle. He instructed Keely and Levi to climb inside and to make room for him. He then took a seat beside them and slammed the door.

CHAPTER 25

Wednesday, January 12

Keely was awakened the next morning when the whelping room door opened.

"What time is it?"

"Eight o'clock," Adam said. "How did it go last night?"

She swung her feet to the floor and considered how much to share with him, deciding on the edited version. "I had trouble falling asleep, but once I did . . . Well, here I am."

He glanced to Pearl and her babies. "That was a horrendous storm last night. But it looks like they did OK."

She nodded. "No issues at all so far. I'm hopeful."

Adam took a seat in one of the two chairs across the room, setting his coffee cup on the side table. "Why don't you go to the house for a while. You can give Titan and Ruby a break, and maybe take one for yourself too."

"Do I look that tired?"

"Yes. But I mostly want you to have time to relax away from the kennel because I need to ask a favor."

"Sure." She rubbed her eyes.

"Sara has baby classes every night this week, and she wants me to go." He wrung his hands. "If I go with her, there's no guarantee I can get back here until ten o'clock or so."

"No worries at all. I don't mind sleeping out here. You take care of Sara and the baby."

"Thanks, Keely. I appreciate your understanding. And I'll be available all weekend to spend as much time as you need."

"That's perfect," she said. "Levi wants me to take Mom to a music thing he's hosting. It's Saturday night."

"You can count on me to be here." He picked up his coffee cup and took a sip. "You go relax for a while. I'll let the dogs out and start cleaning kennels."

"OK . . . Thanks." Keely stood and stretched. "I'll be back at noon. We can eat a sandwich and then get some training done."

"Sounds like a plan," he said as Keely turned to leave.

A few minutes later, Titan and Ruby greeted her briefly and then took off running toward the sunroom.

"I'm sorry, kids. I overslept." She released the lock on the sunroom door, opened it, and hurried to the backyard door to let them out.

Beau Gardner, you messed up my routine with that kiss.

Then she remembered—it had been her who initiated it. What had she been thinking? Life was so much easier without a relationship. Especially one as complicated as hers was with Beau. Who in their right mind would try to rekindle a failed relationship after almost ten years?

She pictured herself as the prototype for one of those face palm emoticons everybody used on social media. And she wondered what Beau was thinking this morning. Probably that it was time to run again as soon as this case was over.

She swallowed her pride and willed herself to relax as Adam had suggested. This wasn't about her. It was about finding the man responsible for her dad's disappearance. And bringing her dad home.

After that, she could move on with her life. With or without Beau.

Please, God, help me find Daddy.

Her phone rang. Beau.

"Good morning," she said cautiously.

"How did it go last night?"

"Oh . . . all right, I guess. I had no problems at all with the pups." She remembered the storm. "How was your drive back into town?"

"Intense. I was wired by the time I got home. It took forever to go to sleep."

"Me too," she blurted out.

He hesitated. "But it was worth it. I'd drive out there again right now if I could get another one of those kisses."

Her cheeks burned. "Don't push your luck."

He chuckled. "I know I caught you at a weak moment. And don't get me wrong, I'm glad I did. But I want you to know I'm not rushing you. I'm lucky to have a second chance. If, in fact, I do."

She didn't speak.

"If you'll just tell me that I have that chance, I'm willing to wait for you. And to earn your trust."

Keely's heart tugged. She wanted to trust him, but . . .

"I—I don't know exactly what to say. Just that I'm not closed to the idea . . . of you and me."

"That's all I want to hear."

"OK."

"Moving on to business, I want to keep you updated. I've spent the morning doing searches for a clown known as Mr. Mike—"

"That's his name? Couldn't he come up with something better than that? Maybe even Mike the Clown?"

"Agreed. But that's what Emma told me he called himself. Even with that, I found several pictures of him online. At least I think they were him. They were snapshots of clowns at children's parties all over town. The outfit, right down to the shoes, look the same."

"That's great! How will that help?"

"My team and I are trying to find a way to identify and reach out to everyone who has hired him in the past. I'm hoping that will give me a lead as to where to find him."

"Good work, Agent Gardner. I'm impressed."

"It's just a plan. We'll see if it works." He chuckled. "But I'm much more hopeful today than I was a few days ago."

"Please keep me updated."

"I'll do better than that. I'll take you to dinner tonight if you'll let me."

"I can't. Adam needs to be out every night this week for baby classes with Sara, so I'll be at the kennel."

"Do you want me to come out and bring food?"

"I can't ask you to do that." She shrugged. "All I had to offer you last night were sweet rolls."

"But they were delicious!"

"How about we talk about doing that Friday night? Or maybe even wait until Saturday. Adam will be back to work over the weekend, and I would love to go to Levi's campfire thing."

"I'm in. What time?"

"I'll find out and let you know."

"Are we taking your mom and Aunt Gigi with us?"

"What do you think? I'm apprehensive about Mom being outside in the elements, especially at night. We're having a warm spell, but it's still January and the nights are cool."

"I'll leave that completely up to you," he said. "I'll support you either way."

"Thank you."

Keely ended the call and walked outside to check on the dogs. They were still enjoying playtime, so she took a seat on the bench beneath the gazebo her granddad Lambert had built years ago. Even in the midst of the fallow season, she could see the potential for hope.

She had read once that winter was the foreshadowing of spring. If winter represented dormancy . . . and death, did that mean that death was a foreshadow of life? That was true in her Christian faith. Christ's death brought life. And hope.

She would choose hope.

Beau gathered everything he had found online about Mr. Mike the Clown and slid it into a virtual folder. He uploaded a copy of the folder to Special Agent Amy Force, who was the TBI's composite sketch artist. He attached a note, asking if she thought it would be possible for her to use the thirty or forty obscure snapshots he had found to compile an artist rendering of the face underneath.

After that, he printed two copies of the folder's contents, one for himself and one for Chris Enoch. Then he put a call into Enoch.

"I'm free right now," Enoch said. "Come on down and let me see what you've got."

Beau grabbed one of the envelopes, along with his cell phone, and took off for Enoch's office down the hall. The door was open, and Enoch motioned for Beau to come in and close it behind him.

Beau laid the envelope on Enoch's desk and took a seat. "This is all I could find, but at least it's a place to start," he said. "I'm convinced this clown is involved in my case."

Enoch opened the envelope and glanced at the pictures. "A real clown?"

"I know, sir. Not your usual suspect."

The corners of Enoch's mouth turned up slightly, and he shook his head. A few minutes later he asked for a more detailed explanation, and Beau explained the thread of evidence that linked Mike the Clown to almost every aspect of his case, including the disappearance of William Lambert.

Enoch leaned back and crossed his arms over his chest. "That's an awful lot of conjecture. Circumstantial evidence at best. And you're relying a lot on the reaction of a dog to tie it all together."

"I realize that, Chris. But my gut tells me we're on the right track." He shook his head. "And quite honestly, it's all I have at the moment."

Enoch nodded. "I would move forward cautiously. But remember, at least right now, you have no real reason to question the guy in the clown suit."

Beau stood. "I agree. But if I can identify him, I can try to learn more about him and hope that will lead to a reason."

"Keep me posted," Enoch said.

"I will, sir."

Beau opened the door to the main hallway and took off down the hall. He was on his way to the atrium for a break when his phone pinged. He had an email from Special Agent Force: *Beau, I'm confident we can put together a composite for you. I'll have something back to you by Monday.*

CHAPTER 26

Saturday, January 15

Keely checked her makeup and hurried to her master closet in search of jeans and a warm sweater. Finally deciding on a black turtleneck and black jeans, she grabbed a pair of black suede Uggs to complete her non-descript outfit. This was Levi's party, and she was content to blend into the background while supporting her brother.

Pink girl had developed an eye infection, requiring that drops be administered every few hours, as well as isolation from Blue boy. Her sleep on the cot had been fitful for two nights. It would be nice to sleep in her own bed tonight. Hopefully, without interruption.

Adam would be taking care of Pearl and the puppies for the next few nights. She had teased him that it was good practice for nighttime ups and down after the baby arrived in June.

She had just finished slipping on her boots when a text came in from Beau.

I'm here.

She hurried through the house, grabbed a jacket from the coat rack in the mudroom, and then remembered she hadn't checked the dogs' water bowl. She topped it off, took two treats from the jar on her kitchen countertop, and gave one to each dog.

"Take care of things," she said. "I'll be back soon."

Both dogs responded with a tail wag, and Keely left, locking the mudroom door behind her.

Beau smiled and got out of the truck when he saw her. He opened her door and helped her climb inside.

"You look nice," he said. "I hope I'm dressed appropriately." He had on a University of Alabama sweatshirt and a pair of faded jeans. "I have a shirt and jacket in the truck if I need to change."

"I thought you went to UT?"

"I did. But who doesn't like Bama?"

"Maybe Auburn fans?"

"Well, there's that." He laughed. "But Alabama colors blend into the background better."

"We think alike," she said. "That's why I wore black."

He closed her door and walked to the driver's side, climbing inside. "We're picking up your mom and Aunt Gigi, right?"

"Yes. Aunt Gigi thought it would be good for Mom to go and see the grandkids. Between us, I think it's more about Gigi wanting to mingle with a few Nashville songwriters."

"Really?" He laughed. "Who will be there?"

"Levi didn't really tell me. He said there would be several writers from his roster, and one or two he works with. He administers their music."

"I have to confess. I don't know what that means," he said.

"Neither do I," she said. "But I hated to ask. Maybe you should and then we'll both know?"

"Oh, sure . . . make me the fall guy." He started the truck. "I'll just do an internet search when we get there. News at eleven."

Keely smiled. "Speaking of internet searches, what have you found out about our clown?"

"Funny you should ask. I expect to have a composite sketch of him early next week."

"How can you do that?"

"We have a composite sketch artist on staff, and she thinks, by looking at the photos I found, she can put together a composite of how he would look without the makeup."

"That's incredible."

"I thought so too. With that, we may have a decent chance of identifying the guy."

Keely's heart caught in her throat. "It feels like we're getting closer." She pulled her dad's dog tag from beneath her sweater. "I'm wearing this tonight. I know he would have wanted to be a part of it."

Beau reached for her hand. "I wish I had known him. I'm sure I would have liked him."

She nodded. "I wish I had known him better. But I'm thankful to have the memories I do have. Levi has none." She thought about that for a minute. "It's funny how he turned out so much like him without even knowing him."

"The power of DNA," Beau said. "I use it a lot in my work. We inherit a lot from our parents. Some good and some bad. Emma is the spitting image of my mom when she was the same age."

Keely studied him. "You don't look anything like your dad."

"I know. I think I'm the milkman's child." He laughed. "Not really. I've been told I look a lot like my grandfather, who I never met. He was killed in the Vietnam War."

Keely pulled her hand away and tucked the dog tag inside her sweater. "I'm glad I resemble my dad. You know my history, right?"

"What do you mean?"

"I was conceived several months before my parents married."

"That doesn't change anything." He glanced toward her.

"It's never bothered me. I knew I was loved." She looked down at her hands. "But that didn't keep people from whispering about me." She sighed. "One reason I'm thankful to have so many outsiders moving into our little town. They have no idea about my background, and they don't care."

"You have a lot to be thankful for," Beau said. "A child can't ask for more than love. I've always doubted that my dad loved me."

"Why? I've never heard you say that."

"I've always been ashamed of it," he said. "I thought it was because there was something wrong with me."

"You've felt that way since you were a child?"

"Mostly since junior high and high school." He stopped at the intersection and turned to her. "It's the reason I left, Keely. I'm sorry it took so long to share that with you."

"But you knew how much I loved you. Wasn't that enough?"

"It should have been. But my dad put too many doubts about my worth in my head. I had to get away. And once I did . . . I couldn't find my way back." He looked at her. "I have a lot of regrets. Not just because of you, but because of my mom. I deserted her too."

"Beau, I had no idea."

He turned into her mother's driveway. "I'll tell you more when we have a chance to talk again."

Beau pocketed his keys, thankful they had reached Maggie's house. He had said too much. Keely didn't need him dumping his problems on her right now. She had bigger ones of her own. And, besides, the truth was that only three people would ever understand what it had been like living with J. G. Gardner. And, of those three, only he and Emma were left.

He got out of his truck, locked it, and then remembered his gun.

"I'll be right there," he told Keely, who was already on Maggie's front steps.

She nodded.

Beau unlocked the passenger side door, reached inside, and pulled his Glock Model 22 service pistol from the glove box. He secured the gun in his waistband holster, pulled his sweatshirt over it, and relocked the truck. They were taking Keely's mother's car to the party because it was more comfortable for Maggie.

By the time he walked to the driver's side of the 2015 blue Buick LaCrosse sedan, Keely and Gigi were escorting Maggie down the sidewalk. Beau opened the back passenger door for her and helped her inside. Then he hurried around the rear of the car to open Gigi's door.

"Did you lock the house?" he asked.

Gigi held up her keys. "I did. Even the back door."

Beau made a mental note to walk through the house after they returned.

The drive to Levi's took over a half hour, and it was almost dark when he made a left into Levi's driveway. Levi and Anna lived in the rural part of the county, off Old Natchez Trace Parkway.

The electronic gate opened as they approached, and Beau could see ten or fifteen cars parked strategically around the circle drive in front of the house with its tall pillars and country style porch. It wasn't exactly the rustic campfire setting he had envisioned. It was better. Much better for Keely's mother, who could sit inside if she became chilled or overly tired.

As soon as they stepped out of the car, Levi came out to meet them.

"Hi, Mom," he said, giving Maggie a kiss on the cheek. "Let me help you and Aunt Gigi inside."

"Isn't their home lovely?" Gigi said, walking to the other side of the car and taking Levi's free arm.

"From the looks of this place, I think I'm underdressed," Beau whispered to Keely. "And I left my sports jacket in the truck."

"You look fine." She grinned. "The songwriters' round will be held on the patio on the east side of the house," Keely said, as they climbed the steps to the front porch. "Levi told me that Mom and Gigi could spend the night with him if they tire too quickly." She took his arm. "I can't wait to show you the house."

Almost immediately after stepping inside, Beau saw Jake Matheson from the Bureau standing in front of the fireplace across the room.

"I'll be right back," Keely said. "I want to check on Mom."

"What are you doing here?" Beau asked after walking over to Jake.

"Beau! I could ask you the same question." He reached to shake Beau's hand. "I'm with Hannah. She's performing tonight."

"When are the two of you getting married?"

"Later this year. Probably October. Hannah's planning it now." He took a sip of his drink. "Speaking of that, didn't I see you walk in with a brunette?"

"Yes," Beau nodded. "We've known each other for years, but business brought us back together a few weeks ago. I'm working on a cold case involving the disappearance of her father. Her mother and aunt are here with us tonight. Her brother is Levi, the man who lives here. I'll introduce you to her when she returns."

CHAPTER 27

Saturday, January 15

Keely found seats on the sofa for Maggie and Gigi, and then looked for Beau. He was standing in front of the large stone fireplace in deep conversation with one of Levi's guests.

And he had been worried about fitting in?

After a trip to the kitchen to fetch glasses of pineapple punch for her mother and aunt, she crossed the great room to join Beau.

"Keely, I want to introduce you to Jake Matheson. We work together at the Bureau." Beau put his arm lightly around her waist and drew her into the conversation. "Jake, this is Keely."

"It's nice to meet you, Jake." She extended her hand. "How do you know my brother?"

"I just met him," he said. "I'm here with my fiancée, Hannah Cassidy."

"The singer?"

"Yes. And songwriter. Levi administers her catalog of songs."

Keely glanced to Beau, who lifted an eyebrow.

"Hannah is performing tonight," Jake added.

"That should be fun," Hannah said.

"So, Levi is your brother?"

"Yes."

"How do the two of you know each other?" He gestured toward Beau.

Keely gave Beau a sideways look. "We went to school together. Elementary through high school." She crinkled her nose. "I have all the dirt, if you need it."

Jake laughed. "That might come in handy." He slapped Beau on the shoulder. "But I know him to be a good guy and a good friend."

Keely smiled up at Beau.

"Jake is the one you want to have on your team when trouble comes down," Beau said. "We've been there together from time to time."

"Are the two of you talking shop?" A slender blonde walked up to them. Keely was sure it was Hannah Cassidy, having seen her photos.

"I'm Hannah." She extended her hand to Keely.

"Nice to meet you." Keely shook hands with her. "Haven't you performed in Leiper's Fork?"

"Yes! At Puckett's several times. Do you live close to there?"

Keely nodded. "It's where Beau and I grew up."

"I love that area. I've been telling Jake we need to check it out some day."

"Why don't you meet us for lunch one Saturday?"

"That would be fun!"

"By the way, my name is Keely Lambert. I'm Levi's sister."

"Are you in music too?" Hannah asked.

Keely laughed. "Not even close. I raise and train working dogs . . . German Shepherds, mostly for search and rescue. We occasionally work with protection dogs."

"Like Schutzhund?"

Keely shook her head. "No. That's another training style. I have my own method."

"I would love to see your dogs sometime."

"I have twenty-one right now. Twenty-three, including puppies."

Levi walked to the center of the room and clapped his hands, asking for attention.

"Welcome, everybody! Anna and I are thrilled to have you at the house tonight. Food is now being served in the dining room. We have a few more guests than we do seats around the table, so please take a plate, and feel free to sit anywhere you would like. We're not fussy. We have kids."

The room echoed with laughter.

"After we finish eating, we'll adjourn to the campfire outside, grab guitars, and enjoy some music."

"Why don't the two of you go ahead and eat so Hannah will have plenty of time before she performs," Beau told Jake, and then turned to Keely. "You're in for a treat. This girl puts on a show."

"Thanks, Beau. You're embarrassing me," Hannah said.

"We'll catch the two of you in a little while," Keely added. "I have my mother and aunt here, and I need to take care of them before we sit down."

"See you in a bit." Jake directed Hannah into the dining room.

Keely and Beau walked across the room to the older women on the sofa. "Are you having a good time, Mom?"

"Yes." Her mother nodded.

"The punch is good." Gigi laughed. "Where did you find that? I may help myself to more."

"I'll refill it for you, Aunt Gigi." Keely reached for her glass. "You and Mom need to hold on to your seats. Beau and I will get your plates and bring them back."

Gigi frowned. "Can we eat while sitting on this beautiful white sofa?"

"Yes. Levi said it was no problem. He wants the two of you to relax and enjoy yourselves. Beau and I will be right back."

Keely refilled Gigi's punch glass and then followed Beau into the dining room in the original part of the house. The rustic round table, which looked to be made of oak or another hard wood, had been naturally distressed by years of use. Anna had found it in an antique store in Hohenwald, Tennessee, and never refinished it. She had simply added mismatched chairs that set it off perfectly.

For tonight's buffet, the table had been covered in a crisp, white linen tablecloth. Antique platters and bowls held large servings of fried chicken, boiled potatoes, crisp vegetables, and biscuits. An attractive older woman, who Levi referred to as Dixie, hovered over the table, as well as the guests, offering a running commentary on the food and handing out glasses of fruit tea. Her assistant was an older gentleman with thick white hair.

"Hi, Dixie," Beau said, approaching the table.

"Beau!" The older woman grabbed him and hugged his neck. "It's so good to see you." She stepped back and refocused her beautiful smile on Keely. "Hi, I'm Dixie Grace."

"Keely Lambert. Levi is my brother."

"It's so nice to meet you, honey. This is Roland."

The older man smiled and nodded but appeared to be content to stay in the background.

"How do you know the caterer?" Keely asked Beau as they walked back to the living room. "You seem to know everybody here."

Beau laughed. "Not everybody. But I met Dixie and Roland working a case with Jake last year. They're nice people. Hannah lives with Dixie."

"She met Jake while he was working on a case?"

"Yes. She was targeted by a trafficking ring. You probably didn't hear much about it. We did our best to keep Hannah out of the papers."

Keely gave a fresh glass of punch to her aunt, and then set the plate of hot food on the table in front of her. "I don't know how you do what you do," she said, addressing Beau. "You're involved in so many dangerous things."

He smiled and set the plate he had been carrying in front of Keely's mom. "Here you go, Mrs. Lambert. This looks and smells delicious. But be careful, it may be hot."

"I'll take care of her, honey," Gigi said. "The two of you need to get a plate and sit with us."

Beau accompanied Keely back to the dining room.

"I love my work," he said. "Having good people to work with, like Jake, makes all the difference. I'll tell you about Hannah's case sometime."

After every person was finished eating, Levi herded the group outside where they took seats around the fire pit. Keely watched through the window as the seats began to fill up. Levi's fieldstone patio had been set up with several groupings of tables and chairs surrounding the fire. Five high boy director's chairs were set up in front of the large retaining wall on the east side, providing a backdrop for the musicians and protecting everyone from the cool east wind. A microphone stand had been placed in front of each chair.

Keely had attended several of Levi's songwriter rounds in the past and was familiar with the general format of the event. Each of the five performers would take his or her turn, performing one or two songs, telling stories, and sharing insights about the music business before passing the spotlight on to the next songwriter. At the end, they would begin another round.

Looking out at the crowd of about thirty people, Keely saw several faces she recognized. But there were many she didn't know. Levi and Anna moved among them, chatting, and making them feel welcome, ever the consummate hosts.

Once the majority of people had found seats, Levi came inside to escort his mother and Aunt Gigi to their seats in a small nook on the north side of the patio, which would allow them a good view of the entertainment but insulate them somewhat from the sound. Since her first accident, Maggie had become sensitive to—and fearful of—loud noises.

Keely followed the three of them to the isolated seating area and helped them take seats. Then she leaned close to her mother's ear. "Mom, I'm going inside to find you a quilt or a blanket to keep you and Aunt Gigi warm. If at any time you're uncomfortable, let me know. OK?"

"OK," her mother parroted.

A few minutes later, Keely returned with a blanket and a cup of hot cocoa for each of the older women. Then she looked around for Beau, finally spotting him across the patio. He was seated at a table with Jake. Hurrying to join them before the lights dimmed, she took a chair next to him.

Where she sat, the crisp night air was sufficiently warmed by the fire pit and the butane heat lamps that Levi had scattered around the patio. She had a clear view of the stage area, the retaining wall behind it, and into the woods behind her brother's property.

The sky above them was dark, absent of stars. In the distance, she could hear the whoo, whoo, whoo of an owl. Was he calling for his mate? Or was he announcing the presence of danger?

A shiver ran down her spine, and she scooted her chair closer to Beau.

CHAPTER 28

Saturday, January 15

Beau reached for Keely's hand and covered it with his own. He had never considered the idea of moving back to the country, but the ambiance tonight could very well change his mind. Sitting under the night sky with the fire pit blazing and the conveniences of the house nearby was far better—as pleasant as it was—than sitting on a three- by six-foot balcony overlooking the traffic in downtown Nashville.

Of course, he could never afford a home like this. One that had been outfitted with the best of everything, from a gourmet kitchen to well-appointed landscaping. But he didn't need five thousand square feet, three garages, and an expansive outdoor living space. Although he would love to have the latter.

If Will Lambert could see his children now, he would be pleased. Levi and Keely had pieced together good lives for themselves. Despite losing her husband so young, Maggie Lambert had raised them well, and without a lot of help from anyone except for Will's elderly parents and her brother Peter. Gigi, who had only recently been widowed, had been living with her husband and children in North Carolina for the last thirty or so years.

There had been rumors that several of Leiper's Fork widowers—apparently Beau's father among them after Beau's mom passed—had tried to win Maggie's interest, but she had remained single. Perhaps, at least for a while, she had held out hope that her husband would return one day.

Beau looked across the patio to where Maggie sat in the shadows. Silver hair now framed her chiseled features, but she was still a beautiful woman. Could it be that an unrequited lover had taken revenge on her, booby trapped her car, and pushed her in the garden? As far-fetched as it sounded, it was possible that Will Lambert had been killed by a jealous former lover or someone who had designs on Maggie. Beau knew all too well from his line of work that love triangles could be dangerous. As dangerous as many of the domestic violence cases he had worked during his tenure at the Bureau. Stalking and the use of tracking devices fit well within that profile.

Then again, maybe Will Lambert had been the catalyst for his own demise. Keely had said that her dad was brusque. Perhaps Lambert had offended someone so badly he had ignited their murderous rage. But why would that person continue to avenge himself on Maggie and her daughter this many years later? It made no sense.

Metro Nashville had grown, and crime had evolved, in the last twenty years, but in 2000 there were few, if any, organized crime rings or gangs to wreak havoc on their enemies. Lambert's disappearance had been an isolated event in a small rural community, with no copycat crimes reported before or after it. As best as Beau could tell, it had not even been reported in the *Tennessean*, Nashville's primary newspaper.

William Lambert's life had been important to his friends and family. But with relatively no fanfare, he had disappeared. From crime annals and from the pages of history. Only his family, and those who lived in or near the village of Leiper's Fork in July 2000, would be able to recall the time he walked among them. And the day he went missing.

It might be time for Beau to knock on every door in town and ask if anyone remembered the crime. And if they did, ask if they had any suspicion as to who might have been callous enough to kidnap a man in the presence of his young children.

Keely leaned into him and whispered. "The guy who is up next is one of Levi's newest songwriters. Levi is really excited about him."

Beau refocused on the lineup of singers in front of him. He had completely missed the first performer.

The second and third performances passed relatively quickly, and when number four was in the middle of her second song, Jake nudged Beau. "Hannah is up next."

Beau gave him a thumbs up and looked at his watch. Eight p.m.

He turned to Keely. "Do you think you should check with your aunt and see how your mom is doing? She may be too tired to stay for another round."

"Oh, I hope not," Keely said. "I'm just now starting to relax."

He stood. "I want another glass of Dixie's tea before Hannah comes on. Would you like one?"

"No. I'm good," she said. "I may run in for a few minutes after I check on Mom and Gigi. They may want something."

Several minutes later, Beau saw Keely in the kitchen. "Gigi asked me to pick up another punch for her and Mom. I think they're having a good time."

"Great." He put his arm around her shoulders and pulled her closer as he walked her to the door. "You can have more time to relax."

Beau opened the patio door for Keely, and she froze. "Where are Mom and Gigi?"

He looked to where they had been sitting and saw two empty chairs.

"Gigi must have taken her to the hall bathroom," Keely said. "That's the only way I could have missed her."

"Here," Hannah handed him the two glasses of punch. "I'll run back inside and check."

Beau kept a low profile as he crossed the patio, trying not to attract attention away from the stage, where Hannah was now performing. As soon as he reached the table and chairs where the older women had been sitting, he set down the drinks and turned around, scanning the outdoor room. The two older women were nowhere to be found. Maybe they had gone for a walk in the backyard?

He stepped around the low planting of shrubbery behind where they had been sitting and made a sharp left at the back corner of the house. From his vantage point, he could see straight back to the woods. There was a play area to the left and a flower garden to the right. But Maggie and Gigi were not there.

He hurried back to the patio and into the house through the double patio doors, almost running into Keely in the great room. "They're not in the house."

"They're not out there either, so where could . . . ?" He noticed that the front door was open and ran to the entry just in time to see Maggie's blue LaCrosse exiting the grounds through the electronic gate.

"Go get Jake," he shouted to Keely before rushing out the door onto the porch, from where he saw the vehicle veer to the left and speed away on Old Natchez Trace.

Why would Gigi have left without them?

It was then he heard what sounded like someone moaning. He hurried down the steps of the front porch and looked around. Nothing.

There it was again. It was the sound of someone in pain. He drew his gun and followed the intermittent groans to a large pine tree in front of the house. When he looked behind it, he saw Gigi. He re-holstered his gun and dropped to his knees, turning her over and propping her head in his arms.

"What happened?" he asked.

"He took Maggie."

Beau's heart pounded. "Who took Maggie?"

"I don't know," she said. "He was dressed like a clown."

"Can you walk?"

"I'm not sure." Gigi made an attempt to sit up. "I'm not hurt. At least, I don't think I am. But he drugged me. He may have drugged Maggie too."

Even in the soft light filtering out from the window, Beau could see moisture in her eyes. She swept the back of her hand across her face. "This has never happened to me before. I'm—I'm queasy."

"Let me try to get you up," Beau said, lifting from his waist. "I need to get you inside so I can assess your injuries."

"I'm not hurt, I promise," Gigi said. "Leave me here. Find the car."

"I'm not leaving you, Gigi. Work with me on this, so I can expedite the search for Maggie."

She allowed him to stand her upright and then leaned against him.

"Can you walk with me helping you?" he asked.

She nodded.

Beau walked her up the stairs and into the house. Keely and Jake met them in the entryway.

"Sit her here," Keely said, motioning toward the dining room. "Where's Mom?"

"A man took her, honey. It's all my fault—" Gigi moaned.

Beau and Jake walked the older woman into the dining room and helped her into the overstuffed chair in the corner of the room.

"What happened?" Jake asked.

"Someone took off with Maggie in her own car." Beau glanced to Keely who was momentarily preoccupied with her aunt. "I need a ride back to Maggie's house to get my truck. Can you take me?"

"Of course," Jake said, reaching into his pocket and pulling out a set of keys.

"I can't believe this happened right under my nose."

"Don't beat yourself up, man. We do the best we can."

Beau shook his head. "That's not good enough. Maggie's life is now in danger." He looked to Keely, who was staring at him with her hand over her mouth and tears welling in her eyes.

"Keely." He rushed to her. "Take care of your aunt Gigi. Jake is going to run me back to your mom's house to get my truck. Do you think Levi can take you home?"

"Later," she said firmly. "I'll stay with Gigi until we're sure she's OK, and then we'll both go to Mom's. I'll spend the night there. Adam is with the dogs. I'll text him to let him know I won't be back."

"That's a good plan," he said. "But you . . . you need to be careful. Have Levi go inside with you when you get there. Lock all the doors and windows—and double check them." Beau remembered the door incident a few days ago. "And don't open the door for anyone, unless it's me or Jake." He pointed to Jake. "Or someone in your family."

Beau started to leave.

"Wait," Keely said. "Do you know who took her?"

Beau hesitated and then shook his head. "It was someone dressed as a clown."

CHAPTER 29

Saturday, January 15

"Let's take Old Natchez Trace to Maggie's house," Beau told Jake on their way out of Levi's driveway. Then he dialed 911, explained who he was and what had just happened, and asked for a BOLO.

"We're looking for a 2015 blue Buick LaCrosse with Williamson County plates. I don't know the tag number, but the car is registered in the name of Margaret Lambert." He waited a beat and then dictated Maggie's home address to the operator.

"We'll get the word out, Agent Gardner," the woman said.

Beau's next call was to Chris Enoch. "I'm sorry to bother you on a Saturday night, but Margaret Lambert, the widow in the cold case I'm working, has been abducted."

"Do you know that for sure?" Enoch asked.

"Yes, sir. I have a witness." Beau recited the details.

"Where are you?"

Beau swallowed his pride. "I was on the scene, but not with her when she was abducted from a social event at her son's house."

"From her son's house?" Enoch hesitated. "You can explain that to me when I see you on Monday."

"Yes, sir."

"Where are you now?"

Beau looked to Jake and then to the road in front of them. They were making good time on their way to Maggie's. "I'm with Jake Matheson. Coincidentally, he was at the same party."

"For the love of everything good, Beau. You had two agents at the house, and Mrs. Lambert was still abducted?"

"Yes, sir. I know, sir."

"What's your next move?"

"I've alerted the local law enforcement. You're my second call. As soon as I hang up with you, I'll call the Bureau and file a report."

"Do you have any idea who might have abducted Mrs. Lambert?"

"That's the only good news, Chris. Apparently, my intuition was right. My witness told me that Mrs. Lambert was abducted by a man or woman who was wearing a clown suit."

"And that's good news because—?"

"Special Agent Amy Force told me on Thursday that she would have a composite sketch to me on Monday."

Enoch sighed. "Great. Keep me updated and let me know how I can help."

"Thank you, sir."

"Let's bring this woman back alive."

Beau swallowed hard and ended the call. Staring out the passenger side window of Jake's Toyota Tacoma, Beau's heart climbed to his throat. They were passing the place where his mother's car had veered off the road before she died.

He turned to Jake.

"Do you have ideas?"

Jake glanced toward him. "Start from the beginning and fill me in."

Beau started from the day Connor disappeared and took Jake through to today. "That's the ten-minute version." They were nearing Maggie's house.

Jake nodded. "First of all, man. You did a great job zeroing in on the perp. Hopefully, Amy's sketch will help you nail the guy."

"Unfortunately, that's two days away. And we're now playing defense."

"Is this it?" Jake asked, pointing to Maggie's driveway.

"Yes."

Jake pulled beside Beau's Colorado and shifted into park. Then he turned to Beau. "I would call the Williamson County Sherriff's Department and ask them to be on the lookout for a car parked off the road, or in a suspicious location, within walking distance of Levi's house."

Beau nodded. "Good."

"If they have the manpower, it would be great if they can do a door-to-door inquiry within, say, a half-mile of there, asking if anyone saw a clown walking down the road. Or if they have video cameras on their property that might have captured something.

"I will ask Levi the same thing." Beau nodded.

"You might also want to call Uber and Lyft and ask if any of their drivers dropped a passenger somewhere in the vicinity of Levi's house shortly before or after the abduction tonight."

"Check," Beau said, making notes on his phone.

"That should give you plenty to do tonight."

"What about tomorrow?"

Jake pulled in beside Beau's truck and stopped. "If you're a believer, I would say go to church. Clear your head. And pray that this guy makes a mistake. You need a lead. If you're lucky, one of the sheriff's patrollers will spot his car, or run into something else overnight that will move you forward."

"This case is too close to me, Jake. I can't rely on luck."

Jake slapped him on the shoulder. "That's where the praying part comes in."

Beau nodded and opened the door. "I'll see you back at Levi's place. I want to check on Keely and do a walk around Ground Zero."

"See you there." Jake put his Tacoma in reverse and, after watching Beau start his engine, backed out of Maggie's driveway on his way back to Levi's.

Beau put another call into the Williamson County Sheriff's Department to follow up on Jake's ideas. After that call, he brainstormed and prayed. He had been too sure of himself, thinking he could waltz right into Keely's life and solve her father's case. Now, he was facing the worst thing that could have happened. Maggie's abduction.

How could he have let that happen? What would he say to Keely when he saw her? *What could he say?* He would have to admit his mistake.

And while he was setting aside his ego, he should call his father. James Gardner may have messed up a lot of things in his life, including his relationship with his son. But there was one thing he had done well. His dad was one of the best law enforcement officer's Beau knew.

And Beau could use his help on this case.

But first . . . he checked the time on the dashboard clock. Why hadn't he thought about this before? He pulled off the side of the road, grabbed his phone, and ran an internet search for Metropolitan Nashville clowns. Scrolling down a few entries, he found what he had hoped to find. An association for Nashville area clowns.

Beau dialed the number and pulled back onto the road.

"I just heard what happened. How can I help?" Keely looked up and saw Hannah standing in front of her and her aunt, who was sitting with her eyes closed.

"I'm not sure what to do," Keely said, wiping tears from her eyes. She had given up trying to hold them back.

She had momentarily been left alone with her aunt. Anna was upstairs with her and Levi's kids, and Levi was saying goodbye to his guests. The evening had ended abruptly after word had gotten around about the abduction. Keely could hear murmurings of concern and the shuffle of feet in the entryway on the other side of the wall.

Hannah pulled up a chair. She leaned into Gigi, putting her hand on her arm. "May I get you anything? Maybe a cold, moist hand cloth?"

"That sounds lovely, dear." Gigi opened her eyes and smiled. "I'm still rather queasy."

"I'll be right back!" Hannah jumped up and hurried out of the room.

"Have you heard anything from Beau?" Gigi asked for the second time in the last few minutes.

"I haven't, Aunt Gigi. He's on his way back to your house right now to get his truck. And I'm sure he has notified all the authorities."

She had no more spoken the words when she looked up and saw a Williamson County Sheriff's Deputy enter the room. It was Russell Wallace. "Ms. Lambert, I'm sorry it took so long, but I was the closest car to the scene, and I came right over."

"Thank you for coming, officer." Levi stepped up behind him.

"How many people were here tonight?" Wallace asked, turning toward her brother.

"Maybe thirty or thirty-five, not including family."

"This is my brother, Levi, Officer Wallace," Keely explained.

Wallace tipped his hat. "Pleasure, Mr. Lambert. Although I hate the circumstances."

"Likewise, sir."

"I'd like to get started with a few questions."

"Of course," Levi said.

"Are you the homeowner?"

"Yes, sir. My wife and our two children live here. Have lived here for about three years."

"Do you have a guest list from the party tonight that you can get to me by tomorrow morning?"

"Yes, sir. No problem at all. I'll have it to you first thing."

Wallace nodded. "Who was the last person to see your mother?"

"That would be me." Gigi held her hand in the air. "I'm her sister."

"Thank you, ma'am. May I have your name please?"

"It's Virginia Bradley. But everybody calls me Gigi."

"Yes, ma'am. Can you tell me where you last saw Mrs. Lambert?"

"Right outside that door." Gigi pointed toward the foyer door. "On the front porch."

"Did you see the abductor?"

"I did."

"Can you describe him for me?"

Gigi shrugged. "I can. But I'm not sure how helpful it will be. He was wearing a clown suit."

CHAPTER 30

Saturday, January 15

Keely watched Wallace take a step backward. "A clown suit?"

"Yes, sir," Gigi said. "Fuzzy hair, red nose, and red and yellow striped clown suit."

Wallace turned to Levi. "Had you hired the clown for entertainment tonight?"

"No, sir. He was not an invited guest."

"I see." Wallace turned back to Gigi. "Have you ever seen this man, um, *clown* before tonight?"

"Let me answer that for you, Officer Wallace," Keely said. "If it's the same man, I have seen him. As you know, Beau Gardner is currently working my father's cold case. And one of his persons of interest is a man wearing a clown suit."

"I see." He looked from Keely to Levi. "Do you know if anyone here tonight saw the suspect other than Ms. Bradley?"

"I'm not aware that anybody did, officer."

"OK. I will follow up on that tomorrow after I receive your guest list." He turned back to Gigi. "Ma'am, can you tell me about the abduction?"

"Yes, sir. My sister, Maggie, and I were on our way back from the bathroom." She pointed behind her. "And the front door opened. You can imagine our surprise when we saw a clown standing on the front porch. He was waving at us." Gigi bit her lip, remembering the unusual scene. "Maggie thought that was the best thing she had seen in a while. She giggled and smiled."

Hannah came back into the room, apparently not noticing Wallace, and handed Gigi the cool cloth.

"Thank you, dear," Gigi said, momentarily holding the cloth to her face. "This is lovely."

"Oh . . . I'm sorry." Hannah noticed the officer and stepped back, blushing.

"It's OK," Keely said.

"Continue when you're ready, ma'am."

"The clown obviously knew he had captivated Maggie, so he waved us unto the porch." Gigi shook her head. "I didn't have any intention of letting Maggie go farther than that, but I didn't think—"

"It's not your fault, Aunt Gigi," Keely said.

"If I'd only had enough sense not to walk out that door."

"Hindsight is always better, ma'am," Officer Wallace said. "What happened next?"

"The rest is almost a blur." Gigi shrugged. "I remember the clown reaching toward me and jabbing something into my arm. It stung! Suddenly, I was lightheaded. And dizzy. I remember seeing him grab Maggie and whisk her off the porch and into her car. I tried to chase after them, but I lost track of where I was." She looked up at Wallace. "And then I remember Beau finding me on the ground next to a pine tree."

Gigi wiped her face with the cloth again and settled into her chair.

Wallace turned to Levi. "Do you have video cameras in the front of your house?"

"Yes, sir. I have cameras on every side of the house. I will be happy to provide you with a copy of the footage from tonight."

"How soon can you get that for me?"

"Is in the morning soon enough, sir?"

"That will be fine," Wallace said, handing Levi his business card. "In the meantime, I'm going to dust your front porch for fingerprints."

"There's no need, officer," Gigi said. "The clown was wearing gloves."

"Are you certain about that, ma'am?"

"Yes, sir. I'm absolutely positive."

"In that case, I won't waste valuable time." He turned to Levi. "You and Ms. Lambert both have my number. If you think of anything else, please give me a call."

Wallace started to walk away and then stopped. "One more thing. I need a physical description of your mother and a recent photo, as well as a list of health issues. Is she on any medication that, if missed, will put her life in jeopardy?"

"I can help you with the medications," Gigi said. "I have the list in my purse." She startled. "My purse! It's in the backseat of Maggie's car."

"I'll make a note of that, Ms. Bradley. There's a good chance the suspect will ditch the car quickly. Our officers will take good care of your purse if we find it."

"Thank you." Gigi shook her head. "I have another list of medications at the house. Can I give it to Keely to give to you?"

"Yes, ma'am. Any concerning medical conditions?"

"Mom has early onset Parkinson's Disease and Traumatic Brain Injury," Levi said. "She sometimes has a difficult time communicating. And she is unsteady on her feet." Levi looked to Keely. "Do you have a good photo of Mom, sis?"

"I do!" Keely started scrolling through her phone. "Here you go, Officer Wallace. I took this about a week ago when I had Mom out for lunch."

"Can you please text that to me, along with your mother's age, height, and weight?"

"Yes, sir." Keely turned to Gigi. "Can you help me with that?"

Gigi nodded.

"Consider it done, Officer Wallace."

"Again, I'm sorry we're in the middle of something so awful," Wallace said. "But we'll do our best to find your mother quickly."

Keely nodded.

"Thank you, sir. I'll walk you to the door." Levi followed Wallace into the foyer.

While Keely texted Maggie's photo and stats to Russell Wallace, Hannah went to refresh Gigi's cloth. She returned to the room and took a seat beside Gigi just as Jake walked through the door with Levi.

"What's going on?" Keely asked, tucking her phone back into her pocket.

"I took Beau to his truck. He should be on his way back here now." Jake walked over to Hannah and rested his hands on the back of her chair. "He's already notified our office and the county sheriff's department."

"Yes. Officer Wallace just left. We gave him a photo and description . . . of Mom." The last few words caught in Keely's throat. She turned away and willed herself not to cry.

"I'm sorry you're going through this," Hannah said. "If I can help you, please call me."

Keely nodded.

"Honey, are you ready to go? I need to get to the office early in the morning so I can fill out paperwork about this case."

"Thank you for your help," Levi said.

Jake reached to shake his hand. "We'll do everything we can to bring your mother back safely."

Levi nodded.

"Beau should be back soon," Jake said.

Hannah walked over to Keely and bent close. "We'll be praying for you and your mom."

Beau was almost back to Levi's house when the call went through. He had expected to get voicemail, but someone answered.

"Hello . . ."

"Yes, sir. I hope I didn't wake you."

"Can I help you?"

"This is Special Agent Beau Gardner. I'm with the Tennessee Bureau of Investigation."

"I understand," the man said. "And how can I help you?"

Beau shook his head. For a clown, this guy certainly didn't have a sense of humor.

"Are you with the association of local clowns?"

"Yes, Agent Gardner. My name is Edgar Wayne. How can I help?"

"Mr. Wayne, I'm investigating a case, and the person of interest is, well . . . a clown. I was wondering if I sent you a photo of him in costume if you would be able to identify him." Beau prayed for a breakthrough.

"If he's a member of our association, I'm certain I can. If you would like, you can text a photo to this number."

"Great!" Beau pulled off the road again, this time into a driveway. "Give me just a minute." He scrolled through the clown's images he had saved to his phone. Finding a good one, he hit send.

"You should have it now."

"Hold on. Let me put on my glasses," Wayne said. "OK . . . Here it is."

Beau waited and prayed again.

"No, sir. I don't recognize him at all. I can tell from looking at his makeup that he's an amateur. We take our organization seriously. What has he done?"

Beau hesitated. "I'm trying to find him in regard to a murder case."

Wayne sighed. "I'm sorry to hear that, and I can tell you, we don't allow those kinds of people in our group. Unfortunately, they give the rest of us a bad name."

Beau pulled back on the road. "I understand. I've had to apologize to people because of something one of our agents did."

"I'll tell you what," Wayne said. "I will keep my eyes and ears open for you. In fact, I will share your photo with a few of our members and ask if any of them know him or know where to find him."

"That is much appreciated, Mr. Wayne. Please feel free to call me day or night."

Beau hung up and checked the clock again. It was too late to call his father. He would call first thing in the morning.

A few minutes later as he approached Levi's driveway, he saw a line of cars coming his way. Apparently, the event had just ended.

He took a sharp left so not to block the single lane of exiting vehicles—or any through traffic that might be traveling down the main road—and pulled into the space that had been designed to accommodate the mailman.

That's when he saw it. A shiny red object lying in the ditch beside the mailbox.

Beau threw his truck into park and hurried out. It was, without a doubt, a clown nose. Maggie must have put up a good fight—and maybe even intentionally thrown it out the car window to leave a trail for her rescuers.

Beau reached into his glove box for an evidence bag, got out of the truck, and secured the nose. He now had his lead. After taking Keely and Gigi home, his last stop tonight would be the TBI lab for DNA analysis.

The line of cars leaving Levi's had finally subsided. He backed up his truck, grateful for the detour, and headed up the driveway. The house was lit up from inside to outside. Beau was willing to bet that no one, except the Lambert kids, would be getting any sleep tonight.

Beau recognized the single vehicle in the circle drive. It was Jake's Tacoma. And he and Hannah were coming down the steps to leave.

"Any word?" Jake asked.

"I may have two leads. I have at least one good one. When I pulled off the side of the road to avoid traffic just now, something in the right of way caught my attention. When I got out to look at it, I confirmed that it was a red nose from the perp's costume."

Jake's expression went from sober to exuberant, and he raised his palm for a high five. "Good work, man."

Beau shook his head. "More like a lucky break. But I'll take all of those I can get."

"No kidding."

"What's been going on here?" Beau asked.

"A deputy from Williamson County left as I was coming in the door. Apparently, he took statements from the family, as well as photo and ID info for a BOLO. It's also my understanding that an EMT checked out Gigi, but she didn't want to be transported. He was fine with that."

"Hey!" Levi hurried down the porch steps. "Do you know anything, Beau?"

Beau repeated what he had told Jake, and then asked, "Do you know who was here from the sheriff's office?"

"Officer Wallace. Keely seemed to know him. And he mentioned you."

"Did he dust for fingerprints? Look for footprints? Anything else?"

Levi frowned. "Not so far. Gigi told him the clown was wearing gloves, so there was no need to dust for fingerprints. And Wallace told me as he was leaving that he would be back in the morning to look for footprints. He asked me to stay out—and keep everyone else out—of my yard to avoid damaging any evidence."

"Good," Beau said. "I'll connect with him. One of us will have a crew out here at daylight."

"Thank you," Levi said. "I don't know what we would do without you, Beau."

Levi's words stabbed Beau in the gut. If only he felt that way. If he had been doing his job, Maggie wouldn't have been taken under his watch.

"I'll see you tomorrow, man." Jake brought Beau back to the moment. "I need to get Hannah home."

"Thanks for your help tonight."

Jake nodded and escorted Hannah to his car.

"I wasn't sure you would be back," Levi said. "I was about to take Keely and Gigi home to Mom's. They're determined to spend the night there. Gigi says she needs her medication."

Beau checked his watch. "If you want to do that, I will drive straight to my office from here. I want to start processing the evidence I found as soon as possible."

"Of course," Levi said.

After a quick check in with Keely, Beau hurried to his truck and left. The time alone to think would do him good.

July 6, 2000

Keely stretched to get a better view of the men in the front seat of the Cadillac, but she could only see the backs of their heads.

"Where were you heading when you had trouble, Lambert?" The man in the passenger seat asked. How did he know her dad's name?

"Kids, jump out. We're going to stay here—"

Keely heard the click of the automatic locks.

"There's no need. Please," the driver said. "Just tell us where you were going. We'll take you there."

"The ice cream shop. A few miles ahead."

The driver shoved down on the accelerator, throwing Keely and Levi back into their seats. She turned to her father for assurance. His face looked pale and drawn. And his fingers twitched.

No one spoke for the next few miles, and then Keely saw the ice cream shop up the road. The driver signaled to turn, and Keely heard her father exhale.

"Thank you," he said, as soon as the car came to a stop. "We'll call—"

"No, please, stay here," the driver said. "Let the children get their ice cream, and then we'll take you home."

"That's not—"

"It's no problem," he said, and he handed a ten-dollar bill across the seat to Keely.

Her dad nodded to her, and she opened the passenger side door of the car and stepped outside. Levi scooted across the seat and followed her.

CHAPTER 31

Sunday, January 16

Keely awoke from a fitful sleep in the bedroom of her childhood. Throwing back the covers, she stood and reached for the jeans and sweater she had worn to Levi's party. Then she slipped on her boots and walked to the kitchen. Her aunt was already there, waiting for a pot of coffee to brew.

"How did you sleep?" Gigi asked.

"About the same as you, I would guess."

Gigi nodded.

"How do you feel this morning?" Keely asked.

"I'm OK, honey," she said. "A few bruises and scratches from losing a fight with that pine tree, but I'll survive." She opened the cupboard door and picked out two mugs. "Do you take your coffee black or with cream and sugar?"

"Disguise the taste as much as you can." Keely took a seat in one of her mom's breakfast table chairs. "I'm not much of a coffee drinker, but I need something to wake me up."

Gigi chuckled. "You're a lot like your mom. She's not a black coffee drinker either."

Their eyes met at the mention of Maggie.

"This is all so unreal," Keely said. "First Daddy, and now Mom. I don't—"

Keely's phone interrupted.

"Let's hope this is Beau with good news." She pulled the phone from her pocket. It was Levi.

"Have you heard anything from Mom?" Levi asked.

"Nothing . . ." Keely said before mouthing her brother's name to Gigi, who walked closer and set a cup of white coffee in front of her.

"How is Aunt Gigi?"

Keely glanced upward to her aunt and hit the speaker button. "I think she's feeling better. She's sore and a little bit banged up from her fall, but she says she's OK."

Gigi took a seat beside Keely. "Don't worry about me. I'm doing fine."

"So, what's going on at your house?" Keely asked.

"I've already talked to Beau a couple of times this morning. He's sending a forensics team out here to look for evidence . . . footprints, fingerprints, DNA. Anything we might have overlooked in the dark." He paused, as if looking at his watch. "They should be here anytime."

"I hope they find what they need to get this guy."

"I've also given Beau access to my security camera files. I'm hoping that will help." He hesitated. "Of course, Aunt Gigi has already told us that the man was dressed like a clown. Now, there's a disguise for you."

"A brilliant one, actually. Not many people would question a clown walking into a party," Keely said.

"Unfortunately, we didn't." Gigi shook her head. "Maggie was fascinated by him. We fell right into his trap."

"Don't beat yourself up, Aunt Gigi," Levi said. "Beau will get to the bottom of this."

Keely took a sip of her coffee and grimaced. "I just hope it's before something happens to Mom."

"Sis, I've got to go. The forensic team is at my door. Call me if you find out anything."

Keely pressed the end button on her phone. Before she could lay it on the table, another call came in. This one was from Beau.

"Hey, what's going on?" she asked.

"I'm at my office. Did you and Gigi go to church?"

"No." She looked at her watch. "Church hasn't started yet, but we're not going. I have too much swirling around in my head right now."

"I think that's a good idea. Keep a low profile. I'm planning to head that way in about a half hour. I need to finish up here first."

"Do you know anything more?"

"Not really. I have a team on the way to Levi's house to collect evidence. And I've sent the clown's nose to the lab for analysis. Have you seen any sheriff's deputies patrolling around Maggie's house this morning?"

"Not that I'm aware," Keely said. "But we're in the back of the house right now."

"I called them last night and asked for increased security surveillance for you. I also have a call into my dad to ask for his help. He hasn't called me back yet."

"Thank you. Gigi and I appreciate what you're doing."

He didn't speak. "I hope it's enough, Keely. I pray that it is. I'll see you in about an hour, maybe a little bit more. I want to pick up something of your mom's to take back to the office for fingerprint samples."

Keely ended the call and sat back in her chair. "I wish Beau had been more optimistic."

"What do you mean, honey?" Her aunt was standing at the kitchen sink.

"I just want this to end, Aunt Gigi. My nightmares are back. And it's not that I can't handle them. I always have. But this time we've lost Mom." She focused her attention on the family photo on the wall. "And just like with Daddy, I feel like it's my fault."

"Oh, Keely . . ." Gigi walked across the room and hugged her. Then, pulling back, she said, "If this is anybody's fault, it's mine."

"No, it's not, Aunt Gigi."

Keely grabbed her aunt and held on to her until they were interrupted by a knock on the door.

A few minutes later they were sitting in the living room with Keely's uncle Peter.

"Are you sure you don't want coffee," Gigi asked for the second time.

"No, Geeg. I'm just fine. Quit fussing."

Gigi smiled.

"I got a call from Beau Garner this morning, and he told me a little more about what was going on. I just wanted to check on you two girls."

"We're doing all right, aren't we, Keely?" Gigi spoke first.

"We're OK," Keely said, although she wasn't convinced how true it was.

Her uncle turned to her. "What's Beau Gardner doing back in town? Didn't the two of you used to be sweet on each other?"

"Stop that, Peter. You're embarrassing her," Gigi said.

"I remember the two of you used to remind me of your parents. Once they met, they couldn't stay away from each other. It was quite a love story." He seemed to be enjoying the memory. "Your parents loved each other, Keely. Don't let anybody ever tell you different."

Keely gave her uncle a sideways glance.

"I've never thought anything but that," she said. "Why would anybody think differently?" She looked to her aunt and then to her uncle.

"They wouldn't, honey." Gigi glared at her brother.

"What's going on?" Keely sat forward in her chair. "The two of you are talking in code."

"Your uncle Peter has just lost his marbles," Gigi said. "And his memory. Let's let the past stay where it is . . . behind us." Gigi repositioned herself on the sofa. "How's your family, Peter? We haven't seen you since Christmas."

"Not so fast," Keely interrupted. "Uncle Peter, what did you mean when you inferred that some people didn't think my parents were in love?"

Her uncle looked from her to her aunt and shrugged his shoulders.

"I didn't mean anything by it," he said and then straightened in his chair. "I was just . . ." He looked to Gigi as if asking for words, hesitated, and then looked back to Keely. "Well—"

"Peter!" Gigi raised her voice. "Not now."

"And why not now?" he asked. "If she doesn't know, then it's time she did. It's not like there's something so wrong about it."

Gigi crossed her arms and sat back.

"Keely, your parents loved each other more than any two people I've ever met. Especially when you consider they didn't know each other that long before they married."

"I knew that, Uncle Peter." Keely relaxed and sat back. "Mom always told me that they met right after Daddy returned from the war. And they fell in love almost at first sight. They were married three months later." Keely looked from her uncle to her aunt Gigi. "That's right, isn't it?"

"Of course, it is—"

"It's not right, Gigi, and you know it."

Her aunt huffed and turned away. "Whatever, Peter. You know best."

Keely swiveled to stare at her uncle. "Well?"

His shoulders dropped, and his expression softened. "Honey, your mom and dad were married soon after they met, but it wasn't quite that soon. They were planning to wait, so your mom could . . ." He looked to his sister. "How do I put this?"

Gigi shrugged. "It's your story, Peter. Tell it however you want."

"So, your mom could tell her fiancé that she had changed her mind."

"Mom was engaged before she met Daddy? To whom?"

"There you go . . . stir it up." Gigi growled.

"Does that really matter?" he asked.

"Maybe not, but I would like to know."

"To James Gardner."

"To Beau's dad? Mom was engaged to Beau's dad? Are you serious?"

"Yes," he said.

She turned to Gigi, and her aunt nodded.

"Oh, my goodness." Keely's hand flew to her mouth. "So, they married right after she told him she was breaking it off?"

"Not exactly," he said. "Your parents married about six months before he returned from overseas. You had already been born, and . . . it was quite the shock to James Gardner when he returned."

"I was born in July, and my parents married in May."

"Yes."

She could feel the color in her cheeks. "Aunt Gigi, I know I was conceived before . . . before my parents were married. Mom told me when I was in high school. She wanted me to hear it from her and not through the grapevine."

"You were a little early in getting here, honey. But you were already being planned. And don't you ever let anybody tell you differently," Gigi said. "Just like your uncle Peter said, your parents were deeply in love and talking about a family."

"I'm OK with that, Aunt Gigi. It's the part about Beau's dad that—" She shook her head.

"Keely." Her uncle shrugged. "I'm sorry I brought any of this up today. You have too much on you right now anyway. It's just that I've thought for a long time that it was something you deserved to know. I'm glad your mom had told you. And the part about James Gardner? I'm surprised that someone else in this little village hadn't already told you about that."

"Not many people knew," Gigi said. "Not outside of the Gardner and Lambert families."

"But Mom and Daddy . . . and James Gardner did."

"Of course," her aunt said.

Keely jumped up from her chair. "I wonder if that's why Beau left?"

She was interrupted by the doorbell. Looking outside, she saw Beau's truck in the driveway.

CHAPTER 32

Sunday, January 16

Beau knew there was something wrong when he saw the look on Keely's face. She stepped aside, and he walked past her into the Lambert living room.

"Peter?"

"Hi, Beau. I'm came over to check on my girls but was just about to leave."

"Is everything OK?" Beau turned to Gigi and then back to Keely.

Keely nodded. But not convincingly.

Peter stood. "Gigi, call me if you need anything."

"Don't hold your breath," she said.

Beau swiveled to look at her. "Gigi? That doesn't sound like you."

The older woman feigned a smile. "Don't worry about it, honey. We had a little family disagreement. And if Peter doesn't leave, I may toss him out on his ear."

Peter shrugged and winked at Beau. "Your turn. I didn't do so good."

Gigi walked her brother to the door and closed it behind him. "Lord, have mercy," she said.

"It's OK, Aunt Gigi. Uncle Peter didn't do anything wrong."

Her aunt opened her mouth to reply but turned to Beau instead. "Are you hungry? It's almost lunch time."

Beau took a seat on the sofa. "I—I could . . ."

"That's enough of an answer for me. I'll be in the kitchen fixing us all something to eat. Why don't the two of you catch each other up?"

"Any updates?" Keely asked, taking a seat in a chair.

"Nothing yet. I'm expecting initial forensic results soon. To finalize those, I need to take something of your mother's with me to have analyzed . . . and Dad hasn't returned my call yet."

She looked away.

"Keely, what's wrong?"

"Why didn't you tell me?"

"Tell you what?"

"About your dad and my mom."

Beau's heart climbed to his throat. "I didn't know if it was true."

She nodded. "It's true. Uncle Peter told me." She studied him. "But I'm not fully convinced that you didn't know."

Beau frowned. "Are we talking about the same thing?"

"Uncle Peter told me that your dad and my mom dated—"

"So, it *is* true? Was it right after my mom passed away or more recently?"

She recoiled. "What are you talking about? I'm talking about before my mom and dad were married."

He winced. "Your uncle Peter told you that?"

"Yes," she said. "You knew, right?"

He nodded. "My dad told me years ago."

"Why didn't you tell me?"

"Because I didn't think it mattered."

"You didn't think it mattered? Is that why you left me?"

"No . . . Keely. I told you why I left."

She stared at him.

"I left because I wanted to get as far away from my dad as I could. He wasn't pleasant to be around. Not for me or anyone in my family." He looked away. "He wasn't physically abusive. But he was mean. He would intentionally try to hurt us . . . with his words. Just like he would have hurt you, if I hadn't left."

"What do you mean?"

"He didn't want you and me to be happy because he wasn't happy. He never got over losing your mom. And you reminded him of her." He looked away and then continued. "I'm embarrassed to tell you that because it tells you what a jerk my dad really is. Or, at least, was. He has tried to do better since Mom died. Unfortunately for him, I think he realized what he had after he lost her."

"I'm sorry, Beau," Keely said. "I didn't know."

"My mom was an amazing woman. She would help anyone who needed help. Even if they didn't ask, she would somehow know and reach out to them. And she was the best mom I could have ever asked for." He thought about that for a minute. "You know, we've both had that," he said. "Both of them good and strong women."

Keely's lip quivered. "I hope I get to keep mine a while longer."

"I hope you do too," he said. "I'm doing my best, Keely. And I'm sorry you're going through this. It feels like it's my fault."

"Don't even think about that. Aunt Gigi and I agreed this morning that neither of us—none of us—are to blame." Keely moved from the chair to the sofa.

"Hey, you two, I have lunch ready." Gigi set a plate of sandwiches on the dining room table. "Beau, what would you like to drink? I have iced tea or lemonade."

"Tea sounds good." Beau took Keely's hand and pulled her up from the sofa.

"Will you do that for me when we're old and gray?" she asked.

He startled. "Can you picture us together that long?"

"Can you?"

"Yes. You'll be beautiful, like your mother." He walked her into the dining room. "And your aunt Gigi."

"What's that?" The older woman set the drinks on the table.

Beau held Keely's chair for her and then took a seat. "I told Keely she would still be beautiful thirty years from now—just like her mother and her aunt."

"He's a keeper." Gigi winked.

Keely unfolded her napkin. "Beau . . . I still have one question. It's about what you said earlier."

He nodded and lifted a sandwich from the platter in front of him.

"You asked if it was true that my mom and your dad had dated recently. What did you mean by that?"

Beau plopped the sandwich unto his plate. He *had* said that, and now there was no way to get around it. He collected his thoughts. "I thought you were substantiating the rumor that has been going around town for a few years."

"What rumor?" Gigi asked.

He looked from Gigi back to Keely. "The rumor that my dad had been trying to convince your mom to go out with him."

"Where on earth did you hear that, Beau?" Gigi asked.

"It's just rumor," he said. "I've heard it from several people. Although I've never really believed it."

Gigi sat back in her chair. "Believe it."

Keely did a double take. "Are you serious?"

"He has been seeing her since I've been here taking care of her. In fact, he has a key to the house."

"What?" Keely looked at Beau, her mouth agape.

Beau shook his head. "Why didn't you tell me earlier?"

"Because you didn't ask," she said. "And the way I have it figured, it isn't anyone's business if those two want to see each other."

"They're just friends, right?" Keely's voice sounded thin.

"If you're asking me about their romantic life, I won't tell you because I don't know," Gigi said. "They may have rekindled that fire at some point, after your mama died, of course." She looked at Beau. "But he's very respectful of her condition now. He stops in to check on her. And to eat lunch with us once in a while."

Beau shook his head. "Gigi, you are blowing my mind. I don't know what to say."

"There's nothing to say," Gigi said. "Your dad and Keely's mom have known each other for a long time. They both care about each other. Those things are never forgotten. You don't just stop loving someone." She shook her head. "You might stop liking them. But loving them? No. Love is forever."

Beau looked at Keely, who was staring at her aunt in disbelief.

"That's why I wasn't too worried about the back door when you found it open last week." Gigi took a sandwich from the platter. "I was sure it was your dad who had left it open . . . Or rather, who had forgotten to pull it shut properly. If it doesn't click, it doesn't lock."

"I'll find out when I talk to him," Beau said.

"There's no need, honey." Gigi smiled. "I called him that afternoon right after you and Keely left. It was him."

CHAPTER 33

Monday, January 17

Fingerprint results for the clown nose were on Beau's desk when he stepped into his office on Monday morning. The lab found prints that matched the sample he had taken in for Keely's mom, as well as partial prints matching those found on both tracking devices. DNA results were still pending.

The lab had also analyzed Levi's home security footage and, within a reasonable doubt, identified the clown who abducted Maggie as the same person in the party photos Beau had found online for Mr. Mike the Clown.

At eleven o'clock, Amy Force delivered the composite sketch.

"So, this is what he looks like underneath all that makeup?" Beau asked.

"It's my best guess," she said.

"I don't know how you do it." Beau couldn't believe the resemblance. It was as if she had stripped off all the makeup and taken a snapshot of the man beneath. "Can you send me digital copies too?"

"Already done," she said.

"Thank you! We're going to catch this guy!"

"I hope so. I heard he abducted a woman. I hope you find her safe."

"From your lips to God's ears," Beau said.

He followed Amy out the door and hurried down to Chris Enoch's office. His boss's door was open, and Enoch was sitting behind his desk shuffling paperwork. Beau tapped lightly on the doorframe.

Enoch looked up. "Come in, Beau."

Beau entered and took a seat in front of Enoch's desk. "I have the composite sketch of our man." He laid it on the desk. "Agent Force just dropped it by my office."

Enoch picked up the sketch and studied it. "You can see the resemblance."

"Yes," Beau said. "She does amazing work. I think it's our ticket to finding this guy. I have a good feeling about it."

"Tell me about the circumstances of the abduction on Saturday night." Enoch set the sketch aside and picked up his pen.

"We were at a party at Levi Lambert's house. Levi is Margaret's son. Everyone was on the back patio listening to music. Mrs. Lambert and her sister, who is our witness, went inside, saw the front door open and a clown standing on the front porch. According to Virginia Bradley, Mrs. Lambert's sister, the clown lured them outside. He then neutralized Mrs. Bradley and took off with Mrs. Lambert in her own car."

"And you and Matheson were at the house when this happened?"

"Yes, sir. Jake's fiancée was performing at the party, and I was there with the Lambert family. Jake and I hadn't been expecting to see each other there."

Enoch tossed his pen on top of his desk. "That makes sense, but it looks bad on paper."

"I know, sir."

"What's your plan to catch this guy? Any leads so far? Any chance this is a for-ransom abduction?"

"Highly unlikely, considering the other circumstances of the case. As to leads, we now have the composite, and I found evidence—the clown's nose—near the scene. It's being analyzed for DNA right now. The lab has already found a partial match for prints on the clown nose and the two tracking devices."

Enoch nodded, seemingly pleased.

Beau took a breath. "Williamson County and our office responded immediately to the scene and followed up the next day, looking for fingerprints and footprints. Nothing significant has been found. Nor has Mrs. Lambert's car been found."

"OK. Get out of here, Gardner. We need to find this woman soon. And keep me updated."

"Yes, sir."

A few minutes later, after emailing copies of the composite sketch to the Williamson County authorities, as well as the distribution office at the TBI, Beau made twenty-five printed copies and left for Margaret Lambert's house. He called Keely on the way.

"Any word?" she asked.

"We're making progress. I'm on my way to your mom's house to pick you up. Can you help me take a few flyers around town? I have a composite sketch of the man beneath the clown suit."

"Sure. I think Gigi's ready to get rid of me anyway. And I desperately need to change clothes."

Beau looked at his watch. "I can be there by twelve thirty. A quarter to one at the latest."

He ended the call with her and then dialed his dad again.

"Yes?"

"Where have you been?"

"I've been out of town for a few days. I met a few buddies of mine in Destin for some deep-sea fishing."

"Have you heard about Maggie Lambert?"

"No . . . what happened?"

"She was kidnapped."

His father cursed. Apparently, some things hadn't changed.

"Do we have any leads?"

"I didn't have much until this morning, but I just sent a composite sketch of the suspect to your office."

"I'm out of the office until Thursday."

"I'll text one to you. I'm driving right now, but I can get it to you within the hour."

"That would be great. How's Gigi holding up?"

"She's doing OK. She was injured in the scuffle trying to protect her sister, but nothing serious."

"I'm sorry to hear that. Keep me updated, OK?"

"Will do, Dad."

Beau ended the call and shook his head in disbelief. His dad had just confirmed Gigi's story. They were on a first name basis.

As soon as he pulled into Maggie Lambert's driveway, Beau texted the composite sketch to his dad. A few minutes later he was sitting on Maggie's sofa showing it to Keely and Gigi. "Does he look familiar?" he asked.

"Not really," Keely said.

"He's rather ordinary looking," Gigi said. "I can't say that I've seen him, and I can't say that I haven't."

"I'll leave a copy with you," Beau said, laying it on the coffee table in front of him. "If you see him, get away quickly and call 911. Then call me."

"I will, honey."

"Are you sure you're OK being here by yourself?" Keely asked.

"I'm perfectly fine," Gigi said. "I'm probably the last person that man cares about. If he had wanted me, he had his chance to take me with him on Saturday night."

Beau chuckled. "I can see your logic," he said. "But be careful." He stood and turned to Keely. "Are you ready? We have a lot of territory to cover this afternoon."

"Let's do it," she said. "We're going to my place first, right?"

"We are."

"Great. I'll be quick. I just want to change clothes."

"You two be careful," Gigi said, standing at the front door as they left. "And please check in with me once in a while."

"I will, Aunt Gigi. Call if you need me."

Beau opened the passenger side door for Keely and helped her inside. "I finally talked to my dad. He's been out of town." He shut the door and hurried to the other side of the truck, then climbed inside.

"Did he know about Mom?"

"No. He was shocked. I sent him a photo of the suspect."

Keely fastened her seatbelt. "I'm still trying to get over what Aunt Gigi told us yesterday."

"You and me both," Beau said. "This little village has more romantic plot twists than a television reality show."

"And most of it involves your and my families."

He gave her a sideways glance. "No kidding."

They both laughed, and then Keely sobered. "I hope my mom's story has a happy ending."

Beau reached for her hand. "We're doing the best we can."

"I know," she said. "And I appreciate it."

In less than twenty minutes, they were pulling into Keely's driveway. Adam was in the outdoor training area when they drove up. He hurried to meet them.

"I'm so sorry about your mom." He gave her a quick hug.

Keely nodded. "We're hopeful."

"Sara and I have been praying for her." He turned to Beau and extended his hand. "Thanks for what you're doing."

"Like Keely said, we're hopeful," Beau said. "We have a few good leads. In fact . . . hang on a minute." He hurried back to his truck for a copy of the sketch to give to Adam. "Have you ever seen this man?"

Adam took the rendering and studied it. "He looks familiar, but I'm not sure. Can I keep this?"

"Yes. And show it to as many people as you can. We're fairly certain he's our man."

"The clown?"

"Yes." Beau nodded.

"What can I do to help?" Adam turned back to Keely.

"You're helping me by staying with the dogs. How are Pearl and the puppies?"

"The pups are growing like weeds," he said. "I think you'll have two good dogs there. I'm anxious to see how they mature."

Beau nudged Keely. "I hate to rush you, but we need to get going." He looked at his watch.

"I'll be right back." Keely took off running for the house.

"How's she holding up?" Adam asked as soon as she disappeared inside.

"She's OK, considering," Beau said. "She's a strong woman."

Adam grinned. "I remember telling you that a while back."

"You did, and you were right." Beau massaged the back of his neck with his right hand. "And so is her aunt . . . and her mom. None of them seem to back down from a fight. Or a challenge." And then he remembered. "How is Sara doing?"

"She is feeling better and better. And we've seen sonograms of the baby." He lowered his voice. "I'm not supposed to say anything yet, but we think it's a boy."

"Congratulations, man. Happy for you!"

"Thanks." Adam's already ruddy cheeks turned a deeper shade of red.

A few minutes later, Keely came running down the hill carrying a coat and a bag.

"Were the dogs happy to see you?"

"They were bouncing off the walls. I promised them I would be home tonight."

"What time do you think it will be?" Adam asked.

"Beau, what do you think? Maybe six?"

He nodded.

"Great! I'll let Sara know to expect me for supper."

"Give her a hug for me, OK?"

"Will do. You two be safe," Adam said. "We'll be praying."

Beau walked Keely to the truck, helped her inside, and then ran around the back to hop in. Almost immediately, Keely opened the bag she had been carrying and pulled out two bottles of tea. "One for you and one for me."

"Thank you!" He took the bottle and slipped it into a nearby cup holder.

"And here's a sandwich," she said. "Nothing fancy like Gigi's. I made them quickly, assuming you hadn't eaten."

"I hadn't. But I was planning to stop at Fox and Locke for lunch. See, I remembered."

She grinned. "You got the name right, but they're not open on Mondays."

Beau groaned. "When am I going to remember that? I've been away from Leiper's Fork too long."

"Yes, you have." She unwrapped her sandwich. "What's our agenda today?"

"I want to post as many of the flyers as we can. That was my other reason to stop at Fox and Locke." He turned to her. "What businesses do you think have the most traffic?"

"How about the post office?"

"There's a post office in Leiper's Fork now?"

"No. I just wanted to see if you remembered."

"Very funny."

"How about we start at The Country Boy and work our way around the block?"

"Let's do it." At the end of Keely's drive, he looked both ways, and then took a left.

"Why don't we pay a visit to Mrs. Arnold too?"

"Our old elementary school teacher? Is she still alive?" He asked.

"I think so. She's not that old, although she's retired. She knows everyone in town. If she didn't teach them, she taught their parents."

"Great idea." Beau took a bite of his sandwich and stepped on the accelerator.

CHAPTER 34

Monday, January 17

The Leiper's Fork Historic District spanned less than a half mile of Old Hillsboro Road from the David Arms Gallery to Props Antiques and back around to the Copper Fox. Within an hour, Keely had helped Beau post flyers inside and in front of stores and alerted as many shop owners as they could find to her mother's abduction.

On their way back to the truck, Keely found a number for Frances Arnold and called her. Their old schoolteacher answered on the second ring.

"Mrs. Arnold, this is Keely Lambert. Do you remember me?"

"Of course, dear. You were that little brown-haired girl with dark eyes. I hope your mother is doing well."

"Thank you, ma'am. Do you think it would be possible for me to pay you a visit this afternoon?"

"That would be lovely," she said. "What time would you like to come over?"

"In the next half hour if that works for you. Where do you live now?"

"That works for me," she said. "My house is the charming little cottage right past the center of town."

Keely chuckled, because every house in Leiper's Fork was charming. "It might be better if you can give me your address."

"Of course, dear." She rattled it off.

"Great! See you soon." Keely ended the call.

"How long will it take us to get there?" Beau asked.

"It depends on if you want to walk or drive?"

"Either is fine," he said.

"It would take about twenty minutes to drive, because we would need to find a parking place," Keely said. "But we can walk there in about ten minutes."

"Easy decision. Let's walk."

"You got it," she said.

"Isn't she's expecting us in a half hour?"

"It'll be OK," Keely said, getting out of the truck. "I'm sure it won't matter if we're early."

Fifteen minutes later they were knocking on Frances Arnold's front door.

"Come in," the older woman beckoned. "Keely, you look beautiful. Just like you did when you were in fourth grade."

"Thank you, Mrs. Arnold. Do you remember Beau Gardner?"

She studied Beau. "Of course, I do. But it took me a minute."

Beau laughed. "I look a lot different than I did in fourth grade."

She led them to her sitting room. "Please, have a seat on the sofa and forgive my messy coffee table. It's just me and the cat since my husband passed away. May I get you something to drink? Tea? Water? Hot chocolate?"

"No thank you, ma'am. We just ate lunch." Keely took a seat next to Beau.

"I'm sorry to hear about your husband, Mrs. Arnold. I lost my mom five years ago." Beau looked around the room.

"Thank you. And I'm sorry to hear about your mother." She settled into her chair. "I try to be thankful for all the time we had." She folded her hands in her lap. "Well, I know you didn't just come for a visit—although that would have been fine too. How do you need my help?"

"You always were intuitive," Beau teased.

"It's a teacher's best survival tool." The older woman smiled.

"I can see why you would need it," Beau added. "I'm sure I was always doing something I wasn't supposed to be doing."

Keely laughed. "Why is that easy to believe?"

"Don't let him fool you," the teacher said. "He was a good boy. And as sharp as a tack."

"Mrs. Arnold, I'm a special agent with the Tennessee Bureau of Investigation now, and I'm investigating a cold case from 2000."

The older woman turned to Keely. "Your father's disappearance?"

"Yes." Keely nodded.

"That was a heartbreaking turn of events. I felt so sorry for you and your brother. How is he doing, by the way?"

"Levi is fine. He's a successful businessman in Nashville. He works in the music industry. I'll tell him you asked about him."

"Good." She nodded and turned back to Beau. "How can I help?"

He gave her a copy of the sketch. "Do you have any idea who this is?" He asked.

"Of course, I do. It's Mike Murdoch. He used to teach at the school."

Keely sat back in her seat and looked at Beau. He held her gaze. Then they turned to Mrs. Arnold.

"We should have come to you sooner," Beau said. "Why was it so easy for you to recognize him?"

She gave the sketch back to Beau. "For one thing, it's the spitting image of him." She turned to Keely. "And I have always suspected that he had something to do with your dad's disappearance."

"You did?" Keely's mouth dropped open.

"Why is that, Mrs. Arnold?" Beau asked.

"I told Sheriff Bannon what I thought right after it happened, but no one ever did anything about it."

"What did you tell Sheriff Bannon?" Beau leaned forward.

"I told him that Mike Murdoch was a likely suspect because your dad had just recently gotten him fired."

"I don't remember that!" Keely said.

"Honey, you were too young to know about it or to remember it if you did know."

"What did William Lambert do, or say, that caused Murdoch to be fired?" Beau asked.

"Well, first of all, Mike Murdoch always was—and probably still is—a strange bird. He was into some kind of weird voodoo historical nonsense. Studying history is one thing, but manipulating it to serve your cause, or satisfy your personal ego, is another."

She sat back and collected her thoughts. "I remember him telling me one time in the break room at school that he was a descendent of some man in the Knights Templar. I think he watched too many movies in the eighties." She chuckled. "The two of you hadn't been born yet, but at that time there were a lot of Holy Grail references coming out of Hollywood."

She took a breath. "And then, it's also just possible that he's a looney tune." She looked to Keely and then to Beau. "I'm sorry. I don't mean to be disrespectful if the man has emotional issues, but I think everyone should respect the law."

She turned to Keely. "After your poor daddy served out his patriotic duty, someone, whether it was Mike Murdoch or someone else, took him away from his wife and his children."

Keely nodded. "Thank you for your kind words, Mrs. Arnold."

Beau shifted in his seat. "Ma'am, do you happen to know where we can find Mr. Murdoch now?"

"I'm afraid I don't." She shook her head. "I wish I could. I was told that he moved out of town and changed his name after he lost his job. But I don't remember ever hearing his pseudonym or his new address."

Beau nodded. "I'm asking because he—or someone who looks like the man in this sketch—has been committing crimes in this area in the last few weeks."

"Oh . . . I'm sorry to hear that."

"Yes, ma'am. He's a person of interest right now in the disappearance of Keely's mother."

The older woman's hand flew to her chest. "That's just awful." She shook her head. "Why didn't someone listen to me twenty years ago? All of this could have been stopped."

"We're listening to you now, ma'am. And we'll do our best to see that this man—Michael Murdoch, or whoever it is—is brought to justice." Beau stood.

"Please let me know if I can help." She slowly rose to her feet. "I'm not physically who I once was, but my memory is sharp."

After walking them to the front door, she gave Keely a hug. "I'm so sorry, dear. You be careful, OK? I'm not so sure he won't try to hurt you. After all, it was what you told your daddy that started the situation."

Keely froze. "What are you talking about?"

"I don't mean to bring back bad memories, but apparently, he said some inappropriate things to you, and that didn't set well with your father. After your dad confronted the school principal, the matter went to the school board, and although there were no formal charges filed, Mike Murdoch's contract wasn't renewed."

"Would any of that information be a matter of public record, Mrs. Arnold?" Beau asked.

"I'm sure it would be. Check with the school board. They should have it on file."

"I'll do that, ma'am. And thank you again for your time." Beau took her hand. "And once again, I'm sorry to hear about your husband."

She nodded and closed the door behind them.

"She's doing great," Keely said. "How old do you think she is?"

"Maybe eighty?"

"Do you believe what she said?"

Beau nodded. "I do, because everything adds up. Even the name. The clown calls himself Mr. Mike."

"You're right! I hadn't even thought about that." Keely shuddered. "How are we going to find out where he lives?"

"I think that part may be easy."

"Really?" Her voice cracked.

Beau pulled the phone from his pocket. "I'll call my dad. He remembers everybody who ever lived here—and usually where they went when they moved."

CHAPTER 35

Monday, January 17

Beau shook his head. "No answer. I don't understand. I just talked to him earlier."

"Have you tried his office?" Keely asked.

"He told me he was off until Thursday."

"Should we drive over to his place?" Beau unlocked the truck door and helped Keely inside. "Or is that a waste of time since he's not answering his phone?"

"Could be. Can you think of anyone else who might know this guy's pseudonym?"

"I've always heard if you want to know where somebody lives ask the postman."

"That's a great idea." He gave her a sideways glance. "You need to join the Bureau."

"No, thank you. But I'll be happy to supply you with dogs."

"Maybe we can arrange for that." He switched gears. "Since there's no dedicated post office for Leiper's Fork, should we try Brentwood or Franklin first?"

Keely picked up her phone. "They're both about twenty minutes from here."

"Do you have their numbers?"

She did a quick search on her phone. "Here's the number for the Brentwood branch."

She read the number to him, and he placed the call, switching to speaker so she could hear.

"Brentwood Post Office."

"Yes, ma'am. I'm Special Agent Beau Gardner with the Tennessee Bureau of Investigation. May I please speak with your supervisor?"

"Yes, Agent Gardner. Hold, please."

Beau turned the volume down, hoping to avoid the hold music.

"Waters. May I help you?"

"Yes, Ms. Waters. I'm Special Agent Beau Gardner with the Tennessee Bureau of Investigation, and I'm trying to find an address on someone who may live in your area."

"Yes, Beau. You probably don't remember me, but I was a friend of your mom's. Gloria Waters."

"I sure do, Ms. Waters. How is your family? Is your husband doing OK now? I seem to remember that he had heart surgery right before Mom passed away."

"He's doing well. Thank you for asking, and please let me know how I can help you."

"I'm looking for a man whose legal name is Michael Murdoch, but he apparently uses an alias. I'm just not sure what that alias might be."

"I know exactly who you're talking about. He's a real complainer. Asking for the supervisor seems to make his day. The name he uses is Michael de Hugues. But, of course, he also has mail delivered to him in his real name."

"May I have his address?"

She hesitated. "I ordinarily wouldn't give it to you without an official request in writing, but since I know you, and you seem to be in a hurry—"

"Yes, ma'am. Someone's life is in danger."

"Hold on . . ." She came back on the line. "I have it right here . . ." She read it slowly for Beau. He glanced to Keely to be sure she was making a note of it on her phone. Keely gave him the thumbs up.

"Thanks so much, Ms. Waters. Please give your husband my regards."

"I will, Beau. Take care."

By the time he ended the call, Keely had already found the address on her GPS app.

"You'll take a right here." She pointed to the approaching intersection. "And then go four lights before you take a left. We're not far from there."

He put his foot on the accelerator and voice dialed a call to his office.

"Enoch."

"Chris, it's Beau. I have a strong lead, and I need backup. I'm on my way to the subject's house now."

"Where are you?"

"I'm almost to the Brentwood City Limits. And I'm on my way to the home of Michael Murdoch, alias Michael de Hugues." He recited the address from memory.

"Is this your POI in the cold case?"

"Yes, sir. And I have even more reason to believe he's the right guy. I just left the home of one of his former coworkers. She said she has always suspected that he was involved in the case—and even went to the authorities in 2000. But no one believed her back then." He took a breath. "She's the one who tipped me off to his alias. She identified him by the composite sketch."

"I'll alert the Williamson County Sheriff's Department. This address appears to be in the county but not inside Brentwood city limits."

"I would say you are correct, sir."

"Be careful. And don't go inside without backup."

Beau disconnected the call and glanced toward Keely. She was staring at him, her brown eyes moist. And her bottom lip was trembling.

"Never promise anything you can't keep," he said.

She nodded, and he held his hand out to her.

"This may be coming to an end," he said. "You may have your mom—and your dad—back soon."

She took his hand. "I just pray she's safe."

"We'll do our best to keep her that way," he said. "And I might as well tell you right now that I intend to go inside if necessary. But I need you to stay in the truck."

"We'll see," she said.

"You don't have any business in there, Keely. Let law enforcement handle this."

"First of all, she is my mom. Secondly, my dogs and I have been in some very dangerous situations. It's part of my job. And finally, I never make a promise I can't keep."

He tried to hide a smile. "You are something else, did you know that?"

She shrugged. "I like to think I'm my father's daughter. He didn't run from anything."

CHAPTER 36

Monday, January 17

Keely typed "Michael de Hugues Templars" into her online search engine and waited for the results. The first entry was enough to explain.

"This guy is interesting. It looks like 'Mr. Mike' takes his name from one of the real Grand Masters of the Knights Templar. Actually, the first Grand Master."

"So that's who he thinks he's related to?" Beau asked.

"Must be."

"Do you know much about those guys?"

She shook her head. "Not really. Didn't they defend Christianity or something?"

"Whatever they did, Murdoch sounds more like a nut. An amalgamation of ancient history and a contemporary clown."

"Creepy . . ." Keely said, typing in a search for the history of clowns. She read through several of the entries. "But . . . maybe not that unrelated. Did you know that twenty-four hundred years before Christ, clowns and priests had similar roles? It says that clowns often played a religious role in society, reinforcing values.

"And . . ." she continued to read, "one site says training as a clown was considered an important discipline, because it required a high level of risk to the performer."

"That fits Murdoch's profile," Beau said. "He enjoys risk-taking, or he wouldn't have stirred everything up again after twenty-two years." Beau glanced her way. "And from what Mrs. Arnold told us, he appears to be a real crusader for his own personal values."

"It's his way or the highway," Keely said. "That's why he and my dad clashed." She sobered. "But I'll never understand why Daddy couldn't win the fight. He was a soldier."

"He was protecting his children, Keely. He chose to be taken away by those men, so you and Levi would be safe."

She wiped a tear from her eye. "I've always known that. And it's one reason I love him so much, even after having only seven years with him."

"He would be very proud of—"

"That's it! Beau, that's his house." She snapped a picture of the large Victorian home. "He must have inherited it. You don't make that kind of money on a teacher's salary."

Beau slammed on his brakes.

"Do you see what I see?" she asked.

"Yes. It's a Williamson County Sheriff's car." He squinted. "It's my dad's car."

"That's why you couldn't reach him."

He shook his head. "I don't like the looks of this."

"What are you thinking?"

"I'm not sure." He pulled the truck off the road, putting a row of tall pine trees between it and the house. "I'm going to walk around those trees and along the side of that field. Maybe I can get the element of surprise. I'll leave the keys in the truck. If someone approaches, or I don't return soon, get out of here and call for help."

"I'm going with you."

"No, Keely. It's too dangerous. Stay here."

"And you'll do what if I don't?" She opened the truck door.

He frowned. "You know there's nothing I can do . . ."

"That's what I thought." She got out of the truck and quietly latched the door behind her.

"Remember . . . the keys are in the truck if something happens."

"Let's hope it doesn't," she said. "Your dad may already have this handled."

Beau grimaced. "I'm not so sure that's what's going on."

"What do you mean?"

"I don't know yet. Let's try to get within range of the house and find out what we can."

"I wonder where my mom is?"

"My best guess," he whispered, "is that she's in one of those upstairs rooms."

They walked to the far side of the pine trees, and then took a left, picking their way along the tree line running parallel to Murdoch's long and narrow front yard.

"The closer we get the creepier this place looks." Keely barely breathed the words.

They were nearing the front of the house when Beau pointed out a 2020 white Toyota Camry to the left. It was parked alongside Maggie's blue sedan, which hadn't been visible from the road.

Keely took a deep breath, trying to ease the pit in her stomach.

"According to my research team at the Bureau, he also owns a white 2010 Ford F-150 truck. I don't see it here."

He motioned for her to follow him along the right side of the house. The south facing windows were covered with thick curtains.

"Maybe he's gone," Keely whispered.

"Maybe—"

Keely heard voices coming from the back of the house. Beau must have heard them too because he waved her to the ground. Putting a finger to his lips, he hurried to the southeast corner of the house and pulled his gun from his holster.

Keely listened and watched, and in a few minutes, the voices emerged as two men, one pushing the other with a rifle to his back. The first man looked a lot like Beau's father. The man behind him must have been Murdoch. Or de Hugues, as he called himself.

So much for a clown. Now that she could see him, he looked more like a bully. Something pinged in her memory.

Murdoch was shouting now. "Get over there in front of the cistern!"

Beau's dad complied without speaking, stopping about six feet from the well, where he turned around to face his adversary.

"You threw Lambert's body in here?" J. G. broke his silence.

Keely recoiled. Her dad was buried in an old well? She fought the urge to jump up and go punch the man, but she knew too many lives were at stake, including her mother's. She continued to wait and watch from her position on the ground.

"It's over, Mike," J. G. continued. "The TBI knows who you are. And that's all your fault." He shook his head. "You wouldn't leave the dead man in his grave. You had to come back for more vengeance. After twenty-two years." He clicked his tongue. "Why?"

"Because they stole my life from me! Don't you understand? They have to pay."

"Who should pay?" J. G. didn't stop. "Lambert's wife who had no part in any of this? Or his seven-year-old daughter, who had no understanding?"

Keely bit her lip, fighting back tears.

Murdoch didn't flinch.

"Why don't you admit it, Mike?" J. G. went on. "You're the one who got yourself into this mess. Not them." He shook his head. "You're the fool. You had it all behind you. No one would have resurrected William Lambert's cold case, but you . . . you had to stir the coals."

"I don't trust you. Or anything you have to say." Murdoch cursed. "You're only trying to save your life. But it's too late." He poked J. G. in the chest with the gun.

Keely's focus returned to Beau. He took a small step to the right from where he had been standing motionless near the back corner of the house, almost straight ahead, slightly to the left, between her and the two men.

Keely knew he was waiting. Waiting to hear more of the conversation. But why? Hadn't they already heard enough to put Murdoch away forever?

She reminded herself to listen. And to memorize everything she could.

"You'll be with him soon," Murdoch said. "And then the only witness—or should I say accomplice—to his death will be gone. I'll have no one left to fear."

"But you're still going to hate, aren't you, Mike? Hate—and vengeance—has destroyed your life. You've allowed it to drive you insane."

Murdoch stepped back. "I'm not crazy. Don't you say that!"

"Crazy as a loon," Beau's father taunted. "In fact, I can get you off with a light charge, or no charge at all, if you'll let me."

"You're lying," Murdoch's face contorted. "You're lying, just like you lied when you said you didn't want me to kill Lambert." He laughed. "You wanted him dead, or you wouldn't have gone with me that day."

"That's not true," J. G. argued. "I told you I only wanted to rough him up. You're the one who decided to kill him."

Keely muffled a scream. Beau's dad was one of the men in the car that day? She glanced to Beau. He had to be devastated. Or had he suspected it all along? Their relationship had never been good.

Please, God, help Beau. Help me. And help my mom.

"That's enough!" Murdoch shouted. "You can plead your case to your Maker. He will sort it out. You can join Lambert in hell as far as I'm concerned. He never understood. And although I think you once did, you've allowed yourself to be tainted by man's law. Man's law and God's law are two different things."

"Just spare Maggie. That's all I ask," J. G. said.

Keely's heart stopped. Did he love her that much? Is that why he was here, to save her?

"Shoot me. But spare her. She's in no shape to witness against you."

"Don't you worry. She's my ticket," Murdoch said. "I don't care about her. I just want to get to her daughter. She's the reason for all of this. You know that."

It was true! Keely gasped.

She had always suspected it. Mrs. Arnold had alleged it. And now . . . she knew.

"She's responsible for a lot of things," Gardner said, "But you need to move on with your life. Why are you allowing her to destroy you?"

What had she done? Were these men delusional?

"TBI," Beau shouted, training his gun on Murdoch. "Put your hands up, Murdoch, and throw down the gun!"

Keely looked up. What had she missed?

Murdoch took a step back and turned toward Beau, pointing his rifle at him.

"Beau!" J. G. shouted. "Stay out of this. You'll get yourself killed."

"Move away, Dad."

"No!" Murdoch swiveled back around to J. G. "Don't you move, or I'll shoot . . . you and your son."

He turned again, pointing his rifle at Beau. When he pulled back the hammer, J. G. froze.

"Murdoch, I'm a special agent with the Tennessee Bureau of Investigation. I have backup on the way. You are under arrest for the murder of William Lambert."

"So, you heard my little confession? In that case, you're going to die, too, just like your father."

"No!" J. G. shouted and ran toward Murdoch.

The clown man turned and fired.

J. G. clutched his chest and fell to the ground.

Murdoch swiveled and took aim at Beau, but Beau fired first. The bullet pierced Murdoch's shoulder, and the clown man groaned, covering his wound with his hand. He stared at Beau momentarily and then turned and ran.

Beau took off after him, but Murdoch had too great of a lead. He jumped into J. G.'s cruiser, started the engine, and backed all the way out of his driveway, nearly three hundred yards. Once at the main road, he stopped, changed gears, and sped away with the car's blue lights blazing.

CHAPTER 37

Monday, January 17

Beau ran to his dad, knelt, and lifted his torso, cradling the older man in his arms. Blood drained from the wound in his chest. Beau silently prayed as he covered it with his hand. "Dad! Can you hear me?"

J. G. Gardner opened his eyes.

"Mag—Maggie is upstairs. Take good care . . . of her."

"I will, Dad."

His father's breathing turned ragged. "I'm proud of you, son . . ."

Beau fought back tears—and bitterness. "I am . . . I'm proud of you too, Dad. Thank you for coming here to save Maggie."

His dad shook his head. "Don't be proud of me. I've been wrong . . . for too long." He strained to get the words out. "But I love you and Emma. I always have." He closed his eyes.

"Dad!"

Keely knelt beside them, and J. G. opened his eyes again. They were filled with love, not hate.

"I'm sorry for all of the pain I've caused you," he said, reaching for her hand. "Maggie raised a good girl. Please take care of my son."

Keely nodded, tears running down her cheeks. "I—I will, sir."

"I never meant for it to end that way. Please . . ." He coughed. "Please know that. Murdoch . . ." He grimaced. "Murdoch shot him before I knew what was happening."

He looked to his son. "And I ran. I *ran.*" Tears filled the older man's eyes. "I could never forgive myself."

"But I forgive you," she said.

J. G. smiled and his eyes closed for the last time.

Beau struggled to maintain his composure. He lowered his father to the ground, as Keely sobbed beside him. Beau gathered his strength, stood, and took Keely's hand. He pulled her up and into his arms.

"Backup will be here in a few minutes," he whispered.

She nodded.

Almost instantaneously, they were surrounded by men wearing uniforms, and Keely pulled away.

"TBI," Beau said, holding his badge in the air.

One of the men moved closer, checking Beau's badge, and then signaled the others. It was at that point he recognized J. G.

"It's your dad?"

Beau nodded. "We need to check the house. The suspect left in Dad's squad car, with Dad's rifle, but there's an older woman inside the house." He gestured toward Keely. "Her mother, Margaret Lambert. Margaret has memory issues. I'd like to go inside with you. She knows me."

"Yes, sir," the deputy said.

"Please have one of your men stay with Keely." Beau turned to her. "I'll be right back. I don't want you going inside until we're sure the house is safe."

She reached for him. "Be careful."

He nodded and hurried to the back door of the house with his gun drawn and three deputies from the Williamson County Sheriff's Department behind him. He slowly opened the door, looked around, and then stepped inside what looked to be the mudroom.

Beau motioned for one of the men with him to turn left into the dining room, and for another to go straight down the hall. Beau and another deputy turned right into the kitchen.

The kitchen, just like the mudroom, looked to be immaculate. Murdoch was likely OCD. Taken to the extreme, it could be part of what was driving his criminal tendencies. The need to order the world in the fashion he preferred. Or more like, required. And it didn't matter what toll it took on others.

Beau motioned to the left toward the staircase hall, hurried into it, and took another left to a place where he could get a visual on the other two men who were both now in the main hall.

"Nothing in there," the man who had gone through the dining room said. "I have a feeling the woman is upstairs."

Beau nodded, and he—with the three men behind him—started climbing the stairs. He stopped every few steps to listen. Nothing.

After reaching the top, he gestured for one man to go right and another to go straight. He and the third man took a left.

An arched window anchored the end of the hall, with two rooms on either side. Beau's partner turned right, and he turned left.

Slowly opening the chamber door, he saw Margaret Lambert lying inside on the bed. She was bound and gagged.

He hurried to her. "Maggie!"

She appeared to recognize him immediately, her eyes widening.

"Are you hurt?" He holstered his gun.

She shook her head.

He quickly removed the gag. "Are you OK?"

"I'm OK."

He unbound her hands, and then her feet.

"Thank you," she whispered.

"He's gone, Maggie. You don't have to be afraid."

Tears welled up in her eyes.

"Keely and Gigi are OK. And you're OK."

She nodded.

"Can you walk?"

She made an effort to lift her head and shoulder off the pillow.

"Let me help you." Beau wrapped his arms around her shoulders—just as he had done with his dying father moments ago—and sat her up with her feet dangling off the side of the bed. One of the sheriff's deputies stepped into the room to assist him and, with one of them on each side of her, they walked her down the stairs. At the bottom, an EMT directed them to the triage area they had set up in the parlor.

"I think she's OK," he said. "I'll get her daughter. That will help her more than anything."

Beau hurried down the hall and out the back door to look for Keely. She was watching two men zip his father's body into a body bag.

"Your mom is fine. Come inside so you can sit with her." He reached to take her hand. "You don't need to be here for this."

"I'm OK." She looked up at him. "He died a hero, Beau."

"Maybe." It was all he could say.

"He wanted to save you . . ."

"I could have done it without him."

She took his hand and started walking with him toward the back of the house. Then she stopped, finding his gaze, and holding it.

"Let him die in peace, so you can live in peace."

He nodded. "Your mom is in the parlor." He pointed her in the right direction, and she hurried down the hall. Momentarily, he heard Maggie crying. No doubt tears of joy upon seeing her daughter.

"I'm sorry, Beau." Sheriff's Deputy Russell Wallace appeared from behind and placed his hand on Beau's shoulder.

Beau turned. "Thank you."

"While they're assessing Maggie Lambert, let's step into the library and debrief."

Beau nodded and followed Wallace down the hall, taking a right into the library. Wallace waited for him and closed the door. "Do you need an attorney?" he asked.

"No." Beau took a chair. "Murdoch killed my father."

"Can you tell me what happened?"

Beau started with his and Keely's conversation at Frances Arnold's house, mentioned his call with Chris Enoch at the Bureau, and then detailed his call to the post office.

"We put everything together, piece by piece, eventually finding our way here."

Wallace wrote while Beau spoke.

"When we got here, we saw Dad's squad car at the top of the driveway, near the house."

"It's not here. Where is it?"

"Murdoch took it when he ran."

Wallace nodded and continued to take notes.

"I didn't want to step into the middle of something already going down and put my dad or Maggie Lambert in more danger, so I parked my truck at the road. Keely and I walked through the field over here"—he pointed to the south side of the property—"trying to remain unnoticed."

Beau thought about the next few minutes.

"As we approached the back of the house, we heard voices. I motioned for Keely to lie flat on the ground. Then I pulled my weapon and moved forward, taking cover behind the corner of the house. From there, I was able to watch everything unfold."

"OK. Go on."

"Murdoch had a rifle to my dad's back, which I believe was Dad's rifle, a Winchester 94."

Russell shook his head and continued with his note taking.

"Murdoch walked Dad from the back of the house to a cistern in the backyard, near where you found his body."

Wallace nodded.

"Murdoch told my dad that he was going to shoot him and put his body in the cistern on top of the body of . . . of William Lambert."

Wallace looked up.

"Yes," Beau said. "We may have finally resolved that case."

"I'm so sorry that Keely . . ."

"She's handling it OK." Beau exhaled. "I waited until what I thought was the right time, and then I stepped away from the house. I had my gun drawn and fixed on Murdoch. He turned and pointed the rifle at me. When he pulled back the hammer, Dad jumped him, trying to save me."

"And he took the bullet."

"Yes," Beau said. "Murdoch shot him at close range. After that, Murdoch turned toward me again. But before he could get off another shot, I fired my weapon, sending a bullet into his left arm."

Wallace studied Beau as he spoke.

"He stared at me for as much as a minute, almost like he was in disbelief, and then he took off running. I didn't want to shoot again, thinking I had a chance to run him down—after all he's twice my age. But he climbed into Dad's car and took off. He backed that squad car all the way to the road, skidded to a stop, and then took off north."

Wallace put his pen down. "I'm glad you and Keely are safe. I understand that Maggie is OK too."

"Yes." Beau nodded. "We're fortunate. It could have been much worse."

"How bad do you think you hurt Murdoch?"

"It was at least a twenty-five-yard shot—and he had the advantage with that rifle—but my bullet penetrated. I'm sure of that. He was bleeding, although I don't think it was a critical wound. He can probably dress it himself."

"Any idea where he might run?"

"I don't know, Russ. But I don't think he'll go far. One of the last things he said was that he wanted to get to Keely."

Wallace sat upright. "Why?"

Beau contemplated how much to tell of the story. It was now up to him—and Keely—to let his dad die a hero. Or to tell the whole truth.

CHAPTER 38

Monday, January 17

"Keely, would you please step into the library with Officer Wallace? He needs to ask you a few questions." Beau beckoned her inside.

"Sure," she said and then hesitated.

"I'll sit with your mom."

"OK."

Deputy Russell Wallace waited for her just inside the pocket doors. "I'll be brief. I know you want to get back to your mother."

She nodded. "Thank you."

"Take a seat."

She looked around the room. Floor to ceiling bookcases—complete with a rolling ladder—lined the far wall. To her left, a large window looked out past the columns of the Victorian porch to the mansion's tree-lined front lawn. And to her right, strange symbols, pictures of clowns, and odd photos from the eleventh or twelfth century covered the wall.

"Unusual art, isn't it?" Deputy Wallace raised an eyebrow.

"Very. But from what little I know he is an unusual man."

"Tell me what you know, Keely."

"Where do you want me to start?"

"From the beginning, as much as you know."

"Wow . . . OK." She took a seat in a red velveteen chair and then thought twice about it. "Maybe I should sit over here." She moved to the straight chair next to the desk where Wallace sat. "Apparently my first recollection of Mike Murdoch should start when I was six years old, but I can't recall it. At least not right now.

When I saw him again this afternoon, something clicked. But I can't quite grasp what it is."

"That's OK." Wallace's face was fatherly. "Tell me what you do know."

Keely turned to look out the window. "Beau and I were in Leiper's Fork earlier today. We were posting flyers with Mike Murdoch's photo and description on them, asking people if they had seen him or knew who he was. I happened to think that Frances Arnold, our elementary school teacher, might know him." She turned back to Wallace. "She knows everybody and everything in town."

"That she does." He chuckled.

"Mrs. Arnold recognized him immediately. She said, 'That's Michael Murdoch, who used to teach at Hillsboro School.'"

"She's sharp."

"Yes . . ." Keely continued. "But it was what she said next that stunned us. She said my dad was responsible for Mr. Murdoch losing his job more than twenty years ago." Keely blinked. "Then she said she had always thought Murdoch was the man who was behind my dad's disappearance."

Wallace looked up from his notes. "Did she say why?"

"She said it had to do with me. That I had told my dad something Mr. Murdoch had said or done . . . and that Daddy called the principal and the school board. She said, eventually Mr. Murdoch was let go."

"But you don't remember any of that?"

She shook her head. "Not really. Not yet . . ."

If she could only remember.

"Mrs. Arnold went on to say that Mike Murdoch had always been rather eccentric—that's my word, not hers—and that he had grand notions about his lineage dating back to the Knights Templar. I looked it up on the way over here. That would have been during the time of the Crusades in the beginning of the Second Millennium."

Wallace looked at the display on the wall behind her. "Now all of that makes sense."

"Yes," Keely said. "She also told us that he had taken a pseudonym and moved away, but she wasn't sure where."

"You obviously found him. What did you do next?"

"We decided to call the post office . . . and the postmaster knew him. She sent us here."

"And when you got here, Beau's dad was already here?"

"Yes." She studied her hands in her lap. "I hate what happened."

"Did you see everything?"

"Yes."

"Those things are traumatic, Keely. If you need counseling, we can arrange for it. Even our most seasoned officers reach out to counselors when they've been involved in a violent intervention."

"I appreciate that, Deputy Wallace. And I will consider it. But I have also seen a lot of things in my work." She hesitated and looked away. "I'll think about it . . ."

"OK," he said. "Let's keep going. So, you and Beau drove up to the house, saw the sheriff's department vehicle, and decided to approach on foot?"

"Yes. And, for the record, Beau didn't want me to get out of the truck, but I insisted."

Wallace nodded. "Did you know your mother was in the house?"

"We assumed so, because the composite sketch Mrs. Arnold identified was the same man behind the clown suit. Michael Murdoch, or Michael de Hugues, as he called himself, was dressed as Mr. Mike the clown the night he abducted my mom at Levi's house. As you know my aunt Gigi was a witness."

"Why do you think J. G. Gardner was already here?"

"Beau and I haven't had time to talk about it, but I assumed it was because he had seen the sketch—Beau said he sent it to him—and recognized Mr. Murdoch."

Wallace continued writing and didn't look up. "What happened after you got to the house?"

"We heard voices. Beau told me to take cover on the ground—in that field." She pointed behind her. "Then he pulled out his gun and sprinted to the side of the house. From my vantage point, I could see everything."

"Did you hear everything?"

"Maybe," she said. "I heard quite a bit."

"Go on."

"The voices got louder and then two men walked into view. I presumed they were coming from the house, since they were walking away from the house. The first man was being held at gunpoint. A rifle, I think. And the second man was shouting at him."

She stopped and visualized the scene. "The first man seemed to be trying to talk the second man down. Naturally, he was trying to convince the second man—who was Mr. Murdoch—not to shoot him. But Mr. Murdoch laughed and said he was going to bury him in the cistern."

She wiped a tear from her cheek. "I'm sorry . . ."

"Take your time," Wallace said.

"Then Mr. Murdoch said he had buried my dad in the cistern. *In the cistern!* Can you believe that? I was outraged, and I wanted to get up and run to him, and . . . I wanted to confront him and ask him why he had killed my father. But I knew it wasn't the right thing to do. There were too many lives at stake, my mother's included."

"Good for you."

"So, I waited to see how everything would play out. And I prayed for it to end peacefully." She looked up. "I'm not sure why, but I got lost in the moment. My mind just kind of refocused. Probably because something had clicked inside me, but I wasn't sure what . . . And the next thing I know Beau was confronting Mr. Murdoch. He told him he was with the TBI and that backup was on the way. He told him he was under arrest."

"Did Mr. Murdoch comply?"

"No. He pointed his gun at Beau and started to pull the trigger. Or, at least, that's what I think happened. It happened so fast . . . and I was probably twenty-five yards away. More or less."

She looked down and then back to Deputy Wallace.

"Can you tell me what happened then?"

"Yes," she said. "Beau's dad jumped Mr. Murdoch, so his son wouldn't be shot and . . . and he was shot instead."

"I'm really sorry, Keely. I know this is hard."

She nodded. "It was awful." She wiped her eyes. "Beau shot at Mr. Murdoch and wounded him, but Murdoch ran to the sheriff's car and drove away. I watched the car back down the drive and take off on the main road to the north. It was after that when I jumped up and ran to Beau and his dad."

"Did Deputy Gardner say anything to you or Beau before he died?"

She nodded. "He asked me to take care of Beau. Then he settled a few things with Beau. He told him he loved him and his daughter, Emma. And he apologized for not having lived a perfect life." She looked away. "But you know, as far as I'm concerned, he died a hero, trying to save my mom . . . and Beau."

Wallace stood. "Thank you. I'm sorry, again, that I had to put you through this. And I'm glad your mom is OK."

"Thanks," she said. "I—I'm ready to take her home now if I can."

"Let's walk in there together. I need to talk to Beau again, and we'll check on your mom and see if we can wrap this up." He walked toward the pocket doors. "If you think of anything else you need to tell me, you have my card."

"Yes, sir. I will call you."

He studied her. "You're a strong and forgiving woman."

"Why would you say that?"

"Today would have been difficult for anybody. But you're standing here holding it together, knowing it may not be the last time you see Murdoch."

"Beau told you what he said about me?"

"Yes."

"I'm not scared of him," she said.

"Why?"

"I'm not sure." She looked away. "I think there's part of me that wants to confront him for what he has done to my family." She focused on the deputy again. "Just like my dad did. And this time everybody will know who he is. And he won't get away."

CHAPTER 39

Monday, January 17

Beau walked toward a mostly purple-colored sky. Only a few streaks of orange remained, where the sun had disappeared below the horizon. Wallace had offered to give him a ride to his truck, but he needed time to think. And to call Emma. He didn't want her to hear the news from anyone else.

At least for now they had kept the press away. But after Wallace filed his report tomorrow, the news would break.

He dialed Emma's number.

"Hey, bro."

"Hi, sis . . ."

"What's wrong?"

"Is Devon there with you?"

"Yes . . . Beau? Tell me what's wrong."

"Dad passed away."

"No!" She screamed. "What happened?"

"He was killed in the line of duty."

"Mom always knew that would happen—"

"He's with her now, Emma."

She broke down, and Beau could hear talking in the background.

"What's going on?" It was Devon.

"Dad was killed today. He was trying to make an arrest."

"Oh, man . . . Beau. I'm so sorry."

"I was with him when he died. Please tell Emma he said he loved her."

"I will." Devon sighed. "How did it happen that you were there?"

"He was killed by the man who put the tracker on Emma's car. But I don't want Emma to know that right now. Give her time before you tell her. She has enough to take in at the moment."

"I agree," Devon said. "Did you get the guy?"

"No."

"Oh, man."

"While I don't think he will bother Emma—or Connor—again, you need to be cautious. I've asked the Williamson County Sheriff's Department to keep an eye on your house. Do you think you can keep Emma at home until the funeral? I'm hoping we will catch up with him by then, or at least have some idea about where he is before he hurts someone else."

"You can count on it. I'll tell her we need to stay home for the kids. I can work from here for a few days. So, who do you think he's after?"

"Keely. I heard the words straight from his mouth."

"Beau, I'm so sorry. She doesn't need anything else on her right now. Tell her our prayers are with her."

"I will." Beau climbed into his truck. He engaged the engine and shifted into drive.

"It sounds like you're rolling," Devon said.

"I'm on my way to pick up Keely so we can meet her mom at the hospital. Maggie was found safe, but they transported her by ambulance to check her out."

"I'll tell Emma. She's been worried."

"Please tell her that I'll call her later, if she's up to it."

"I'm sure she'll want to talk to you," Devon said. "We're glad you're safe. Take care of yourself."

"Will do."

Keely was waiting with Wallace when Beau pulled up to the house. Wallace opened the passenger side door for Keely to climb inside.

"You two stay safe," he said, holding the door. "Call me if you need me, Beau."

"I'll check in with you soon about dad's arrangements," Beau said.

Wallace nodded.

"Deputy Wallace," Keely spoke. "When can we pick up Mom's car?"

"We need to go over it first," Wallace said. "And, by the way, Beau, we found a tracker under the front left fender."

"So that's how he—"

"Knew she was at Levi's house the night he took her?" Wallace finished Beau's sentence. "Yes. I had wondered about that myself." He closed Keely's door. "Have a good night."

Beau put the truck in reverse and started backing down the drive.

Two hours later, when they pulled into Maggie's driveway. Gigi flew out the door to meet them. Peter followed closely behind her.

"The whole family's here, Mom." Keely pointed to her siblings, and Maggie smiled. "You're tired, aren't you? We'll get you to bed as soon as we get you inside."

After Maggie was in bed, Gigi suggested coffee.

"Do you have any more of that chicken salad?" Keely asked.

"My goodness, haven't you kids eaten supper? I sure do. Peter, can you help me in the kitchen? We need to get these two fed."

Peter got up from his chair and followed his sister.

"How are you feeling?" Beau turned to Keely.

"Exhausted. Anxious. Maybe a little worried. How are you?"

"I'm OK. Emma didn't take the news very well, but she'll get through it with Devon and the kids there to help her. By the way, Devon said to tell you that they would be praying for you."

"Me?"

"I told him that Murdoch got away."

Keely shrugged. "He'll be found. I'm confident of it."

"You're anxious about your dad, aren't you?"

She nodded. "I can't get it off my mind that his body has been in that cistern for over twenty years. I want to give him a hero's burial."

Beau didn't speak.

"What's wrong?" she asked.

"We're both planning funerals for our fathers at the same time. That doesn't seem real, does it?"

She stood and walked to the sofa where he was sitting. "God will get us through it, Beau."

He turned to her. "What did you tell Wallace?"

She took a seat next to him. "The truth . . ."

Beau nodded.

She continued. "That your dad died a hero's death."

"You didn't . . . ?"

"No. Did you?"

He hesitated and then shook his head. "I conveniently left that out. It just didn't seem—"

"Relevant."

"Is that the word?" He asked.

"It is as far as I'm concerned," she said.

"How can you forgive him so easily, Keely?"

She grew quiet. "He died trying to save my mother." She shrugged. "That doesn't make up for his part in my father's death, but he asked for my forgiveness, and I owe it to him. You need to forgive him too."

"I'm not sure I can."

"You're making progress. You only told Wallace what was appropriate. A dying man's conversation with his son should remain private."

Beau took her hand. "My family has . . ."

"Your family has been responsible for good things and bad things, just like the rest of us. But you're one of their greatest achievements, Beau. And your dad knew that."

"Hey, kids, the food is ready." Gigi walked into the living room with plates in her hand. Peter followed with drinks.

"It looks great," Beau said. "Thank you."

"So, tell us about your day."

Keely looked to him and nodded. "The main thing is that we got Mom back."

"Don't you know I'm grateful! Thank you, Lord!" Gigi threw her hands in the air. "I was feeling so guilty about that."

"Gigi, get over yourself," Peter said. "None of us is perfect."

Beau winked at Keely, and she smiled.

"But as soon as you finish eating, we'd like to hear the details."

"I'll go first," Keely said, munching on a carrot stick.

She told them about meeting with Frances Arnold, Beau's conversation with the woman at the post office, and what she had found online on their way to Murdoch's house.

"Who knew somebody like that lived around here?" Gigi said.

Beau took over from there. "My dad's cruiser was in the driveway when we got to Murdoch's house. He had gone on his own to make the arrest, and he was somehow overpowered by Murdoch."

He collected his thoughts. And his words. "Dad . . . was shot and killed."

"Beau!" Gigi's hands flew to her chest. "I'm so sorry."

"I appreciate it, Gigi."

"I'm sorry too, son," Peter said. "Losing your father is not easy."

"Keely knows something about that." Beau glanced her way.

She nodded. "We also found out what happened to Dad."

"Oh, honey . . ." Gigi wrung her hands. "Please tell us."

Keely looked to Beau. He nodded. "We overheard Murdoch telling J. G. that Dad's body was buried in the cistern."

"Oh, Keely. Does Maggie know?"

"No. She also doesn't know about my dad. We didn't think it was a good time to tell her," Beau said.

"That's just too much for her to take in at once," Gigi said. "It won't be easy for her."

CHAPTER 40

Tuesday, January 18

The next morning, Keely filled Adam in on the details of Maggie's rescue, while waiting for Beau to pick her up. When he arrived, the two of them hurried to meet him.

Adam stuck out his hand and then pulled Beau into a man hug. "I'm sorry to hear about your dad."

"Thanks," Beau said. "We had quite the day yesterday. Has Keely told you about her dad too?"

Adam nodded. "When do you think you'll know for sure?"

Beau put his arm around Keely's shoulders. "We have a crew there today."

Keely's breath caught in her throat. "I can't believe it." She fanned her face. "I'm anxious and grateful at the same time."

"Let me know how it goes, Keely," Adam said, as she climbed into Beau's Colorado. "And don't worry about the kennel. You have a lot to do today."

She nodded. "I appreciate it."

As soon as they started rolling, Keely turned to Beau. "Where are we going first? My mom's house?"

"That's what I had planned. Then we need to pick Emma up. Our appointment at the funeral home is at one thirty."

Keely checked her watch. "And after that?"

"We'll take Emma home and see what happens."

"If they find him today, what happens next?"

"They will take his remains to the Medical Examiners Lab and do an autopsy."

"What can they tell after twenty-two years?"

"Probably quite a bit. Science has come a long way."

"How he was killed?"

"Yes, probably."

"That's incredible," she said, and then took a deep breath. "I hope it brings peace."

"I hope so too." He reached to take her hand. "You and Levi deserve it. And I hope your mom understands."

"Levi and I had a long talk this morning. He's as relieved as I am about it. In many ways, though, I think he's most relieved for me. Because he doesn't remember dad, the need to find him it hasn't been as critical for him." She turned to Beau. "He wanted me to tell you that he's thankful for all you are doing."

"You know how I feel about that," Beau said. "I'm honored that I can help your family find closure."

She studied him. "You love your work, don't you?"

Even before he spoke, the smile on his face said it all. "I love what I do, and I work with some of the greatest people in the world." He turned to her. "When all of this is behind us, I would like for you and me to go out with Jake and Hannah."

"That would be fun. I feel awful that I missed her set Saturday night."

"I'm sure she understood."

"Can you believe so much has happened in three days?" Keely leaned back into her seat. "Is that why I'm so tired?"

Beau squeezed her hand. "Do you know what you're going to say to your mom this morning?"

She shrugged. "I'll only tell her about your dad. We don't know anything else for sure until we find my dad's body."

"I agree." He grimaced.

"What are you not telling me? I can see it in your face," Keely asked.

"They found Dad's cruiser last night."

"Where?"

"About a mile from Levi's house."

"Let me guess. He dumped it and left in his pick-up truck, which had been waiting since he stole Mom's car on Saturday night."

"That would be my guess. But we're still not sure where he had the truck parked. There were no truck tire tracks near the cruiser."

"That guy is a magician." She thought about what she had just said. "Of course, he is. He's a clown. A master illusionist. Just like what I read online."

"I'd be more likely to call him a con artist."

Keely laughed. "Mrs. Arnold called it voodoo religion. But I call it creepy."

"Yes." He nodded.

She twisted in her seat. "Beau! I just realized something. Is Murdoch's truck white, like his car?"

"Yes. It's a white Ford F-150 Lariat, or at least that's what is registered in his name."

"Of course, it is. The truck I saw him drive away in at Emma's house the day of the party was white. And his car is white, too, right?"

"Yes. You saw it. A 2020 Toyota Camry."

"This is so obvious now that I know it. That's why my mom doesn't like white cars."

"You didn't tell me she didn't like white cars."

"I didn't think it was important until now. But—and I can't believe I just realized this—she must have been referencing Murdoch's car. And maybe his truck too."

Beau looked her way. "That makes sense. He was probably stalking her long before her accident."

"Before both accidents," Keely said.

"Yes."

"And remember, in the restaurant that day when she said she saw him? It could be that she saw a white car—or even *his* white car—go by."

"Maybe."

"Beau!" Keely's heart went to her stomach. "Do you have a picture of him? Like a real picture, not the sketch?"

"I do. We have an APB/BOLO out on him. It has been uploaded to our most-wanted page."

She typed "TBI most wanted" into the search engine and the link came up immediately. She clicked on the link, and there he was. The man who had waited on her at the toy store. "You're not going to believe this."

"Try me."

"I bought Connor's birthday gift from him."

He swiveled in her direction. "What was the name of the store?"

"The Unique Toy Store, near the Galleria," she said. "I knew there was something funny about him that day at the store. Of course, I had no idea who he was or what he looked like, but when I picked out the stuffed dog and took it to the register, he said, 'He's going to like this,' and I asked him how he knew I was buying for a boy."

"What did he say?"

"Something about having just bought one for his grandson, so he had assumed." She turned to look out the window. "God has protected me from him so many times."

"And He will again," Beau said, turning into Maggie's driveway.

They were about to get out of the truck when Beau's phone rang. "Gardner."

Keely waited, holding her breath.

"You did." He looked at her. "OK . . . Let me know."

He ended the call and slipped the phone into his pocket. "That was one of my guys on our forensics crew." He reached his hand out to her. "They found human remains in the cistern."

Keely covered her face with the palms of her hands. Then, grabbing her stomach, she rocked back and forth silently. Was she going to be sick? She forced herself to breathe and tried to settle her mind.

It was him. After all these years.

He had been waiting for her to find him. And now . . . she had.

Beau reached to lay his hand on her back but didn't speak. A few minutes later, she sat up and stared out the front window of his truck. Finally, she turned to Beau.

"It may not be him, Keely. Wait until we get DNA evidence."

She shook her head. "It's him. I know it is." She bit her bottom lip to keep it from trembling. "And I thank God for finally letting my family have him back."

The tears finally came. After all these years, they were free to fall. And she was free to grieve. She had held it back for so long, waiting and wondering.

But she finally had her answer.

Beau sat with her in the truck for another few minutes before they went inside. Gigi was waiting for them at the door.

"Is everything all right?" she asked. "I saw you out there, but I didn't want to bother you."

"They found my dad's remains." Keely spoke so softly her aunt had to ask her to repeat what she had said. Then she nodded, and her eyes filled with tears.

Gigi put her arms around Keely's shoulders and escorted her into the living room, where Maggie waited in her favorite chair. But something was different. Today she was singing, more like humming, an old gospel song.

Keely turned to her aunt with a puzzled expression.

Gigi nodded. "She's been singing all morning. Somehow, I think she knows."

Keely looked to Beau, who appeared to also be on the verge of tears. He walked around the women to the sofa and took a seat in his usual place. Keely went directly to her mother's chair and kneeled beside her.

"How are you today, Mama?"

"OK," Maggie said, but she didn't turn to look at Keely. Instead, she stayed focused on something in front of her. Something in the distance. Something no one else could see.

"What are you singing?" Keely asked.

"'Amazing Grace'," she said, turning to her daughter. "I was once lost. But I'm now found."

Keely knew the words weren't exactly right, but the meaning was there. She took her mom's hands and cupped them in her own. "Mom, they found Daddy's body today. We can give him a proper burial now."

A tear ran down Maggie's cheek. "Good," she said.

The irony wasn't lost on Keely or anyone in the room. Maggie hadn't said, "OK," as she usually did. She had said "good," because the news was much better than just OK. It was probably the best news they could have gotten today. Or any day for the last twenty-two years.

Her daddy was coming home.

July 6, 2000

Levi walked back and forth, from one end of the glass case to the other, contemplating the multi- colored buckets of ice cream. But Keely's concern was with her dad. When it was time for her to choose, she asked for a strawberry sundae.

After contemplating his choices, Levi settled on a vanilla cone. Keely gave the ten-dollar bill to the clerk, who smiled and returned her change.

She stashed the money in her pocket, walked her brother to the door, and hurried him around the corner where the black car was waiting to take them home.

But the car was gone. And their dad was nowhere to be found.

CHAPTER 41

Wednesday, January 19

Beau opened the truck door for Keely. She had put one very difficult thing behind her. It was now his turn.

"I'm sure you're happy with the way that went." He slowly backed out of Maggie's driveway.

"I think she somehow knew," Keely said.

"I don't know how she could have. But that whole scene was unreal." He glanced toward her. "I'm glad you didn't mention Dad. It would have been too much today."

"She was at peace. And I couldn't risk taking that away from her. Not today."

"You can tell her in due time."

"Yes. Eventually." She turned to him. "So, when do you think you'll have your dad's funeral?"

"Either Thursday or Friday. That's what the funeral director told me when I called yesterday."

"How much did you tell Emma yesterday?"

He hesitated. "I told her the truth. Without all the unnecessary details."

"I'm proud of you, Beau."

He shook his head. "I don't understand how you can be so quick to forgive."

"It's God's way. I had no choice but to follow it." She reached out to him. "And I'm at peace with it."

"Good."

"I hope you and Emma can agree on the arrangements. That will help you."

"I do too," he said. "As soon as we have worked out the details, I will call Russell Wallace and ask for a minimal police escort."

"Is that something the family can request?"

"I don't see why not."

Thirty minutes later, Beau turned into Emma's drive. Both Devon and Emma were in the front yard. Devon had baby Jessie in his arms.

"Where's Connor?" Beau asked.

"Watching cartoons."

"It's better than video games," Emma said. "This stay-at-home thing can get tiring fast."

Devon chuckled. "It has only been a day."

"Yes. But they'd only been back in school for a couple of weeks. Christmas vacation and that birthday party sent me over the edge."

"Climb inside, grumpy sister," Beau said and then winked at Devon. "We'll keep her for a while so you can have a break, Devon."

"Very funny." Emma leaned in to kiss the baby and then her husband.

"Love you. Be careful," he said.

Keely slid closer to Beau, and Emma climbed into the front seat.

"How are you, Keely?" Emma asked.

"I'm doing alright."

"I hope your sweet mama is holding up through all of this. I was sorry to hear the news about your dad."

"Thanks," Keely said. "Mom is doing remarkably well. And I'm sorry you're going through the same thing."

"Unfortunately." Emma looked down and then to Beau. "Can we talk about the arrangements before we get to the funeral home?"

"Of course."

"I would like for him to have a full military funeral."

Beau glanced to Keely and then to his sister. "I'm all right with that."

"Oh . . . good. Thank you. He was always so proud of his military service."

"I agree."

"Will you be the one who arranges for the police procession?"

"What do you mean?"

"You know, when an officer dies in the line of duty, fellow officers usually pay final tribute to them."

"I don't want to do that, Emma."

"Why not?"

When he didn't answer, she turned to Keely. "Don't you think that would be the thing to do?"

"Me? I'm staying out of this," Keely said, putting her hand up. "This sounds like a family disagreement, and I don't have a vote in the matter."

"That was a cop out." Beau chuckled.

"Beau, that wasn't nice," Emma scolded. "Do you agree with him or me, Keely?"

"No. Not going there."

"Well, somebody has to break the tie."

"Good idea," Beau said. "Daddy will."

"What does that mean?" Emma asked.

"He didn't want that kind of thing, Em."

"How do you know that?"

"I promise you. I know."

"*How* do you know?" she insisted.

"Because he expressed a lot of regret to me before he died. He said he was sorry for the way he had handled things in his life. And he regretted not doing some things he should have done."

"Beauregard Gardner, are you taking revenge on Daddy for all the disagreements you had with him? This is not the right time to get even." She crossed her arms and stared at him.

"That's not even close to the truth, is it Keely?"

"Actually . . . I can take Beau's side on that last point, Emma. They cleared the air."

"Daddy and I made our peace, Em. I promise."

His sister uncrossed her arms. "Well, it had better be. However, I still don't understand why we can't have the police procession."

They rode in silence for the next few minutes, and when they arrived at the funeral home, Beau dropped Emma and Keely at the front door before finding a parking place. Once stopped, he took the time to check his messages, hoping he had received an ID on the remains from the cistern.

He did have a message from his office, but it wasn't what he had hoped. Instead, it confirmed that partial prints on the second tracking device matched those on the first. Similarly, the second device came back as unregistered.

The best news was that those same partial prints matched full prints taken from Murdoch's house. Michael Murdoch was not only J. G. Gardner's killer and Maggie's abductor, but he was also the owner of the two tracking devices. Murdoch would be put away for years once they found him.

Beau tucked his phone into his pocket and joined the women inside. A while later, as they finished up with the funeral director, a call came in from Christopher Enoch. Beau took it and walked into the other room.

"Gardner, I want to offer my condolences," Enoch said. "Losing your father is a hard one. And I understand that you're now without both parents?"

"Yes, sir. Thank you. I'm glad I was with him when he passed."

"I understand he was a hero. You should be proud."

"My dad didn't consider himself a hero, sir."

"The real ones never do," Enoch said before switching gears. "I'm also calling to congratulate you on your good work on the Lambert case. Based on dental records, we have tentatively confirmed the identity of the remains in Murdoch's cistern as those of William Lambert. Final confirmation is pending DNA test results."

"Thank you, sir."

Now to tell Keely.

Beau put his phone away and went to find the girls.

"Here he is," Emma said. "Beau, we need to sign paperwork and then we'll be finished."

He followed the two women into the funeral director's office and took a seat at a small table.

"Who will be signing?" he asked.

Emma looked to Beau. "You're the eldest."

"I don't mind doing it," he said. "Are both of you happy with the choices you've made?"

"Yes, it will be a nice service," Emma said.

Keely nodded.

Beau quickly read through the two-page contract, signed his name, and slid the paperwork across the table.

The funeral director saw his signature and looked up. "I'm so sorry . . . but I just realized that you're Beauregard Gardner." His emphasis was on Beau's first name.

Where was he going with this?

"We had the strangest inquiry yesterday. A man called and asked if we were the funeral home in charge of the Beauregard Gardner funeral."

"What did you tell him?"

"I didn't take the call, but the person who did said, 'No, but we have the J. G. Gardner funeral.' Is your dad's first name Beauregard by any chance?"

"No, sir. It's not." Beau looked at Emma. She shook her head.

"It must have been a strange mix-up," the funeral director said. "It was just odd."

"Do you happen to have the caller information?" Beau asked.

"I don't think so. But our receptionist took the call, let me check with her."

A minute later, the man reentered the room. "No. She said the caller ID was blocked."

"Thanks for letting me know." Beau's phone rang. "Excuse me." He answered and stepped out of the room.

"Hey, Beau. It's Jake. I was sorry to hear about your dad. You're in the middle of a rough patch."

"Thanks." Beau lowered his voice. "We're at the funeral home right now making arrangements."

"That's why I'm calling," Jake said. "Everybody here knows you're out for a few days, and something just landed on my desk. They gave it to me since I'm somewhat familiar with the Murdoch case. I thought you should know about it as soon as possible."

Beau searched for a pencil and pad but couldn't find one. "Do I need to write something down?"

"Not at all. I just wanted you to know that we have a team at Murdoch's house going through his files. They found a bunch of weird stuff. He's into some odd things."

"Yes, I know."

"They found one thing, however, that really disturbed me." Jake hesitated. "It's a detailed architectural drawing of the interior of Keely Lambert's house, as well as her kennel."

"Are you kidding me?"

"No. And it gets more interesting. He even has a plat of her farm, complete with fencing and gate information."

"We need to get a security team on her property twenty-four seven until we find this guy."

"I'll put the order in right now."

"And Jake, one more thing. Keely told me that she remembers having seen Murdoch at a toy store near the Galleria Mall in Franklin. It's called The Unique Toy Store. You might want to check it out and see if he just works there or if he owns it."

CHAPTER 42

Wednesday, January 19

Keely said a silent prayer for Beau as she slid to the center of the seat. Emma climbed in behind her, and Beau closed the door and hurried to the other side.

He had been quiet since taking his last phone call inside the funeral home. Had he received disturbing news? Or had this day—or his dad's death—finally gotten to him?

"Are you all right?" she asked as he took a seat beside her.

He nodded, but still no words.

"Emma," he finally spoke when he was stopped by a red light. He thumbed his fingers on the steering wheel. "I'm taking Keely to a late lunch in Leiper's Fork, if you'd like to go with us."

"I appreciate the offer," she said. "But I need to get back to Devon and the kids. Besides, you would have to drive me all the way back here after we ate. I'm sure you have a lot more important things to do."

"We would love to have you join us," Keely said.

"Maybe we can all get together soon." Emma looked down at her hands. "It's just us now, you know."

Beau nodded. "We'll get through this, sis."

"I'm thankful for you, big brother. And you too, Keely." She gave Keely a sideways hug.

"We've been through a lot together," Keely said. "I feel like you're family."

"You are!" Beau said.

"Yes, you are," Emma agreed and then hesitated. "If you'll have us. We're a bit dysfunctional at times."

The three of them laughed.

"I don't know about you, but I needed that laugh." Emma wiped tears—no doubt bittersweet—from her eyes and then continued. "All of this drama gets to you after a while. First Connor, then the nightmare with Keely's mother."

Keely turned to Beau. "What do you think about that prank call to the funeral home?"

The muscle in his jaw tensed. "It was probably Murdoch. He likes to play psychological games. It fits his profile." He glanced her way. "It's how he keeps his 'victims' on the run and afraid."

"You're right . . . he does!" Keely said. "First Connor, which was all a charade. And then the dog tag. And finally, the tracking devices, which were so easily discovered."

"That's creepy," Emma said.

"My thoughts exactly," Keely turned to Emma.

"And then he took your mom, but thankfully didn't harm her."

"Her situation is different," Beau cautioned. "I'm fairly certain he was behind both of her accidents."

"She has had more than her share of pain from him." Keely nodded.

"I'm sorry, Keely," Emma said. "He's a nasty man."

Keely turned to Beau. "What was that last phone call about?"

She saw Beau's jaw twitch again. "I had planned to wait and tell you later. It's just more of Murdoch's psychological drama."

"What?" Keely asked.

"Don't become overly concerned about what I'm going to tell you."

"I don't like the sound of this." Emma visibly shuddered.

"Tell me . . . please." Keely stared at Beau.

"It was Jake who called. He has been assigned to help with the case, while I'm out for Dad's arrangements." Beau glanced toward her. "He has a team of people going through Murdoch's things, looking for evidence and possible clues about where he may be hiding."

Beau stopped at another traffic light. "This morning they found a detailed architectural rendering of your house . . . and your kennel, as well as a plat of your land."

"Keely!" Emma grabbed her arm.

"I admit, it's creepy. But maybe he was hoping we would find it, and he's just playing me." Keely sighed.

"I don't know . . ." Emma said. "He went to a lot of trouble and expense just to play you."

"True." Keely agreed.

"The two of you need to relax," Beau said, turning into Emma's driveway. "I've asked for a twenty-four seven security detail at Keely's place until this is over."

"Good idea," Emma said. "Please be careful, Keely."

At the end of the drive, Beau put the truck in park and looked at Emma. "I want you to be careful too. If you see anything suspicious, call me. I can get a detail assigned to your house as well."

"I will, and I appreciate it," Emma said, opening the truck door. "But I have Devon, and he has a small size armory inside the house."

Beau laughed. "I've always liked him."

Emma scrunched her face and smiled. "Love you both," she said. "Take care of each other, and I'll see you on Thursday evening for visitation."

"Love you, too, sis." Beau waited for his sister to step inside her house and close the door before he turned around in her driveway and took off toward Leiper's Fork.

Keely's hand flew to her mouth. "I almost said something back there that I shouldn't. I'm glad I stopped myself."

"What? It can't be that bad."

"Oh, yes it was. I was thinking about that psychological game thing—and I realized that was what he had probably been doing to your dad for years."

Beau turned to her. "I think you may be on to something," he said. "I will never argue my dad's innocence, but Murdoch is a master manipulator."

"I was going to wait and tell you over lunch, but I will go ahead and tell you now."

Keely studied his face.

"My supervisor called right after you and Emma got out of the truck at the funeral home. And based on dental records, which are almost one hundred percent accurate, they have confirmed the identity of the remains in Murdoch's cistern."

"Daddy?"

He nodded. "Yes."

That now all-too-familiar pit gnawed at her stomach. Was she about to be sick? No . . . the tears began to flow. These were easy tears. Tears of gratitude. And relief. She let them cleanse.

It was almost over.

"Thanks for telling me in the truck. I much prefer crying my eyes out here than in the middle of the restaurant."

Beau nodded. "There's a box of tissue in the backseat."

She reached to grab one and came back with a fistful. She wiped her eyes. "I can't help but wonder what else this man will do before he's caught. He's full of surprises, isn't he?"

"I suppose that's one way to put it."

"I can tell you now"—she dabbed her eyes again and sniffed—"if you ever have him on the run, I would love to help search with my dogs. I'm sure Titan would track him down." She looked at Beau. "Although I'm not sure I could hold him back next time. It's almost a shame, I did last time. It might have saved us a lot of grief."

"Except that we might not have found your dad."

"Yes . . ." Peace swept through her. "You're right. God's plan is always the best."

"It can be tough going through it."

"We set ourselves up for some of that."

"Me? I've never brought trouble on myself," he teased.

The windshield splintered with a loud POP. Beau fought the steering wheel, and the truck skidded off the road. "What was that?

Keely clutched his arm. "Are you all right?"

"Yes. Are you?"

She caught her breath and tried to look through the web of shattered glass. Then she saw it. There was a hole in the center. "A rock hit the window!"

Beau shook his head. "That wasn't a rock," he said calmly. "That was a bullet. Look at the way it came through here . . ."

She watched as his eyes followed an imaginary path from the windshield to the dashboard, to the floorboard, and then back up. Then he froze, and she saw fear in his eyes.

"Look here." He pointed. "It's embedded into the seat behind us."

Keely screamed and jumped back. The bullet had passed dead center between them. "What do we do now?"

"If you're all right with it, and I can see well enough to drive, I'd like to take it directly to our lab." He picked up his phone. "But first, I'm calling Russell Wallace to ask for as many squad cars as he can get to scour this area."

"So, you think . . ."

"Who else would it be? It's too late for deer season."

"Beau, if Emma had been in the car, I would have been sitting closer to you and . . ." She took deep breaths. "What was I just saying? God has a plan." She looked at him. "Please keep reminding me of that."

"As soon as I'm off the phone with Russell, I want you to call Gigi and Levi. I'll call Emma. This guy is playing more than psychological games. He's playing for keeps." He steered the truck back onto the road. "And he's not only high tech, but he's also sophisticated enough at actual warfare to be extremely dangerous."

CHAPTER 43

Wednesday, January 19

Beau drove as fast as he dared with a cracked windshield during rush hour traffic in Nashville. At four fifteen, they arrived at the lab, and fifteen minutes later, a crew of forensic technicians were examining his truck. Inside and out.

Keely waited in the staff lounge, with special permission from Chris Enoch, while the bullet was extracted from the leather seat and quickly analyzed. It was easily determined that the cartridge, a round nose 30-30 type, could have been fired from J. G. Gardner's Winchester Model 94 rifle. But did the lands and grooves match? Because forensics had catalogued and uploaded photos of the bullet that had killed J. G., it was easily confirmed that it did.

They had been shot at—and narrowly missed—by his father's gun, leaving little doubt that Murdoch had been the shooter. Michael Murdoch alias de Hugues was now confirmed as an armed and dangerous man with vengeance for the Lambert and Gardner families.

In under an hour, Keely and Beau were on their way to Leiper's Fork in a government issue SUV, and Beau was praying for the wherewithal and the wisdom to stop Murdoch before he hurt someone else. Like it or not, Beau had stirred up the devil when he showed up in Murdoch's backyard. Would Murdoch have been satisfied to take out J. G., the only man who knew the truth about William Lambert's disappearance and subsequent death? Or would he have continued his pursuit of Keely?

Of course, he would have. Murdoch had said it himself. His hate-fueled rage began and ended with Keely and William Lambert. Whether Beau liked it or not, Keely was center of target, and his inserting himself into the matter would only temporarily divert Murdoch's attention, not forestall it. All he could do was surround Keely with as much security as possible, while trusting his gut, as well as his many talented peers at the Bureau.

Rush hour was winding down as they made their way toward Leiper's Fork.

"You're quiet again," Keely said. "That always scares me."

He glanced her way and smiled. "You're beautiful, did you know that?"

"Now, you're really scaring me."

"Why?"

She pointed to her wrinkled white blouse and shoeless feet, because her high heels had been tossed aside earlier. "You may not be able to see well enough to drive."

He engaged his turn signal, pulled into a church parking lot, and motioned for her to come closer to him. She complied with a mischievous smile, and he reached to pull her in. Hesitating slightly, he leaned into her. When she didn't resist, he kissed her lightly on the lips. She pulled away, looked into his eyes, and then let him kiss her again.

"Now," he said, a few minutes later. "Have I convinced you yet?"

"I'm not sure," she teased. "We might want to discuss that thought again at a future date."

He grinned, put the SUV back into drive, and took her hand in his. A few miles down the road, he checked his watch. "What do you think? Do we have time to stop at Fox & Locke for supper?"

"They close at seven o'clock," she said.

"Let's do it." He accelerated enough to set her back in her seat.

"This has been an interesting day, to say the least," she said. "I can now say I have a better understanding of your job."

"I'm not sure *interesting* is the best word to describe our day," he said. "But I'm grateful we're still here to talk about it. That bullet came close to changing everything."

"Please be careful." She looked at him. "I know you love your work, but I would appreciate it if you would love me more—and stay alive."

Had she really said that?

"Did that kiss back there mean I have a chance at keeping you in my life?"

"You've always had a chance." She bit her lip and then smiled at him.

He laughed and squeezed her hand.

Fifteen minutes later, they were sitting in the restaurant eating hamburgers and waiting for the live music to begin.

"That was as good as I remembered," he said.

"I was so hungry. I could have eaten the packaging and been happy." Keely laughed.

"Oh, I forgot. You eat breakfast at seven in the morning, don't you?"

"Six-thirty, usually, but you're close enough."

"Every time I think I would like the country life, I remember how different it is," he said. "Living downtown, I'm closer to my office. And we have good hamburgers down there too."

"If hamburgers are your criteria, I can see why you might choose the big city," she said. "But there's so much more to life than that."

He nodded. "You're right. And there are always weekends."

She glanced to him and smiled. "Except in my business."

"Are most of your SAR calls on the weekend?"

"Yes . . . it never fails. I'll have something planned—even if it's just to rest from a hard week—and then some hiker will decide to get lost. The next thing I know, it's Monday morning again." She laughed. "But I'm blessed to be able to do what I do. It's what I have always wanted to do."

"It's not much different for me."

"I had already figured that out." Her eyes lit up with understanding.

"Any idea who this act is that's coming on?"

"It may be a writer's round, like Levi had at his party."

"Oh . . . Gotcha. Are you set on staying?"

"Not me. I thought you wanted to stay."

They both stood at the same time, and he followed her out the door.

"Keely, I have a bad feeling . . ."

"What?" She jumped back.

"I think we need to change Dad's funeral arrangements."

She caught her breath. "Oh, good. You scared me. I was afraid you'd seen somebody on top of a building with a gun."

He took her hand and hurried her along. "I'm sorry. I'm thinking way ahead of myself. But the idea of someone on the roof with a gun isn't a good thought. Let's get to the truck, and then I'll share my other thought with you."

They were almost to her place when he finished sharing. "Even though I signed paperwork for a visitation tomorrow night, I think we need to cancel it. Keeping the funeral secure will be difficult enough."

"Emma will be disappointed."

"I understand that. But I've requested high profile presence from the police—don't look at me like that, I know what you're thinking—for everyone in attendance at the funeral. If we drag this out over two days, we're taking up valuable police time." He thought for a minute. "I would rather they use their resources to find Murdoch, instead of cover Thursday night visitation."

"Good point," she said.

"Let's call Emma." He picked up the phone, connected to Bluetooth, and voice dialed her number.

"Thanks for calling. I was worried."

"We just left Fox & Locke, and I'm taking Keely home."

"That was a late lunch," she said.

He glanced toward Keely. "That's because we had a little incident after we dropped you off."

"What happened?"

He told her about the shot fired into the truck. "And we're all but sure it was Murdoch who did the shooting."

"Beau, please be careful . . ."

"I want you to do the same. I've put in a request for twenty-four-hour security at your house. You, Devon, and the kids need to stay close."

"We won't go anywhere until Thursday night, I promise."

He hesitated. "That's also why I called. We need to cancel visitation tomorrow night and have the funeral only."

"Why?"

"If we have only one service, we're taking up less law enforcement time, and they can be looking for Murdoch. Plus, we're cutting our exposure, and our guests' exposure, to this guy in half."

She didn't respond immediately, and Beau traded glances with Keely.

"Emma?"

"I agree with you. Do you want me to call the funeral home and let them know?"

"Yes, please. Thank you. Oh . . . and I just thought about something else. We need to let them know that we will be checking IDs at the door on Friday."

"Got it."

"If you know someone who is planning to attend you might want to let them know."

"Will do."

"Love you, sis."

He ended the call as he pulled into Keely's driveway.

"Never in a million years," she said, "would I have thought we'd be planning a funeral for someone we love and asking for police to check IDs at the door."

CHAPTER 44

Friday, January 21

Beau left his condo at nine o'clock sharp Friday morning. Keely had offered to ride with Adam and Sara to the funeral to save him the drive to Leiper's Fork. But he would feel much better having her with him.

Although they had originally planned for Gigi and Peter to bring Maggie, the security risk outweighed any possible benefit. Beau had also called Levi and requested that he and his family stay home.

Having less instead of more of the Lambert and Gardner families made sense. And, for the first time, he was glad he didn't have to take the risk of having his mother there. The responsibility of keeping Emma and her family, as well as Keely, safe was enough.

Most of the other attendees would be members of the law enforcement community who had worked with J. G., and all of them were prepared for the risk. At this point, he almost regretted having dismissed the hero cop procession Emma had wanted.

Almost. But the truth now was, every officer attending the service or driving in the procession would be a working officer. The idea of a tribute was more of an afterthought.

When he got to her place, Keely was standing in the front yard looking like a million dollars. She was dressed in a navy-blue suit and high heels. How had he ever walked away from this woman?

He opened the passenger side door of the black SUV and helped her step in. Not an easy task for her in that skirt. But he enjoyed the view, and she laughed when he told her so.

"How has your morning been? Or is that a good question to ask?" She studied him. "I'm guessing it was stressful."

"Good guess," he said. "I'll be glad when we have this behind us. Then we'll be back on offense. It's safer."

"How can I help you today?" she asked as he secured his seatbelt.

He reached to take her hand. "If you're standing beside me, it's enough."

She smiled and squeezed his hand, and they rode in silence for most of the trip. What was there to say when he was on his way to bury his father? Especially one with whom he'd had a contentious relationship for years.

Funny enough, that didn't seem as important now. Had he really made peace with James Gardner at Murdoch's house a few days ago? In many ways, he believed he had, and that would make moving on a little bit easier.

Beau entered the funeral home property from the back and parked his car behind the hearse. The hearse that would carry his dad to his place beside his mother. A generation that had forever passed.

And way before their time. Neither of his parents had seen retirement age.

A member of the funeral home staff opened Keely's door, and Beau hurried around the back of the vehicle to take her arm. When he did, he saw Russell Wallace standing at the back entrance door, and a sense of relief settled over him.

Wallace and the rest of his men had this. There would also be a covey of undercover TBI attending for an additional measure of security.

"How's it going?" Beau asked as they approached.

The deputy nodded and tipped his hat. "It's all good, Beau. We have it covered. You go in there and honor a man who served his country and his fellow man."

Wallace's words punched Beau in the gut.

In all his worrying and guilt about his father's part in William Lambert's death, Beau had forgotten the times, both before and after that life-changing mistake, in the war and at home, that J. G. Gardner had served ordinary citizens, making their lives better and keeping them safe.

Beau had heard countless stories during his time at the Bureau about his dad's service. And he had been told time after time that J. G. Gardner was one of the best law enforcement officers in the business.

But Beau had always been quick to write him off. He knew the real man. Or so he thought.

Beau escorted Keely through the double doors and across the viewing room, up to the casket that held his father's body. J. G. looked good in his dress greens. Momentarily, Beau had a vision of a younger James Gardner serving his country overseas. Fighting one of the toughest wars in history, not that any war was easy, and coming home with only one thought. That of marrying Margaret Bailey. What a shock it must have been to learn that she had not only married, but she had a baby on the way.

For the first time, Beau put himself in his father's shoes, trying to understand the difficulties and the disappointments he had faced in life. Of course, he had added to his heartache by acting out his anger. But he had paid dearly for that too.

He had lost his peace forever the day William Lambert died. And he had lived the rest of his life trying to make up for it.

Beau squeezed Keely's hand and looked down on the man who had done his best in recent years. His best, whatever that meant for him. It was different for each of them.

"I'm sorry, Dad."

Beau spoke softly, almost inaudibly into the casket.

"I hope my forgiveness now is enough. And I hope you were somehow able to look through all our disagreements and understand that I, too, was doing the best I could."

It was at that moment that Beau realized his father had understood . . . and forgiven him. Hadn't he died trying to save him? The forgiveness was now complete. And in the hands of God.

Keely put her arm around his shoulder as he quietly wept. She wept along with him.

"Let's sit down," he finally said.

Within a few minutes, guests were filing through the open doors in the front of the room. Neighbors, church friends, old high school buddies, and cops of all ages walked to the casket to pay their respect and then stopped to speak encouragement to Beau and Emma.

Beau thanked each of them for coming, especially in these circumstances, and told them their presence had made a difference.

"Dad would have loved to see you today," he said over and over. And he knew it was true. Because, as often as Beau had tried to make his dad the consummate villain, he knew it wasn't always so.

J. G. had friends in this world. A lot of them. But he had chosen to leave them to save his son. He hadn't hesitated.

Beau bowed his head and did his best to keep it together. He was grateful to have Keely at his side, and he thought about what his dad had told her with his last breath.

"Take care of my son."

He smiled. Because she was.

The service passed quickly. The pastor's message was uplifting. And there was no sign of trouble. J. G.'s comrades had stood by him one last time and protected those he loved.

As soon as the opening chords of the recessional sounded, Beau, Keely, and Emma, along with her family, stood. They filed by the casket and left through the side door to their respective vehicles. Beau walked Keely to the SUV and helped her inside. Then he hurried around the front and climbed inside.

"Thank you," he said. "You have no idea how much it meant to me."

"I can't think of anywhere else I would want to be." She took his hand.

At two thirty sharp, the hearse left for the cemetery, which was only a few miles away. When they arrived, the grave was surrounded by well-wishers. People who had chosen to take time out of their day to spend a little more time with J. G. Gardner and his family.

At the end of the short service, Beau led Keely to his mother's side of the stone. He paid his tribute by remembering a hundred little things she had done for him, and then escorted Keely down the hill.

"I don't know how you did that in high heels," he said, trying to lighten the mood.

"I could say it takes practice, but I would be lying. I never wear high heels." She smiled and her brown eyes danced. "This girl is much happier in boots and sneakers."

"Please don't ever change," he said.

She squeezed his hand as Emma caught up with them.

"Do the two of you want to come to our house for a while? We have a lot of food that the church brought over. Only a few close friends will be there."

Beau looked to Keely. "Are you up for that?"

"Sure," she said. "It might do us good."

"We'll see you in a few minutes, sis," he said and then helped Keely into the car. Within seconds, she had taken off her high heels.

"I wish I'd brought a change of clothes."

"Me too." He loosened his tie.

Keely's phone rang as Beau engaged the car engine.

"It's Greg McAllister," she said before answering. "Hi, Greg. Good to hear from you . . . No, we don't. Your timing is good . . ."

Beau could hear conversation on the other end but not what was being said.

"Tomorrow? Sure. What time? Do you remember how to get to my place?" She laughed. "See you then."

"What was that all about?" Beau asked after she ended the call.

"He wanted to know if we had snow on the ground, and I told him we didn't. He said his supervisor had asked him to make another trip to town when there wasn't snow so he could see my dogs work again."

She bit her lip. "I hope that's not bad news."

"He loved them the first time, and he'll love them more this time," Beau said.

"I needed that, thanks." She put the phone in her purse and looked at him. I hope this isn't a bad time. You know with the threat of Murdoch."

"It shouldn't be a problem," Beau said. "And certainly not from McAlister's point of view. He's familiar with danger. I doubt he will be too worried about Murdoch."

"You're probably right," she said.

CHAPTER 45

Friday, January 21

A government-issue SUV was waiting at the entrance to Keely's drive when Beau brought her home at seven thirty. A second car was parked at the top of the hill next to her house.

"Beau?" She looked at him. "What is going on?"

"At least one agent will be here all night," he said. "Several sheriff's deputies will also be patrolling the area. Both by car and on horseback."

"That sounds like too much," she argued. "Although I appreciate it."

"I have to keep my girl safe."

"What about you? When will I see you next?"

"I'll be here first thing in the morning, unless you need me sooner."

"That means ten o'clock, right?" She teased and stepped out of the car. "Or is ten thirty more realistic?"

His smile tugged at her heart. "I could be here at six thirty, but I need to go to the office first to get my truck."

"I won't wait breakfast then."

He laughed. "Good idea."

"I know one thing," she said. "I'm ready to be done with these high heels. They're a lot more comfortable when they're in the back of my closet."

Beau agreed, took off his tie and tossed it into the backseat of the SUV. "Do you want to check your house first, so you can change into your sneakers? Then we'll check the kennel." He got out and walked around to her side of the vehicle.

"There's no need to check the kennels. Adam was here earlier to cover the evening chores."

"Don't you need to check the puppies?"

"Not since they're older. They're still in the whelping pen, but that will change soon too."

"So, you're not going out there tonight?"

"No."

"Then let's check your house." He took her arm, and they started walking up the hill. "I'm not leaving until I've made sure you're safe for the night. What time will Adam be here in the morning?"

"Probably nine o'clock or so. He's only coming in because McAlister wants to watch the older dogs work." She turned to him. "And I realized earlier that he might be interested in one of the new pups. Adam and I both think they're extra special."

"What time do you expect McAlister?"

"He's flying into Nashville at ten thirty, so he should be here before noon."

"Those military guys travel light," Beau said. "He may not check luggage."

"He didn't have much last time." She reached for the handle to the mudroom door.

"Keely, your back porch light is out."

"I know. I need to replace the bulb. It went out last night, but I didn't get to it."

Beau frowned. "I'll do that for you before I leave."

She opened the door to two rambunctious shepherds. They seemed to be as eager to see Beau as they were her. That thought warmed her heart.

After he had checked her house and changed her outside light bulb, he took her in his arms. "I hate leaving you tonight," he said. "Call me if you need anything. Even if you just want to talk. But especially if you have a bad feeling about something. I've learned to trust my gut. Sometimes it's better than reason."

"I will . . . and I'll be fine," she said. "Don't worry. You're leaving me with plenty of security. Not to mention Ruby and Titan."

"I'm glad you have them," he said.

Keely shuddered.

"Are you all right?"

"Yes." She nodded. "I had a chill, but I'm OK."

She prayed and backed away from him. Maybe the fuss about security had gotten to her, but for some reason, danger—and even death—seemed to be closing in. She shook it off and reminded herself that they had buried Beau's dad today. And identified her father's remains. It would be easy to let those feelings linger. But this felt more like the gut feeling that Beau had talked about.

Or God sending her a warning to prepare. *For what?*

Returning to the moment, she stood on her tiptoes—having already tossed her high heels into the corner—and touched her lips to Beau's.

"I could stay—"

"I'll see you tomorrow," she said, giving him a playful push. "Be safe, Beau Gardner."

She blew him a kiss as he walked away, and after closing the mudroom door and locking it, she turned toward the dogs.

"I've missed you two."

Eager faces invited her to play.

She picked up a ball from the floor, threw it into the next room, and was immediately rewarded with havoc. And hair . . . lots of hair. She would vacuum in the morning.

"Do you two want to watch a little TV before bed?" she asked them. "We can cuddle and watch something you like. I promise . . . You can pick." She laughed out loud, then laughed again, knowing if someone heard her talking to her dogs, they would think her crazy.

Only dog people, and the occasional cat person, understood.

The three of them moved into the bedroom, and Keely turned on the TV before changing clothes. Loose jeans and a cozy sweatshirt so she could let the dogs out one more time before bedtime.

A few hours later, she awoke to an alarm.

Six thirty already?

She reached for her phone, picked it up and saw that it wasn't ringing.

So, what was that sound? Even the dogs heard it. They were whining and jumping in and out of the bed.

The fire alarm!

She jumped up, pocketed her phone, and put on her boots. She didn't smell smoke, so what could it—?

It was the kennel!

Rushing to the window, and pulling back the curtains, Keely saw flames licking the top of the trees above the metal building. She grabbed her phone, scrolled for the kennel door app, and pressed the button. Now . . . the dogs would be safe in the yard, while she dialed 911.

And then she remembered the whelping pen. Pearl and the pups couldn't get out!

"Stay," she shouted to Ruby and Titan as she rushed out the door, closing it behind her.

Oh, dear God . . . help me save my dogs.

Keely ran as fast as she could down the hill, and then fought to slide her key into the lock. After it released, she stepped inside.

Smoke was everywhere, and she could hear the fire popping and cracking. The sound of dogs in the distance, howling and barking, assured her that the eighteen were safe. Now to rescue the three in the back.

Why hadn't she thought about a wet cloth? Why hadn't she called 911?

It was too late. She had to move quickly.

How long could they breathe this air and survive? How long could she hold her breath?

One more step . . . Was it this way or was it the other way? She was beginning to feel woozy.

And disoriented.

Keely! She chastised herself. *Stay awake! Find the dogs and run for your life.*

She finally made her way to the whelping room door, threw it open, and hurried inside. Pearl was cowering in the corner, and the puppies were crying.

"My poor babies!" She bent and picked up one puppy and then the other. She cradled them close to her breasts, trying to shield them from the smoke.

"Pearl, come with me." *This way!*

The dog followed her out the whelping room door and into the main hall, where the smoke was thick. She could see a light in the distance. It was one of her solar yard lights. Focusing on it, she put one foot in front of the other.

Hurry . . .

She stumbled.

Stay awake and run . . . run . . . run . . .

She couldn't—

Cooler air enveloped her. She had made it outside!

She took a deep breath of the almost fresh air.

And then someone grabbed her from behind and pulled her. She couldn't fight back. Her lungs were too tired from breathing the smoke.

Was this a dream?

She let the puppies fall to the ground. *But where was Pearl?*

Keely could see in the smoke filtered light in front of her that Pearl was lying on the ground and the puppies were running around her.

"Pearl? Are you . . . ?"

The darkness overwhelmed her.

CHAPTER 46

Saturday, January 22

Beau awoke to ringing. Who would be calling him—he looked at his watch—at three in the morning? Reaching for his phone on the nightstand, he saw the caller ID. It was Vernon. But why?

Vernon! He was working security for Keely tonight.

"Gardner here."

"Beau, Keely's kennel is on fire."

Murdoch!

"Is Keely OK?"

"I'm not sure," the agent said. "We can't find her."

Beau was already up and dressing. "How did this happen?"

"I was out of my car, stretching my legs," the older man said. "The next thing I know, I'm waking up on the ground, and there's fire coming from the kennel."

"Is the house on fire too?"

"No . . ."

"But you can't find Keely?"

"She's not in the house. We've looked."

Pearl and the pups! Beau's heart took a plunge.

"She must be in the kennel. Have you looked in the kennel?" He grabbed his coat and his keys and headed out the door.

"The firefighters are here, but it's too hot to go inside."

Dear God.

"I'll be there . . . soon."

Beau took the stairs to the parking garage, ran to the SUV, and accelerated out of the lot. If there was any good news, it was that traffic was light this time of night and he had police lights on the

SUV. He activated the lights, made his way to Interstate 40 West, and then shoved the gas pedal to the floor.

He'd had a bad feeling when he left her. Why hadn't he stayed?

Adam! He voice dialed Adam's number. One ring. Two rings. Three . . . *Adam, please don't have your Do Not Disturb on.*

Beau was about to hang up and dial again when Adam picked up.

"Where are you?"

"I was in bed, man. What—"

"The kennel is on fire. And Keely is missing."

"I'll be right there." Adam disconnected.

Who should he call next? *Devon? Levi?* He would call them both. And, of course, they were both asleep but said they would meet him there.

Who should he call next?

Enoch.

Beau dialed his boss, briefly filled him in, and promised to keep him updated. Enoch said he would call Jake, so it was time to pray.

An hour later, Beau was standing in front of a still smoking kennel, waiting, and continuing to pray for good news about Keely. The firefighters were now inside looking for her.

Adam stood beside him calling the play by play. "She would have released the automatic locks and set the eighteen free to escape in the play yard. Then she would have run inside to save Pearl and the puppies."

The eighteen were in the big yard. But Pearl and the puppies weren't here. That wasn't a good sign. Keely must have gone inside and been overcome by smoke.

How long would it take to pass out? To succumb to smoke inhalation?

Beau knew all the answers, but his mind refused to bring them to the top. He couldn't. Rational thinking might cause him to lose hope. And hope was all he had.

"Has anyone checked the house?"

"I haven't," Adam said.

"Me either," echoed Devon and Levi.

"My men checked it earlier, but I'll run up there," Beau said. Maybe Keely had slept through the whole thing and somehow they had missed her. Wouldn't that be wonderful? It would be the best news he could think of right now.

He ran, focusing on that outcome, and when he got to the back door, he wasn't ready for what he saw. Pearl and the puppies were curled up together on the stoop. Her instinct had told her to take them to the house.

"Where is Keely, Pearl?"

The dog didn't respond. Beau could see she was having trouble breathing.

"Adam!"

"What is it?" Adam was at his side in a flash.

"Something's wrong with Pearl. Can you help her while I go inside and look for Keely?"

"Sure."

Beau nodded and put his hand on the back doorknob. It was unlocked. Was that good news or bad? When he stepped inside, he found two anxious German Shepherds. Both were looking eagerly behind him for Keely, and he knew instantly she wasn't there.

But he had to be certain. He ran through the house shouting her name. In the bedroom, in the bathroom, and upstairs.

Nothing.

He opened the sunroom door and ran into the backyard, the dogs romping after him. But there was no Keely, so he hurried back into the house.

Before he slipped out the mudroom door, he gave each of the dogs a treat, just as Keely would do.

"Don't you worry," he said. "I promise. We'll find her."

Once outside, he ran down the sidewalk toward the kennel and saw Adam and an EMT holding an oxygen mask to Pearl's face. Her two puppies were snuggled beside her.

With all other options exhausted, Beau knew he was waiting on bad news. Either Keely had lost consciousness in the burning building . . . or Michael Murdoch had taken her.

His heart climbed to his throat. Because he feared the second scenario the most.

March 1, 2000

"Daddy, why can't girls be warriors?" Keely asked.

"What do you mean, honey?" Will Lambert set aside his newspaper and turned to his daughter. "Girls are warriors all the time. I fought in the war with girls who were warriors. And your mother is a warrior. She's a strong woman, Keely. She cooks and cleans and manages our home—"

"But I want to be a real warrior like you when I grow up, Daddy. Not the stay-at-home kind."

Her daddy smiled. "Well, you can be, if that's what you want."

"A teacher at school told me I couldn't. He laughed and said that girls should stay home."

"Who told you that, honey?"

"Mr. Murdoch. He's not my teacher, but he came to our classroom today to talk about stuff, and he asked each of us what we wanted to be when we grew up."

"And you told him you wanted to be a warrior?"

"Yes. Like you. I told him I want to be like you."

"I'm proud of you, honey. And do you know what?"

"What?"

"You're already a warrior."

"I am?"

"Yes. You did exactly what a warrior would do. You stood up for yourself. You defended what you believed."

"What do you mean, Daddy?"

"When that man told you that you couldn't do something, you told him you could. And do you know what's even better than that?" He got up from his chair and knelt beside her.

She giggled. "What?"

"You believed that you could. Do you understand?"

"I think so."

"Keely, I want you to remember two things for me, OK?"

"OK."

"Do you promise that you will never forget?"

"I promise."

"I want you to remember to always . . . always believe in yourself."

"OK."

He gave her a hug. "And I want you to always remember that I love you."

CHAPTER 47

Saturday, January 22

Keely awoke lying flat in a dark, enclosed space with no sense of motion or sound. She felt neither hot nor cold. She had no pain. Except for a burning in her chest.

The fire! She stifled a sensation to cough.

Where was Pearl? And the puppies? The older dog had been lying still on the ground and then . . .

"Are you awake?"

Keely startled.

Murdock?

She eased to a sitting position just as Michael Murdoch pulled back the curtain. Daylight flooded in. Keely blinked, and then with Murdoch in the foreground, she quickly scanned the background. A small kitchen to the right. And a skinny sofa and breakfast table to the left. The exit door was straight ahead. And closed.

They were inside a camper. A cab-over model that was most likely in Murdoch's Ford F-150.

She returned her focus to the clown man. His graying, sandy colored hair protruded from his scalp in disarray rather than a style.

"Oh, my dear . . ." He walked closer. "You have been the most difficult prey to catch. I do believe you really might be a warrior. That is except that women can't be warriors." He laughed.

Her dream! She remembered it now. All of it. What he had told her in the classroom that day had been the beginning of everything that had gone wrong.

"But I was seven years old!"

"You were seven years *too* old," he said. "I wish you had never been born. Do you know how difficult you have made my life? When is your birthday?"

"You know when my birthday is," she spat back at him. She would not cower to his insolence. "That was the day you took my daddy from me."

"You're smart too. So, you remember me?"

"I remember the presence of evil," she said. "I was too young back then to put a name to it, but I understand now."

Murdoch laughed again. A vile, guttural sound. But she wouldn't let him get to her, especially now that she knew about his psychological games. Beau had been right. Murdoch was weak. And he preyed upon the weakness of others. She would have to be strong to best him.

"You have always been what I wanted," he said. "You and your troublemaking father."

Keely clenched her teeth. He was taunting her, and she wouldn't fall for it.

"I didn't care anything about that boy in the woods. Or your mother really. Although she was a party to your birth."

Keely refrained from calling him crazy, remembering his reaction when J. G. had called him that. "You're the clerk in the toy store," she said.

"When did you figure that out?"

"I won't lie. It took me longer than it should have."

He laughed. "You're honest. That's good."

"So how did you set my kennel on fire?"

"Keely, I like you. You're inquisitive."

She hated hearing him say her name. "So how did you do it and get past the security guards?"

"It was easy," he said beckoning to her. "Please step down. I trust your accommodations are adequate. As my honored guest, I wanted you to have the best bed in the . . . house, so to speak."

Keely waved off his offered hand and took two steps down to the main floor of the camper. He gestured for her to take a seat on the small sofa, while he remained standing, leaning against the kitchen counter.

"I set the fire by drone. And then, after that . . . chaos. I was able to take down each of the guards before I got to you."

"Where are we now?" She reached for her phone in her back pocket.

"Don't worry about your phone. I took it. It's a long way from here, lying in the middle of your burning kennel."

She flinched. "So where are we now?"

"You're in my camper."

"On your truck?"

"Right again."

"If we're in your camper, then may I ask if we're going somewhere?"

"You may. But I'm not telling you yet."

Hopefully, not the cistern.

"Well, I guess I'm all out of questions for now."

He laughed. "You really are clever. In some ways, you're still that seven-year-old girl."

Keely thought back to that time, and she agreed with him. She was the same.

"Seven-year-olds like to ask questions," he said.

Maybe that was her ticket out of here: to keep asking him questions while she watched and waited for the best way to escape.

Adam and Beau would be looking for her. Adam with the dogs, and Beau with his team of law enforcement officers. Still, she needed to be proactive. Staying inside this camper wasn't a good way to be found. She had to lure Murdoch outside. She needed to mark a trail for her dogs. For the rescuers who were looking for her.

Or *would* be.

How much time had passed? Had it been three hours or three days? Or more?

What she did know was that she would be better off running from him outside and getting caught than to stay and die inside the vehicle. According to Beau, they had been looking for Murdoch's truck for days and not found it. If that's where she was now, she suspected she was off the beaten track. Or, at least, someplace not easily discovered by the authorities.

"I would love to get some fresh air." She risked showing her hand.

He studied her, and a slow smile spread across his face. A face, she now noticed, with a rough and somewhat ruddy complexion. Keely guessed he had never been popular with the girls. There was nothing about his personality or his looks that was pleasing.

"But, of course, we can open the window," he said.

Keely didn't try to hide her disappointment. "Oh . . . OK. If it doesn't get too cold. I was just hoping to stretch my legs."

"You *are* impetuous." Murdoch chuckled. "Did you know that? Just like a child."

"So . . . I'm guessing you like children. You used to teach them. And you're a clown too. Clowns have to like children, right?"

"Not necessarily. Some clowns like to scare children." He shrugged and then lunged toward her. "Boo!"

She jumped.

"Ha! But you're right. I do like children. They're much more honest than grownups. Don't you think?"

"By far," she said. *Score one for Keely.* Now she knew that she had to keep up the seven-year-old-girl thing, because he liked kids better than adults. If that was her chance of getting out of here, she would take it.

"Do you like games?" She asked.

"Games? What kind of games?" He raised an eyebrow.

"I don't know. . . . Board games? Card games? Piñata? The last one is a birthday party game. You've probably seen a lot of those as a clown."

"You're fascinated by the clown thing, aren't you?"

Keely shrugged. "I mean, isn't everybody?"

"No. Not really. Some people hate clowns."

"I don't understand that." *Was that a white lie?* "Well, maybe I do understand it. But I don't hate them."

"What do you like about them?"

He was creeping her out again. "I don't know. What's your favorite part of being a clown?"

"You're a smart little girl," he said.

Little girl? Interesting.

"I just like questions." That was innocuous.

"You know, Keely. I do too. And I have one for you."

Uh-oh. "And what would that be?"

"Are you ready to sleep now?"

"Sleep? No. I can't say that I'm sleepy."

"But I am," he said. "And if I'm to sleep, then you'll have to sleep."

"Oh, all right. Well . . . good night." She stood and took a step toward the bed, where she had been sleeping earlier.

He laughed. "That's not good enough," he said, reaching to cover her face with a wet cloth.

Once again, darkness overtook her, and she fell into his arms.

CHAPTER 48

Saturday, January 22

While Beau was on the phone with Chris Enoch, Adam was readying the dog teams. McAlister would be here soon, and they hoped to put him in charge of a team. Titan and Ruby were both ready to run.

"Another abduction under our noses?" Enoch was repeating himself, which meant he wasn't happy. "How did that happen?"

"I was at home, sir, and Vernon called me about three o'clock this morning"—he looked at his watch—"about three hours ago, to tell me that Keely's kennel was on fire, and she was missing." Beau took a breath. "I threw on some clothes, and by the time I got here, the fire department had most of the fire controlled. They had just gone inside to look for Keely."

Enoch didn't comment, so Beau continued.

"While we were waiting on the firemen to check the kennel, I checked her house, so I knew it came down to one of two things. She had either lost her life in the fire, or Michael Murdoch had her."

"I thought we had two agents on duty out there?"

"Yes, sir. We did. But Murdoch managed to neutralize them before taking Keely."

"I don't like anything about this. Please tell the agents on the ground that I will expect a full report."

"Yes, sir."

"In the meantime, you're off this case, and I highly recommend that you extend your family leave. Jake Matheson will continue in charge. Please see that he has a good photo and stats for Keely

Lambert so we can get the word out. Has anyone notified the Williamson County authorities?"

"Yes, sir. They are on horseback right now checking the perimeter of Keely's farm. They will also be sending a helicopter and drones."

"Excellent." Enoch paused. "Is there anything I can do to help you personally, Beau? Your family has been through a lot in the last few weeks."

"No, sir. Nothing I can think of except what you're doing. And I appreciate Jake's help. I'll have Keely's personal information to him within a few minutes."

"Keep me posted," Enoch said and ended the call.

Beau looked around the grounds for Adam or Levi. He found them deep in conversation.

"Do either of you have a current photo of Keely you can give me for uploading into our system?"

"I do," Levi said. "But not with me."

"Why don't you just use the one on her website?" Adam suggested.

Beau shook his head. He wasn't thinking clearly. Enoch was right. This had gotten personal.

"Do either of you have any idea about her height and weight?"

"Wow . . . I don't know," Levi said. "Five feet seven and one hundred and twenty pounds? Something like that."

Adam nodded.

"Great," Beau said. "I'll get this to my office, and then I can help you with the dog teams."

Beau went to Keely's website and copied and shared her photo with Jake. Then he texted a short profile.

> 28 years old. Brown hair. Brown eyes. 5 feet 7 inches and 120 pounds.

As soon as he had finished, he walked back to Adam and Levi. Devon had joined them.

"Are we ready to get the dogs on the trail?"

"Almost," Adam said. "I'm thinking we start with one dog. Neither Devon nor Levi have experience with dog handling." He checked his watch. "McAlister won't be here for a few hours, and if they want, Devon and Levi can set out on foot in the meantime."

"Yes. I'm ready to go," Levi said. "I don't want to stand around here wasting time."

"Which dog are we taking?" Beau asked.

"We'll take Titan. That leaves Ruby, our most experienced dog, for McAlister. Titan will respond well to me and Keely, but I'm not sure he's ready to work with a stranger." Adam chuckled. "McAlister will love Ruby. Wouldn't it be great if she could cinch Keely's deal with the army while she's away? That would make a nice little surprise for her when she returns."

Beau appreciated Adam's positivity. They *would* find Keely and bring her back safely. "What can I do?" he asked. He was as eager to get started as Levi.

"Why don't you run up to the house with me. I'll get Titan leashed up and find something of Keely's for the scent. Not that he needs it. I can assure you there's nobody these dogs would rather find than Keely."

Beau and Adam took off for the house, and Adam handed him a backpack.

"If you would, grab a couple of bottles of water out of Keely's fridge and put them in here. Unfortunately, the back of the kennel was hit worse, but Keely keeps spare gear at the house so she can be out of the door quicker if she gets a call."

Beau did what Adam requested and was waiting in the mudroom when Adam returned from the bedroom waving a couple of ziplock bags. "Keely's pillowcases. I hope she'll go easy on me when she returns."

Beau sent up a silent prayer for that possibility, although he suspected Keely would give Adam a hug instead of a piece of her mind.

As soon as they returned to the kennel area, Adam sought out Devon. He and Levi were still together.

"Hey man, instead of going with Levi, can you stay here and keep us posted on the latest information? Maybe we'll get lucky, and Keely will wander in, stunned from the smoke, but safe."

"Wouldn't that be great?" Levi said.

Adam gave Devon and Levi each a walkie-talkie. "Beau and I will have one with us too. These babies have a range of more than thirty miles. Keely and I use them all the time when we're in the field."

"Levi, you can probably buddy up with one of the Williamson County guys. They're sending a fresh team over and should be here anytime. In the meantime, as you know, we're expecting a dog handler from the Lackland Air Force Base to get here sometime before noon. Devon will recognize him. He was here when Connor was lost last month."

It was after eight when Beau and Adam set out with Titan. At the fence line, behind the kennel, Adam let Titan smell the pillowcase, unleashed him, and told him, "Go find Keely."

The big black German Shepherd perked his ears and looked around. Then with his nose in the air, he took the lead. Keely had taught Beau that a good air-scenting dog could cover a swath of one to three hundred feet, depending on the vegetation and the direction and velocity of the wind.

It was Beau's job to map their progress, but he had a difficult time keeping his eyes off Titan and his mind off the last time he and Keely had worked the dog at Beaman Park when he found Connor. He hoped Titan could do as good of a job this time.

He couldn't imagine what Keely was going through. She had agonized over her mother's abduction, and now it was her. She had witnessed her dad's disappearance, and subsequent death, at the hands of the same man who now had her in his grasp.

Beau tried not to let his mind go there. The thought of Keely's fate being in Murdoch's hands was too much to stand. Instead, he studied their current GPS quadrants and familiarized himself with the territory around them.

At one point, Titan stopped and loitered, his nose on the ground, excitedly sniffing in a six-foot circle. Adam allowed the diversion for a few minutes as he continued to walk up the trail. Then he shouted over his shoulder, "Let's go," and Titan took off running, passing Adam, apparently freshly motivated.

As the sun continued to climb in the sky and the day grew considerably warmer, Beau started to worry that Titan had lost the scent. And then they reached the fencerow between two fields about five miles from the kennel. That's when the dog went crazy, jumping and barking and trying to get Adam's attention.

As soon as Beau caught up with the dog, he saw what had captured his interest. Apparently, a sweatshirt or hoodie had caught in the fence, and the piece that had been torn off had attached itself. Adam recognized it as one of Keely's shirts. Once they had crossed the fence, they found fresh tire tracks.

"Don't those look like truck tires?"

Adam nodded in agreement.

"Murdoch has an F-150."

"I would say that could be the right size."

Beau took a photo of the tracks and the physical surroundings, and texted both along with the GPS coordinates to Jake. They might have their first good lead. But they had also reached the end of the trail.

To save time getting back to the house, Beau texted Levi to ask if he could bring his car and pick them up.

CHAPTER 49

Saturday, January 22

Keely awoke to the smell of bacon. She sat up and looked around. The smell was coming from outside, and Murdoch had the camper door open. This was her chance.

She swiveled in the bed, dangling her legs over the side, and jumping to the floor as quietly as she could. She tiptoed to the door and descended the steps slowly.

If Murdoch saw her hurry, he would think she was trying to escape. But that wasn't her plan, at least not right now. She wanted to drag her scent over as much ground as she could.

"What are you doing?" He turned and frowned.

"I'm stretching my legs."

She took a seat on a log and massaged her calves. Then she rubbed her bare arms, trying to exfoliate as many skin particles as possible.

"You sure do have odd habits."

She bit her lip. The proverbial pot calling the kettle black. "That smells delicious. What are you cooking besides bacon?"

"Grits, of course." He laughed.

"You don't sound at all like a southerner." She smiled. "You're joking with me, aren't you?"

He stuck his thumbs in his ears, wagged his hands, and stuck out his tongue. A clown making a clown face. Funny. If this guy wasn't a psychopathic killer, he could be a comedian. She reminded herself about the former.

"Seriously, what's really for breakfast?" she asked.

"Bacon and eggs," he said and then refocused on his work.

She assumed there would be no toast. Instead of asking, she looked around trying to decide where she was. It was quiet here. But . . . was that traffic in the distance?

"It's a pretty day," she said. "What do you have planned?"

It might be something she didn't want to know, but it was too late to take the question back.

"There you go again, asking questions." He said the words, but he didn't seem to be annoyed. The thought that he might like her, in a creepy, I'm-going-to-kill-you-later kind of way chilled her. She brushed her arms again and did her best to put the thought out of her head.

"Are we staying here or moving on?" She tried to ask nonchalantly, but it must not have come across that way.

"Who wants to know?"

"Just asking . . ."

"Keely," he said, getting up from his three-legged stool. "I really can't share everything with you. You're starting to get on my nerves."

Somebody had gotten up on the wrong side of the bed. And it might have been her. "I'm sorry."

He nodded and turned toward the camper door. Was he going inside? Could it really be this easy? Could she run? She could probably best him in the three hundred meters, but a half marathon? Especially not knowing where she was.

Maybe running was a bad idea, she thought as he climbed the stairs with his back to her. Maybe that was his plan. Maybe it was a trap?

Or was this an opportunity for her?

She stood slowly and pretended to dust off her hands, careful not to make a noise. Was he watching her in his peripheral vision? Did he have a scope on that rifle of his? *Another unpleasant thought.*

She sent up a silent prayer, asking for wisdom, and a cloak of peace settled over her. The time wasn't right. She remembered what Beau had told her last night. *Trust your gut.* Sometimes reason will get you in trouble, he had said.

Reason told her to run, but her gut told her to stay. She made a mental note to severely reprimand herself if she found out later this had been her one chance to get away. In the meantime, she would rest in the belief that she had made the right decision.

When Murdoch stepped out of the camper, he seemed almost surprised to see her there. She processed that nugget of information and filed it away.

Reading body language was everything when it came to working with dogs, and Keely didn't want to give away her secret. As far as he was concerned, she was a dumb seven-year-old girl. One she hoped he liked, despite their bad start twenty-something years ago. Of course, reason and her gut instinct told her she was fooling herself about that one.

As Beau climbed into Levi's Cadillac Escalade, he was struck by the realization that it didn't matter how much money you had when you were fighting for your life. All the luxury cars in the world couldn't bring you back. And none of them could save you.

The only thing that could save Keely right now—besides God's intervention, and he was praying for that—was a streak of good luck and good police work. He rang Enoch.

"Any word?" Beau asked when his boss answered.

"Every network in town is covering the story," Enoch said. "It seems that 'cop killer abducts twenty-eight-year-old woman' has a ring to it. Especially when you drop in a subhead that the killer tried to take out a kennel full of dogs. We've fielded calls from animal rights activists and rescue shelters all morning."

Beau cringed at the thought of his dad's story being out there, but if it helped find Keely, it was all good. Whatever works, worked for him. Having the news carry her story would only help her.

"In the meantime, we've tried to ping Ms. Lambert's cell phone. Nothing. My guess is that he threw it into the fire."

"I'd say you're right," Beau agreed. "He's a smart tech man, and he loves playing games."

"Maybe we should play games with him," Enoch said.

"Exactly. I'm hoping Keely picks up on that. We talked about it one day. If she remembers, it might help keep her alive." Had he just admitted that there was a possibility she wouldn't stay alive? He wouldn't let himself go there again.

"I wonder if this guy has a news source. We can't play games with him if we can't get to him."

"No idea, sir." Beau took in the scenery passing by his window as Levi drove them back to Keely's place. The countryside in Williamson County was some of the prettiest in Middle Tennessee.

Wait! That was it.

"Chris, I have an idea. Humor me on this. I realize that your missing person alerts have been going out all over the state. But is it safe to say that law enforcement is focused mainly on Williamson County because both the victim and the suspect live here?"

"Yes. I would say that's accurate. I think that's true for the general public too. Most people connect more with the news in their own backyard. People in Williamson County are most likely to be watching for the white pickup truck."

"I think we've been looking in the wrong place."

"Really? Why is that?"

"If you'll remember, this whole thing started when Murdoch scared a little boy, my nephew, at Beaman Park in Northwest Davidson County. That's over in the Ashland City area. A far reach from Franklin. A totally different demographic."

"Go on . . ."

"I think that's where this guy may be holed up. We both know that crimes are usually committed within a few miles of someone's running territory."

"Yes."

"Well, the first crime took place in Beaman Park. My best guess—and this is only an instinct—is that Murdoch has a place in the Beaman Park area. Can we find out if he has or had relatives with property in that area?"

"We can try. I'll put people on it and get back to you."

"Great!" Beau said, now reenergized as he disconnected the call.

"That's an interesting idea," Levi said, glancing toward Beau.

"I agree. Good thinking." Adam leaned forward from the backseat. "We've obviously lost the trail here, and I think we should just go for it. It isn't like there's another place to search right now."

"I agree," Beau said. "And I know the right guy to help us. I'll call Dan Rodgers at Beaman Park."

A few minutes later, Beau had Rodgers on the phone.

"How are you, Beau?" he asked.

"I've been better," Beau said. "I need your help again."

"Sure, what's going on?"

"Keely is missing. We're almost certain she has been abducted by the same man who killed her father. By the way, we found her dad's body in a cistern in Williamson County."

"That's terrible news. On both counts," he said. "I will do anything I can to help, you know that."

"Until now, we've been concentrating our search efforts in the Williamson County area, but I have a hunch. I think he may be holding Keely somewhere close to Beaman Park."

"Interesting thought. I assume it's because you think he's familiar with this area."

"Exactly."

"What can I do to help?"

"First of all, if you could have your rangers keep an eye out for anything suspicious, that would be great. As soon as we hang up, I'll text you information about Murdoch, the killer, and Keely. You might even want to post it in the nature center so hikers will recognize one or both if they see them. And let me warn you—Murdoch is deadly. He just killed a police officer."

"I'll do it. What else can I do?"

"Do you mind if we set up a small base camp in your parking lot?"

"Of course not. You can use my facilities if you would prefer."

"That would be great, Dan. We're going to pack up right now so we can move everything over there as soon as possible. Thanks so much."

"See you soon."

Beau hung up and gave Adam and Levi a thumbs up. "We're moving our operations to Beaman Park Nature Center."

By the time Adam had the dogs loaded and ready to go and a few things packed, Greg McAlister had arrived. Beau gave him a quick update, and he was one hundred percent onboard with helping.

"Thank you," Beau said. "We can cover a lot more territory with two dog teams."

Adam's vehicle was big enough to hold both dogs, so McAlister hopped in the car with him. Beau drove the Bureau's SUV so he would have the technology he might need. Levi rode with him. Devon stayed at the house in case Keely should turn up, and to watch over Pearl and the pups, who were all doing well.

When their caravan arrived at Beaman at one o'clock that afternoon, Dan Rodgers was waiting for them. "I'm really sorry again about Keely," Rodgers said. "We have her photo—and Murdoch's—posted in the center. Everyone on my crew is informed and are actively looking for any sign of them."

"Much appreciated." Beau reached to shake Rodgers's hand.

"I'm Keely's brother," Levi said. "Thank you from our family for your help."

"Are you all ready to move your things inside?" Rodgers asked. "I'll set you up in my office, and I'll work in our naturalist's office while you're here."

"No need to move," Beau assured him. "We don't want to inconvenience you. And if you're in the same room, we can keep each other better informed."

"That works," Rodgers said.

They had just finished moving everything and were prepping the dogs when Enoch called. "We're on top of your idea, Beau, with one caveat. I'm telling the press that we're pinpointing our search in Williamson County, while broadening our efforts in all of Davidson County. That way, if Murdoch catches the news and he's in the Beaman area, he'll think he's bested us. We want him to let his guard down."

"That sounds good, Chris. A much better idea," Beau said. "We now have a mobile headquarters set up at the Beaman Park Nature Center and two dog teams ready to start a search. We're working with Ranger Dan Rodgers at the park. Dan was a big help to us when we were here in December looking for Connor. He already has park rangers on the ground. As you know, it's a massive area, covering two thousand acres. And there are a lot of homes scattered along the perimeter. We have a considerable amount of ground to cover, but we have good support."

"Great," Enoch said. "By the way, Jake Matheson is here with me. I've asked him to update you as well."

"Hey, Beau. I wanted to let you know that I've called the city and state police in the Beaman Park and Ashland City area and asked them to get involved. I've also sent an alert to the Davidson County Sheriff's office. We'll be posting flyers in public places near the park as well."

"It's a good plan," Beau said, ready to hit the trail. "Now, we get to work and hope for a lucky break."

CHAPTER 50

Saturday, January 22

"How soon can you have the dogs ready?" Beau asked.

"We're ready when you are." Adam gave him a thumbs up. "Greg's a good man to work with." He glanced toward McAlister and grinned.

"Great," Beau said. "Dan has offered all-terrain vehicles if we need them." He turned to Rodgers. "Where do you recommend we start?"

Rodgers walked to the large map of the park that was hanging on the wall outside the nature center. "My crew is covering the center of the park." He drew an imaginary circle around the bull's eye area in the middle of the park. "We're leaving the perimeter to you." He enlarged the circle he drew. "I can tell you now, there will be quite a few hikers out today, since it's Saturday and the temps are relatively mild."

"Let's just hope they don't stir up a hornet's nest." Beau grimaced. "Murdoch is armed and dangerous."

And Keely is with him.

Beau prayed he hadn't missed the mark when he moved the focus of the search to Beaman. It felt right, but Keely's life was at stake. And the sooner they found her the better. Murdoch was a time bomb that had been ticking for the last twenty years. And he had already killed twice.

Grief swept over Beau when he thought about his father, who had only been laid to rest the day before. A lot had happened since then. Murdoch was no doubt operating on little sleep, fueled by adrenaline and rage. Hopefully, Keely could play him, and slow him down, until they got to her.

Beau again partnered up with Adam and Titan. And Levi would be working with McAlister and Ruby. Both teams left Ground Zero at two fifteen in the afternoon. They had about the same amount of time as they'd had in December with Connor to find Keely before the sun went down.

Beau could tell that both dogs were motivated. Both took off running when they went off leash. Because they wanted to do a perimeter search, neither team would be staying on the trail for long, and they separated shortly after leaving the center. Titan's team went left, and Ruby's went right.

Although Adam reminded Titan every few minutes why they were here, Beau suspected the dog knew more than they did. And, then again, he may have been extra excited about another opportunity to work the park that had brought him so much attention the first time.

As before, Beau stayed a few paces behind Adam, who was several yards behind the dog. Both men did a visual search while the dog searched primarily with his nose. Beau kept an eye out for physical boundaries between the park and private property and jotted down GPS coordinates every time the dog appeared to be exceptionally motivated.

A niggling of doubt kept trying to penetrate his peace, his hope that they were searching in the right place. But it was the intersection of both his instinct and his reason that had brought him here. Beaman Park just made sense. Then again, maybe he was like Titan, and he liked being surrounded by his past successes. And maybe he felt closer to Keely here.

It had been an emotional week—and that stood to escalate. For some reason a conversation with his mother came to mind. It had come at another important intersection in his life, a time when his passion told him to marry Keely, but his father was doing everything to drive them apart.

Beau's mom had set him down at the kitchen table one morning and told him "not to let his angel get away." He remembered her words clearly, and exactly as she had said them. If only he had listened to her instead of running away. It could have saved him a decade of regret.

Ironically, it was just like God to bring Keely back into his life when he would need her the most. And, coincidentally, she had needed him too.

But then again, he didn't believe in coincidences.

Without his passion to reopen Will Lambert's cold case, her father's body might never have been found. J. G. Gardner and William Lambert might have shared a watery grave. And neither the Gardner nor the Lambert families would have had closure.

When the next hour passed, and Titan didn't seem to be especially motivated, Beau looked at his watch and estimated the amount of daylight hours remaining. Not one member of their team planned to pack up and go home at sunset, but nighttime searches could be far less productive and a lot more dangerous in this case. They needed to get the jump on Murdoch and not the other way around.

A second hour passed. And then another. If Beau had calculated correctly, they would soon be at the point when both teams would meet on the far side of the park. And that didn't leave him with a good feeling. If that happened, they would have to reconsider their approach. He prayed to God for providential protection and wisdom. Especially for Keely.

It was almost five o'clock when Beau's phone vibrated. He picked it up. It was Rodgers.

"We've had a hiker sighting of a white pickup truck with a cab-over camper parked just over the line from the park's boundaries." He gave Beau the GPS coordinates.

"Did you let McAlister know too?"

"He's my next call."

"Would you please notify the local authorities too?"

"I will."

"Dan, if you're a praying man, I think we're going to need your prayers."

"I am. And you've got them."

Beau ran ahead to catch up with Adam and told him the news. They were already heading in the right direction. All they had to do was step up the pace, not an easy thing in such rough terrain.

Beau had them figured to be about a mile and a half away when Adam cried out in pain. Beau ran to him. "What happened?"

"I've twisted my ankle. Beau . . . it's bad." He grimaced. "I can't go on."

"But you have to," Beau said. A pit settled into his stomach. "I need your help."

"No. We're close. You take Titan and go get Keely. You can do it. Besides, you may not need the dogs since you have coordinates."

"Titan won't respond to me."

"Yes, he will. You've seen this done. Just remember to tell him to 'stand down' when he sees Keely or Murdoch, so he doesn't go crazy."

Beau nodded.

"You can do it." Adam repeated, rubbing his ankle. "And it's better this happened to me and not to you. Keely needs you more. You're prepared to take Murdoch down. I couldn't shoot my way out of a paper bag. And my negotiating skills are nonexistent."

Beau debated for less than thirty seconds and realized there was no other choice. "Will you call for an ATV to pick you up?"

"Yes. And you be careful. Our girl needs you to be well after all this is over."

Beau nodded and took off running, taking charge of Titan, and reminding the dog to find Keely. In under twenty minutes, the two of them had covered another mile.

Keely watched as Murdoch stirred something that looked a lot like stew over a small outdoor stove. Something in her spirit—would Beau call it her gut?—told her to start praying. But she wasn't sure for what.

She also wasn't sure whether to engage her captor in conversation. He had been impatient with her all afternoon, but she decided to make another attempt.

"Can I help you with supper?" she asked.

He looked up from the portable stove he had secured between two rocks and shook his head.

Not a promising response.

She decided to get up and walk. He had allowed her that luxury off and on all day, and she had tried not to abuse it. She didn't want to set him off when she was trying to buy time.

"That looks like stew. Do you need fresh herbs? My grandmother taught me how to find herbs in the wild."

"What kind would you find?"

"This time of year? I've found wild onions. Sometimes mushrooms. And maybe, but not likely, rosemary. Any of those would be delicious with a stew."

"Go ahead."

"Awesome!" Keely prayed for direction. And that she could find the right herb, but not too soon, giving her time to look around. At one point this afternoon, she'd thought she saw a hiker in the distance. That could mean they were close to a park. But what park? Were they even still in Tennessee?

Judging from how long she was out when Murdoch put her to sleep this morning, she guessed they were still close to where they had started on her property.

It broke her heart to think about the kennel. How much of it remained? And her dogs. Was Pearl safe? How about the puppies? She had so many questions.

She moved across the perimeter of the woods, foraging for anything she could find. Hoping, especially, to find mushrooms. She needed something to make Murdoch happy. He was much easier to be around when he was in a good mood.

She had almost given up when she saw a few wild mushrooms peeking from beneath a log. Perfect. They would provide a meaty addition to the rudimentary stew Murdoch had thrown together. And she knew they were safe. Her grandmother had taught her that too. It was a knowledge that came in handy when she was on a search and needed something to eat.

She harvested the mushrooms and continued to look around. Over there . . . a few wild onions.

She hurried back to Murdoch and held out her treasure. "I found these mushrooms."

He sat back. "I don't trust you."

"Look," she said, and then popped one into her mouth. "They're good. Do you want one?"

He backed away. How ironic. He was afraid to die.

"Shall I throw them away then?" she asked.

"Do what you like, but I'm not going to eat them."

"All right. But I also found wild onions."

She held the onions out to him, and he took them. "Thank you."

"I'll try to find a few violets now," she said. "They're good for dessert."

He shook his head and let her go.

CHAPTER 51

Saturday, January 22

Beau's phone vibrated with a text from Levi. They were approaching the GPS coordinates Rodgers had given them, and Levi wanted to know if Beau was nearby.

He texted back that he was, that Adam was down with an ankle injury, and that he and Titan would approach cautiously from their side.

He called Titan to him, leashed him, and urged him to walk on. Within five or six minutes, he caught sight of the truck. And was that Keely?

His heart pounded. *Keely, look up!*

When she didn't see him, he moved slowly and deliberately in a sideways direction that might put him more in her line of vision. This time, when she looked up, she saw him. He signaled for her to stay quiet and remain calm.

The smile on her face simultaneously broke and warmed his heart. What he did next mattered, because she was still closer to that madman than she was to him. Every move he made from now on had to be deliberate.

He looked to his right and saw Levi, McAlister, and Ruby approaching. Titan saw them too. It was hard to hold him back because the dog also saw Keely.

"Stand down, Titan," Beau whispered, and the dog complied.

Beau gestured for Keely to go to the left, and she slowly started walking that way. Simultaneously, Beau withdrew his gun from his holster, and that's when he saw Murdoch.

Beau strained to see if he had his father's Winchester rifle beside him, but he appeared to be unarmed. Of course, there was no way to count on that.

Was it time?

Beau calculated McAlister's position. He was within firing range. And Keely was off to the left, out of the direct line of fire.

Beau pulled himself to his full height and shouted. "TBI, Murdoch. Put your hands up!"

Murdoch looked up. From the expression on his face, it was obvious they had taken him by surprise. He looked around frantically for Keely, who had ducked behind a tree.

Beau approached rapidly with his gun drawn, Titan walking beside him. "If you have a weapon, throw it down and put your hands in the air."

Murdoch appeared to comply and then reached behind him and brought out a pistol. Titan pulled away from Beau's grasp and took off running, lunging at Murdoch, just as he had at Connor's birthday party.

From where Beau stood, the dog was in his line of fire. Should he shoot? Or should he let Murdoch get his shot off?

A gun fired. The bullet and the blast pierced the air in front of Beau. And then Murdoch fell to the ground.

"Help me," he cried. "Get this dog off me or I'll kill him."

Keely took off running toward the dog, but Beau shouted, "No! Go back! It's a trick."

Beau took aim, fired, narrowly missing the dog, knocking the pistol out of Murdoch's hand.

Keely called off Titan, and the dog ran to her side. Then she dove to the ground, just before Murdoch grabbed the Winchester rifle, which had been lying on the ground in front of him. He aimed it directly at Beau, and then turned to shoot Keely.

"Keely!"

It was too late. A gun fired. And then a second shot.

Beau's heart surged. "Keely!"

But it was Murdoch who fell backwards. McAlister had put two shots in him. Surely, he wasn't still capable of firing.

"Stay on the ground, Keely."

She nodded, and Beau walked closer. Murdoch moved, his body twisting upward. He had the rifle—Beau's dad's rifle—pointed dead center at Beau's chest.

But this time Beau had a clear shot. He fired.

And the bullet hit Murdoch in the heart.

EPILOGUE

Tuesday, February 15

Keely clutched Beau's hand as twenty-one shots were fired, and William Allen Lambert's bones were lowered into a grave at the Lambert family cemetery just off Natchez Trace Parkway near Leiper's Fork, Tennessee.

Her mother, Maggie née Bailey Lambert, sat quietly between her siblings, Keely's aunt Gigi and uncle Peter. Levi, his wife, and their children sat nearby. Not many people had attended the service, because few people in their small town still remembered Will Lambert.

Frances Arnold was there. So were Dan Rodgers and his wife, and Russell Wallace and his wife. Of course, Beau's sister, Emma, and her family were there. Along with Adam and Sara Hunt, who were expecting their first baby, a boy.

Greg McAlister was also at the service. His father, a veteran military war dog handler had insisted on being there too. Keely's family story had captured Sergeant McAlister's imagination almost as much as her dogs had captured his heart. And Keely couldn't wait to hear stories about her dad from the elder McAlister, who remembered him.

The most unexpected guest at the service had been Roy T. Peyton II. The son of Will Lambert's former real estate partner, Roy Sr. The younger Peyton had finally returned Beau's phone call, explaining that he now operated the family real estate business and that he had waited to call Beau until he could reach his father, who lived on an island in the Caribbean. At his father's request, Roy Peyton II had brought a "small gift" for Maggie Lambert. A check for $100,000 to help take care of her future needs, along with a note offering his family's condolences on the loss of "a great man."

Will Lambert had left his mark on the little village of Leiper's Fork, Tennessee, during his too-short time here. A lot had changed in their community in the last twenty-two years. Some of it for the better. Some of it not. Keely wondered how much, if any of it, made sense to her mama, as she sat wiping her eyes and humming the tune to "Amazing Grace." But she hoped she now had closure.

She hoped they all did.

Autopsy results for Keely's dad listed the cause of death as blunt force trauma to the head and a gunshot through the heart. He was being buried today with his dog tags. Keely had made sure of it.

The complete investigation into Michael Murdoch de Hugues's background revealed several aliases, a degree in ancient religions, as well as one in elementary education. They had also learned that he was an ex-Marine who had served only a small amount of time before he was granted an Entry Level Separation. Several family friends from Murdoch's parents' hometown in Ashland City, Tennessee, maintained that he had never married because of his religious beliefs. A great aunt had bequeathed the Williamson County Victorian to him with explicit instructions that it would be given to the county Victorian society upon Michael Murdoch's death and used as a museum.

Earlier in the week, Keely had received word from her insurance company that her kennel would be restored to its original condition, in addition to an amount required to take care of her dogs while it was being rebuilt.

Keely and Beau had decided to wait until after the funeral to announce their engagement, although most of the family knew it was inevitable. Much like the love affair between Maggie and Will Lambert, which had become something of legend to those who knew them.

ABOUT THIS STORY

After I finished the first draft of *Deadly Conclusion* on an almost impossible deadline, my agent's first words were, "It's a miracle." And I agreed with her. I had wanted to give up so many times during the long nights and early mornings that define writing on a tight deadline. It was only knowing that so many people were praying for me that kept me going.

And then God stepped in.

When I needed information about military war dogs, the first person to come to mind was a business acquaintance from 2013. I searched online for his updated contact information and couldn't find it. And then, out of the blue, I received an email from him. His help was a literal godsend.

Conversely, when I started doing research on search and rescue (SAR), I had assumed that would be the easy part, because I have a lot of friends and acquaintances who are dog breeders, trainers, and even past SAR handlers. When none of them had the information I needed, I started making cold calls. But no one had the time or inclination to help. That's when I knew that God was nudging me away from a technical SAR story and moving me toward a restoration story.

I'm so glad He did.

I have had this book in my heart for years, but when I finally sat down to write it, it didn't turn out as I had planned. What started as my idea, turned into His idea. And, in the end, it became a story about two fathers who, although both imperfect, sacrificed themselves for their children. That thought brought tears to my eyes when I realized how it mirrored our Heavenly Father's love in giving His *perfect* Son to be sacrificed for each of us.

The opening scenes of *Deadly Conclusion* were inspired by the real-life rescue of a twelve-year-old Boy Scout in the Blue Ridge Mountains of North Carolina. After three days of a massive search party trying to find him—and when the boy's chances of survival were diminishing—a Shiloh Shepherd dog by the name of Gandalf and his handler, Misha Marshall, who were on their first official SAR run—just like Titan in my story—found the twelve-year-old boy safe. Gandalf and Misha were immediately thrust into the public limelight, and the story became personal for me when I learned that my dog, Glocken, was a close relative to Gandalf.

You can read more about Gandalf and Misha in this *Reader's Digest* article: www.rd.com/article/gandalf-and-the-lost-boy/. You can read more about the Shiloh Shepherd breed in Tina Barber's book *The Shiloh Shepherd Story: Against the Wind—A Breed Is Born.*

Facts About Military Working Dogs

The human-canine connection goes back thousands of years, and dogs have fought beside us for almost as long. History records dogs going into battle as early as the seventh century.

Canines have been used by the United States military since the Revolutionary War. Many have achieved exceptional notoriety. Chips, a mixed breed, earned a Purple Heart, the Distinguished Service Cross, and a Silver Star for saving soldiers' lives during World War II. Rin Tin Tin, widely known for his acting career, was first a MWD rescued and trained by an American soldier during World War I. And Cairo, a Belgian Malinois, made headlines as a member of Seal Team Six on the mission to take out Osama bin Laden. You can read about many, many more of these four-legged heroes at the Department of Defense site listed below.

- About 1,600 military working dogs currently help keep our country safe.
- The Department of Defense (DOD) finds its canine recruits from elite breeders around the world, and a select group—about 13 percent—are born and bred into the US military

through the DOD Military Working Dog Breeding Program, also known as the Puppy Program. These puppies come from the 341st Training Squadron at Joint Base San Antonio. The squadron has been training MWDs at the base since the 1950s.

- Whether they have Puppy Program pedigrees or outside credentials, would-be canine troops must graduate from the Military Working Dog Training Program to enter regular military service. Most dogs that successfully complete the 120-day program qualify to be dual-purpose dogs that either patrol and sniff out explosives or patrol and detect drugs.
- At about one year old, dogs are evaluated for entry into the Military Working Dog Training Program. The 341st Training Squadron uses the "consignment test" on them—the same test any dog must pass to be recruited by the Department of Defense.

Source: U.S. Department of Defense. Learn more at www.defense.gov/Multimedia/Experience/Four-Legged-Fighters/.

For more information about Military Working Dogs, read John C. Burnam's interview on my website (https://kathyharrisbooks.com/john-c-burnam-writing-history-a-monumental-task/) or visit the US Military Working Dog Teams National Monument website (https://myairmanmuseum.org/military-working-dogs/).

For more information about Kathy Harris,
visit www.kathyharrisbooks.com.